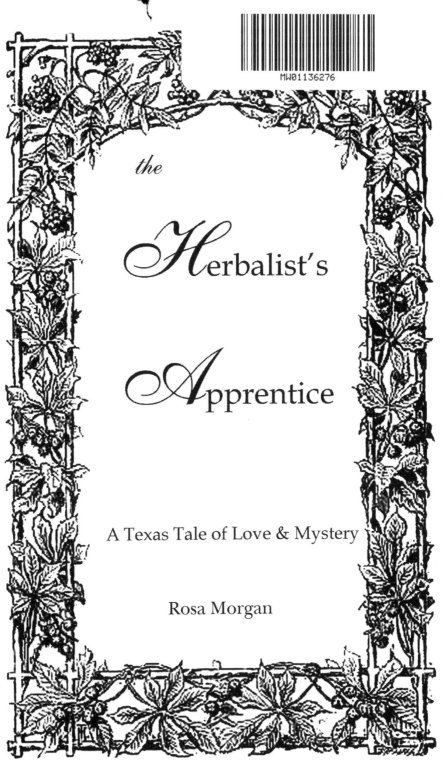

the

Herbalist's

Apprentice

A Texas Tale of Love & Mystery

Rosa Morgan

ISBN: 1495212610
ISBN-13: 9781495212611

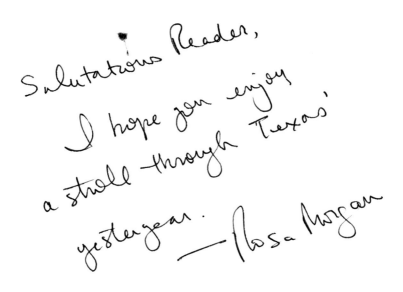

Salutations Reader,

I hope you enjoy a stroll through Texas' yesteryear.

— Rosa Morgan

To Tim, with love, who was there for me through the Dark Passages,
as well as on the Sunny Paths.

CONTENTS

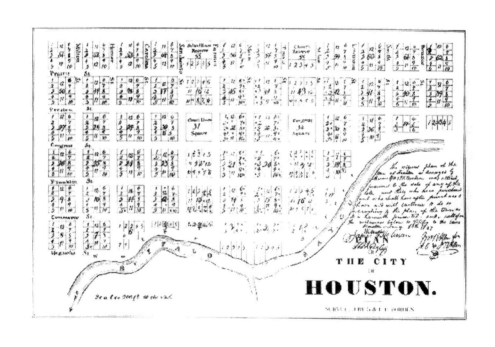

CHAPTER I

LAVENDER SCENTED MEMORIES

March 1850

I propped open my bedroom window, and breathed in the fresh air of that glorious spring day. Dogwoods glistened in the sunlight like fallen snow, and wisteria scented the air with a heady perfume. Amidst this transformation, I remained cocooned, not quite ready to emerge. At seventeen I'd taken up the chores of running a household for Pappa and my three younger brothers. Folks referred to me as a young lady. Plenty of men, I assumed by their unrestrained glances, considered me the ripened object of their desires. If only one more degree of warmth or a gentle shower could awaken me as easily as they had the blossoms. If only Mamma were here to guide me.

"Well, howdy there, Miss Mia. Or should I call you Senorita Stein? Fine day to be sitting so prettily upon your windowsill in your Easter finery. I can't do a lick of work, it being the Good Lord's Sabbath and all, so perhaps you'd care to join me in a stroll after supper?"

In the middle of Texas Avenue, the widest street in Houston, stood Mr. Elijah Jackson, proud proprietor of the Capitol Hotel.

The building, which once served as the center of our Republic under President Sam Houston, had fallen into disrepair after Austin was chosen as our new capital. With a fresh coat of peach blossom paint and plump feather-ticked mattresses, Mr. Jackson had resurrected the forlorn property into a most enviable boarding house. Despite a stagecoach bearing down upon him with bone weary passengers seeking the before mentioned bedding, he bowed gallantly before me, hat in hand.

Like a frightened child, I was on the verge of hiding behind the curtain when a group of parishioners on their way to First Baptist Church, noticed Mr. Jackson's preoccupation and glanced up at me.

Mrs. Haley, a nearby neighbor, along with her son and daughter, paused to talk. "Hello, Mia. Just wanted to say thank you for coming by last week. The tobacco juice and chalk is already starting to work on Ralph's warts."

Her son, embarrassed by mention of his affliction, pulled nervously at his persistent cowlick.

Mrs. Haley continued, "And the gunpowder and vinegar has done wonders for Jane's ringworm."

The darling girl's dress was hopelessly spoiled by a jelly handprint, but she curtsied politely nonetheless.

"Glad to be of help," I replied.

Mr. Haley, who had stayed quiet during mine and his wife's exchange, tipped his hat politely as they parted. Several others gave me a friendly hello, the exception being Cora, Preacher Hornsby's wife, who shot an evil eye in my direction.

I was not surprised by this woman's haughty contempt for me, though it still smarted. She was the town gossipmonger and her views reflected her husband's fiery sermons of damnation. She was as rigid as a flagpole, with a tightly pulled bun emphasizing her sharp cheekbones. Her wordless stare chastised me for being a

Catholic, little better than a heathen in her mind. It was all to be expected, considering I was raised motherless and had Mexican blood coursing through my veins.

Church bells rang their final peal, and the street, emptied of parishioners, still held the expectant Mr. Jackson waiting for my reply. He peered up at me with a hopeful grin, his eyes squinting into the sun. "Come now, Miss Stein, I'd be pleased as Punch if you'd accept my proposal."

The possible misinterpretation of his words brought a flush to my cheeks and doubled my impulse to flee without answering. However, Pappa's previous admonition to put away my playthings and act like a proper young woman rallied my courage, and I fleetingly considered saying yes to him. He was not bad looking and was certainly respectable, but he was also a widower with seven motherless children. I replied, "Thank you, Mr. Jackson, for your kind offer, but I'm afraid a previous engagement precludes my joining you. Good day to you, sir."

My rejected would-be suitor deliberated his next move, shuffling dirt beneath his boots. Several men taking their leisure on his veranda jeered his failed efforts. Embarrassed, he resignedly put his hat back on, tipping it genteelly in farewell, then slowly turned away. The ensuing conversation was beyond my hearing, but Mr. Jackson's reddened face indicated the men teased him mercilessly.

There was always a crowd gathered at the Capitol Hotel, and because of my advantageous view, I watched their comings and goings with great interest. There were those I called the Observers, who planted their spurs solidly against a post and required little to amuse themselves other than watching passersby. The Vultures were men who perched on the railing, whittling industriously until they swooped down for the next game of poker. Then there were the Personages, esteemed by wealth or old age, who commandeered the highly prized rocking chairs. Though proffering a splinter to the backside upon a hasty departure, the chairs provided easy access to the spittoons.

Unfortunately, the men watched me as closely as I did them. I was apprenticed to Miss Emily, Houston's esteemed midwife and herbalist, and when I ventured out to visit her or my patients, all eyes were upon me. Miss Emily was a high-yellow freed slave, linked to

Mamma as tight as a honeysuckle vine clinging to a window frame. Her daughter, Hannah, had been my best friend until one wintry day several years back.

Bitterly cold, the chickens' water had frozen solid and the strange phenomena of snow dusted the muddy streets white. I ran the six blocks to Hannah's house, eager to share this wonderland. Miss Emily kept her house neat as a pin, the dirt yard swept and the picket fence garlanded with rambling yellow roses. However, on this day, garden tools were left in disarray and muddy footprints mucked up the porch. I ran through the dogtrot, stopping dead in my tracks as a tarred 'X' loomed above me on the door.

The horrors of prejudice, I thought, especially against freed Negroes. I continued angrily toward the door, but before I reached it, Miss Emily appeared. Through the narrow crack I saw her tear-stained cheeks and hair unplaited. Miss Emily was of solid character, not shaken by the most difficult of deliveries or the fiercest hurricane rattling the windows. Seeing her so agitated meant a catastrophe had surely occurred.

"Get away with you, child," she cried sternly. "Don't you know what that 'X' means?"

"I thought..."

"We're quarantined. Hannah's got diphtheria. Nobody's to come or go. Didn't Klaus tell you?"

"I left before Pappa was up. Didn't tell him I was coming."

"He'll be worried sick if he wakes and finds you gone a missin'."

Desperate to help, I asked, "Have you a tried mustard rub? How about syrup of acacia? Pappa always gives it to us when we're sick."

"Don't you think I've tried everything?" she said in desperation. "Now, get on back home. Hannah will be seeing you..."

Miss Emily's words broke off in a sob, and I knew with certainty I'd never see my dear friend alive again.

I later learned Miss Emily had indeed tried every known cure to save her child, including cutting a hole in the false membrane suffocating her. My sorrow turned into a determination to become a healer, and though I was still just a child and Miss Emily grief stricken, we began almost immediately upon my studies. My father admired my newfound vocation, though there were many hateful people of our town who gossiped, saying gallivanting around the city with a Negress was a disgrace.

My attention was drawn once more to the Hotel's veranda, now empty of Mr. Jackson and the other men who had retired for Easter dinner. Slipping from my bedroom, I listened for stirrings downstairs before heading to the locked dressing room, once belonging to my mother. The skeleton key hidden on the dusty doorcase fell into my hands, then turned the rusty lock. Though five years had passed since her death, the room still smelt of lavender. It was a difficult herb to grow in Houston's humid climate, but Mamma loved to make sachets from it and so always managed to keep a plot of it alive.

Smelling the sweet herb brought back long buried memories of her. I could imagine her sitting at her marble topped vanity, pulling a silver brush through her raven mane; her curls falling across her brown shoulders, and a thick fringe framing her almost black eyes. She was a mestiza, a Spanish Castilian with Mayan Indian blood, and her looks reflected this heritage.

"Remember, Mia," she instructed, "One hundred strokes and you'll have strong, shiny hair like mine."

"But Mamma, I can't get through the knots and my arm is tired," I whined. "Maybe I should shave it off and become a nun," I teased. "Your father would have liked that."

Making the sign of the cross, she said, "All blessings for the Holy Mother Catholic Church. However, if you recall, my father left the priesthood to wed my mother and I tell you it was her hair, her crowning glory, that lured him. Wait and see, it will play an important part in your future too."

"How Mamma?"

"By the time of your quinceañera you will..."

I interrupted, "When does it come?"

"Seven years from now, when you're fifteen."

"And what will happen then?"

"We'll have a big party to celebrate your becoming a woman, and a ceremony in church to give you a blessing. You'll have to be tamed though, as will your hair. No more climbing trees or wearing braids hanging down like a child's, instead you'll coil your hair atop your head like mine. Then when you're married, only your husband will see it down at night, like Pappa sees mine. Come now Mia, it is time for our morning prayers."

Retrieving the rosary from her apron pocket, she knelt upon the hard wooden floor. Her belly was full with child, and getting down was not easy. She began, "Hail Mary full of grace. The Lord is with thee..."

I don't know if it was the crucifix hypnotically swaying as she fingered the beads, or her melodic chanting, but the ritual slowed the hands on the clock and brought a peace and awareness to my mind. She finished her prayers, reverently kissing the tiny Virgin Mary upon the bedroom altar.

Feeling confessional, I cried, "Oh Mamma, I can't be good all day, even when I try."

"Nor do I, but we must make an effort or never improve. Come now," she said, rising with difficulty. "I hear the milkman's bell, and Pappa will be leaving for work soon. Mind you, be quiet and don't wake your brothers."

I rushed downstairs to find Pappa at the table, reading the *Texas Telegraph's* obituaries. He poured his hot coffee from the cup into his saucer, then sipped it from there. The froth of the cream clung to his beard and he licked it clean. He was as regular as clockwork with his paper and breakfast, just like Mamma's routine with her morning prayers.

"Pappa, can I have a sip?" I asked, coyly climbing into his lap.

"Ja, but only a small one," he answered in his thick German accent. "It's not a drink for little girls."

"Why does yours always taste better than Mamma's?"

"Cherry brandy for the coffee is one of my family's tradition," he declared. "One my mother raised me on."

"Where is your mother, and why does she never visit us?"

Ignoring my questions, he turned back to the obituaries, "Sometimes you can decipher more of a man's character by how he died than how he lived."

"Oh Klaus, you've a morbid preoccupation," Mamma scorned as she washed the dishes. "Besides I don't see any connection with who I am and how I'm to die. I'm sure I'll have no say in the matter."

How prophetic these words proved later, but during those years of innocence our days were only filled with kisses and laughter. My parents' discussion of the greengrocer's list was sprinkled with terms of endearment. With a mischievous grin, Pappa teased he wouldn't go into work, but Mamma shooed him out the door nonetheless. He swung me up in the air, then gave me a bear hug, his beard tickling my cheek.

With a smile on his face and his hat tilted jauntily, he headed straight for T.C. Laconte's Barber Shop Extraordinaire in Building Number Two. Aside from the Capitol Hotel, it was the hub of social activity for the male population. Both locals and newcomers alike enjoyed five cent shaves and ten cent haircuts with gossip and politics gratis. Klaus' arrival prompted a respectful welcome of firm handshakes and jovial pats on the back. He was one of Stephen F. Austin's Old Three Hundred, the first Americans to brave hunger and snakebite in order to tame the Mexican territory of Tejas. He was also a veteran of the Battle of San Jacinto, and ran a thriving furniture store on Mercantile Row. His accomplishments were enough for most folks to overlook that his wife was a Mexican.

I pulled open the vanity drawer and retrieved the one daguerreotype we had of Mamma. She appeared happy and triumphant, cradling my youngest brother. It was his baptismal day and there had been a heated debate between my parents as to what he should be christened. Mamma insisted upon Santiago Ancelmo Manuel, arguing her other sons' names bore not a trace of their Spanish lineage. In the picture Pappa stands proudly behind her, his hands caressing her shoulders. He looks pleased too, for though he acquiesced to the name she insisted upon, he always called my brother Sam for short. My other brothers, Emmett and Christian, and myself are nestled amongst her silk skirts. In the wheel of life, Mamma had been the steady axle to our spinning spokes, and without her, we were dreadfully off kilter.

"Mia, what are you doing in here? You know this room is to be kept locked."

Pappa's stern voice shattered my dream world where Mamma still lived.

"I'm sorry Pappa, I was just looking for a ..." Being a dismal liar, my words trailed off into guilty silence.

"Then your headache must be better. Come now and see what the boys and I have been cooking."

Relieved he wasn't too unsettled at finding me in forbidden quarters, I pressed my luck, "Before we go, can you tell me about when you and Mamma were married?"

My father gazed around the room as if painful memories resided in the furniture and draperies themselves. His eyes fell on the image of my mother, and he tenderly took up the picture. A wistful smile replaced his furrowed brow, and he was seemingly transported to a happier time. "In thirty-six just after the revolution, the Allen Brothers bought six thousand acres on the south bank of Buffalo Bayou. They hawked it up and down the seaboard, selling an acre for a dollar. They named their new city after Sam Houston, the Texian general who had led us to victory. We were called the New York of the Gulf, and chosen as the capital of our newly founded Texas Republic.

"Soon folks from across the country and Europe wanted a piece of the dream, as did your mother and me, who arrived in thirty-seven with five dollars between us. We had only you and Emmett at the time, with Christian on the way. There being more people than houses in this town, I took up work as a carpenter. Mind you, building a house in a day wasn't my idea of craftsmanship, but it was a heap better than a tent. Business slowed down after the capital moved to Austin, so we opened the furniture store and carried on real well. People always need pieces for their houses."

"That's all very interesting Pappa, but what I'm most curious about is yours and Mamma's relationship. It seemed you never argued like most married folk. Except over Sam's name, that is."

Pappa chuckled, "As I recall it wasn't much of a row. We always found a way to compromise. Francesca Castillo," he trilled, letting my mother's name roll off his tongue. "was the most beautiful woman I ever saw and the sweetest. Doesn't mean life was always easy. There were floods and war, and well...the issue of our differing backgrounds."

"Is that why Grandmother and Grandfather Stein never visited us? Because Mamma was a Mexican?"

Despite my father's bushy eyebrows twitching in displeasure, I continued to press my point. "Pappa, I need to understand these things. How can I live in the present when my past is hidden from me? I don't even know how Mamma died, and yet you've preserved her room like a shrine."

He stood up abruptly, his hand trembling as he replaced the photograph on the vanity. "I don't have time for any more fool questions. Now, come on down before the food is spoilt. And Mia, I want this door locked, do you understand? The past is dead and no amount of talking will bring it back to life."

I placed Mamma's beautiful face back into the drawer. Pappa could make me lock away the room, but never the lavender scented memories it held. I swore that one day no matter the price, I'd uncover secrets of my family's past, including how my mother died.

CHAPTER II

AN UNINVITED GUEST

Our home, Holly Cottage, got its name from the tree growing in our backyard. It was an old yaupon, gnarled and twisted, but it was special because my parents had carved their initials and a heart into its bark. As a young girl, I loved to climb the tree and practice skin-the-cat from its branching arms. I knew exactly which steady limbs to reach for and where to settle a sure foothold. It's where I found solace after Mamma's death five years ago, and where I hid my tears from Pappa and my little brothers.

Holly Cottage reflected our rising prosperity, growing from a one-room log cabin into a two-story clapboard house with a double front porch and turret in front. We had a cozy parlor, a paneled dining room, three bed-chambers, and an attic fitted out for my eldest brother, Emmett. At fifteen, he was between hay and grass, and gladly endured boiling summers in exchange for a bit of privacy.

Pappa built a stone kitchen that stood separately out back to prevent a fire from spreading through the house. I followed the cobbled path to it, meandering past our cistern and gardens. I still felt unsettled by thoughts of my mother, and my brother's peevish attitude did not help.

"Where you been, Mia? Supper is practically done and with no help from you."

"Don't be unpleasant, Christian," Pappa chastised my middle brother.

"He can't help it," Emmett offered in his professorial voice. "He was ornery enough to be born in thirty-seven when everyone was dying of yellow fever."

Pappa huffed, adding a stick of wood to the stove. "Your sister does the lion's share of work around here, and I expect you boys to pitch in when she's under the weather."

"Girls," Christian declared derisively, as he pushed his smudged glasses up with floured fingers. "they're always having their headaches and moods."

I went over to the youngest of my brothers, Sam. He was sitting precariously at the worktable atop stacked pillows, his feet dangling above the floor's oilcloth. He looked up at me, then pointed to the bowl with the brown sugar loaf in its middle.

"I see you're making a cake, and is this the sugar island?" I asked.

Sam nodded his mop of golden curls, and his cheeks dimpled with a shy smile. My brother was seven, fully capable of talking, and yet he remained mute except when speaking alone to me. Miss Emily explained sometimes folks went dumb due to a severe shock. I wondered if Mamma's death had impacted him, though I was certain he didn't even remember her.

"Here comes the snow," I said, sifting the white flour. A gill of milk poured down like rain, the wooden spoon stirred up an earthquake, and Sam squealed delightedly as I dropped three speckled eggs from a perilous height.

"We've made quite a mess now," I said, picking out the pieces of broken shell.

Of all my brothers, Emmett with his olive skin and dark hair had my mother's looks. However, in temperament and eagerness to enter into scientific debate he took after my father. "Reminds me of Lyell's *Principles of Geology,*" he observed, peeking over his book.

"I can't imagine how," I said.

Needing no further encouragement, Emmett began, "Some folks think that just like you stirred up that flour and sugar, so did God stir up the earth. In a matter of days, He supposedly pushed the land around to form mountains and valleys, lakes and rivers, but Lyell contends our landscape is shaped by geological forces. And that it took millions of years for these changes to occur."

"I couldn't have explained it any better," Pappa said proudly. "It's good to delve into these subjects, but remember most folks aren't as open minded on these matters. You're challenging long held beliefs, which in the past would've cost you your life. So, remember discretion is key."

"Meaning keep your mouth shut," Christian piped.

"I hate to disrupt such a scholarly subject," I remarked, "But Emmett, your pokeweed is boiling over!"

My absentminded brother loped over to the stove.

Christian chided, "If Emmett didn't always hide his nose in a book, he'd see the important thing that needed stirring was his pot, and our dinner would be ready by now."

"On the contrary," Emmett countered. "If I'd not previously read Mrs. Beeton's cookery book and learned to drain pokeweed twice in order to rid it of its poison, I might have killed our family. Cooking is a science, one devises a receipt much like a hypothesis, develops it through cooking or experimentation, examines the proof or rather tastes it, and finally draws a conclusion. The proof is in the pudding or in this case the pokeweed."

"By gum, my conclusion is your cooking and theory stinks!" Christian said, snubbing his nose.

"Entire family dies of pokeweed poisoning," Pappa mused. "That indeed would make an interesting obituary."

Dinner was ready to be served when someone appeared at our screen door. It was Cora Hornsby with her squinty eyes flitting nervously about the room.

"Good day, Mrs. Hornsby," Pappa said, opening the door. "This is an unexpected pleasure. Will you join us for supper?"

"Thank you, but no, Mr. Stein. I don't condone social visits on our good Lord's day of rest, and especially it being Easter. However, Christian duty compels me to make an exception on account of your daughter's unseemly behavior."

"You have come on a fool's errand if you're referring to my Mia. I'd bet a month's wages she'd do nothing to shame our name."

Bug-eyed, Cora shrieked, "Gambling is a sin!"

Pappa retorted, "It was merely a figure of speech. Now, Cora, tell me what this is all about, so my family can have their dinner before it gets cold."

Pointing her finger at me, Cora said, "Why don't you ask her if she wasn't entertaining a man from the hotel at her bedroom window. And I'm not the only one to have witnessed this shameful act. Half a dozen parishioners from my church can testify its truthfulness."

I turned beet red at her obscene accusation.

Wound up with emotion, Cora ranted, "Mia has already got a sullied reputation, doing devil's work with a witch doctor. Negroes are the cursed descendants of Noah. God brought them into this world for us to have dominion over, just as we do the horses and cows. Cursed be Canaan, the lowest of the slaves will he be to his brothers. Straight from the Good Book, Genesis, chapter nine, verse twenty-five. And these half-breed children of yours would be bible learned if you and them attended my husband's sermons instead of listening to those priests' Latin gibberish. Everyone knows it ain't easy for a man alone to be raising a family, and you've got our sympathies, but... Well, that's all. I've said my piece and know the Good Lord approves."

With her tirade spent and waiting for a response, Cora's bony fingers fiddled with the ivory broach at her neck. Pappa's temperament was as easygoing as a flatboat sailing a calm bayou, but Cora's venomous tongue had exceeded the idle scuttlebutt he was accustomed to. His jaw muscles contracted and his fists clenched, but the only sound breaking the awkward silence was the chicken fat hissing on hot coals. By the time Pappa resumed his composure, Cora's pale face was a mass of nervous twitching.

"I remember when I first met you, Cora. It was at a harvest moon dance. Do you remember the lovely gathering in thirty-nine? You were just a young thing, and your dance card was filled up, so I didn't even get a chance to give you a twirl. What a beauty you were, and I mean inside and out. Somehow Josiah Hornsby won your heart that night. Now, being a parson's wife is no easy row to hoe, especially riding the gospel circuit from one end of Texas to the other. When you settled back in town I'd hoped to get reacquainted, but you'd changed. Tell me Cora, what's happened to make you so bitter a woman?"

Pappa had reached down into Cora's tortured soul, and exposed the raw nerve she concealed with malice. Her pale lips trembled as if to speak, then gulping air to stifle her sobs, she ran from the kitchen.

"Whew, you got her goat, Pappa," Christian said with satisfaction.

In frustration, our father threw the towel down on the table. "The woman deserves only our pity," he said, leaving the room.

Cora's words haunted me as I prepared the dining room for supper. The mean things she said about me and Miss Emily weren't easy to let go of. I knew full well there were other folks who believed the same way she did, and yet to hear it spoken in so caustic a manner was painful to bare. I was mad as a wet hen, and yet I saw how Pappa had skillfully turned his anger into real concern for her. How did he do it, I wondered.

I spread a fresh cloth on our old oak table that glowed from my diligent rubbings of linseed oil. Easter dinner merited our fine red transferware and crystal glasses. The silver caster set was filled with the cucumber ketchup and watermelon chutney I put up last fall, and hard-boiled eggs dyed with onionskin and daisies from the garden were the centerpiece. The beautifully set table was only missing our napkin rings, each engraved with our initials. A pang of mournfulness always came over me when retrieving them from the sideboard, for Mamma's ring remained behind, looking lonely.

With dependable regularity our dinner began when the clock struck five. Grace was said, and though Pappa bought the third pew from the front for us children, he refrained from joining in. He was a man without faith, which I assumed occurred after losing Mamma.

"I've been reading about Da Vinci," Emmett began as soon as our prayers ended. "Did you know he was ambidextrous and wrote his notes backwards?"

"Then you can read it in a mirror," I said.

Christian barked, "I could go on living the rest of my life without needing to know that. Besides it being a waste of my conjuring abilities."

Undeterred, Emmett continued, "Perhaps you'd find it interesting to know Da Vinci studied the anatomy of cadavers in order to paint realistic portraits." Noticing he had sparked little Sam's curiosity, he asked, "Are you wondering what a cadaver is?"

Sam nodded his head shyly.

"It's a dead body," Emmett explained.

"A dead body?" Christian repeated with interest. "Finally something of note to talk about. Was this Vinci fellow a grave robber?"

"Most likely hired somebody else to do the dirty work," Pappa said, stabbing the roast chicken. "A fellow could get arrested for such dubious activity."

Emmett added, "Michaelangelo is known to have stolen bodies from the morgue for his study of anatomy."

It didn't matter if the biscuits were burnt, the pokeweed bitter, and the cake lopsided, I loved our dinners and animated debates. With forks jabbing the air to punctuate a point of view, crumbs dropping higgledy-piggledy, and shins kicked beneath the table in retaliation, our discussions exceeded the boundaries of small town convention.

Pappa sat at the head of the table, proudly observing his rambunctious lot. If thoughts of Cora Hornsby's vicious words crossed his mind, they left no trace of agitation upon his face, though they remained a splinter in my side.

CHAPTER III

THREE PARTS LOVE

ext morning, I threw on a cotton shift, and headed for Miss Emily's house. Standing at the corner of Capitol and Brazos Streets, it was a short six blocks away, but Sam's insistence on examining every leaf and critter along the way extended our journey to nearly an hour.

Stopping for a moment, Sam asked thoughtfully, "Mia, why didn't Mrs. Hornsby tell Pappa the reason she was so unhappy?"

This was the type of insightful question my youngest brother so often expressed when he was alone with me. It was proof of his intelligence and curiosity, and only furthered my perplexity concerning his usual muteness.

"I think whatever is bothering Mrs. Hornsby hurts too much to think about, much less tell someone." Sensing his continued concern, I asked, "Is there anything bothering you?"

Sam grimaced, and I was certain something laid heavy on his tiny shoulders. I pressed him, "Come now, you can tell me anything."

Hesitatingly, he answered, "I heard a boy in school say something kinda like Mrs. Hornsby. He said a Negro's skin don't feel heat or snake bites like a white man's. It's why they're good at being slaves."

Stifling my anger, I asked, "And do you believe that?"

"I only need to touch Miss Emily's soft cheek to know better. Besides, nobody aught to be a slave."

I was relieved to drop such a dreadful topic when his attention turned to a tree growing beside the street.

"Look, Mia, it has three different kinds of leaves. One looks like my mittens."

"It's a sassafras. We'll pull these saplings up for tea. Its bark makes a good blood purifier."

"Did Miss Emily teach you that?" Sam asked, filling the basket.

"Of course, she's my teacher, and I'm her apprentice."

"And is she a voodoo witch doctor like Mrs. Hornsby said?"

"She's an herbalist and midwife, something to be proud of."

We reached Miss Emily's house and found the garden abloom. The window boxes overflowed with Indian paintbrush and wine cups, hollyhocks stood as sentinels, and yellow roses blanketed the picket fence.

Like a pixie, Miss Emily sprung up from behind the rosemary hedge she'd been trimming. She welcomed us with a motherly embrace smelling of earth and sunshine.

"My, your garden sure looks fine, Miss Emily."

"One part breeze off the bayou, two parts manure from the livery stable, and three parts love," she said with a smile that always lifted my spirits. "The last part, love, being what all livin' things are most needin'."

"And this gorgeous rose is a new one, isn't it?" I said, bringing the dark red petals up to my nose for a sniff.

Miss Emily nodded, "I gave Miss Penelope down at the

café, senna for her bowels, and she give me half a rhubarb pie and this rose bush. She calls it Archduke Charles, sounds fancy don't it?"

"Its scent would make a lovely rosewater. I bet we could sell it for two bits a bottle at Ophelia's millinery shop."

"A fine plan, Mia," Miss Emily said as she deftly untied my braid and plaited it tighter. "Always can use extra pin money. What you got fillin' your pockets, Sam?"

Sam shyly revealed the varied contents of katydid skins, doodlebugs, and a fine specimen of a bullfrog, which he promptly handed to Miss Emily as an offering.

"That's mighty generous of you, Sam. I reckon he'll be quite at home here in my garden."

I opened my basket, "I brought those mugwort cuttings you said you needed for Mrs. Beale's womanly complaints. And a book, Linnaeus' *Systema Naturae* that Pappa borrowed from the Lyceum."

"I'll never understand why in heaven's name your father keeps company with such harebrained society? The latest outrage they be spewing is that a woman can't improve her mind as well as a man. Chew on that one for awhile."

"We know Pappa doesn't believe such nonsense, and I say let's prove the others wrong."

Miss Emily led us down a stone pathway to her backyard where creeping thyme grew between the stones, emitting a citrus scent with each step. Pappa had built her a table and chairs from birch twigs, and she'd set these up for our lunch under a canopy of redbud blossoms. The lacy tablecloth was dappled in sunlight, and never before had bean soup and chickweed salad looked so appetizing.

"Everything you do is filled with magic," I said admiringly.

"I do what I enjoy and there *is* magic in that. Now, you two dig in, and tell me what's goin' on at Holly Cottage."

Between bites, I began, "Well, Christian had a bicycle wreck the other day. Broke his spectacles and tore up his knee pretty bad."

"A bicycle? I thought your Pa had more sense than to throw his money away on one of those contraptions."

"It actually belongs to Tommy Price, and you know whatever is the latest rage up North his daddy Rufus will be shipping down the bayou for him."

"Penny-wise and pound-foolish, that's the Prices for you. Tell me, how'd you treat his knee?" Miss Emily asked, easily slipping into her role as teacher.

"Cleaned the wound with lavender water, stopped the bleeding with burnet leaves, and bandaged it with a comfrey poultice."

Sam tugged at my skirt and whispered into my ear.

I relayed Sam's message, "He said soldiers in the American Revolution drank burnet tea before fighting in battle."

"Why I believe we have a buddin' herbalist amongst us," Miss Emily said proudly. "I remember the day you were born, Sam. Your ma and me knew you were goin' to grow up to be somethin' special."

Sam blushed with the excessive attention directed toward him, then scampered off next door to find anonymity amid the blacksmith's bellows.

"He's a dear one," Miss Emily said, refilling our cups with sweet hibiscus tea. "Has he started to talk any more?"

"I'm afraid only with me."

"Give him time, I'm sure he'll grow out of it. And what of Emmett, how's it workin' out with him down at your pa's store?"

"He says he'd rather be holed up in the attic reading, but Pappa says he's got a real talent with woodworking. Thinks he'll be the one to take over the shop one day."

"And what of Klaus, I mean your pa. Is he back from his trip to New Orleans? I hope he took the blue jacket I mended for him. It do bring out the color in his eyes."

"Pappa's back and busy building a bedroom set for William Rice's bride-to-be. You know the money from that quarter, so it will be a masterpiece, I'm sure. Pappa sends his regards and promises to come by week's end to chop up that rotten oak of yours. He's afraid it's coming down on your house with the next big wind."

Miss Emily observed the imposing tree. "Hardwoods do fall over quicker than pines. Had any patients lately?"

"I saw to Mr. Kinkaid's corns the other day. He missed a day at the gristmill, they were grieving him so much."

"Did you cut them off?"

"I couldn't 'cause of the moon waxing, but I applied a house-eleek plaster and told him I'd be back in a week's time to look at them."

"Your reputation will soon precede you, Mia."

"I think it already has to a certain degree. Just yesterday I was in Byrne's Stationary Store up on Long Row, when a woman approached me. Told me I'd cured her cousin's rickets, and begged me to look at her husband. He's postmaster Issac Wade, no less."

Miss Emily nodded knowingly, "From what I hear, it's his heart and he don't have much time left. To ease his suffering, I'd recommend pigweed and angelica seeds steeped in Spanish wine."

"Why don't you go see him yourself? I mean, I can handle corns and headaches, but something as serious as this... What if I do something wrong?"

"Do you think Doc Abbott with his cuppin' and bleedin' and full as a tick half the time considers doing somethin' wrong? No treatment is fool proof. We just got to do our best. Besides, you have the touch."

Miss Emily had taught me the laying on of hands. Even though my hands tingled as if warm water flowed from them and patients swore they felt relief from their pain, I remained skeptical of the phenomena.

Miss Emily propped her slender legs on a tree stump and rested her chin in her palms, "Well, when you gonna read from that fat book you brought? I's ready for some learnin'."

As a former slave, Miss Emily was prohibited from learning to read, which made it all the more astounding she'd gained all her knowledge of healing by word of mouth. Taking up the thick tome, I carefully turned its brittle yellowed pages to the scarlet ribbon marking my place. "It's written by Carolus Linnaeus, a Swedish doctor from the eighteenth century. He spent countless hours collecting plants and preparing drugs from them."

"Sounds like my kind of man," she mused.

"He's mostly known for a system he created, called binomial nomenclature. It's a way to classify all plants and animals by two names, the genus and species."

"Binomial what? Mia, go no further. It's plain as day this is beyond my ability to reckon."

"Be patient, you'll soon understand. Let's say you need an herbal treatment for kidney stones. Someone offers you Joe Pye weed, another person suggests Queen of the Meadow, while somebody else swears Gravel Root is the right medicine for you."

Miss Emily was stumped. "Why, they're all talking about the same plant. It just has different names it goes by."

"Exactly! But what if someone didn't know it had different names. It could get awfully confusing right away. So, Linnaeus realized there needed to be one official name, a scientific one. For Joe Pye weed, it's Eupatorium purpureum. Now, there's no more confusion in identification."

"But the name itself is confusing."

"Latin may sound a little strange at first, but it gives information about the plant. In this case, Eupatorium comes from Eupator, King of Pontus, who discovered the herb was a poison antidote, and purpureum describes the plant as purple. Can you see how it's much more descriptive than Joe Pye weed?"

Miss Emily seemed skeptical. "I see your point, but..."

"Here's a bit of Linnaeus' poetic writing, you'll like this.'The flowers' leaves serve as bridal beds, which the Creator has so gloriously arranged, adorned with such noble bed curtains, and perfumed with so many soft scents, the bridegroom with his bride might there celebrate their nuptials with so much the greater solemnity...'"

"A bed of flowers," Miss Emily hooted. "That's what every honeymoon should be like."

"Is that how yours was?"

By her scowl, I knew it was the wrong thing to ask.

"Never did jump the broom with Hannah's daddy," she answered sullenly.

"You mean you never married him?" I asked, shocked.

Like a play's final curtain, our congenial conversation came to an end. "I'm sorry I mentioned it," I said tentatively.

I was curious about her past, knowing it was a painful one. She'd been captured by an English slaver and sold on the block, but the rest remained shrouded in mystery. I was certain it held the key as to why a beautiful and intelligent woman of thirty-four wasn't married, and why she had no gentlemen callers. I also knew this was not the right time to ask what she knew about Mamma.

CHAPTER IV

ABOUT TOWN

*S*aturday bath was a luxury I looked forward to all week. It required a fair amount of labor, hauling fifteen gallons of water from the cistern and heating it for two hours. It was worth all the effort when I finally eased myself into the tin tub behind the kitchen stove. Being the only girl in the family, I had the privilege of bathing first, my brothers following in order of age. After I was scrubbed clean and dressed, I headed downstairs to pass muster with Pappa. It was the precursor to our family outing about town.

"Well, Pappa, what do you think?" I asked with a smart curtsy.

Absorbed in the latest edition of *The Telegraph,* my father mumbled, "Hmm?"

"I want to know how you think I look."

His eyes raised above the paper with a perfunctory glance. "Sehr hübsch, Mia."

"This is the dress, Miss Emily helped me sew. It's from the linen you brought back from New Orleans."

He continued distractedly, "Uh, huh."

"She asked me the other day if you wore the blue coat on your trip. The one she said she mended."

"Ja, you can tell her I did."

He raised his paper again, and I couldn't help but feel he was trying to obscure his expression. "The obituaries must be particularly interesting today or is something else capturing your fancy?"

"Death notices are always fascinating, why here's one you'll find of particular interest. A patient of yours, I believe. '*It is with much regret we announce the death of postmaster, Issac E. Wade, aged 42 years on Sunday morning. Mild and unobtrusive in his manners, tender and affectionate in all his intercourse.*'"

"To be sure, Miss Emily and I were just discussing his case. I'm afraid it was quite hopeless, his heart you know. Why he was only two years older than you, Pappa."

"Death is a certainty. That's why we've got to live each day to its fullest. Speaking of which, where are your brothers, I've a lot to do today."

Pappa hollered and my brothers were soon lined up before him. They were in their best bib and tucker with spit shined shoes and oiled back hair. Emmett was weighed down by a satchel of books, which he insisted was light reading he'd pursue in lax moments. Pappa shook his head at the ridiculous sight, but could not condemn such noble efforts to enhance one's mind nor one's muscles by the look of their weight.

Sam smiled shyly, his dimpled cheeks rosy from the scrubbing I gave them. He loved Saturday outings, for they always meant some special treat for him. My mischievous brother, Christian, was uncharacteristically subdued. He was clean and in order, but his eyes were averted, and he wore his straw boater conspicuously low upon his head.

Noticing an alteration in Christian's usually rambunctious ways, Pappa asked, "Son, what are you up to?"

The answer to Pappa's question came when Emett stole Christian's hat, revealing my brother's once thick mane of hair was replaced by bald patches and crudely bandaged nicks.

"What happened to you?" Emmett queried. "Been to a blind barber?"

Christian retrieved his hat, and swiftly covered the offending sight. "Cut it myself, and it's a pretty good job except a few spots where the scissors slipped."

"You're handsome just the same," I said in a feeble attempt to relieve his embarrassment.

Pappa chuckled, "For the time being your hat will make a fine compliment to your wardrobe. Now, let's get going."

We generally walked to our destinations in town, but stocking up on supplies at Market Square required conveyance in our old buckboard. With a gentle touch to the reins, Pappa guided Bess, the old mare, and Joe, the pinto gelding, up Main Street. After three days of rain, the dirt road was a quagmire, and the shoddy springs made the ride a rough one. However, the sun was now out, and we were all in high spirits with the prospects of the day before us.

We turned onto Travis Street, and I, sitting in the front with Pappa, smiled and waved at our acquaintances. My father, being handsome and profitably employed, was considered a catch and incited much notice from the single women we passed. We came upon a group of women particularly excited to see him, whereupon we noticed Cora Hornsby in their midst. With her puckered face turned directly at us, she shot us an evil eye cold as an outhouse seat on a winter's night. Turning back to the women with an urgent communication, they huddled about her, their heads bobbing from Cora to us and back again. I was certain their titters were the result of mean-spirited gossip Cora was spreading.

My father, who showed previous restraint in regards to Cora, abruptly reined in the horses. They were unaccustomed to rough handling and responded with wild prancing and snorting. I had no idea as to his intentions, however Cora sensed danger and hastily departed from her companions who cackled with surprise. Pappa, thinking better of further confrontation, directed the horses into a dramatic galloping departure.

"I need a drink! We're going over to Kessler's."

This was an extraordinary declaration, for it wasn't Pappa's custom to imbibe spirits before noon, nor to take his children to an arcade known for betting on which Texas town had the most murders for the week. Emmett tied our horses to the hitching post, and we had no sooner entered the arcade than Pappa was approached by Mayor Francis Moore, who shouted and waved at us with his one arm. His loss of limb during Texas' Revolution had not slowed down his aspirations. He'd served as surgeon with the Buckeye Rangers, was thrice mayor of Houston, father of nine children, and current editor of the *Telegraph*. There was no rest for Francis Moore, and he liked it that way.

Moore jovially patted my father on the back. "Klaus Stein, just the man I've been lookin' for. I'll gladly buy you a drink if you can convince these Third Ward aldermen on the error of their ways."

"A deal indeed, Francis," Pappa said, making himself comfortable on a nearby tree stump. "A gin toddy sounds mighty fine right now."

The mayor asked, "Klaus, have you been over to see the new courthouse?"

"Not yet. Been meaning to though. Business has kept me hopping."

"I know your eye for detail, and I think you'll find the workers did a fine job. However, we're needing the interior finished out and the quotes exceed our budget. I thought perhaps you'd consider offering a counter bid, thereby proving to these fine gentlemen we don't need to be robbed to get good work done."

An excruciatingly drawn out negotiation began, which then progressed into discussions on the quality of our bayou's water and the threat of cholera, Santa Anna's recent activities in Mexico, and the census results of our city's two thousand inhabitants. Emmett had been wise to bring his books, and he contentedly settled down to reading them in the shade of a nearby tree. Christian had no trouble with the waiting, for his attention was drawn to the gamblers' finer points of betting. As for me, each minute was agony as I deflected men's unsavory glances, and contended with Sam pulling on my skirts with complaints of hunger. Finding no natural pause in my father's fervent conversation, I demurely whispered my desire to leave. Taking no heed of my gentle entreaty, I repeated my request a bit louder. Still disregarded, I at last raised my voice, "Pappa, Miss Penelope will be expecting us. Hadn't we best be going?"

With its fine porcelain and real silverware, Penelope's Cafe was a genteel refuge in our rough and ready town. And though its proprietor had a heart as big as all outdoors, she fell short in comportment proper to an unmarried woman. She was a minx with her sights set on Pappa, and I knew the mere mention of her would provoke a reaction from my father and his companions.

"Ah, Miss Penelope McGuire," Mayor Moore hooted. "A fine Irish gal whose hips are made for birthing. Klaus, have you two set a date yet? You're not getting any younger."

My father's face reddened. "Idle gossip, Francis, we are merely friends. Mia, why don't we just eat here?"

Offended by such an absurd suggestion, I grabbed Sam's hand and made an abrupt departure. Laughter and snide remarks regarding strong-minded women followed after me, but I was not deterred, and by the time I reached the cafe's blue and white striped awnings, Pappa had arrived with Emmett and Christian in tow.

We entered the establishment and were unexpectedly seated by a woman we didn't recognize.

"Lucky Pappa, I believe *she's* not here today," Emmett observed.

Without Miss Penelope's usual unsolicited advancements, Pappa enjoyed his meal more than ever, and thought he'd escaped her completely until he asked for the check and caught sight of her flaming red hair.

"She's making a bee line for us and looking awfully man hungry," Christian said.

"She's shameless," Emmett added.

"That's enough nonsense," Pappa reprimanded under his breath.

An unnatural silence prevailed as the subject of our discussion approached.

As Miss Penelope bent over to crumb the table, Pappa's eyes fleetingly rested on the ample freckled breasts threatening to burst her bodice's pearl buttons. "How were your chicken and dumplings, Klaus?" she asked in her lilting Irish brogue.

Nervously clearing his throat, he answered, "Very tasty, Miss Penelope, thank you. We always enjoy dining here. In fact, Mia insisted we go nowhere else."

Miss Penelope glowed, certain Pappa's praise for her establishment was equal to a declaration of love. "And Miss Mia, what a charming linen dress you have on today. You're such a pretty lass. Now, don't you slouch down like you're trying to hide. There's nothing to be ashamed of when someone takes notice of you. Did you dance around the Maypole this morning? I hear they were going to have a lovely celebration."

I answered, "No, ma'am, I think I'm too old for that now."

That's how Miss Penelope was, always to the point. I recalled the time we'd run into each other at Torri Dunn's Hardware Store. Standing in the aisle between hatchets and whipsaws, she confided to me her painful life story. How she'd witnessed her parents and half her village die in Ireland's potato famine. Her tears flowed as she disclosed the dream she and her husband had of making a new life in America, but that he tragically died on the crossing. The indention her wedding ring had made in her flesh was long gone, but the mark on her heart was indelible.

I remember her saying, "It was a dismal welcoming when I arrived on these shores, for 'No Irish Need Apply' was posted in all the shops' windows. So, it was the squalor of the poorhouse for me, eating nothing but watered down gruel and hardtack. The deprivation inspired me to open a restaurant. I wanted to serve the most delicious food, where no one went away hungry. When I heard about the Allen brothers starting up a city and found out they were Irish, as well as the mayor, I thought that's the city for me. There'd be no difference between the shanty or the lace curtain Irish. We'd all be Texians together."

My attention returned to the scene before me; Miss Penelope giving kind attention to each of my brothers in turn.

"And you lads, find everything to your liking?" she asked. "Did you all get full?"

"Yes, Ma'am," Emmett said, batting his eyelashes in imitation of hers. "Best buffalo tongue I ever ate. A real epicurean delight."

"Epicurean delight?" Miss Penelope squealed. "Well, that does take all! I might use it in my 'vertisement if you don't object. Klaus, more coffee? I know how you like it, straight black with no sugar or cream."

Pappa accepted the offer. "You do make the best coffee, Miss Penelope. I sure wish you'd tell the secret to my Mia."

"It's the eggshells, nothing else takes the bitterness out as well. How about a slice of rhubarb pie? My receipt for it won first place at the Fair's bake-off last year."

"I remember your triumph and it's well deserved," Pappa said. "However, I promised Sam a trip to the confectioner's, and he'll be up with a tummy ache if I add pie on top of it all. Maybe, next time."

"Well, we can't have Sam with a sore belly," she said patting the top of my little brother's head as if he were a favorite pet.

Talk of sore bellies jogged Sam's memory and to our astonishment, he spoke in public for the very first time. "By the way, Miss Penelope, did the senna help with your bowels?"

The woman went crimson with embarrassment, but managed to say, "Thank you, they're just fine. Now, if you'll excuse me."

She skedaddled as my older brothers convulsed with laughter.

"Gadzooks, Sam!" I cried. "The discussion you overheard between Miss Emily and myself concerning Penelope's health or any other patient is confidential. That means we don't talk about it with others."

My scolding brought tears to my little brother's eyes, and I realized I'd ruined his brave effort to conquer his shyness.

"Never mind the slip," Pappa declared. "Miss Penelope's skin is thick as leather and she'll soon recover. What matters is that Sam talked and that was wunderbar!"

All ears in the cafe were trained on our table's drama, and no one was more enthralled than Darlene Campbell. She was president of the Daughters of the Texas Revolution, and a member of my sewing circle, so I knew her well. Once beautiful with a patrician stature to match the high opinion she held of herself, she was now in her seventies and stooped with a dowager's hump. She perpetually wore widow's weeds out of respect for her heroic husband who died at the Battle of San Jacinto.

Captivated by every word of Pappa and Miss Penelope's discourse, she'd dunked her doughnut absentmindedly till the pastry was a soggy mess and the table linen covered in spilt coffee.

"Come over here a minute, Miss Mia," Darlene beckoned with her crooked finger. "Did I just witness a lover's quarrel?"

I'd have to be guarded with my words. Darlene was as much a gossipmonger as Cora, and the town could easily be privy to everything transpiring in that café by end of day. "Miss Penelope was merely checking up on how we liked the food. She's a very good hostess, wouldn't you say?"

"Don't try to pull the wool over my eyes, young lady. That woman went beet red before hightailing it to the back room. It's about time your father settled down. Five years is too long for a respectable man with his own business to stay a widower. Besides he could do far worse than Miss Penelope."

"What do you mean by far worse?"

"Just that. There's talk of your father stepping out with someone unsuitable."

"You must be confusing Pappa with someone else, he's not seeing anyone. Now, if you'll excuse me, my family is waiting. I will see you on Thursday at the sewing circle."

We left the cafe and headed to Market Street. If the bayou was Houston's artery, then Market Square was its heart. With a maze of stalls covering a square block and vendors hawking their wares, it had the perpetual atmosphere of a fair. We stocked up on sugarcane and flour brought in from the nearby plantations, and dried beans and lye, then headed over to the confectioner's. The boys' pockets were soon bulging with saltwater taffy and licorice sticks, and I bought sweetmeats for Sunday dinner. Emmett and Christian then went off to peruse rifles and Bowie knives, while Pappa accompanied Sam and me to Percival Gray's Emporium.

Percival was a young fastidious cockscomb who kept each hair in place by aid of a thick pomade. Through persistent industry and bold advertisement, he had expanded his wares from a single cart to a string of counters equaling half the block.

"Good day, Mr. Stein, Miss Stein, and young Master Samuel, I believe." Percival spoke in a fast clip, reflecting his nervous energy. "How may I be of service? At Gray's Emporium, we promise everything necessary to outfit a house, yet sold cheaply enough to satisfy all classes. As you see we have a new shipment of Chinese porcelain, and there's a beautiful Wedgwood dinner service for eight, that you might like, Miss Mia, for your hope chest."

I warily eyed Sam's swinging limbs beside the stacked dishes.

"Nope," Pappa replied succinctly.

"Perhaps some castor oil?" Percival persisted.

Sam's tongue stuck out in disgust.

"Do I look in need of a dosing?" Pappa asked perplexed.

"Begging your pardon sir, of course not. Why you're the very picture of health. It's just that... To be honest I'm overstocked and obliged to offer my customers an incredible discount on it."

"Sorry, I can't help you out Percival, I'm not in the market for castor oil today nor any other day if I had my druthers. I *am* in want of a new collar, though."

"Right this way sir. The finest haberdashery awaits you."

I knew of no upcoming wedding or funeral, and because my father was not a churchgoer, there was little occasion for him to dress up. Darlene's suggestion of his stepping out with someone unsuitable came back to me. "A new collar, Pappa? Having second thoughts about Miss Penelope?"

His stony silence squashed further inquiry.

"Here's the very one, Mr. Stein?" Percival said, opening a box. "I'm certain you'll find it to your liking. It's our newest item, the Elliptic Three Fold Collar, quite unique in design and singular in operation. Allow me to fit it to your shirt."

Pappa bristled, "No need for any fuss, I can manage myself."

Percival took no heed as he manipulated the collar. "No trouble at all, why it's my pleasure. Notice the ease with which the patent elastic fastener attaches, and as you can see it opens back or front. It's our number one seller, and of course I always guarantee one hundred percent satisfaction. Sam Houston, himself, came by here not an hour ago and purchased a dozen of these very collars. Said he was leaving for Washington to see to his senatorial duties."

Sam's eyes widened in awe at the mention of the formidable Mr. Houston. Pappa had fought under his command during the Revolution, and we had espied the impressive gentleman from afar on several occasions. His charismatic personality always drew a quick crowd.

"Shall I get you a dozen too, Mr. Stein?" Percival asked hopefully.

"One will suffice," Pappa maintained.

Not easily deterred, Percival pressed, "Perhaps a new shirt and cuffs to go with it then? I've broadcloth vests on sale. A man of your position needs to maintain a certain image in the community."

"Just the one collar will do me fine."

"What about you, Miss Stein? I just received several bolts of gingham and calicoes. All the ladies been saying they're the smartest colors they've seen in quite some time and will make up fine summer dresses."

Percival's enthusiastic sales pitch was cut short by the unexpected appearance of Sheriff Willoughby Franklin holding Christian in his firm grip. Emmett ran up closely behind them, along with a sweaty faced salesman. It seemed a chase had transpired, ending with the apprehension of my brother.

Sheriff Franklin, dark as tanned leather and famous for fighting scalawags on the western border, drawled, "There's been an unfortunate occurrence, Mr. Stein."

"Oh my, very unfortunate," Percival mumbled.

Squirming under the stronghold of his captor, Christian's straw boater fell off, revealing his badly shorn head. Nervous laughter rippled through the gathering crowd, and I hoped my brother's trespass wouldn't forever be handed down as a scandalous strike against his character.

"If you'll kindly unhand my son," Pappa said. "I'm certain whatever offense you believe him to be guilty of doesn't warrant such rough handling."

Sheriff Franklin loosened his grip and instructed Christian to confess his misdeed. With downcast eyes brimming with guilt, Christian pulled his hands out from his pockets. A small pin knife appeared, covered in sticky taffy.

The muscles in Pappa's jaw contracted. "What do you have to say for yourself, son?"

Christian muttered pitifully, "I'm very sorry."

Turning to the aggrieved salesman, Pappa asked, "Excuse me, sir, what is your name?"

"It's Todd Blakely, sir."

"Well, Mr. Blakely, let me also apologize for my son, though his actions are inexcusable. Christian will be in your service for a month to work any odd jobs you come up with. Do you agree that's enough compensation?"

"Mr. Stein, it's really not necessary," the salesman answered. "My property has been recovered and it appears the boy has learned his lesson."

Pappa shook his head in disagreement. "We all make mistakes in life, but we're not apt to learn from them unless we feel the full brunt of their consequence. I'm sure Christian agrees."

My brother gazed up meekly. "I'd rather have a birch twig to my backside than indentured service."

"Then you shall have both," Pappa replied.

The sheriff and salesman laughed, breaking the tenseness of the moment, and the crowd dispersed. Pappa finished his transaction with Percival and my family was able to find a secluded spot to discuss our plans.

"Mia, I've got to drop by the sawmill to check on a lumber order that's late again," Pappa said. "Don't know what Sam Allen is up to, but if he don't start running things better, I'll be taking my business elsewhere. The boys will come with me."

"Can we stop by the barbershop?" Christian pleaded. "Please Pappa, to fix my haircut."

"Nope, I think I'll leave you just as you are. Let it be a reminder to not have sticky fingers in the future."

Sam showed me his fingers covered in a thick candy coating. "Not that kind, little brother."

"I'd like to go to the barbershop too, Pappa," Emmett said, stroking the barely visible fuzz above his lip. "I think it's about time I get a shave."

"Emmett, you can't get a shave, you're not a man yet," Christian said scornfully. "Though you smell like one. Mia, you'd better make some coriander tea for his armpits."

Pappa gave Emmett a proud slap on the back. "Well, you *are* working now, so I suppose it's time you get your own mug down at the barbershop."

"I've one more errand to run," I said. "I'll meet you all back home."

Sam attached himself to my skirts, imploring me with his big blue eyes to take him with me. Fortunately, Pappa convinced him he'd have far more fun with them, and so I was given the rare opportunity to be left to my own devices.

CHAPTER V

RACHAEL ROTHSCHILD

I headed directly to Ophelia Thomas, a milliner on Franklin Street. My intention was to treat her rheumatism and pitch my idea of her selling my rosewater. In order to reach her establishment, I was obliged to walk past Hook and Ladder Company Number One, an unnerving experience for an unchaperoned woman. The firemen were generally brazen flirts, but today I was fortunate enough to find a solitary man out washing the horses. By his Dundreary whiskers and large drooping mustache, I recognized him as a fellow member of Pappa's Lyceum club.

"Good day to you, Miss Stein," he stammered. "I have acquaintance with your father."

"Yes, Pappa has mentioned you."

"Pardon my manners, I'm Evan Clark, ma'am."

There passed an uncomfortable silence, whereby he nervously bit his lip, looking heavenward for inspiration on what to converse. His reputation as an eloquent club debater apparently excluded discourse with the opposite sex.

"The horses seem especially frisky today," I offered as a jumping off point. It seemed more original than commenting on the weather.

Relieved to direct his attention toward the animals, he replied, "Yes, they're anxious for exercise. Haven't had a call in weeks."

"*The Telegraph* mentioned your getting a steam-operated pumper. I'd think it a heavy load for the horses to pull."

"These Morgans are some of the strongest draft horses, they can handle it. We'll be showing the pumper off at the Fourth of July fair. I know that's not for a couple of months still, but do you plan on attending?"

"Yes, I'm working a booth with the Daughters of the Texas Revolution. We're selling lap quilts and such."

"Then I'm certain to see you there, if not before." Evan paused, then asked, "I've heard you're a kind of healer, is it true?"

"Yes, I'm apprenticed to Miss Emily."

"Well, my mother is grieving something awful with a toothache. Could you recommend something to help her with the pain?"

"Have her chew willow bark or cloves work even better. Of course, you might call on Doc Abbott. He'll see if it needs pulling."

Mr. Clark scowled. "Ever since he tended Mother's last delivery, she refuses to see him. I shouldn't say anything as I don't like bad-mouthing folks, but he's a butcher, not a physician."

"I'm sorry to hear it. Did the child die?"

Mr. Clark solemnly shook his head in affirmation, "And she holds him responsible for it. Not the baby's death, but what happened afterwards was... well, I can't rightly say more. Miss Stein, it's not proper conversation with a lady."

"Those who deal with the infirmed are not allowed the luxury of a squeamish sensibility. Please, Mr. Clark, tell me what happened."

"I'm certain you've seen your share of unpleasant cases, but I don't reckon you've experienced the atrocity the doctor performed. Mother was in labor for nearly two days straight, and we all thought she wasn't going to pull through. The baby died inside of her, so to get it out, Doc crushed its skull with scissors, then with hooks brought him out piecemeal. It was the most gruesome sight ever, one I wish I could forget."

Despite wanting to prove my stalwartness, I shuddered at the scene he depicted. "I'm so sorry, Mr. Clark. And your mother, has she recovered from the trauma?"

"She's a strong woman, but you can sympathize with her aversion for the doctor. My father has considered wringing the man's neck."

"Would she be inclined to my calling on her? I could bring her the cloves then."

"Thank you kindly, Miss Stein. I'm certain she'd most definitely enjoy your company."

As I turned to leave, a herd of loose hogs crossed the road and upset the horses, who in turn kicked the bucket of soapy water onto my dress.

"How dreadful!" Evan said, rushing forward with a dry towel. Not taking into consideration the impropriety of his actions, he patted me down as if I were one of his horses.

I pulled away, feeling the soft pressure of his hand still on my leg. "I really must be off, Mr. Clark. No need for apologies, I'm fine."

Despite my placation, the man was beside himself with chagrin, and I could still hear his pleading for my forgiveness when I rounded the corner and entered the milliner's. The jingling bell announced my arrival, bringing forth Ophelia Thomas from a curtained backroom. "Dear Mia, what has happened to you? Your lovely dress is soaked through, and with not a cloud in the sky."

"It's no matter for concern, it will dry soon enough," I said, avoiding an explanation.

"Well, I'm glad you came no matter your peculiar state. Just look at my fingers all cramped up. Why, I can't even manage a needle and thread."

I held Ophelia's twisted fingers gently in my own till the warm tingly sensation of *the touch* passed between us.

"I swear I'm already feeling better with just you being here," she exclaimed cheerily. "I think you must be a miracle worker."

"Far from it," I argued. "What will do you far more good is the yarrow tea I brought."

Alarmed, she asked, "Oh, my, isn't that called the devil's plaything? I've seen Chinamen throw down stalks of it in a divination. Are you sure it's safe to drink?"

"My mother used to call it plumajillo, which means little feather for the shape of its leaves, and it's a very useful and safe herb.

I prescribe two cups a day, one in the morning and one at night. It's rather bitter, so you might prefer it sweetened with treacle."

"Thank you, Miss Mia, you've saved my very livelihood. Please take a look around and pick out something nice for yourself, my treat."

I glanced disappointingly at her lace trimmed shelves. They were piled high with outrageously decorated bonnets and parasols of so sheer a lace as to not perform their function. "I don't have much need for fancy things," I admitted.

"A young girl like you must have a string of beaus and opportunity to be walking out. Here take a look at this new shipment of kid leather shoes. Should I look for a pair in your size?"

"No ma'am, my shoes are still in good standing, so to speak."

"What about some violet water. This very morning, Esther Price bought six bottles for Charlotte's bridesmaids. June weddings can be pretty, though it be fiercely hot."

"June? I thought Charlotte wasn't getting married till August?"

"They moved up the date. I'm sure it's a week to the day because I told her I'd have the embroidered handkerchiefs ready by then."

"I wonder what the rush is all about?"

"The girl is already twenty-five and homely as sin. She best be getting hitched soon or else no amount of her daddy's cotton money will be enough to snag a husband."

"Charlotte and her family are our next-door neighbors," I said, thinking this sufficient to stop her gossip.

"I know very well, Miss Mia, and I can't say a word against poor Ester, whose born her husband a child every two years like clockwork 'til they have a dozen towheaded children impossible to tell apart. But Rufus is another matter entirely. Everybody knows he's a cruel master, keeping his slaves underfed and overworked."

Though I couldn't disagree with Ophelia's opinions, I wasn't going to add my two cents worth. "I notice you don't carry any rosewater. Miss Emily and I plan to make a batch. Would you consider selling it here?"

"It'd be a pleasure and the least I can do considering all the help you've done me. But, you still haven't picked out something special for yourself. Here now let me choose something if you won't. I've got the perfect thing in mind. You'll see, it's absolutely precious!"

Her once stiff fingers rifled nimbly through the hatboxes until she came upon the particular one she was searching for. Leaf by leaf the scented tissue paper was removed until at last a diaphanous bonnet emerged. It was covered in pink satin roses, and she positioned it upon my head with the pomp and ceremony befitting a coronation.

Ophelia cooed as she circled me. "How lovely. Note the melon crown with its strips of whalebone going across instead of around. It sets off your dark hair to good affect. And the brim hits just above your eyebrow, providing that hint of reserve and mystique that every woman seeks to attain. It's the quality that surely draws the men in."

"Yes, it's beautiful," I agreed. "but what would I wear it with? It's far too elegant an adornment for my plain wardrobe. I really don't need it."

"Since when does a woman *need* to buy pretty little things except for the pure enjoyment of owning them. This dainty little confection is the latest fashion and sure to elevate your wardrobe. Besides, it's your obligation to bring beauty to our Houston streets, as did your mother in her own way."

My ears perked up at her reference. "You knew my mother?"

Ophelia blanched. "Not really. She never came into my shop, actually hardly ever saw her on the street. She was a mystery of sorts, but when she did appear, no one could deny her beauty."

"My mother a mystery? How do you mean?"

"I've misspoken," she stammered. "I meant to say..."

Ophelia's explanation was interrupted by the doorbell jingling and the arrival of a young woman wildly stomping her muddy feet.

"Hang this mosquito infested town and everyone in it," she railed. The harsh words sounded incongruent with the girl's refined British accent. She continued, "It's impossible to take a step from my phaeton without ruining my skirts and shoes. I shall soon be called a mud turtle, for that is what the rest of the country considers Houstonians."

Rolling her eyes in disapproval, Ophelia murmured, "The hoity-toity has arrived."

I raised my dress hem to reveal my stodgy boots, the only sensible shoes for our streets.

The brash young woman swished toward us. Despite her spoilt satin slippers, she appeared as a vision stepping off the pages of Godey's Lady's Book, the definitive authority on style. Her dress was a blue taffeta, its skirt most certainly five yards at the hem with several petticoats beneath. It flared to such immense proportions so as to completely conceal the chair she boldly took beside me.

Ophelia forced a smile. "Miss Mia Stein, allow me to introduce you to Miss Rachael Rothschild. She's the niece of Captain Charles Biggs," Ophelia explained. "You'll recall his lucrative commerce on the high seas during our revolution."

Ophelia was referencing the infamous captain making money hand over fist by selling arms to the Mexicans. I assumed it's why my father hated him and forbade us to even pass by his grand house, Mosswood. To encounter his relation intrigued me. "A pleasure to meet you, Miss Rothschild."

Rachael offered her limp gloved hand, and purred, "How quaint. You're a darling child."

I was perplexed by her remark, for though she was painted and coiffed, I was certain she was similar in age to myself and in no position to pretend otherwise.

"I see you've gotten into a puddle or two yourself," she continued tartly. "Or are wet dresses the rage these days? I admit I'm ignorant in the ways of this backward town. You really should do your hair altogether different, Miss Stein. The manner in which your braids hang down detract from the bonnet's exquisite artistry. If you must wear plaits, a Grecian braid encircling your head would suit you far better. As for your dress, Gigot de mouton sleeves are terribly last season. Don't you agree Miss Thomas?"

I was shocked by her denouncement of my appearance, and grateful for Ophelia rising to my defense.

"Mutton sleeves *are* outmoded, but Miss Stein is wearing *engageantes*, and they are all the rage. Now, if you will excuse me ladies, I have a pressing matter to attend."

I was certain Ophelia referred to her ironing, and was envious of her escaping this most ill-mannered girl.

Miss Rothschild appearing impatient with me and perhaps life in general, tapped her muddy slipper. She asked curtly, "Are you buying the bonnet?"

"Yes, in a manner of speaking. It's payment for services rendered to Miss Thomas."

"Do say, are you in trade also?"

"I'm an apprentice to an herbalist and midwife. I gave Miss Thomas a remedy and she in turn gave me this bonnet."

Twirling her parasol between porcelain white fingers, she coyly offered an affected smile. "What oddities one finds in this swampy outback." Finding amusement with her own remark, she burst out in a haughty laughter until she gasped for want of air and pain contorted her delicate features.

"Are you alright?" I asked with genuine concern.

"Yes, of course, don't be silly," she managed to say while fanning her flushed face with one hand, and gripping her side with the other.

Certain I knew the source of her troubles, I offered, "It's your corset constricting your lungs. They're unnatural contraptions exacting a severe price for beauty. Let's go to the backroom, and I'll help you loosen the strings."

Her eyes bugged with disdain. "You dare lecture me on beauty and health? I know what's best on both counts, and it's that bonnet atop your head that will allay this pain. I'll pay you double its worth."

It was obvious the girl was addlebrained. "How will my bonnet ease the pain in your side? No, I will not sell it to you."

"I see you're a shrewd bargainer. Then make it triple the price. Surely you cannot refuse so dear an offer."

My conscience was torn. On principle, I didn't want to give into the whims of this spoilt girl, and yet to turn my back on so substantial amount of money was prideful folly. Considering it seed money for my rosewater endeavor with Miss Emily, I reluctantly removed the coveted bonnet. Surprisingly in doing so, I realized my own desire for the pretty little thing.

Throwing her own beautiful bonnet on the ground, Miss Rothschild greedily snatched up mine. "Don't you think it handsome against my blond ringlets?" she asked, primping in the mirror. "I'm blessed with naturally curly hair, you know."

If it were true then it was surely the only natural thing about her.

"American goods are inferior on all counts, and most shops aren't worth patronizing. Thankfully, Miss Thomas imports her merchandise from abroad."

Reaching my limit for Miss Rothschild's barbs, I countered, "With such strong prejudices against my country, I think you'd prefer living in your homeland."

"Amour, my dear, is the irresistible lure that draws me here," she giggled. Then fearing another fit, she checked her enthusiasm. "And I'm not ashamed to admit I'd brave the Atlantic a hundred times over to be by my cousin, Daniel's, side. Unfortunately at present, his days are filled with work, leaving me to my own devices. And as I'm so newly arrived, I'm at a loss with how to fill the long hours. Why don't you join me for tea at Mosswood. Let's say Wednesday at one o'clock."

This peculiar creature perplexed me to a high degree. She'd insulted my city, country, and person, audaciously procured the very bonnet off my head, only to invite me to tea. Yet, despite my vexations, I accepted her offer. To be sure it was not for the enjoyment of her company, but rather I couldn't deny my only opportunity to see inside Mosswood, the palatial estate of Captain Biggs.

With butterfly kisses brushing both my cheeks and a sweet adieu, Miss Rothschild took her leave. Ophelia timidly reappeared, and together we watched with amusement as the English girl tiptoed daintily to her awaiting barouche. She signaled her driver to move on, but the small painted ponies couldn't dislodge the wheels stuck in the mud. The slave earnestly tugged at the horses' bridle, but still the animals struggled. Despite her abusive rant upon her driver, her beauty alone attracted attention from a passing party of young gentlemen. Rachael ceased her tantrum and transformed herself into a genteel lady, her coquettish smile a prize for her saviors.

Ophelia shook her head disapprovingly. "Happiness isn't always getting what you want, but rather wanting what you already have. Mark my words, that spoilt missy will never be happy."

I walked out onto the street, mulling over Ophelia's words. I'd heard the trite platitude before, maybe even believed it at one time. But in that moment, I only felt loss and envy as the bonnet of palest pink, covered in satin roses, slowly disappeared down the street. Shamed by my shallow thoughts, I turned to the lame beggar woman, who was squatting at her usual corner. She thrust her tin cup towards me with a hopeful snaggletoothed grin. The bundle of bills, Miss Rothschild had paid me, suddenly felt too heavy for my purse, so I stuffed them into her cup and walked on.

CHAPTER VI

MYSTERY AT MOSSWOOD

outh of the courthouse, running east from Main to Crawford, stood the majestic houses of Quality Hill. Each edifice had a generous swath of verdant lawn and a brick wall to enclose it. They were ostentatious proof that the homeowner had prospered in what Rachel Rothschild described as a mud hole. For years, John Andrews' three story Greek revival, known as *The Castle*, had been the pinnacle of architectural extravagance. Mosswood, Captain Biggs' estate, had stolen the title, and he was now king of the hill.

How imposing his property appeared before me, as I stood at its edge. The tea date I'd agreed upon with Rachael had arrived, and I, through deception, had received Pappa's approval for my outing. I gave him the Rothschild name without disclosing her relation to Captain Biggs. I was ashamed by my ruse, but not enough to cancel my visit and the opportunity to meet the illusive captain.

Rachael's pretentious appearance gave rise to my own self-consciousness and a desire to prove Houston women could be just as fashionable. My walking dress was a pale green watered poplin, one of my best, and the chemisette was an embroidered muslin. My straw hat tied with a nosegay of violets didn't compare with the bonnet of satin roses I had possessed so fleetingly, but I felt I was presentable enough.

Pushing open the heavy wrought-iron gate, I found my palms sweaty and my heart racing with anticipation of what lay ahead. I soon realized I had mistakingly entered a side entrance, for a shelled pathway led me through a series of garden rooms rather than directly to the house. Each plot was a unique oasis enclosed by towering yew hedges. The first was a perennial garden consisting of all white blossoms: knee-high cosmos lining the path, Madame Plantier roses arching over an arbor, and gardenias scenting the air. The second allotment was a formal boxwood parterre with topiaries precisely clipped into frolicking bears. The third garden room held a reflecting pool bordered by espaliered persimmon trees. So golden and enticing was the fruit, I found myself plucking several to eat. No sooner had I touched the tasty morsels to my lips that an enormous mastiff bounded toward me with bared fangs and lathered growl.

Screaming, I ran and climbed the nearest tree without delay, and was there stranded with the ferocious animal nipping and barking at the tree's base.

A man, who I presumed was one of the captain's slaves, appeared and called out, "Come here Cerberus, that ain't no way to greet a young lady."

His sharp rebuke subdued the terrifying beast into a playful pup proffering his belly for a good rub. This wasn't what I had in mind when I imagined my genteel invitation to tea. "Cerberus, guard of the underworld? The captain must have a sense of humor to come up with such a name."

"Wouldn't know, Miss, but, ya shouldn't have run. Only stirs him up more. Let me help ya down. It's a shame your hem got torn. Not too many visitors come round here. Are you lost?"

"Miss Rothschild invited me to tea, but I came in the wrong way and I'm a little late."

"Well, go right on ahead then and don't mind Ulysses up at the house. Cap'n just bought him in New Orleans, and he thinks he's high and mighty above the rest of us. Well, I best be off. Just keep to the right, and ya can't miss it."

Following an avenue of crepe myrtles, I came upon a spectacular view of the house. It was a grandiose structure with an overhang supported by pink granite columns, each topped with intricate curlicues, and double hung sashes of six over six lights covered its facade. I was most impressed by its beauty, and yet I wondered if it could offer the comfort of my much smaller home. Approaching the massive door bookended by a pair of ferns, I felt an apprehension grip me. The lion's head doorknocker seemed to be daring me to enter this world of privilege.

My knock echoed through the cavernous house, and after some delay, Ulysses the butler answered the door. He was an imposing figure in white gloves and blue velvet suit, and after a cursory glance at my torn and dirtied dress, he said, "The service entrance is round back, Miss."

I was grateful the old man had forewarned me about the haughty servant, for I found the nerve to respond with indignation. "You are mistaken, sir. I am Miss Mia Stein, here for tea with Miss Rothschild."

Ulysses peered out the door and down the drive for the carriage which must have conveyed me, then uttered under his breath, "Highly irregular." Presenting me with a silver tray, he directed, "Your carte de visite, if you please."

I rustled through my purse, pretending to be in possession of a calling card, then said, "I'm sorry sir, but I seem to be all out today."

Raising an eyebrow in disdain, Ulysses directed, "Take a seat upon the settee. Miss Rachael will be told of your arrival."

The slave disappeared up the winding staircase, leaving me to take in the details of the lavish hall. Had Pappa not held such strong prejudice against the captain, he'd have enjoyed seeing the house's superior workmanship. I would regale him over dinner with details of the neoclassical door topped by a colored fanlight, and the intricate marquetry of the Louis Quinze commode.

Curious to see more, I ventured down the dimly lit hall only to come face to face with the despised blackguard, Captain Charles Biggs. To be sure it was only his portrait, however the flames refracting through the crystal chandelier had eerily captured his arresting blue eyes making them appear lifelike.

Recovering my composure, I took in the artist's skillful execution. Instead of flattering his patron, he'd depicted him with harsh realism. Sagging jowls revealed Biggs' age, his bulbous nose and bloodshot eyes were surely signs of debauchery, and his furrowed brow and scowl conveyed a sour, even perhaps malicious temperament. I'd heard tell that he lost an ear in a duel, but thankfully the portrait did not reveal this grotesque feature.

I defiantly announced to the visage before me, "Well, Captain Biggs, you don't frighten me in the least, nor does your rude servant or big dog. I've been properly invited, and plan to stay until I receive my promised tea. Even if you were to materialize upon the spot this very minute, I'd boldly stand my ground, for I am Klaus Stein's daughter, and he's far more respected in this town than you with your piles of ill-gotten money. Do not fear, I promise to show good manners and not stare at your missing ear when I do finally meet you, no matter how curious it proves."

Off in the distance a door opened and shut, and with approaching footsteps echoing off the marble floor, my boastful prattle dissolved into trembling fear. The relief I felt upon seeing Rachael's welcoming face cannot be fully expressed.

"Mia, what a delight," she chirped with outstretched arms.

Striding toward her with too much enthusiasm, my muddy boots slipped on the polished floor and hit the edge of the hall table. If not for Rachael's quick response, an ugly vase decorated with drunk looking men would've shattered into a thousand pieces.

"Dash it all, Mia! You almost broke Uncle Charles' Ming vase. It's the Eight Immortals, a priceless objet d'art. I dare not consider his tirade we would've had to suffer. Come now, don't look so frightened. Here, clean your shoes on the boot scraper. Did you have trouble finding us? I'd almost given up on your coming."

"Not at all. I've known of Mosswood for many years, and confess I've been keen to see its interior. Is Captain Biggs at home today?"

"He's not been here for months. Off to the Dark Continent on a big game safari. No telling when he'll return. Besides he's not a man to socialize. Come, I shall give you a precursory tour since you've shown such an interest."

"I saw the captain's portrait," I said, eager to hear Rachael's views on it.

"Doesn't do him justice," she fumed. "But at least it obscures his disfigurement. I don't suppose you'd know, but my uncle has only one ear. Lost it in a duel over a woman, which I consider terribly romantic, don't you?"

Rachael led me down dark twisted corridors covered in the longest piece of Brussels carpet I'd ever seen. There were a myriad of rooms, each more fantastically decorated than the previous. One bedroom resembled a sultan's lair with tented ceiling, sumptuous pillows scattered on the floor, and even a hookah on a side table. Rachael's room appeared as if it were the inside of a clamshell, every stick of furniture and linen a pearlescent pink or ivory.

"The house exceeds my imagination," I said. "How many rooms are there altogether?"

"I've never cared to count, but I know we've five water closets."

"Indoor plumbing?" I said with undisguised envy.

"But of course. At first I thought them a vulgar luxury of the nouveau riche, but now living without the convenience is inconceivable."

Arriving at a paneled gallery, Rachael waved her hand toward the hanging portraits. "Miss Mia Stein, may I introduce you to my illustrious ancestors. Here's my dubious Great Grandfather Sir Roger Rothschild, hung for treason by Queen Anne. And this is Great Great Grandmother Sarah Biggs, a courtesan in the court of King Charles I."

I was duly impressed by the historical connections, but thought the man appeared too daft to be a threat to any crown, and the thick necked woman, too matronly for a courtesan. "So, the Rothschild and Biggs families have been linked throughout history?"

"Their bloodlines first crossed centuries ago. They say I've got the temperament of a Biggs and features of a Rothschild."

"If the captain's portrait is true to his likeness, then you certainly don't resemble him. Who is this woman, it appears to be newly painted?"

"That's Aunt Edna, the captain's sister. She's ... Come into my uncle's library, where we can talk in private. The slaves are always about with their big ears."

The book lined room, smelling of tooled leather bindings and sheaves of old paper, seemed the perfect room to while away the hours. I could easily imagine the old captain sitting in one of the club chairs or standing at the refectory table studying his antiquarian prints. Rachael seemed uneasy, and I was certain she was about to disclose an insight into the mysterious Biggs family.

"You see, Aunt Edna is not quite all there," she said pointing to her head. "Unhinged, you know. It began when she was very young and Captain Biggs was her legal guardian. She fell in love with a man, whom my uncle believed was after her money and well below her station in life. Even with threat of disinheritance, she accepted her beau's proposal and ran off with him. Can you imagine such folly? Thankfully the Fates saved her, and the man died soon after the elopement of some horrid malady. My uncle generously accepted her back into the family, but her foolish actions were as good as signing a death decree to her social standing. She's lived the life of a recluse ever since, becoming odder with each passing year."

Rachael's disclosure further whetted my curiosity and I boldly asked, "And what happened to Captain Biggs' wife? They had a son, Daniel, whom you mentioned you were in love with."

My mention of the young man brought a flush to Rachael's pale cheeks. "Captain Biggs' wife was my aunt, Anne Rothschild. She died when Cousin Daniel was only a boy. Uncle was terribly distraught over her death, and to escape his grief, he left England for Mexico to make his fortune. He's a difficult man to know, and there's no subject he's more reticent to discuss than that period in his life. All I know is that a further misfortune befell him while there, resulting in a duel over a woman, which I mentioned before. I believe it happened in San Antonio."

"It seems odd for the captain to return after all these years to a locale which caused him sorrow."

Rachael shrugged, "Who can explain the mysteries of the heart? I, myself, have shamelessly chased Daniel here, only to be left alone most of the time. He's recently traveled to England on Uncle's business, but you're sure to meet him on his return. Then you'll see why I find it impossible to deny him my affections. Stay here while I see about our tea. I'll be back in a moment."

I was content to be left alone in this room, for I felt it revealed much of the captain's character, whom I was dreadfully curious about. The books on the shelves covered a wide range of interests: philosophy, art, poetry, and the sciences. Then I noticed a glass fronted cabinet that was locked. The volumes within were visibly older than any I'd ever seen, and I was desperate to discover their contents. Running my hand along the cabinet's back, I found its corresponding key attached, and soon had the door opened and one of the books upon the table.

It was a medieval bestiary filled with illuminated engravings of grotesque creatures. As I thumbed those forbidden pages, the images and descriptions of their supernatural powers simultaneously attracted and repulsed me. I was lost in my imaginings of the captain studying those very images when to my dismay I leaned against a paneled alcove and the wall gave way. Falling back into a hidden chamber, the door closed behind me.

Trapped within the darkened room, I frantically searched for an escape, but to no avail. I came to Mosswood with curious intention, and it appeared I had stumbled onto the captain's secret hideaway. The room was decorated with exotic tokens from his far flung travels: masks and spears carved by African natives, tusks and animal skins from safari, and silk kimonos from the Far East. These were all expected elements of a seafaring gentleman's decor, however, I was not prepared to take in the rest of what I discovered. Paintings hung gallery style depicted men and women engaged in congress and the most disturbing one showed a woman with an animal.

In the center of the room stood a low divan piled with pillows and furs, and beside this a table with what appeared to be various tools of torture. I shuddered to think what horrors transpired in this den of iniquity. Then I noticed a niche carved in the wall. It was a candlelit altar shrouded by crimson curtains, and smelling of lavender, the scent I associated with my mother. Though fear gripped me, I felt compelled to open and discover its contents, certain it held the key to this horrible man.

On the point of making my discovery, the door swung open to the library and a Negress appeared. With her head wrapped in a blood-red scarf and two serpents scarified on her arm, she was both beautiful and menacing. Miss Emily had described to me slaves who practiced Voodoo, and I suspected she was one of them. She stared at me as if in recognition, though I couldn't recall having met her. Then hissing like a snake and grabbing my arm, she demanded, "What are you doing in here, girl?"

Not waiting for an answer, she roughly pushed me from the chamber, her heavy gold rings swinging from her elongated earlobes and bangles jingling at her wrists. Frightened by the threatening woman, I fled the library and found refuge in a nearby parlor. A blazing fire heated the room oppressively, and heavy brocade drapery expunged all signs of the spring day outdoors. As my eyes grew accustomed to the darkness, I saw every available surface was covered with gaudy bric-a-brac. A stuffed peacock adorned the mantelpiece while porcelain figurines and vases of dead flowers crowded the tables. There were busts topping pedestals and a bear rug staring up at me with vacant marble eyes.

I was on the verge of leaving when I heard across the room, low gurgles that grew by steady measure to a thunderous roar. Though still shaken by my experience in the hidden chamber, curiosity moved me toward the noise, first hesitatingly then more boldly after suspecting Rachael was playing a game.

When I rounded the high backed chair I discovered the source of the strange noises was an elderly woman and her companion pug dog snoring in their sleep. Dressed in a beaded silk evening gown, with her face caked in heavy powder and cheeks defined by conspicuous spots of red, she seemed ready for the dim foot-lights of the stage. Comically, a band of red faux curls contrast-ing sharply with her gray hair had slid down her forehead and over her eyes. I was thinking she must be Rachael's unbalanced aunt when the ugly dog stirred from his sleep and began bark-ing, and the crone's gnarled fingers grasped my wrist as if in a vise.

"You're a pretty little thing," she said, licking away the bubbles of saliva from her thin lips. "I know why you're here. It's to see my brother, isn't it? He loves you very much, but it's not fair. He can't have you if I can't have my lover. You must leave this house imme-diately or trials and tribulation shall rain down upon you."

Recognizing the deranged look of madness and not wanting to disturb her further, I tried to gently pull away, but she held firm with both hands. "You must be Miss Biggs," I said in a sooth-ing voice. "I think you've mistaken me for someone else. I'm Mia Stein, come to visit your niece, Rachael. As for your brother the captain, I've never met the man, and am certain he's not in love with me."

"I know you're name is Stein now. I remember everything about you; that curly hair, those Cupid's bow lips. I can see you anytime I want to. You're a dark secret hidden away, but I know all about you."

Rachael entered the room looking disturbed. "Mia, there you are. I've been searching the house from top to bottom."

Upon espying Rachael, the hag released her grip and instantly transformed into a sweet old granny. Even her dog settled down, contentedly chewing the chair's fringe. Had it not been for the red marks encircling my wrist as proof of her dementia, I'd almost imagine the bizarre encounter hadn't happened.

Rachael fussed over her aunt, readjusting her hot water bot-tle and propping her bandaged foot on a stool. "I see you've met my Aunt Edna. Sometimes she's befuddled after waking from her nap, but she is harmless. Pardon the warmth of the room, but we must humor my aunt's abhorrence of drafts and fear of taking chill. Aunt are you feeling well today?"

"Perfectly," she drawled, pushing up the faux curls from her face.

"This is my new friend, Mia Stein," Rachael said with genuine joy.

"Very glad to meet you Mia. I'm *Miss* Edna Biggs," she said, emphasizing the title.

I thought of the sorrowful engagement she'd suffered in her youth, and could not but pity the woman.

"I wasn't asleep," she swore. "No, no, only resting my eyes a moment. My stereoscope fatigues them exceedingly. Did you say Stein was the name?"

"Yes, Ma'am," I replied, settling into the sofa's lumpy horsehair cushions.

"Hmm, the name rings a bell," she said, her milky blue eyes appraising me. "Does my brother have a connection with your family?"

I considered my father's prejudice against the captain and answered, "No, ma'am, I'm sure he doesn't. Perhaps you've heard of Stein Fine Furniture, the shop my father owns."

"Oh well, no matter, it will come to me eventually. Do take a look at my stereoscopic pictures. The new ones of Niagara Falls are executed to noteworthy advantage. I find them absolutely breathtaking, and they save me the trouble of having to visit them."

Gazing into the instrument, I declared, "Very clever how the two images come together to create one, however, I don't imagine pictures alone can do justice to such a splendor of nature."

Posturing like a cock fighter, she examined me through her raised lorgnette, "You express your opinion too boldly for someone so young and ignorant of the medium. Platt D. Babbitt is the most accomplished landscape photographer of our time, and these are examples of his finest work."

The similarity between her contemptuous expression and that of her brother in his portrait was uncanny. "Forgive me, I didn't mean to offend. I'm sure they're the next best thing to traveling to the Falls yourself."

Grimacing with a wave to her bandaged foot, she asked, "Young lady, is it not obvious I'm in no condition to undertake such a trip? Well, now that you've so cavalierly dismissed my stereoscope, I'm at a loss as to the direction of our conversation. I'd planned to entertain you with it for at least half the tea."

"Please know my intention was not to be contrary. I'm accustomed to conversing within my family circle where it's a matter of course to debate each issue. I would like to see more of your pictures."

Ignoring my apology, the cantankerous aunt sulked in silence and her pug growled at me. I nervously studied the table's cabriole legs until Rachael mercifully suggested tea be served. With a flick of her hand, she called forth a young slave who had been silently hovering in expectation of her mistress' command. The girl, no more than nine years of age, struggled with the weight of the silver tea service as she placed it down on the teapoy.

"Here let me help," I offered.

The girl smiled appreciatively, then nervously lowered her eyes in submission upon seeing Miss Biggs' disapproving scowl.

"Sissy, you're acting all too familiar," Miss Biggs barked. "Now, get on with you."

Like a turtle protecting itself, the girl hunched her shoulders, nearly cowering as she timidly backed away.

Miss Biggs counseled me, "With Negroes and savage Indians, one must maintain a firm grip on them or they *will* take liberties."

It appeared Rachael's aunt had two completely different personalities; the stodgy matriarch obsessed with etiquette and the lunatic who had held me in her own firm grip not a half hour before.

She continued her harangue, "Just the other night we had a runaway. He was a clever one, shaking pepper in his shoes to throw off the dogs. Then brazen as can be, he stole one of the captain's horses and got as far as Jones' Ferry on the Brazos. Someone saw him try to cross and said he reined up the poor horse as if to strangle the animal. The man was lucky he drowned, considering the lashing he'd have received from my brother, Charles. So, you see, my vigilant control over them is for their own good."

Outraged by her nonsensical reasoning, I exclaimed, "Forgive me, but I can no longer hold my tongue. Negroes and Indians are not savages. They are as intelligent as any white man and are only at a disadvantage due to the circumstance of their environ, and as for the poor man who drowned..."

Rachael's swift kick to my shin to censor me was unnecessary, for the old woman had slumped down into her chair and was mumbling incoherently.

"You'll have to excuse my aunt," Rachael said sadly. "Her spells come and go of their own accord. It's one of the reasons we don't have many visitors. I thought you might understand, you being a healer of sorts."

"Has she been seen by a doctor?"

"Countless ones, and Doctor Abbott most recently.

"Has he prescribed anything?"

Before she could answer, Miss Biggs revived herself once again and took up her previous train of conversation as if there'd been no interruption. "As I was saying, we must be diligent in controlling our servants. But enough of that. Mia, do you play whist? When Daniel returns we will need a fourth player."

"I've never played the game, but I'm fair at chess," I answered.

"I cannot abide such a boring game," she affirmed with a flare of her nostrils. "Sitting for hours doing nothing while any attempt at conversation is scorned for breaking concentration, that's not my idea of amusement."

Attempting to alter the combative tone of the conversation, Rachael said cheerily, "Come now, ladies, let's enjoy our refreshments."

I needed no further encouragement to delve into the delights that tray held. Should I eat a watercress sandwich tied daintily with a chive ribbon or a scone with lemon curd, I wondered.

"Sugar or cream?" Rachael asked pouring the tea from the silver urn with an affected lift of her pinky finger.

"Both, please," I said, trying not to sound greedy.

She dropped the sugar and cream in first, pouring the tea on top.

"That's interesting," I noted. "I've always done it the other way around. I mean the tea first and then the cream."

Miss Biggs pounded her ivory tipped cane onto the table like a judge calling court, and I braced myself for another of her pontifications. "Taking tea is the foundation of domestic happiness, and there's a precise science in its preparation. You'd do well to take note, young Miss Mia who thinks she knows everything. First, one must rinse the teapot's interior with scalding water to remove its chill. This helps to maintain the beverage's temperature later. Choice of tea is next..."

Trying to participate in the long winded conversation, I interjected, "Camellia sinensis?"

"Of course, my dear, what other?"

"But there are countless plants one can make tea from," I asserted.

"Those are tisanes, not tea," Miss Biggs corrected. "As I was saying, Darjeeling is the preferred tea for discriminating palates, and the leaves from the first flush is superior as it possesses a musky spiciness without undue astringency. Most definitely, one is never to imbibe tea harvested during the monsoon season."

She went on to describe the optimum temperature the water must be: just to the boil but not rolling, and the length of time to steep: exactly three minutes. As for which to pour first, tea or cream, she explained it was definitely the cream, so as to prevent the cup's glaze from cracking.

I would've been bored to tears with her diatribe except that during its entire delivery she stuffed her mouth voraciously, taking two sandwiches in one bite, and if custard was not oozing from her lips then crumbs were falling down the gap between her sagging breasts. My first impulse was to slurp my tea from the saucer, like Pappa, and tell her in no uncertain terms what she could do with her clotted cream. However, I reminded myself of her mental instability, and so instead took satisfaction in a helping of strawberry sponge cake topped with sugared pansies.

"Do you speak French or play the piano?" Miss Biggs asked, offering her pug dog a pastry.

"I'm afraid neither. I've no ear for languages, except for the Latin associated with plant identification, and my brother, Christian, is the only musical member of our family."

The old woman asked condescendingly, "Then what are your accomplishments?"

"I like to read, and I know quite a bit about herbs."

Miss Biggs laughed at my response with such hysterics that she spilt hot tea into her lap and bumped her bandaged foot. She then cursed uncharacteristically for a lady, and I thought she'd slipped once again into madness until she said, "Did you hear that Rachael? She said '*erbs*?'" She shrieked again, tears streaming like rivulets through her powdered cheeks. "Miss Stein, you've dropped the *h*, like a commoner. The correct pronunciation is *herbs* with the '*h*' fully enunciated."

For the life of me I didn't see the humor in the situation, nor was I going to not defend myself. "I dare say you will find differences in dialect as you travel throughout our country. However, I'm certain Mr. Webster agrees this particular variation in elocution is equally correct as your suggestion."

Miss Biggs' eyes narrowed to slits, and her pasty complexion reddened as she countered, "It is obvious, we English, know the proper way to pronounce the Queen's language. It is *our* mother tongue after all. Having grown up in such an uncivilized land as Texas, you were bound to learn an inferior version of the language, and are blameless for your ignorance. You are a pretty girl and doubtless clever, but your social skills are atrocious and must be corrected. Otherwise, you'll find socializing in genteel circles, and catching a suitable husband an impossible task."

Rachael's nervous entreaties to pray hold my temper failed to quiet me. I shot back, "Your notions of socializing are archaic, and the mastering of an instrument or proper articles of speech are artificial standards by which to judge a person's worth. What is of import is the substance and character of an individual. As for my future betrothal, I don't plan on *catching* anyone. To wed without mutual love and respect is a hypocrisy to the sacred commitment of marriage."

I expected Miss Biggs to retaliate with another round of arguments, but instead the self-proclaimed arbiter of propriety settled back into her chair. Perhaps she recalled how she'd flaunted convention for her one true love, or maybe she was simply worn out.

She harrumphed, "Put up the fire screen, Rachael, the heat in here is unbearable."

Rachael repositioned the stitched sample of Berlin woolwork and fanned the overwrought woman. "Aunt, you must calm yourself. Doctor Abbott gave strict orders against any agitation."

Miss Biggs pouted as she repositioned her sore foot. "My gout is acting up fiercely again, but alas Miss Stein has no sympathy for the many crosses I must bear."

The affliction of the rich and overfed I thought, before responding, "I've often treated gout, and am familiar with several herbal remedies to allay its symptoms?"

"Now, Mia," Rachael chided. "My aunt isn't interested in nostrums."

Offended, I said, "My methods are far from quackery. Mrs. Briscoe found excellent relief, and will readily give testimony."

"Anecdotal," Rachael asserted dismissively. "Besides, Doctor Abbott is the finest of physicians, and Aunt trusts him implicitly. Isn't that right?"

"To be sure I have an outstanding practitioner, and he's so very attentive coming round each week."

"I'm well aware of the doctor's reputation," I said, omitting any mention of his intemperateness and the fireman's recent tale of butchery. "However, you mustn't dismiss the effectiveness of herbal treatments so offhandedly, for their use has been proven over centuries. The Papyrus Ebers was an Egyptian text written in fifteen hundred BC and contains references to more than seven hundred herbal remedies. It's only during recent times our apothecaries have substituted these ancient cures with chemical concoctions."

"Dover's Powder and laudanum always work for Aunt Edna's pain," Rachael said defensively.

"Alcohol and opium," I said. "Don't you realize these drugs can unsettle the mind?"

"Mia, I don't think my aunt cares for your innuendos."

Miss Biggs cut off Rachael, "Wait a minute, dear niece, I appreciate your concern, but I believe we should hear Miss Stein out. It appears this is the one subject she has command over. Proceed, please."

Accepting her backhanded compliment, I continued, "Gout is caused by an accumulation of uric acid, which settles painfully in the joints, most often the big toe. It is..."

Again the crotchety woman interrupted. "I don't give a fig about the pain's cause, and I'm already well aware of where it has settled. Make haste to the remedy, dear girl."

"Very well, first, you need to limit your consumption of meat."

Miss Biggs argued, "Decline Cook's scrumptious sausage rolls? Why, they're a staple of my breakfast."

"Your very pleasure is your poison. You need to eat lighter fare, and plenty of cherries along with a tincture of comfrey root. I can make that up for you. And there's to be no alcohol whatsoever. It inhibits the body from ridding itself of the uric acid."

Rachael shook her head in disagreement. "Mia, this nonsense directly counters Doctor Abbott's prescription of two glasses of sherry with dinner to aid her sleep."

"I have often found my counsel to be at odds with the aforementioned doctor, therefore you must decide whose suggestions to follow according to your own good judgment."

Placing her spoon in her empty cup to signal the end of tea, she smiled approvingly, saying, "None of Miss Stein's advice sounds harmful. I'll order Cook to make the necessary alterations. Rachael, why don't you show your new friend the conservatory, she will no doubt enjoy our specimens. And please do come again; I look forward to another of our lively debates."

The eccentric woman dismissed me with a kiss to both my cheeks, and her once antagonistic pug licked my hand goodbye. My first visit to Mosswood had far exceeded what I had imagined.

CHAPTER VII

A FAINTING

achael took me into the conservatory where sunshine streamed through glass walls and a fountain trickled melodically amid a tropical oasis of palms and ferns.

"Thank you, Mia," Rachael said, as we took a seat beside the fountain.

"For what?" I asked, distracted by the colorful parrots flying overhead.

"For understanding about my aunt or at least trying to. She's vexing in the extreme and even scary at times with her odd behavior, but still she is my aunt and I love her dearly."

I thought of the captain's hidden room, and longed to ask if she knew of its existence and what its horrible significance was, but feeling guilty of trespassing where I didn't belong, all I could manage was, "And how does your uncle respond to his sister's moods?"

Rachael stammered, "Aunt Edna is locked away when he's home. He won't tolerate her, says she's dangerous. In fact, he's unaware we allow her her freedom in his absence. I tremble to think of his reaction if he knew the truth."

Just as my white gloves concealed my purple fingers stained from picking dewberries, the beautiful facade of Mosswood hid the dark secrets within. My perception of the captain was evolving moment by moment. I imagined eventually all the pieces would fit together into a monster like the ones he studied in his leather clad library.

Sensing I was forming a bad opinion of the captain, Rachael said, "Don't think too badly of my uncle. Just look at the little jungle he's created here with flora collected from around the world. You two will have a common interest in plants to discuss when you finally meet. Have you ever seen this plant before? Their leaves when rubbed emit a fragrance as pungent as a freshly peeled orange. Uncle Charles brought them from South Africa last year."

I tested other similarly shaped leaves and found a feast for the senses with strawberry, mint, and even a chocolate aroma. "I think they're pelargoniums," I said with interest.

"My Mum loves to make potpourri with them," Rachael said, rising and walking outside. "Does your Mum do those sorts of things?"

"My mother died five years ago."

Rachael turned to me with a tear glistening in her eye, "Oh, you poor thing, I'm so sorry."

A compassionate side of the selfish girl I'd met in the millinery was emerging, first regarding her aunt and now towards me. I presented a cheerful smile to relieve her of pitying me, and said, "I live with Pappa and my three brothers. They're a handful to watch over and vex me at every turn, but truthfully I'd be lost without them."

"Brothers! You don't say. Tell me are they dashing specimens of manhood? Don't doubt my love is all for Daniel, but light flirtations are necessary distractions for a girl."

"Sorry to disappoint, but they're all younger than me. Why don't you come meet them and afterwards I'll show you my herb garden. Holly Cottage is modest in comparison to Mosswood's conservatory, but you're sure to find something of interest."

"I'd love to go, but Aunt may not allow it."

"Does it really matter what she thinks? I mean..."

"Of course there are times she hasn't her wits about her, but for my own sanity I carry on as if she does."

To our horror, we looked up to see Miss Biggs climbing out her third story window and standing on the facade's stone ledge. With her evening gown rustling in the wind, she appeared oblivious to her elevation and the consequence of a misstep. "It's come to me," she announced, pointing at me. "Like a vision in a dream your face materialized and I know your true identity. You thought you'd fool me with those green eyes, but you can't; I'm more clever than all of you think."

Ulysses appeared at the window along with the exotic looking slave who had terrified me in the captain's hidden chamber. They both reached for a wailing Miss Biggs who protested their interference. It was unclear to me whether they were hindering or helping her progress. After they spied us, I thought they put forth more effort in retrieving her, though it may have been my imagination running riot. In the ensuing tousle, her necklace broke and pearls rained down upon us.

Mercifully, Miss Biggs disappeared into the safety of the room, and Rachael and I ran upstairs where we discovered her lying in bed in a stupor. The Negress pocketed a small amber bottle, which I recognized as opium and I presumed to be prescribed by Doctor Abbott. The slave eyed me contemptuously as if I were to blame for the old woman's mania, and then departed. Checking the prone woman's pulse, I found it depressed, and suspected her caretakers were overdosing her.

"She'll be fine now," Rachael said assuringly. "She'll sleep like a baby till tomorrow and won't remember a thing about this dreadful episode. I only wish I had the same inclination."

Unable to dismiss the situation so easily, I asked, "Who was the woman that was just in here?"

"You mean Rita?" Rachael answered. "She's the captain's favorite at the moment, if you know my meaning. She's also the one who locks up my aunt when necessary." With eyes downcast, she said, "My aunt is completely barmy on the crumpet, and I wouldn't blame you if you choose to never come here again, seeing all that you did today."

She was unaware of half the frights I'd suffered. I was also beginning to think the captain was legitimate in his desire to lock up his sister, if not as a danger to others then for her own safety, and yet I wasn't ready to turn my back on Rachael nor Mosswood. "Don't be silly. Your aunt has her eccentricities, but it does nothing to alter my opinion of you. Come now, I think we deserve a bit of a lark."

We were departing, when to my surprise, Miss Biggs sat straight up in bed. Despite having been dosed with opium, her eyes were clear and her speech intelligible. I was intrigued how readily she slipped back and forth from dementia to lucidity, and wondered if Miss Emily had experience with such a patient.

Miss Biggs clawed at her neck, demanding, "Where are my pearls? I'm certain I was wearing them earlier. No doubt one of those thieving slaves has pilfered my necklace. Rachael, I demand you bring the whole staff up here this moment so I may question them."

Rachael said coolly, as if nothing out of the ordinary had transpired, "Dear Aunt, I saw your pearls in the parlor. You must be forgetting that you left them there. I'm going to take the air with Mia. She wants to show me her house, and on my return I'll bring your necklace back up to you."

Miss Biggs pushed up the faux curls that persisted on sliding down her forehead. The crazed look she'd demonstrated on the house's ledge had completely vanished, replaced by the concern of a doddering old aunt. "It is highly improper for girls to ramble the countryside unchaperoned, and you're bound to fall into mischief. Have Ulysses drive you there."

Loathing the idea of her pompous slave accompanying us, I said, "Miss Biggs, believe me, it is but a cursory walk, which I often take safely alone. It will be good exercise for Rachael, and she'll bring back the comfrey drink I prescribed you. Remember the remedy I mentioned for your gout? The sooner you begin treatment, the sooner you'll feel relief."

The old woman appeared doubtful. "Do I have your word there will be no discourse with strangers? I'll not have you cavorting about without proper introduction. We must keep our standards of conduct above reproach, even if we live in this unsophisticated environ."

Rachael gave her a reassuring hug. "Absolutely, Auntie, you needn't worry."

"Your father entrusted me as your guardian, so it is my duty to worry," Edna Biggs countered. "However, I agree with Mia, fresh air would be good for your health, and you don't socialize enough for a girl your age. Mind you, I can't stress enough the importance of your parasol as a constant companion. A fair complexion is a lady's testimony to her genteelness. Mia, where is your parasol? Your skin has turned rather brown."

I fear I don't possess such an item. I come by my coloring naturally, and the sun doesn't bother it in the least."

Dismayed, she said, "Rachael, I'm having grave doubts about this outing. Perhaps we should schedule it another time when I can accompany you."

"Please, Aunt Edna. Mia is the first girl my age I've befriended here, and with Daniel away... Don't you want my happiness?"

Miss Biggs succumbed to our persuasion. "This goes entirely against my better judgment, but I will allow you to go. Ulysses will come round to pick you up at four sharp, and know this occasion will serve as a test of your trustworthiness."

It was obvious there was a close tie between the two, despite the elder's gruffness. Rachael gushed, "How can I ever thank you? You're simply the best aunt a girl could ask for."

Mrs. Biggs brushed away her praise. "You may show your gratitude by following my instructions to a tee. Remember, keep a dignified comportment at all times."

"Yes Auntie, of course Auntie!" Rachael said, backing out the door.

When we reached the property's outer gate, I glanced back once more toward the house. There was a movement at Miss Biggs' bedroom window, and fleetingly I feared a reenactment of the bedlamite walking the ledge. Instead it was the slave, Rita, staring at me with an undecipherable expression.

"Don't dawdle, Mia, I've not much time," Rachael ordered, ditching her parasol behind the nearest bush and with it all of Miss Biggs' cautionary instructions. We made our escape from the oppressive house and its mysterious inhabitants as eagerly as the captured parrots would have flown from their artificial jungle, had they the chance. No matter how beautiful Mosswood was, in truth it was a prison to a youthful spirit.

"The direct manner in which you spoke to my aunt was extraordinary," Rachael said. "Do you conduct all your conversations with elders in such a forthright manner?"

"Pappa taught me to speak my mind without affectation or guile, no matter who I'm addressing."

"Whatever your charm is it worked, for you overturned her initial bad opinion of you and won her approval."

"Perhaps she senses my sincere concern for her welfare."

On our way home, I took a detour to a meadow bordered by Austin and Capitol Street, where I often gathered native plants for medicinal use. The cerulean sky and yellow spotted swallowtails flitting amongst the wildflowers proved surprisingly invigorating to Rachael, for she pointed toward the shadowy verdant line of trees, shouting, "I'll race you." Hiking up her voluminous skirt, she dashed wildly across the field, and had the North wind been prevalent, I'm certain her billowy dress would've caught sail.

"If only your aunt could see you now," I shouted, running beside her. "You've thrown all comportment to the wind and are acting like a heathen."

"What she doesn't know won't hurt her," Rachael shot back.

"I think she'd approve if she saw the results; your cheeks are as pink as a rosebud."

"Don't fool yourself. Flushed cheeks or not, Auntie would send me straight to bed without supper if she saw me behaving so." Rachael stopped dead in her tracks with tears rolling down her cheeks.

"What is it?" I asked.

"Can't get my breath," she gasped.

"Come rest in the shade. It's that detestable corset constricting your lungs again. You'd certainly run with more ease without one."

Aghast, she asked, "You mean to say you don't have one on?"

With a sense of pride, I answered, "Never have worn one on preference and principal. They're horrid contraptions that men created to control women."

"That's rather brazen of you. I thought only women of the night didn't wear corsets."

"If it's true then they must be sensible."

Rachael's breathing came easier as she rested. "I don't think I've ever ventured to sit down in the grass before. I was always afraid of dirtying my dress. It's really very lovely. Who planted all these flowers?"

Stunned by her inexperience with nature, I answered, "They're sown by the birds and the wind. This is a wild carrot called Queen Anne's Lace, another herb that would effectively treat your aunt's gout."

Rachael twirled the white flower clusters above her head. "Do you think Aunt would approve of my parasol?"

"I know I do, it's much prettier than your other one."

"Mia, how do you know so much about flowers and herbs?"

"I read a lot of books, and I also learn from my friend, Miss Emily."

Rachael frowned. "Is she your best friend?"

"Oh, I don't know. I've never considered her in that way. She's much older than me, and I've known her all my life. She's more like a mother."

"Could I be your best friend?"

Rachael's vulnerability was in sharp contrast to the acrimony I'd first seen upon meeting her. It was similar to her aunt's vacillating demeanor, and I wondered how long it would last and which was her true nature. "I suppose time will tell," I answered. Sensing her disappointment, I asked sunnily, "What do you like to study?"

She threw her head back, laughing, "Nothing, absolutely nothing. I'm through with schooling. My governess left off when I turned thirteen, and Father discouraged me from further education. He took it on our physician's good authority that too much learning sends energy wastefully to the brain. It diverts it away from the normal development of a woman's body."

"Good grief, Rachael, you don't really believe such nonsense, do you?"

She shrugged, "I don't know, haven't really given it too much thought. I readily admit I'm not a deep thinker like you. The sensational novels are what excite me. *Clarissa* or *Pamela*, now they are stimulating. Have you read them?"

"No, though I can easily guess their plot. Let me see, first there's a young woman who is usually orphaned and in the care of an ogre of a relative. This heroine searches for her knight in shining armor, and in the meantime various misfortunes befall her. When she finally discovers her one true love, they are at cross purposes until the last chapter when she conquers her troubles and the two live happily ever after."

"I think you *have* read them," Rachael declared, picking up a long blade of grass. Moving her finger along each seed, she sang, "Tinker, tailor, soldier, sailor, rich man. Brilliant, I'm going to marry a rich man!"

"I've no doubt you'll marry exactly the man... Dear me, that reminds me. Charlotte Price is to be married this very day, and if we hurry we may just catch a glimpse of the wedding party before they leave."

Rachael clapped her hands in glee, "Hooray, I love weddings!"

With the clanging of bells announcing the happy union, we arrived as Charlotte and her newly betrothed husband, Gunther Eberhard, emerged from Christ Episcopal Church. Though Charlotte had a poxed sallow complexion and sour disposition, standing there in her white satin dress and tulle veil, she looked radiantly beautiful.

Gunther had arrived in our country four years previously. He'd planned to live in the Mainzen Verain in New Braunfels as part of Prince Solmes' German settlement, but had fallen ill with malaria and was left high and dry on Galveston Island. Charlotte's father, Rufus Price, was doing business on the island when he came upon Gunther and hired him as a wagoneer. Within a year the ambitious young man was betrothed to Charlotte, and with his future father-in-law's aid, opened a wagon repair shop in Houston along Greasy Row.

Gunther, looking pleased with himself, lifted his new bride into the carriage, as she gazed adoringly at him. Then with much ballyhoo from the crowd, Gunther gave her a passionate kiss, one not often seen in public. The men cheered their approval of so brash an exhibition, while women blushed and looked away. The groom then snapped his whip, and they were eagerly off to their newly built home in the German's Frost Town.

Amused by the ardent kiss, Rachael said, "I'd bargain they've been practicing that quite a bit beforehand. Mia, have you ever been kissed?"

"No, of course not. One doesn't do such things unless you're engaged to be married."

Rachael giggled, "What a silly girl you are. I've kissed several boys, and though Daniel is the man I shall marry, our lips have never met."

I tried to hide my confusion. "If you really love him, it seems you'd wait for his affections alone?"

"One day he'll be mine, but until that glorious day I don't want to miss all the fun. Have you ever seen a naked man?"

Shocked, I blurted, "Rachael, you go too far!"

She laughed hysterically. "I suppose you believe sex is for reproductive purposes only. How provincial you are. My governess told me when the time comes, I'm to lie still and think of England, but I think I'll like it and want to wiggle quite a bit."

I could hardly believe my ears and began to question the propriety of bringing her home. It was too late though to turn around, for my house was before us and we were greeted with the all too familiar racket of Christian on our desperately out of tune pianoforte. Whether it be a music hall ballad or a snippet of Bishop's opera, my brother's internal metronome was stuck and he pounded out the music at the same feverish tempo.

Rachael fussed with her hair in the entrance hall mirror. "I'm a sight."

"You look fine," I said, opening the French doors to the parlor. "They're my *younger* brothers, remember."

"Yes, but there's only one first impression."

To be honest, I was thinking along similar lines as far as Rachael's opinion of my home. Whereas Mosswood was dark with heavy drapery closing out the light, Holly Cottage was sun-filled with delicate swaths of lace at the windows. I'd summer dressed the furniture with white muslin slipcovers and stored the rugs in the attic with pennyroyal, leaving the polished floors bare. Instead of surfaces crowded with knick knacks, our two worktables held a pair of moderator lamps and a bouquet of honeysuckle to scent the air. Our family's books, few but treasured, were neatly arranged in a large oaken bookcase. I hoped our home illustrated the inherent beauty found in function and simplicity of form.

"Your home is lovely," Rachael shouted over the din. "It reminds me of our summer cottage in Bath, all light and airy."

Her praise was lost on me, for I was shamed by my brothers.

"You're driving me crazy with that infernal racket!" Emmett yelled.

"Go fry an egg!" Christian snarled.

"Do your brothers always ignore common courtesy?" Rachael asked, wringing her handkerchief in obvious dismay.

"This is mild. You should see them at dinnertime. Boys!" I shouted over the mayhem. "Can you please give me your attention? We have a guest."

Emmett turned, saying, "Excuse me, I had no idea someone was here."

Christian pounded out a final chord, "Nor I."

"Visitor or not, you boys need to behave more civilly to each other. Allow me to introduce my acquaintance, Miss Rachael Rothschild. Rachael, this is my oldest brother Emmett and the virtuoso is Christian."

Rachael curtsied coquettishly, then surprised us by taking a seat beside Christian at the instrument. With a precision born of much practice, her delicate fingers moved skillfully over the keys as her voice high and clear brought forth a melodious rendition of *Bonnie Annie Lowrie*. Never had the ballad sounded so sweet, nor our ill tuned pianoforte so harmonious.

My brothers were mesmerized, including Sam who had slid down the banister to join our recital. After rapturous applause and further encouragement, Rachael entertained us with several more songs from her evidently vast repertoire.

Enamored with Rachael's charm and beauty, Emmett and Christian shouted "Bravo," and Sam eager to be a good host, whispered to me.

"Rachael, this is my little brother Sam," I introduced. "He'd like to show you his snail collection."

Rachael scrunched her nose in disgust, "I detest slimy creatures."

Sam's bottom lip quivered at her curt response, but he was undeterred in enticing our guest with another offer. Unfortunately, his gift of a garden snake was promptly denounced as horrid.

Emmett's offer was next as he shyly advanced. "Perhaps a collection of sea shells and butterflies in my room might better suit Miss Rothschild's delicate sensibilities."

Rachael giggled, whispering into my ear, "Cheeky devil, an invitation to his bedchamber? And what would Aunt Edna say?"

I cringed at her innuendo, "It was an innocent suggestion."

"Your collection intrigues me," Rachael cooed, "But I've already promised to tour your sister's garden. Perhaps on my next visit?"

Emmett bowed his acceptance with a panache belying his youthful inexperience.

I proudly presented my garden to Rachael, identifying each plant by its common and Latin name, as well as its medicinal and culinary use, until her yawns of boredom could no longer be ignored. Disheartened by her disinterest, I was leading her back to the house when bumblebees began circling. I explained there was no danger if she would only remain calm, however, Rachael's hysterical screams and flailing arms soon agitated the bees to alter their lazy roundabout dance into frenetic movements. To my dismay, the poor girl violently shook, then fainted straightaway. Her unconscious body was held upright momentarily by the rigid hoops of her petticoats before she toppled limply to the garden path. Any chance of a pleasurable afternoon together had evaporated as surely as the morning dew upon greeting the sun.

I fanned her face furiously. "Oh, dear! Wake up, wake up!,"

"Sam, go tell your brothers Rachael fainted, and I need their help."

Eager to assist, he ran as fast as his little legs could carry him and returned just as quickly with his brothers in tow.

Christian leaned over her. "By golly, a prostrate girl. What a sight!"

Emmett looked at her tenderly. "I've brought a pillow for her head. What on earth happened?"

"She was frightened by the bees and fainted, that's all. When she overexerts herself, she has difficulty breathing due to her corset. We should let out the stays."

Grinning mischievously with the prospect, Christian offered, "By all means we should relieve her discomfort, and I shall help."

"Have you no decency?" Emmett railed. "Let's carry her inside and try to revive her by other means."

Finding assurance in the natural rising and falling of Rachael's chest, we dragged her leaden body to our parlor's chaise longue and argued over what the best course of action was. I insisted pungent herbs would revive her, Emmett called for a wet cloth to the forehead, Christian insisted the laces be cut, and Sam wanted to place hot bricks to her feet. Before any of our measures were carried out, she awoke wild-eyed and screaming.

Taking her hand in mine, I comforted, "Calm down, Rachael, you're safe amongst friends."

Christian laughed, "Too bad, I was liking Sam's idea of the hot bricks."

Rachael sat up. "Hot bricks? What happened? How did I get here? Has my physician been called for?"

"Believe me it's not necessary," I asserted. "The bees were upset, but you weren't even stung."

"Look here," she cried, frantically. "I'm certain those beastly insects stung me. I want to go home right now!"

Examining the spot, I pointed out, "But Rachael, that's only a freckle."

"Bees smell fear, it's probably why they were agitated," Emmett explained.

"Are you saying I'm responsible for the attack?" Rachael shrieked.

"I've had enough of all this crying," Christian said retreating.

Emmett knelt down beside her, "Take heart, Miss Rothschild, bees are enough to upset anyone. I'll hitch up the horses and take you right home. Where do you live?"

Fearing Rachael's disclosure of her connection to Captain Biggs, I quickly spoke up, "It's kind of you Emmett, but it's almost four and her driver will soon be picking her up."

Distressed, Emmett asked, "Then can't we do something for her now? What about one of your herbal salves or something? You're a healer, aren't you?"

Despite thinking it ridiculous, I prepared a vinegar compress for the offending freckle, while Emmett coddled the whimpering Rachael. Mercifully for all concerned, Ulysses arrived on time and carried our feeble guest into her carriage.

Feeling bad for her, I said, "Rachael, I'm so sorry for the upset."

"I would've fared better to have listened to Auntie. I'm a delicate creature, and the outdoors does not suit me."

Without bidding farewell, a sullen faced Rachael departed, and with it came the end to one of the strangest days I'd ever experienced: the hidden chamber, the unhinged Edna Biggs, and the quixotic Rachael, sweet and tender one moment, acerbic and spoiled the next. I wondered if I'd ever see her again or return to the mystery of Mosswood.

CHAPTER VIII

DANIEL & HENRI

espite the almanac's prediction for a rainy Fourth of July, almost all two thousand Houstonians descended upon the bayou fairgrounds to celebrate our country's independence. There was something to entertain everyone: baseball, horseshoes, one legged races, and military pageantry. Adding to this excitement, we Steins anticipated the arrival of Mamma's brother, Manuel Castillo. I'd not seen my uncle for two years, but through correspondence we learned he'd been briefly married before heading to California. There were countless tales of women abandoned by husbands with dubious get-rich schemes, and I feared my uncle's scandalous divorce was due to gold fever. Tío was now returning home a wealthy man, and promised a dramatic arrival. My brothers imagined him being conveyed in every mode of transport from a golden coach pulled by white stallions to a rainbow-colored boat arriving at the bayou's dock.

"It's Fannin's Artillery and the Houston Dragoons!" Christian exclaimed excitedly, as our wagon pulled up.

"Can we go watch them, Pappa?" Emmett asked, barely able to restrain himself.

"Alright, but keep a sharp eye on your brothers. Remember last year a man lost his arm lighting the cannon."

Empowered by his new authority, Emmett declared, "Hear that Christian? You're to mind me, and no sticky fingers."

Pappa and I headed to the bandstand where the Milam Guards, resplendent in starched military dress, were striking up the 'Star Spangled Banner'. Up went the six flags, which at one time or another, flew over our land. There was one from Spain, France, Mexico, the Republic of Texas, the state's lone star, and our country's Red, White, and Blue. Though the tuba played off-key and the flags hung limply in the stifling heat, Mayor Moore's patriotic speech brought tears to everyone, including Pappa who swore he had dust in his eyes. When the mayor announced California's newly formed statehood, bedlam broke out with hats flying and pistols shooting skyward. The excitement didn't die down until William Marsh Rice, one of the richest men in Texas, stepped up to the podium.

Rice began, "Ladies and gents, it's a pleasure and an honor to declare this year's Cotton King, the planter who's brought in the most bales this season. However, allow me to digress for a moment with another announcement that is dear to my heart. As a young man, having lost my belongings at sea, I arrived penniless in our fine city. Through diligence and the aid of fine folks, I made my fortune. I'm not ashamed to disclose that my early entrepreneurial efforts consisted of selling a quart of popskull for a buck at the Milam Hotel. My business along with my partner, Mr. Nichols, has evolved over the years, but alas my true happiness has come this very day, for I shall marry Margaret Bremmond."

Someone in the crowd heckled, "Hey Rice, you'll be losing your independence on Independence day."

"There's no fairer lass, I'd rather lose it to," Rice laughed good heartedly. "So, due to this wonderful circumstance, I believe you'll understand why I must cut short my attendance at these happy festivities. However, before I go, I want to bestow this gold cup to the new Cotton King."

The crowd looked expectantly toward, Rufus Price, who had won this coveted award for the past four years. The farmer grinned with a gap toothed smile of self-assurance.

To everyone's surprise, Rice announced, "And the Cotton King is... Mr. Randall Topper! Congratulations, Mr. Topper. I believe you were the overwhelming winner despite your cotton worm."

Rufus Price's defeat didn't sit well with him, and he let out a slanderous rant toward the winner. Thankfully, the band struck up a lively tune to drown him out, and the crowd, led by their noses, disbanded toward the barbecue pits of venison and cabrito. Pappa and I made our way to the shade of a red bay tree where we spread an old quilt to enjoy the contents of our picnic hamper.

"The deviled eggs have overturned into the sweet potato pie, but everything else fared well," I announced.

"Hmm, the fried chicken sure looks good," Pappa said hungrily. "All we have to do is open the hamper and here come the boys."

Seeing Sam and Christian covered in mud from head to toe, while Emmett was clean as a whistle, Pappa said hotly, "Emmett I told you to keep an eye out for your brothers. Explain to me what in tarnation they've been up to."

"Pappa, that's blasphemy!" I chided.

"It's what comes of being provoked," he said, shaking his head.

Between bites of honeyed cornpone and gulps of lemonade, Emmett explained, "We've been in the biggest tug of war contest you ever did see. It was strung over the bayou and half the town was pulling on that rope. Wanting to keep my britches clean, I chose the team James Oren was on. He's a blacksmith whose arm muscles are the size of a woman's waist. I pressed it upon my brothers to follow suit, but they refused and chose their own course, thus their muddy attire."

Pappa fumed, "Emmett, being in charge of your brothers means telling them what to do, not asking. Sam has ruined his new sailor suit, and they both could've drowned in that bayou."

Emmett argued, "I swear they were at the end of the rope, and in no danger."

By the time we finished our meal, Miss Penelope had appeared and brazenly linked her arm through Pappa's. "Klaus, I've been looking for you all morning. You've got to come with me to see the bucket brigade's exhibit. They've acquired some new contraption, and I'm sure no one could explain it to me as well as you."

"It's their steam operated pump. Should be interesting," Emmett offered.

"Now, Klaus, please don't say no," Penelope pouted, batting her eyelashes. "You can't imagine how disappointed I'd be if you didn't accompany me."

What a pickle poor Pappa found himself in. He could promenade the fairgrounds with Miss Penelope and have the town's gossipmongers arrange their nuptials before sunset, or refuse her request and end up with a hysterical woman on his hands. "Miss Penelope, there's no doubt your offer is most tempting, but unfortunately I must decline on this occasion, for a prior commitment precludes it."

All trace of coquettishness vanished as Miss Penelope's eyes narrowed and her arms were planted akimbo. "And what previous commitment might that be, Mr. Stein?"

To my astonishment Pappa pulled Miss Penelope to his side and whispered a secret communique.

"How exciting, and I promise to keep *our* secret," she said slinking off like a Cheshire cat.

"What was that all about?" I asked.

"All will be disclosed at three o'clock in front of the bandstand. And now I must be off. Remember to be there at three sharp," Pappa announced mysteriously as he gathered a bundle and left.

"Do you think Pappa is keen on Miss Penelope?" Christian said, scrunching his nose in distaste.

I shrugged, "Who knows. He's acting awfully strange. What's for certain is we've only two hours before meeting up with him, so let's make the most of it. What should we do first?"

It was unanimously decided upon to go straight to the watermelon seed-spitting contest where contestants entertained us with their comical techniques. Percival, the fastidious Market Square salesman, looked like a human slingshot. Swinging his head slowly back and then jerking it violently forward, he sent his seed into third place.

Next came an elderly gentleman, whom I expected greatness from because though he laid down his two canes in order to take up the watermelon slices, his smile revealed a spacious gap in his front teeth, perfect for spitting through. However, his performance proved sorely disappointing as one seed after another dribbled down his chin.

When Evan, the fireman, came up to the line, he tweaked his mustache and winked at me. I felt the color rush to my cheeks, and was duly impressed when by the power of his puckered lips and a strong pair of lungs, he successfully sent the seed the farthest distance of the day.

"Mia, you know you could beat all of them," Emmett declared proudly. "And a giant watermelon is first prize. Just think of the rind preserves you'd make with it."

"It's not refined behavior for a young lady," I argued.

"You spit seeds at home," Sam whispered to me.

"That's different."

"Aren't you always saying girls should have the right to try and accomplish everything a man does?" Emmett asked. "Must I call my own sister a hypocrite?"

Christian joined into the argument, "What about the pie baking contest? You convinced me to enter it even though I'm the only boy! Come on, Mia, throw your hat in the ring."

They were right of course, but I didn't overcome my reticence until Evan had returned to his steam-pumper and there were few observers around to see me make a spectacle of myself. I stepped up to the starting line and tied back my braids to prevent them from swinging forward and breaking my rhythm. With the gravity of receiving communion, I accepted the juicy slice with trembling hands and extracted the seeds, holding them between the tip of my tongue and pursed lips. With feet planted firmly, I bent my knees tight like a coiled spring, then straightening them, I rose on tiptoe much like a released jack in the box. I repeated this eating, coiling, springing, spitting routine, while at the same time trying to maintain as much decorum as possible. The technique proved effective with each successive seed flying further until the fifth one slipped prematurely from my lips, dropping at my feet. All confidence was now dashed, for once you lose your spitting rhythm there's little hope in regaining it.

"Go for broke, Mia," Emmett cheered.

My brother's encouragement boosted my flagging confidence, and to my satisfaction my last seed flew the farthest. The judge solemnly measured the distance twice, shaking his head in disbelief. "Fifty-four feet and three inches," he proclaimed. "As of now it's the farthest for the day by a quarter inch!"

I was jumping and shouting with pink watermelon juice dripping down my white summer dress when I found myself face to face with Rachael and her companion, a young man who definitely cut a swell. It was the first time we'd seen each other since her ill fated faint in my garden. I could only manage to stammer, "What on earth are you doing here?" It was a stupid question, but knowing her loyalty to the English crown, I didn't think she'd want to celebrate America's independence from the mother country.

"The better question is what are you doing?" she asked in disdain. "Eating melon straight off the rind and spitting seeds? Never could I imagine a more base public exhibit."

I frantically searched my pockets for a clean handkerchief, but found none. "Just having some *American* fun," I retorted.

Rachael's companion offered me the much desired article. "Please allow me," he said gallantly.

I shyly accepted his handkerchief, saying, "It's evident I'm in dire need, but I fear I will ruin it."

"This is my dear dear cousin, Daniel Biggs Esquire," Rachael said effusively.

There stood the young gentleman, Rachael had endlessly gushed about, and I admit he was nothing like I'd imagined. He was undeniably handsome with a clean-shaven face, except for the sideburns defining his jawline. His figure, well-proportioned with broad shoulders and trim waist was stylishly clothed in a blue frockcoat and striped trousers. His top hat, silver tipped cane, and gold watch fob dangling from his vest pocket dandified him, however his tanned complexion and curly brown hair tousled by the wind suggested outdoor activity. It was odd I took note of every detail of his appearance, and yet I was drawn to do so. In every regard he didn't resemble his father, the captain, except for his piercing blue eyes.

Rachael continued the introduction, "Daniel, this is Mia Stein, the girl I've been telling you all about. And these are her brothers, I'm sorry I don't remember your names."

Crestfallen upon hearing Rachael's forgetfulness, Emmett nevertheless bowed genteelly. Daniel Biggs bowed in return, then firmly took my sticky fingers in hand, keeping a steady gaze upon me. "Pleased to make your acquaintance, Miss Stein." He then heartily shook my brothers' hands in turn, asking for their names and what they liked best of the fair so far. Noticing Sam's refusal to talk, he even tried several times to entreat him from his shyness.

"Don't bother with him," Rachael said curtly. "The cat got his tongue."

Kneeling down to Sam's level, Daniel said, "I think you're very wise to choose when to speak. Many of us would benefit by such discretion."

My little brother beamed at the man's praise, and I couldn't help but smile in gratitude for his compassion.

"Daniel just arrived from England yesterday," Rachael chattered. "I hoped to amuse him with the locals' quaint customs, and I believe I have, courtesy of you, dear Mia."

Ignoring Rachael's mean-spirited ways, I turned to the gentleman, "And how did you find your crossing, Mr. Biggs?"

"Please, I insist you call me Daniel. I'm afraid I've not my father's sea legs, but I will spare you the gruesome details."

"I sympathize with you, sir. I get seasick with the slightest of movements," Emmett said.

"Did you see Mia spit?" Christian asked proudly. "Her seed has gone the farthest, and she's the winner so far!"

Daniel smiled, "Most fortunately I did watch your sister, and was impressed by her skills of concentration and delivery."

"Dear Cousin, don't tease her so brutally," Rachael tittered, tweaking his tie. "False praise only encourages foolishness."

Daniel's blue eyes sparkled as he opined, "I don't speak falsehoods when I say most girls wouldn't be so daring, and that in itself impresses me."

Rachael was flustered. "What nonsense, let us speak of things of import. Mia, what do you think of my new dress? It's a Balmoral tartan, homage to Queen Victoria and my mother country."

"I'm sure the monarch would be pleased," I answered, trying to sound earnest.

Rachael continued with her barbs, "One day I will take you shopping for fashionable clothing, something reflecting the Paris designs. They are the true arbiters of good taste."

Daniel interjected, "I'm no expert in fashion, but as a man who knows what he likes, I think Miss Stein's dress is quite lovely."

"Melon stain and all?" Rachael queried sharply.

Uneasy with Daniel's attentions towards me and Rachael's increasing antagonism, I was relieved when Christian suggested we take our leave to watch the pie eating contest.

I offered politely, "It was very nice to see you, Rachael, and to meet you, Mr. Biggs. I mean Daniel."

The young gentleman unexpectedly asked, "Mind if we tag along? It's unbearably forward of me, but I'm certain if you'll serve as our guide, the fair experience will be enhanced. Don't you agree dear cousin?"

With hand to forehead and eyes fluttering, Rachael whimpered, "Actually, I'm so fatigued, I fear I may faint. We'd best return home posthaste."

From our prior experience, I didn't doubt her, however, Daniel accepted none of her foolishness. "Come now, take my arm for support. There is so much still to see, and the exercise will do you good."

Emmett chivalrously offered, "Shall I escort you home, Miss Rothschild? It would take no time at all to hitch up the wagon."

Rachael shook her golden curls as if her spell had passed. "Thank you, dear boy, but my cousin's attentions have revived me, and if I'm allowed to lean upon his strong arm, then I feel confident to proceed."

With our unexpected escort, we headed en masse to the large tent where contestants, bibbed in red-checkered tablecloths, were ravenously consuming pies.

"What a spectacle!" Rachael exclaimed with disgust. "Their faces are covered in meringue and fruit fillings. They're certainly heathens one and all."

I countered, "To be sure, all the participants are clergymen. Houston has five churches and to capitalize on their inherent rivalry, they hold this fundraiser. Everyone makes 'offerings' on behalf of their own preacher. It's quite successful."

Daniel leaned in toward me, "Must be humble pie, they eat."

Rachael shook her head. "It is simply gorging and nothing Christian about it."

"The judges are Harry and Augustus Allen," Emmett explained. "They're the two brothers who founded Houston."

"You see I was right, Miss Stein," Daniel beamed enthusiastically. "The fair is far more entertaining with your family as guide. Now, tell us, who are the clergymen participating?"

I pointed out, "The man at the end of the table is the Baptist preacher, Josiah Hornsby, and the woman standing beside him is his wife, Cora."

"By the looks of his waistline, he doesn't preach restraint, and his wife looks meaner than parsley," Rachael commented.

I couldn't argue against her insightful commentary, but was not going to disclose my dislike for Cora Hornsby. "The man next to him is the Methodist preacher. I can't recall his name, but his church was the first brick building in Texas, and he's ever so proud of it."

"And who's that poor fellow?" Daniel asked with concern. "The one with his forehead beaded in perspiration. I fear what pie he manages to swallow may directly come back up again."

"That's Reverend Hughes, Christ Episcopal," I answered. "And the elderly gentleman next to him is the Presbyterian minister. Rumor has it he'll soon retire due to his congregation's pressure."

"And his swan song is an eating contest?" Rachael laughed haughtily. "This shall have to be adopted in my home's parish. Our vicar would love it."

"Last of all there's my own Father Muldair. Solitary in nature, and yet, never has there been so dedicated a priest."

Daniel mused, "It seems incongruent for the disembodied voice of the confessional to struggle with an overfilled rhubarb pie."

Rachael pointed out, "Mia, your priest has gotten off to a slow start. Perhaps you better say a few Hail Marys for him."

The crowd was cheering on their favorite competitor until a most unusual party gathered to watch.

Rachael whispered, "I say, are those women what I think they are? I mean, I didn't think trollops gad about during the day."

Houston had several houses of ill repute, but none was more heralded by men or scorned by women than the one down by the depot. I explained, "The woman with the red hair is Madam Henrietta Tildy, and those are her girls."

"Those strumpets are long past the distinction of being a girl," Rachael pointed out.

Madam Tildy's friendly how-do was ignored all round. Some of the gentlewomen present turned brusquely away, pulling their husbands along with them, while others couldn't resist staring at the women's painted faces and garish clothing. Despite the social snub, Madam Tildy kept her chin proudly up. Daniel politely tipped his hat, as he would to any other woman. Feeling the pain of her ostracism, I smiled civilly, and she gratefully returned the gesture.

Attention shifted from the women back to the contest when Mayor Moore blew the whistle, announcing the robust Reverend Hornsby had won.

"It appears gluttony has triumphed over piousness," Rachael quipped.

"It's two-thirty," Emmett reminded. "We'd better head over to see Pappa."

"This has been an extraordinary day, might we commemorate it with a likeness taken at the daguerrian gallery?" Daniel asked. "It's right over there, and would take only a minute of your time, Mia."

"What a splendid idea," Rachael gushed. Then shooing my brothers as if they were pests, she directed, "You boys run along, and I promise your sister will join you on time."

Emmett looked at me questioningly.

I stood there in a quandary, but with further persuasion from Daniel Biggs, I relented. "Emmett, I'll catch up with you shortly. And this time keep an eye on your brothers and hold onto Sam's hand."

Daniel directed us into a tented salon where Mr. Whitfield arranged us on a settee with Daniel in the middle. Sitting primly with her ankles crossed, Rachael boldly took Daniel's hand into her own, then Daniel with his eyes twinkling mischievously took my hand in his. The photographer instructed us to remain perfectly still while the exposure was taken. The pleasant sensation of my small hand cradled in Daniel's larger one contrasted sharply with the fear of Pappa discovering my association with Captain Biggs' son and niece. As soon as the powder flashed, I jumped to my feet and ran out from the tent without explanation.

"Until we meet again, Miss Stein," Daniel shouted after me.

Slipping through the crowd, I joined my brothers to listen to the unexpected speaker. Dressed letter perfect as a patriot from our country's revolution, the gentleman had a pony-tail hanging from a three cornered hat and wore knee britches, buckled shoes, and most notably a new Elliptic Three Fold Collar. It was our very own Pappa who was standing at the podium.

Reading our country's Declaration of Independence, Pappa began, "We hold these truths to be self-evident, that all men are created equal. That they are endowed by their creator with certain unalienable rights..."

"Yea, everybody but the Coloreds!" came a derisive shout from the crowd.

Jefferson's words caught in Pappa's throat, and a collective gasp arose from the gathering. Everyone turned to identify the heckler as no other than, Rufus Price, who after his defeat as the Cotton King had become thoroughly inebriated.

Rufus continued in a drunken slur, "Let's not fool ourselves, everybody knows the coloreds are content with the existing state of affairs. They're like children wanting to be taken cared of, not having to worry where their next meal is comin' from. It's liberal Yankees and men like Klaus Stein who put fool ideas of equality and freedom into their heads. They're the ones causing all our problems, and if we don't stop 'em now, our country will be divided in a civil war."

I could comprehend how a cheap jug of moonshine and the bitter taste of loss had loosened the tongue of a man like Rufus, but it didn't explain the nods of approval by so many in the crowd.

Pappa's peace loving disposition had been pushed too far, and he wasn't about to let Rufus have the last word. He argued back, "No one has the right to another man's labor without compensating him, and to own another man like chattel is a down right abomination. Everybody in this town knows you treat your hunting dogs better than your slaves. They're forced to live in hovels and their backsides are raw from lashings, women and children included."

Not backing down, Rufus growled, "I paid good money for my slaves, and that entitles me to treat my private property as I see fit. We all know you, Mr. Stein, like Jefferson, is a lover of hired help. But alas, I won't speak of your private life in the presence of ladies."

The crowd parted as Pappa stepped down from the bandstand and confronted the wild-eyed Rufus who was fuming with rage. "My love for a person isn't decided upon by the color of their skin. As Jefferson said, 'Due rights and proper respect are accorded to all humans.'"

Seeing the tension between Pappa and Rufus had reached fever pitch, a bearded frontiersman, dressed in buckskin and coonskin cap, placed himself squarely between them. Like many short men who are confident of their physical prowess, he swaggered like a banty rooster.

His black eyes flashing contempt at Rufus, he declared, "If it weren't for men like Monsieur Stein who risked his life fighting with Sam Houston, you wouldn't be celebrating our independence in a state called Texas. Nor would you be riding high on your cotton money."

Pappa's recognition and gratitude toward the Frenchman was curtailed by Rufus, who spat squarely in my father's face. This vilest of actions surprisingly did nothing to alter Pappa's calm countenance. As if wiping sweat off on a hot day, he slowly removed his handkerchief from his vest pocket and cleaned his face. Turning

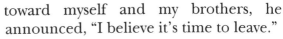

toward myself and my brothers, he announced, "I believe it's time to leave."

I'd never been prouder of my father, however, his fine example of self-restraint was not practiced by the Frenchman. His punch landed squarely on Rufus' unsuspecting jaw, rendering him prostrate upon the ground.

"Right in the chops," hollered Christian approvingly.

"Free fight, boys!" yelled somebody, and the crowd erupted into pandemonium.

Anger over slavery had simmered for quite some time in our city, and it took only a nudge of encouragement for them all to join the rumpus. It didn't matter who was on which side of the argument, for fists flew helter-skelter. Women took cover behind nearby wagons; the exception being Darlene Campbell, whose longing for revolutionary days inspired her to utilize her hatpin as a weapon. Poking men's behinds proved an effective means of attack, for no one dared retaliate against so respected a denizen of our community. She continued unabated until Bailey, Pappa's shop foreman, encountered her sharp jab. With a gentle hand, he plopped Mrs. Campbell into the horse's trough. She remained there, realizing it was a most advantageous spot for observing the action.

Sam enjoyed every minute of the fracas, especially watching John Kincaid, owner of the Congress Street mill, fight one of Rufus's wagoneers. John was as big as an ox and with every punch he took, a cloud of cornmeal puffed out from his clothes. Then there was Pappa's civilized fight with a dockman, each politely taking turns with their blows. Emmett and Christian found boys near their own age to tousle with, and Rufus, who had started the whole mess, scurried off like a scared rabbit.

A few fought like Kilkenny cats, but thankfully bowie knives and guns weren't brandished, so no one suffered more than a black eye or busted lip. By the time Sheriff Franklin shot his six-shooter into the air, everyone was tuckered out and willing to go their separate ways.

When all had settled, Pappa searched out the Frenchman, who had come to his defense. Offering his hand in gratitude, he said, "Why if it isn't Henri Dubois."

The rugged frontiersman kissed both of Pappa's cheeks. "Klaus, it has been too long."

"Ugh, he just kissed Pappa," Christian pointed out.

Emmett shrugged, "When you can fight like him, I guess you can get away with that sort of thing. Besides it's what the French do."

"Henri, you've a nasty gash to your forehead," Pappa noted. "Mia, come see what you can do for my dear friend."

"Please, don't bother, I'm fine. I've had a lot worse, as have you."

Pappa persisted, "It's the least we can do for such a show of valor. You spoke up in my defense, and I'm obliged."

"No less is expected for a brother-in-arms and the man who saved my life."

Sam's eyes widened with interest, and I knew he longed to ask, as did we all, what was behind the Frenchman's statement.

Pappa dismissed his claim with a wave of his hand, "Henri, you exaggerate. I did my part at San Jacinto, just like every other soldier."

Concerned for the Frenchman's bleeding cut, I offered, "Shall I take a look at it, sir? I don't have my bag with me to patch it up properly, but I'll do my best."

His eyes moved up and down me approvingly. "How can I decline so generous an offer."

Carefully removing strands of raven black hair matted in the bloody cut, I found, like most head wounds, its severity didn't match the profuse bleeding. Then washing out the embedded dirt, I apologized for the necessary rough treatment and for causing the bleeding to start afresh. I applied a poultice of mashed juniper berries, which I found growing nearby, then modestly raising my hem to tear a strip of cotton underskirt, I bandaged his head.

Throughout the whole of this procedure, Mr. Dubois watched me closely, and when I exposed my limbs there was no doubt his gaze lingered. Feeling increasingly embarrassed, I avoided meeting his eyes until I was finished, only to then suffer the intensity of his steady fixed look. The fair and its throngs of people seemed to recede, leaving us two alone. "You'll be fine," I stammered, looking away. "Just make sure you change the bandage everyday."

The Frenchman's accent was seductively smooth, "And how may I repay your kindness, Miss Stein?"

Again I was drawn to look at him, "I'm in *your* debt, sir, for your aid to my father."

I felt saved by Pappa's booming voice, "Have you been in Houston long, Henri? I recall you planned to return home to France after the injury you received at San Jacinto."

"I did go back for several years, but now I make my home in Galveston. I'm a customs officer there, but my business often brings me to Houston."

"The wild frontiersman has an office job?" Pappa laughed. "Picturing you behind a desk is difficult, especially in that getup. You look ready to hunt down wild boar."

Henri's brow cocked. "You'd be surprised how at times the life of a customs officer is indeed a hunt."

"Now, you intrigue me," Pappa said. "Have you a place to stay here in town?"

"I've let a room at City Hotel over on Franklin. It suits me well as it's not far from the docks where I handle much of my activity."

Pleased, Pappa said, "Why, it's not a block from my shop. Promise me you'll come in for a visit; better yet, accept my offer to dine at our home. Mia is an exceptional cook."

"Klaus, I'd like nothing more than to accept, but I'm afraid I must return to the island this evening. In fact, I must now rush to catch my boat, but it would give me much pleasure to take up your offer on a future visit and taste Miss Stein's cooking."

"Of course, anytime," Pappa said with a friendly slap to his back.

Their easy interaction portended of a renewed friendship as the two men embraced once again in the French custom. Mr. Dubois then bid me adieu with his full sensual lips pressed against my hand. I felt dizzy with perturbation as he turned and disappeared into the crowd.

"Mia, aren't you supposed to work the sewing booth at this hour?" Pappa asked, bringing me back to earth.

When we arrived, Darlene Campbell was there, still soggy and disheveled from her encounter with the horse trough. It didn't deter her from exuberantly hawking our handiwork for the betterment of unwed mothers. "Mia, wherever have you been? I'd scold you if it weren't for the incredible success of your rosemary pincushions. They've proven to be our biggest seller. And dear, Mr. Stein, let me shake your hand, sir. You stirred a passion within all of us today with your speech. We must fight the injustices of the world one by one, and you're truly a leading soldier in our crusade."

"And you, Mrs. Campbell, were in the thick of things yourself," Pappa said.

"I try to do my part. My, what's all the commotion over there? Look a crowd is gathering in the meadow."

An Uncle Sam figure on stilts rushed by, shouting, "Been sightings of a hot air balloon. Looks like it's trying to land at the fair."

Darlene Campbell pulled down a tarp over the booth. "You go on Mia with your family. I was planning to close up shop anyway."

I didn't need further encouragement, for the balloon was heading straight for the field.

"I can make out the word Daedalus on its side," Emmett said, looking through his spyglass.

"What's a day da las?" Christian asked, straining his eyes toward the floating object.

"The question is not what, but who," Emmett explained. "Daedalus was a figure in Greek mythology who was imprisoned with his son Icarus. To escape their cells, he created feathered wings for them to fly away, but Icarus flew too close to the sun, and the wax holding the feathers together melted. He fell to his death in the ocean."

"I hope wax isn't holding the balloon together," Christian mused.

As the airship floated closer the pilot shouted down, "Mia, Mia, I see you. This is for you."

"I can't believe my eyes," Pappa exclaimed. "It's our very own Tío Manuel flying that contraption."

Our uncle dropped a basket attached to a tiny parachute, and a man who caught it, read the attached note, "Happy Early Birthday, Mia. Say, who is this Mia?"

"She's our sister," my brothers answered, as they retrieved the basket.

I was embarrassed by the attention, but thrilled with the contents of the basket: two mewing kittens, one white and the other black. Tío threw out the drop lines, and the townsfolk clambered to pull the gondola and its occupant safely to the ground.

Mayor Moore tipped his top hat and greeted our uncle with a hearty handshake. "Salutations and welcome to Houston. What, sir, may I ask is your name, and from what faraway region have you traveled?"

"I am Manuel Castillo, and I've successfully completed a flight from the distant California territory."

The crowd was enthralled and encouraged my uncle to tell of his journey. A showman at heart, Tío needed little encouragement. "My flight across our fine country held many adventures and breathless vistas. There were deserts glowing crimson with the setting sun and lakes shimmering under a silvery moon. I brushed the tops of redwood forests and watched wild mustangs graze peacefully below me, and though these were extraordinary sights of a lifetime, nothing made my heart beat faster nor fill me with more joy than when I crossed the Rio Grande and knew I'd arrived in my beautiful home of Texas."

The crowd cheered their approval, and helping him from the basket, lifted him to their shoulders like a returning hero. After further questions were answered and invitations to dinners and dances generously proffered, Manuel, who was relishing every moment of his celebrity, was finally left to his family. We hadn't seen him in two years, and though his travels must have been trying at times, he appeared an impeccably dressed dandy. The only difference I noticed in him was that his once black hair, kept in place with Macassar oil, had turned grey, as had his curled and pomaded mustache.

Hugging us each in turn, he whooped, "I've missed you so much, you can't imagine. And my, how you've all grown up. My Mia es muy bonita. You are the very image of my beloved sister, Francesca, may she rest in heaven."

"Thank you for the kittens, Tío, you're so thoughtful."

"A girl turns eighteen only once, and I won't be here in August for your special day. This early surprise will have to do."

"And what a surprise," Pappa said. "You promised an unusual arrival, but never did we imagine you descending from the heavens."

"My brother, the balloon is the future mode of transportation. Haven't you read Edgar Allen Poe's story in the New York Sun? It tells of travel across the Atlantic carrying passengers from Europe to America. Mark my words, it may be fiction now, but not for long."

Intrigued, Sam was examining the balloon's riggings when Manuel spoke to him. "And who is this? Why, you must be the baby," Manuel teased. "You were knee-high to a grasshopper, the last time I saw you."

Affronted, Sam managed to speak up, "I'm not a baby, I'm Sam!"

Everyone laughed at his indignation.

"Excuse me, young man. You're absolutely right. No one wants to be called a baby. And Emmett and Christian? You both look like you've been in a fight. I hope not with each other."

"No, Tío, but you should see the other fellows," Christian crowed. "And Pappa started the fight."

"Your father throwing a punch? That's utterly impossible to conceive."

Pappa grinned, "We have many stories to share, but it's late now and I'm sure you're tired after such a journey."

"To be sure, tonight all I want is a hot bath and a good night's sleep. Tomorrow I'll regale you with tales of my life out West, and I'll hear all about the Stein men fighting and Mia's adventures with her doctoring."

Fireworks exploded across the night sky and the band played their last song as we hitched up our wagon. I sat up top with Pappa, while the boys gathered round Tío.

"Too bad, you didn't win the seed spitting contest," Emmett shouted up to me. "I heard the fellow who took the prize home was a bricklayer with years of experience spewing tobacco."

"And I'm sorry Christian lost the pie-baking contest," I said.

Christian pouted, "Page eleven, rule forty-four of the cooking handbook, 'Hard liquor will not be allowed in the making of a pie.' But whiskey is what makes my chocolate nut pie so delicious!"

"Miss Penelope always wins," Emmett concluded.

Pappa relaxed the reins and allowed the horses to lead the way home. He suddenly looked all worn out, and I knew it disconcerted him to see men, whom he regarded as friends, side with Rufus. How grateful I was Miss Emily was delivering a baby, and didn't witness such hatred.

The kittens mewed hungrily, the boys settled down to the rhythm of the gently swaying wagon, and the moon followed us home. In my quiet moment of rumination, the touch and glance of Henri Dubois and Daniel Biggs came to mind. Two men so different in appearance and manner had crossed my path and surprisingly stirred my heart.

CHAPTER IX

CHRISTIAN'S PROPHECY

y dreams were a jumble of confusing images; the warm touch of a hand, blue penetrating eyes turning black, buckskin and waistcoats interchanging until I awoke restless in a sweat. I knew it was my encounters with Daniel and Henri that disturbed my slumber. It had been remarkable to meet Rachael's dashing young cousin, whose gentlemanly behavior most certainly differed from that of his scandalous father. Their peculiar relationship intrigued me, for Rachael's fondness for him was obvious, whereas I was dead to rights he didn't return her affection in kind. Then there was Pappa's long ago friend, Henri Dubois, to consider. His dark allure enhanced by his mature confidence was undeniably seductive, though his unrestrained observation of me was unnerving.

As I finished my toilette, my perfunctory glance in the looking glass aroused unexpected dissatisfaction. My long braids hanging down suddenly looked unsophisticated, and my summer dress too plain. I wondered if Rachael's criticism was influencing me or if it was something else spurring this new found attention to my appearance. I fiddled with one hairstyle after another until I settled upon the same manner in which my own mother once wore her hair, a stylish chignon secured with tortoise shell combs. I then fashioned a belt from a pink satin ribbon to accentuate my waist in the sack like dress, and descended the staircase, satisfied with what I was convinced was a more mature look.

After baking bread and tidying the house, it was near upon noon when I discovered my brothers whispering conspiratorially on the kitchen stairs. "And what mischief are you boys are up to now?"

"We haven't seen Tío all morning, so we thought we'd better check up on him," Emmett answered.

Sam put his finger to his lips indicating it was a covert mission.

"Actually, we want to see what souvenirs he brought us," Christian stated matter-of-factly.

"Let me make myself perfectly clear, young men, you are to wait until your uncle comes down on his own. He's endured a long journey and may not rise till this evening. And mind you, I don't want you fishing for any presents either. He will offer them when he is good and ready."

"Did I hear presents mentioned?" Tío asked, poking his head around the corner with the much sought after bag in hand.

"I thought you were asleep," I said.

"I've been up since five; sunrise being the best time to practice yoga and meditation."

Our uncle preceded to show us what he meant by plopping down on the kitchen floor and crossing his legs atop each other. Closing his eyes, he breathed in a strange rhythmic fashion, then with the greatest of ease, he raised himself on his hands into a headstand.

Christian crowed with laughter, "You could work for P.T. Barnum's sideshow alongside the Bearded Lady and Tom Thumb. They'd call you Pretzel Man or the Human Knot."

Sam limberly copied our uncle's pose.

"Where'd you learn how to do that?" Emmett asked.

"In California," Tío answered. "A hundred thousand people from all corners of the world came there in search of gold, and I had the good fortune to befriend Jahan, a gentleman from India. He stayed at my boarding house where we, along with two other men, shared an old straw mattress and the bedbugs to go with it."

"Four to a bed?" I asked incredulously.

"Yes, and twenty to the room, including women. Of course, they were provided a modicum of privacy behind a curtain divider, but soap was hard to come by, so you can imagine the stink. I confess I was a driven soul back then, frantic to find gold and strike it rich. When I met Jahan, I saw he was on the same hard and fast mission, and yet he remained calm. He explained it was the result of his physical and spiritual regimen, and so longing for the same positive affect on my frazzled nerves, I asked him to teach me his foreign ways. You might imagine the other miner's reactions when they awoke to find the two of us in such odd poses. Now, I think you boys are ready for the real business of the day."

"Presents!" they squealed to my dismay.

With a dramatic flourish, which we had come to expect from our uncle, Tío pulled a long strip of white fabric out of his bag and twisted it around Christian's head until he'd formed a turban. "Ah, this suits you very well. You look just like the mysterious people of the East. And now for little Sam, a prized arrowhead from the Maidu Indians. They are very good natured, as most Indians are unless you try taking their land."

Our uncle rummaged through his bag until to our astonishment he brought out a chunk of gold the size of his fist. "A fair size nugget wouldn't you say?"

I said in wonder, "It must be worth a small fortune."

"I give it to Emmett," Tío announced. "Does my present satisfy you?"

Coolly accepting the gift, Emmett replied, "Thank you, Tío, though I don't think I'll be able to buy much with Fool's Gold."

"You've a keen eye, Emmett. Far better than mine. I found this piece of pyrite on my first day of digging and believed it to be gold. You can imagine my elation and subsequent depression when I discovered its true value was only as a fire starter, and at that the quality is poor, for it smells awful when burning. Perhaps as a conversational piece it will prove its merit."

Emmett turned the shiny object over in his hand. "I thank you Uncle. It has a good story to it and an even better lesson."

I'd not noticed Christian's absence until he reappeared dramatically dressed in his turban, a colorful table scarf draped around his shoulders, and a mustache fashioned from ashes. He positioned himself cross-legged and with a flurry of exotic sound-ing gibberish disclosed a crystal ball, which in truth was the globe to our parlor's oil lantern. "Gather round, people of curiosity. Let me introduce myself, I am Swami Knowitall. Through the powers of the unknown darkness I am able to foresee the future. Miss, I can see you wish to know your fortune. I will gladly disclose all for only three pennies."

"Swami, I am making bread for our mid-day meal and some-thing hearty besides, perhaps you will dine with us in lieu of payment."

"I accept your generous offer," Christian said solemnly. "Now, if everyone will hold hands. This will increase the magnetic field necessary for my vision, so we may see what lies behind the veil of ignorance. Please Miss, I must ask once more if you're *sure* you want to know what lies ahead. All may not be as you wish?"

I played along, "Yes, whether it be good or bad. I want to know."

It seemed all the elements conspired in the make-believe, for a cloud darkened the sun and the birds stilled their singing.

Christian's eyes fluttered, "I see a figure on the horizon. I can-not make it out. Ah yes, now I see it is a man who will soon be com-ing to visit our Mia."

I laughed nervously, "You must be seeing the past, and our uncle's visit."

Christian shook his head, "No, this man's means of travel is definitely not a balloon. He comes in a fashionable carriage pulled by a spotted horse. He's a young man with eyes the color of the sky. The crystal is clouding... Wait it clears again and there appears a different man and with him comes the dark cloak of danger. One of them will open the door to the past. Be prepared, Miss Mia, your simple life will soon alter."

I wondered how much Christian was alluding to Daniel and Henri, and how much was simply coincidental. Whatever the case may be, I knew Daniel Biggs would never come to call on me.

"Do you dare hear more?" Christian asked, while rubbing the crystal ball with the practiced hand of a seer.

"No thank you, Swami. I'm not sure we should foresee too much of our destiny."

The front door opened, and Pappa entered, asking? "What's for supper?"

"You mean what's for chow," Tío said. "That's what we gold diggers called our meals."

"Mock turtle soup with black beans," I answered.

Tío groaned, "In California we had beans every meal and every day. I couldn't bare to see another one, as long as I live,"

"Don't look at us," Emmett said. "We have to eat whatever she makes."

"You'll all go hungry if I hear one more word of complaint," I cried. "Now, go out on the veranda where it's cooler, and I'll bring some of the ale we brewed last winter."

My offer of drink was premature, for apparently we'd put too much sugar in the ale and the bottles had exploded, leaving a mess on the cellar floor.

Settling into a comfortable rocker with a glass of lemonade, my uncle tried to make the best of it by saying, "At least we're safe from the The Sons of Temperance. I wouldn't want the law upon our head."

Pappa tapped his pipe against the sole of his shoe and emptied its ashes before pontificating, "Reverend Hornsby declares drink destroys thousands of folks each year. He's gone so far as to say drunkenness can lead to combustion of the human body. I'll not argue many a man has fallen into degeneracy with a bottle of cheap whiskey by his side, but I assert that if a man's moral character is deficient, then the bottle merely serves as his excuse."

"And what of your hero, Sam Houston?" Tío asked. "I'd say he's a man of good mind and character, and yet his overindulgence of drink almost ruined him."

"You've got a good point there, Manuel, and though Houston does have a good mind and character, one or the other must have a weakness."

"As do we all," Tío concurred.

"But not you, my dear brother-in-law," Klaus said glowingly. By traversing this vast country of ours and returning triumphantly with fortune in hand, you've shown courage and determination to follow your dream in the face of much adversity. I can only hope my own sons will grow up to have such a stalwart constitution."

Looking embarrassed, Tío countered, "Klaus, your praise is far too generous."

Settling down with my sewing basket, I pleaded, "Dear uncle, you promised to tell us more of your time in California. I'm certain you have some exciting adventures to reveal."

Tío tweaked his mustache, and asked, "Will a duel suit your curiosity?"

My brothers enthusiastically chimed their approval, and so my uncle began his tale, not noticing the scowl on Pappa's face. "One morning at the boarding house, a fellow who recently arrived from France and was one of our bed companions, woke up and began to frantically search his pockets and saddlebags for his money. Despite the language barrier and his state of agitation, it became apparent he was accusing me of robbing him. Of course, I denied any hand in the matter, and reminded him of the drunken state he'd been in the previous night. I maintained he'd either misplaced the money or more likely squandered it. The Frenchman, taking offense at my suggestion, slapped my face with his glove and challenged me to a duel. With my honor at stake, what alternative did I have but to accept his challenge?"

"Did you kill him?" Christian asked excitedly.

"Patience, my boy. One does not jump prematurely to the end of a story. Now, where was I? Ah yes, arrangements were made according to tradition, with the time of two o'clock agreed upon and a pair of revolvers provided. News of our upcoming duel spread quickly through the miners' camp, and a crowd, eager for diversion, formed. Like the true friend he was, Jahan, offered to take my place, but I declined, knowing his knowledge of firearms was even less than my own. I'm not ashamed to admit I was near collapse with foreboding by the time my opponent arrived. Had the competition been with a lariat, I would have won hands down, for my father taught me this ranching skill better than anyone I have since met. Give me a rope and I can lasso you a chicken, picking which leg I'll catch."

"Don't tempt me," I said, "Or I shall take you up on your offer come dinner time."

"Uncle, please get back to the duel," Christian pleaded.

"Yes, yes, of course. Well, all the preparations were arranged and it was nearly the appointed hour when the Frenchman came to me red faced with shame. Pointing to the tip of his boot, he pulled out the misplaced wad of money which might have caused one or both of our early demise. Apparently, in his drunken stupor he had hidden it there for safekeeping, then promptly forgotten. Never have I seen so sudden a reversal in character. He was all apologies afterwards, and treated Jahan and I to a bath at Miss Scarlet's and as many rounds of drink we cared to indulge in.

"A happy ending," Pappa said, looking relieved. "And on that note, I'm afraid I must leave your storytelling. I've got to make a quick trip to the mill for a delivery, and a double check of the board keeps Hank honest.

Tío continued with his tales until the boys spied a copperhead and ran off to wrangle it. With my uncle and I left alone, I broached the intimate issue of his marriage and what had caused its dissolution.

With his head hung in shame, he confessed, "Like a dog with a bone, I couldn't let go of the notion that what I had to offer Neeva Jane wasn't enough. And so struck with gold fever, I headed West, hell-bent on making my fortune. There's no excuse for my foolishness, and I've had to pay dearly for it."

"Oh Uncle, how terribly sad," I said. "Is there no hope of you winning her back?"

"She went back East to her family, and though I've written her countless times asking for forgiveness, never has she replied."

"As you know, when Pappa married your sister, he had little money, and though his own parents were against their union, he followed his heart. So, Tío, if you truly love your Neeva Jane, do not forsake her."

"Mia, your father has done well raising you on his own. You've learned love above all things is essential to our happiness. I only hope it's not too late for me to benefit from the same lesson. After my visit here, you've given me the courage to head directly to see her. Now, tell me what you're working on, is that a quilt for your dowry?"

"It's taken me forever," I said, running my fingers across the appliquéd top. "but I'm just about ready to sew the three layers together.

"You've chosen interesting pictures to depict. Do they mean something special?"

"Each square symbolizes a different aspect of marriage. The laurel branch brings good luck to the newly wed and the playful dogs represent fidelity, and the linked rings are the union of heart and soul."

"And the basket of eggs?" he asked. "Does that promise the wife will be a good cook?"

"No, it means the husband will," I shot back.

"Ah, you're getting saucy just like your Mamma was. Tell me Mia, why are you picking up a needle for such fancywork? Have you a beau I should know about?"

"No one," I stammered, thinking of Daniel and Henri. "It takes years for a girl to finish all the linens for her future household. If she were to wait for an engagement to start, it wouldn't be done on time."

Upon delivering my disavowal of an attachment, our attention was averted to an approaching horseman. Shivers ran up my spine as I recalled Christian's divination of a man visiting me. Identical to his description, the gentleman was driving a fashionable gig pulled by a spotted horse, and he was no other than Daniel Biggs himself.

His dark green morning coat was tailored to perfection and his knee-high Wellington boots showed his calves to good advantage. Repeating the impression he made upon our first meeting, I had a heightened awareness that a refined and well-favored gentleman was before me.

Alighting from the carriage with an agility reflecting his youthful vigor, Daniel doffed his leather riding gloves and greeted Tío with a hearty handshake. "Good afternoon, Mr. Stein."

"I'm afraid you mistake me for my brother-in-law, Klaus. I am Mia's uncle, Manuel Castillo. Good to make your acquaintance, and your name sir?"

"I beg your pardon, I'm Daniel Biggs. I was introduced to your niece yesterday at the fair by way of my cousin, Rachael, and realizing I was in the vicinity, decided to pay her a call and make her father's acquaintance."

Removing his top hat, Daniel bowed before me. "It's a pleasure to see you again, Mia. I hope you don't think ill of me, popping in unannounced."

My anxiety over Pappa finding the offspring of Captain Biggs at our home was countered by the pleasing sensations I was feeling with his proximity. "Not at all, Mr. Biggs."

"Daniel to you," he reminded me.

"Yes, Daniel, I'm not usually one to stand on ceremony. Did you see my uncle's grand entrance at the fair, yesterday? He arrived in a hot air balloon, flying all the way from the California territory."

"Unfortunately, I missed that remarkable sight. Rachael was fatigued, and we left shortly after your sudden departure.

His coy smile rekindled the embarrassment I'd felt the day before. He must surely think me a foolish child, running away as I did, and yet his opinion must not be too low, for he had made a call upon me.

"How did you find life in California, Mr. Castillo?" Daniel asked politely.

"I'd say untamed is the best way to describe it," Tío responded, eager to recount his experiences. "Few laws and an excess of alcohol brings out the worst qualities in men, and if you add the risky business of searching for gold, you end up with utter chaos. If you were lucky enough, and most men weren't, to actually strike gold, it was wise to keep the knowledge of it to yourself or you might find your throat slit."

"Indeed," Daniel said, as he adjusted his collar. "I understand your country just recently took control of California. How do they justify the conquest of these Mexican territories?"

"Manifest destiny, my young man, the same way we took Texas. You see, I'm in a peculiar position because I'm both a Mexican and a Texian. This is my homeland either way I look at it, and yet at times I'm considered an outsider by the good citizens of this land. Mia's mother, Francesca, also endured difficulties when she came to live in Houston. After the Battle of San Jacinto, the Mexican soldiers who hadn't been slaughtered were forced into slavery. They worked alongside the Negro slaves clearing the land to make this city. So, even if you're a Mexican who fought on the side of the Texians, you're not beyond suspicion and prejudice."

Being English and new to our country, I was certain Daniel had little knowledge of what my uncle discussed, and talk of the prejudice my family endured made me uncomfortable. Intent on redirecting the conversation, I asked, "Tío, were there many women in California?"

"They were a rare sight indeed, perhaps one for every twenty men, and most of them were married, so, you can imagine the commotion when a single woman came to town. It's a difficult life out there, but a woman with housewifery skills usually made more money than the men digging for gold."

"You mean to say, washing clothes and cooking could make me flush?" I asked incredulously.

"Consider the men who worked all week in the worst conditions, sleeping at their claim or in crowded mining camps. When Saturday came they poured into town ready to pay high dollar for a bath, clean clothes, and home cooking."

"That settles it, I'm packing my bags tonight," I teased. "I can run a boarding house and sell medicinal remedies on the side."

Believing my proposal, Daniel said, "Sounds horribly dangerous, Miss Stein,"

"She'd be fine with a gun strapped to her hip," Tío said.

I continued my ruse, "Me, brandishing a weapon? I think it would be much more lady-like to discreetly conceal it upon my person. Perhaps a small colt revolver."

Daniel's face reddened, and so did mine when I considered the delicate nature of what I suggested.

"Extraordinary," Daniel said.

"You realize our Mia is pulling your leg, don't you?" Tío asked, taking up his whittling.

Daniel swore he knew I was teasing, though his look of relief said different.

Tío continued, "I'm telling the truth though, when I say my niece is an accomplished healer. I once had a catarrh in the head that threatened my very life. Mia, do you remember the treatment you advised for me?"

"I believe it was a mixture of gum Arabic, gum myrrh, and bloodroot," I answered.

Tío proclaimed, "I was well within the week. Yes indeed, our Mia is a wonder."

Daniel looked admiringly in my direction. "Doesn't surprise me in the least. Your niece seems to be a woman of many talents. I know nothing of medicine, but it is a field which interests me. Perhaps Mia, you will take me under your wing for instruction. I promise to be a willing pupil."

"I believe now, you're teasing me," I said.

"I am completely in earnest."

My uncle smiled encouragingly at the two of us. "Mia, why don't you show Mr. Biggs your herb garden. It could be the first of many lessons."

I considered the inappropriateness of my walking with a gentleman without a chaperon, but dared not refuse Daniel's sincere smile and proffered arm. We enjoyed a delightful meander through my garden, and true to his word, he was curious about each plant and its corresponding medicinal property.

Reaching the end of my allotment and corresponding instruction, we sat upon a bench next to the holly tree, and I asked, "You mentioned the necessity of leaving the fair early because of Rachael's fatigue; is she faring better today?"

Making a wry face, he answered, "I anticipated her spontaneous recovery upon our return home, and was delighted to see it come to fruition. I'm sure you've noticed my cousin is accustomed to getting her way."

"Rachael is ... how can I say it?"

"Willful," Daniel offered.

"Yes, the very word I sought. However, you shouldn't discount, out of hand, all her complaints. Her health is problematic. Did you know she suffered a fainting spell in this very garden?"

"It doesn't surprise me in the least, and I'm certain she'll completely ruin her constitution if she doesn't put her mind to some activity other than cards. It seems you're kept quite busy."

"Yes, I'm always at some task and I try to eat well, and of course, I don't wear a corset. Please excuse me, I don't know why I mentioned that last thing. You will think me quite unmannered."

"On the contrary, it's refreshing to meet a woman without affectation. I see you've done up your hair differently today. It's very becoming, though I hope it's not as a result of Rachael's criticism. Her tongue can be sharp at times."

"Thank you, sir, for noticing the alteration. My hair could resemble Medusa's and my family wouldn't perceive a difference. To them, I'm as inconspicuous as the wallpaper, until it's supper time, and then their only query is to what we will be eating."

Daniel mused, "I dare say it's the way with most families. We're blind to those we live with, but it's obvious your brothers adore you. They were most proud of your seed spitting abilities."

"Your Aunt Edna reprimanded me for not fostering enough accomplishments. You'll have to inform her of my latest acquired skill; I'm certain she'll think it quite barbaric."

"So, you've met her," Daniel said, looking slightly disturbed. "Yes, she can at times be a stickler for protocol. Old guard, you know."

"Rachael told me you're an only child."

"Yes, my mother died when I was a boy. There had been a terrible cholera epidemic in London, and like you, she went out amongst the poor to give aid. In a cruel twist of fate, the very people she worked to help, ended up killing her. You see, many came to believe doctors and the government poisoned the water in a plot to collect bodies for anatomical dissection. In truth, inadequate sanitation contaminated the water, but the hysteria couldn't be stopped and my mother was killed during a riot."

"How very tragic. I'm certain it brought you and your father close together."

"Ironically, I hardly know the man, and it's a bit awkward to find myself in America helping him with his work. He left for the states immediately after my mother's death, putting all his energy towards his commerce. I suppose it was his way of coping with his loss. I was passed between relatives for a couple of years, excluding my Aunt Edna. Since you've met her, I believe you'll understand why it wasn't arranged. Eventually, I was sent to boarding school, and only saw my father on the odd holiday."

Unable to suppress my curiosity concerning his father, I conjectured, "I've not had the opportunity to meet the captain, but from what I gather, he's a bit of a mysterious character."

"It's true he avoids society, but I'm sure it's due to his devotion to his work. He owns two cargo ships and exports English goods around the world. Perhaps my coming here and lending a hand with the business will help to alter the reputation, you say he's acquired. That is, if he ever returns home. He's on an African safari, mixing business with pleasure. Ghana, I believe."

"So, your future is as a sea merchant?"

"Oh no, as I revealed before, I don't have the sea legs for that. I plan to handle the land-based end of things and coordinate our steamer between here and Galveston."

"Expect tough competition with the Houston Navigation Company," I pointed out. "They've secured all the mail contracts, and whenever another business tries to compete, they always undercut their fares."

Undaunted, Daniel declared, "I'm just now acquiring the rudiments of the operation, but perhaps we'll be the dark horse that will win."

Trying to damper my enthusiasm for such a proposal, I asked coolly, "Then you plan to make your home here? I mean to stay?"

"Yes, if all turns out as I hope. I almost came to live here in Texas as a boy, when my father was to remarry. However, my plans were altered when the engagement was broken."

No doubt the woman he dueled over, I thought. "Do you know who his intended was?"

"I know little about her, other than she lived in San Antonio and was very beautiful. What happened to end the betrothal is a mystery to me, but I know it altered my father forever."

I was intrigued. "Perhaps he returned to find her."

Daniel humored me. "Anything is possible when it comes to love."

Venturing into sensitive territory, I posited, "You lived with Rachael's family for a time; you two must be very close."

"It isn't gallant of me to disclose, but I was as close to her as a boy could be to a younger girl, whom he considered a pest. However, the years have narrowed the gap between us, as it is want to do, and we have gotten to know each other in a different way."

I felt a pang of jealousy mixed with further curiosity, but I dared not press him further on the issue.

Daniel continued, "She told me that you too lost your mother at an early age."

"I'm surprised Rachael speaks at all of me. Our first get together was a bit of a disaster, and you saw how caustic she was toward me at the fair."

"She's actually quite captivated by you, and I wouldn't be surprised if she takes up spitting seeds after seeing your triumphant performance."

"You say she admires me, then why does she find pleasure in belittling me?"

"She recognizes and is drawn to your strength of character, and yet it threatens her. For all her efforts to hide it, she's a very insecure person, so you mustn't take what she says to heart."

"I try to ignore her insults, but I fear one day her provocation will go too far and I may give her a dose of her own medicine."

"I trust whatever action you take will be warranted, but I ask you to keep in mind what I may call the formation of her character. Her father was an indifferent and distant figure in her life, and her endless succession of nurses and governesses were of the same cold temperament. Rachael was kept practically a prisoner in the nursery, except for the odd occasion when she was paraded out for the amusement of her father's guests. I'm certain she was scarred by this lack of affection."

"But what of her mother?"

"Didn't Rachael tell you? No, I suppose she wouldn't. Mrs. Abigail Rothschild is permanently residing in a lunatic asylum. She is far worse than our Aunt Edna."

I was shocked by this revelation. "Poor Rachael, I had no idea. To grow up motherless in a loveless home must have been unbearable. It seems you were dealt the same harsh fate, and yet you have fared well."

"It's true I was young when I lost my mother, but her unconditional love for me created a sense of security, which sank deep and steady like an anchor, so that no matter what storm arises, I'm always tethered safely."

"You must miss her terribly, as I do mine."

"It's an emptiness I hope will be filled one day by another's love."

I was so enraptured by his and Rachael's life story that I found myself completely at ease when his hand embraced my own. However, our tender moment was destroyed by raucous laughter and jeering from my three mischievous brothers, who were hiding behind the garden shed. Mortified that they'd witnessed our tête-à-tête, I shouted vengeance upon them like an old nag, and Daniel laughed heartily at them and me.

"I'll fix his wagon if he tries to kiss our Mia," Christian bellowed.

He then tousled with Emmett, knocking over pots and gardening tools, before making their escape. Sam, alone, stood glaring at Daniel. He seemed to be in a dither as to what action to take. Then he settled upon sticking out his tongue before scrambling away.

I moaned in agitation, "I'm afraid you'll have to excuse my uncivilized brothers. They test my patience daily."

Daniel smiled understandingly, "Don't begrudge them their fun. I was up to the same shenanigans when I was a lad, if not worse. Besides, I should be off. Rachael is sure to be waiting supper for me. May I give her your regards and say you'll visit soon. She has wanted for some time to extend another invitation to Mosswood."

"Yes, please do, and ask her if she'd like a kitten. My uncle gave me two adorable ones, and I think one of them would make a perfect companion for her."

"A splendid idea; I know she'll love it. Now, I must bid farewell. I've enjoyed our time together, and I hope I may call on you in the future. Oh, I almost forgot this."

From his vest pocket Daniel retrieved the daguerreotype that we'd made at the fair. It captured Rachael looking adoringly at Daniel, I, on the edge of my seat ready to flee, and Daniel in the middle looking pleased with himself.

I was about to express some flippancy regarding my ridiculous appearance when Daniel generously offered me the picture as a gift. Then bowing, he kissed my hand tenderly. I was aflutter with emotion, and when his gig moved down our street, I almost broke into a playful dash after him. On further consideration, it dawned on me this childish behavior wouldn't suffice for the mature woman I aspired to be. My petals were beginning to unfurl; I was blossoming.

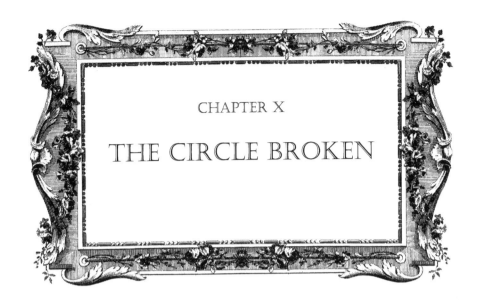

CHAPTER X

THE CIRCLE BROKEN

That summer in Houston, the black vomit of yellow fever stained many a bed sheet, and widow's weeds and mourning wreaths became painfully ordinary. Those who could afford to travel, fled to the countryside, not returning until the oppressive heat let up and the incessant drone of deadly mosquitoes quieted. I linked my arm with Miss Emily's, and with a handkerchief to our noses, to avert the acrid stench of smoking tar barrels, we made our way down the deserted streets.

Amid this pall of death, our own President Taylor succumbed to typhoid fever. Fillmore stepped into his place, and it was his confidence in resolving the slavery issue, which spurred my own idealistic efforts to protest the injustice of inequality. It was Thursday morning, the customary day for my sewing circle, and I was boldly, or perhaps naively, bringing Miss Emily to join the other ladies.

It wasn't until we started up the long shelled pathway to Darlene Campbell's front door that Miss Emily wavered. "You're a fool Miss Mia, and so am I for goin' along with this crazy idea of yours. Those women in there ain't never gonna accept me."

"Nonsense," I affirmed. "Once they get to know you, they will love you, as do I."

Miss Emily sneered. "I already know them ladies as well as the back of my hand. I delivered six of Esther Price's ten children, treated the boils of her uppity daughters, and pulled teeth from that cantankerous Philadelphia. As for our hostess Darlene; fourteen years ago when her husband died at the Battle of San Jacinto, she took to her bed and nearly joined him in his grave. That is, 'til I prescribed the cold-water treatment of Beauchamp Springs and wild lettuce to calm her nerves."

"I can't argue that you know them well enough as patients, but..."

"No buts about it," Miss Emily said firmly. "I know full well they'll holler for a colored woman if they're ailin', but they'd rather die than give me the time of day on the street. Girl, you've got good intentions, but what you're plannin' is just not done."

"I reckon you might be right with most of them, but it's different with Darlene. You didn't see her at the fair on the Fourth, fighting like a wild cat against slavery. I know she'll accept you, and when she does, the rest will follow. Besides, Liza sits with us."

Miss Emily's hoots of derision ceased with the crunch of footsteps on the shelled path. Towards us walked, Charlotte Eberhard, whose appearance was altered for the good, since having gotten married. Her usual drab outfit was perked up with colorful passementerie, and spiraling curls framed her pocked cheeks. Her mother, Esther Price, was beside her. She looked fagged with dark circles beneath her eyes, a testimony to having produced a child every two years of her marriage. Bringing up the rear was Esther's faithful slave, Liza. She was a Guinea Negress who came from West Africa aboard Jean Lafitte's pirate ship. She'd been bought as a childhood playmate for Esther, and remained as indoor help when she grew up. Her smooth hands and straight back was evidence that she'd avoided the brutal eighteen-hour days of harvesting cotton.

This was my first encounter with the Prices since Pappa and Rufus had come to blows at the fair, and I expected a few uncomfortable exchanges before matters smoothed themselves out. "Good morning, ladies," I said with a hopeful smile. "My dear friend Miss Emily will be joining us this morning. I believe you have already met. We've brought each of you a bottle of rose water, which we'll be selling at Miss Thompson's millinery. I hope you like it."

Apparently, Charlotte's mean-spirited disposition hadn't been transformed with her appearance, for she stared at myself and Miss Emily with unveiled disdain. Esther accepted my rose water offering, but then walked briskly to the front door where she engaged Darlene in a lively conversation on how to cook the perfect coddled egg. Liza defiantly stopped to give us a welcoming smile until her mistress called her to follow.

Darlene's initial response of seeing my companion was one of mild shock, but recovering quickly she said, "Why, welcome, Miss Emily. Of course your face is a familiar one to me."

"Yes, our paths have often crossed," Miss Emily replied. "And how you feelin' today?"

"Fair to middling," Darlene responded with a wipe to her brow. "It's this heat, I expect."

Miss Emily stood at the door, hesitant to enter. "I hope my visit don't cause too much trouble. Mia has spoken so often of your gatherins, I was pleased when she asked me to join. Your home is most comely. I don't think I've ever seen it from the front."

"Had it shipped all the way from New Orleans," Darlene said proudly. "Each plank and beam was numbered, dismantled, and methodically reconstructed on the very spot we stand. The veranda's ironwork is a French design fashioned after Malmaison. You know, where Empress Josephine lived."

Miss Emily's blank expression reflected she hadn't the foggiest idea of what Darlene was talking about. Nonetheless, I was thrilled with the civility of their discourse. Darlene ushered us in, and we all stood around uneasily pursuing small talk.

Esther pointed to the gray cameo pinned to our hostess's black crape and bombazine blouse, "Darlene, is that a new pin you're wearing?"

"This old thing," Darlene answered. "It's a souvenir I picked up in Pompeii on my Grand Tour. The jaunt was doctor prescribed, and thanks to that and Miss Emily's remedies, I've regained my joie de vivre. Come now ladies let's take our places in the parlor. I'll be serving orangeade and bird's nest pudding during our break.

I expect Fanny and my sister, Philadelphia, shortly, but there's no reason for us to delay our work."

"Idle hands are the devil's tools," Esther agreed.

"Amen, sister," Darlene chortled. "We were a stupendous success at the fair, selling every item we stitched. We made twenty-seven dollars and fifty-five cents, all funds going to the Society for Unwed Mothers. They have graciously sent us a letter of appreciation for our efforts."

"I heard a girl from Harrisburg has found herself in a predicament," Charlotte remarked, flaring her nose in contempt. "I don't see why they ride the horse before hitching it."

"Now, daughter, it's not our business to judge wayward souls," Esther pointed out. "It's our Christian duty to help them out as best we can."

"Well spoken, Esther," Darlene observed. "Now, our Christmas bazaar will be upon us before we know it. So, let's get to work."

It was a cozy scene of domesticity as we took to our chairs in the beautifully appointed room. With an eye for detail, Darlene had stenciled a tasseled frieze at the top of the walls to clever effect, and coordinated the pink calico curtains with a hooked rug of cabbage roses. A series of Currier and Ives lithographs hung on the wall between two candle sconces of punched tin.

Liza sat in a corner at a respectable distance from the table, and began her mending, for slaves were not allowed to do fancywork. She was treated kindly by Esther, at times their conversation was as intimate as two friends might share. However, an unspoken boundary existed, and she knew to cross it might endanger her genteel livelihood.

My chair was near a large bay window, the light illuminating the tiny stitches I strove to achieve. A petite demilune table with carved acanthus leaves encircling its edge provided a surface to place my sewing basket. Without delay, I began crocheting double chains on the scalloped edge of my table scarf before realizing all sides of the table had been commandeered and Miss Emily was at a loss as to where to sit.

I was relieved when Darlene thoughtfully remedied the awkward situation. Pappa had designed a unique quilting table for her, so by way of rope and windlass, she could lengthen it. "Miss

Emily, it would please me if you take this seat alongside me," she said as she made the alteration.

Noticeably shocked that Miss Emily wouldn't take her place aside Liza, Esther and Charlotte seemed to be considering leaving when Darlene said, "I recall Miss Emily from the good old days when Houston was just getting off the ground. Back then we were nothing but gambling houses and saloons, with not a single house of worship. It was surely a rough place for a single lady to set down roots. Remember when President Anson Jones declared the Republic was no more? Why, there wasn't a dry eye in our city. Well, we're all Texians now, aren't we," she asked rhetorically, while looking around the table for any signs of dissent.

There was no denying Darlene had her annoying ways, but her inclusion of Miss Emily placed me forever in her debt. For a group of women accustomed to a cacophony of babble, we worked for nearly half an hour in awkward silence until the tiny patter of Molly Moffitt's patent leather shoes skipped into the room. The darling six-year old was the daughter of Fanny, and was as sweet tempered as she was adorable.

Fanny followed her in, quickly settling down to smocking a dress for her daughter. She was a relatively new member to our circle, who often stirred up impassioned debates with her suffragette opinions. She sometimes threw me into a muddle, making me feel my life would be cooked and scoured away. "Good day ladies, it's lovely to see you all again. A new face is amongst us today."

"This is my friend, Miss Emily," I said. "You may know her by her reputation of being the finest herbalist and midwife in town. Miss Emily, this is Fanny Moffitt. She's a familiar sight in the mornings, delivering bread from her bakery."

"Her rye loaf is the best in Houston," Darlene proclaimed.

"Praise indeed," Fanny said. "I always say burnt fingers and sleepless nights are worth the effort if I don't have to rely on a man."

All of us present knew of Fanny's troubles and the simmering hatred it had cultivated in her. She was a grass widow, divorced from her Texas Ranger husband after he threatened her with a clitoridectomy; a procedure Doc Abbott recommended as a sure-fire way of settling her down.

"Molly, quit hiding behind my skirt," Fanny chided. "You'll not get far in this world if you're scared as a mouse. Now, show everyone your best curtsy."

Molly timidly followed her mother's directions, daintily holding her white frilly pinafore out as she bent at the knee. Shy as she was, I realized she'd make a good playmate for my Sam.

"She's not been sleeping well at night," Fanny said of her daughter. "Her ear's been aching her."

Miss Emily offered, "Ear drops of paregoric and sweet oil, warmed to the touch, will bring her relief."

"Mighty kind of you," Fanny said. "I'll try that."

Darlene petted the child's head. "Molly, you poor thing, earaches are the worse. You run along to the kitchen and ask Cook to give you some East Indian sweetmeats I just bought. Mind you, remember to wash your hands before you come back in here."

"Yes, ma'am," Molly said politely.

Fanny parted the sunblind, then as was her custom, she wasted no time in delving into an intimate exchange, "Mia, I was wondering which church you attend?"

Knowing I was the only Catholic in the group, I loathed her question, and reluctantly answered, "St. Vincent de Paul."

"Your father isn't a churchgoer though, is he?" Esther demanded with a snarl. "Perhaps he's a nullifidian?"

The question hung uneasily in the air, for everyone there believed a person without faith was as good as the devil. I answered, "He prefers to take communion under the shade of a tree with the leaves as his witness. However, I don't think he holds anything against churchgoers, at least not on principle."

"Why I never!" Charlotte gasped in indignation.

Miss Emily playfully kicked my shin under the table. I stomped her toes in return, causing her to prick her finger. It was then I noticed she was darning a pair of Pappa's socks. It touched me how she was always doing things for our family.

Darlene spoke up, "I couldn't live a day without God's hands guiding me, and I warrant most folks benefit from regular church going, but if a man as good as Klaus Stein finds peace of mind under a tree, then I've got nothing to say on the subject."

Darlene's elderly sister, Philadelphia, shuffled into the room, her head bobbing in and out from the loose folds of her neck. Fearing drafts of any kind, her customary place was on the apple-green velvet sofa, where the hearth gave comfort whether lit or not.

"Sister, we have a guest today," Darlene announced. "This is Miss Emily, Mia's friend. I recall she has treated your sundry ailments in the past."

Philadelphia offered no word of recognition, though as our conversation resumed and her knitting needles feverishly clicked, she often glanced with curiosity toward Miss Emily.

Esther looked up from stitching ribbonwork on her reticule, "Does anyone know how our Cora is faring? She canceled our bible study meeting this week."

Fanny volunteered, "Yellow fever has hit her hard, but she's on the mend. Josiah came in the shop on Monday, saying her fever had broke and my custard pie was the only thing she could stomach. She was nothing but a rail to begin with, but we all know she's too ornery to give-up the ghost that easy."

Darlene clucked her tongue, "Remember back in forty when the fever hit so bad? Between everybody dying and moving to the new capital in Austin, I thought Houston was done for, but we rallied then and we'll do it again."

Finally appearing at ease, Esther asked, "Have y'all seen that sewing machine Percival is selling at Market Square? I've been thinking about getting one."

"I think it's a frightful invention," Darlene said. "It will surely be the end of sewing circles. How are we to talk over such a racket?"

"You could do your heavy sewing on the machine," I said. "And leave the fancywork to do by hand."

Esther agreed, "Mia is right. It could never replace intricate stitches, but I reckon it would cut mending time in half. And with my brood it would be heaven sent."

Charlotte seldom engaged in actual sewing, and this occasion was no different. As she occupied herself with arranging stickpins into patterns on her strawberry pincushion, she reached toward the center of the table for another needle and ostentatiously showed off her new diamond ring.

"What a rock!" Fanny exclaimed."

"And did you see her wedding gown?" Darlene queried. "Simply breathtaking. And her nuptials were unarguably the best of the season."

Charlotte smiled, revealing her buck teeth. "It was a success due to Fanny's scrumptious confections. Gunther's mother wanted me to go with the new baker on Main Street, who is English and has quite the reputation for sponge cake. But I emphatically said no; Fanny is my only choice, no one can match her chocolate tortes."

"Thank you, Charlotte, loyalty means a lot to me. I've lost a few orders to him already because of undercutting my prices."

"I heard not everything went smoothly after the ceremony," Darlene ventured, "something of a ruckus on your honeymoon. Those Germans in Frost Town keep up the tradition of a chivaree. Am I right, Charlotte?"

Tears of embarrassment sprung to the newlywed's eyes.

"Now, Darlene, spare the child your teasing," Esther scolded. "Can't you see such a lewd reference pains her?"

"We're all friends here," Fanny relentlessly pressed. "Come now give us the details of the night."

With Fanny ignoring them, Darlene eagerly filled in the details. "It seems several men from the wedding party came round in the middle of the night and made a scene in front of Charlotte and Gunther's house. They banged pots and pans and set off firecrackers till the preoccupied groom was forced to pay them off with beer at Floeck's Brewery."

"I don't see the problem," Fanny laughed. "I'm sure Gunther had Charlotte awake no matter the hour."

Charlotte squalled, "Congress between husband and wife *is* necessary. Isn't that right Mamma?"

Seeing Charlotte distressed, Miss Emily extended her hand sympathetically. "You poor thing, such a night can be quite frightenin'."

Instead of showing gratitude for Miss Emily's consolation, Charlotte only glared in her direction. The rising tension in the room was once again broken by Darlene. Tightening the sample in her tambour, she asked, "Have you heard of Mrs. Clark's loss? She is absolutely bereft."

"Her husband has died?" Fanny asked.

Darlene shook her head. "No, far worse. He's gambled away their life's savings and gotten arrested to boot. Can you imagine five thousand dollars on keno and faro?"

"Election time is coming or else Sheriff Franklin wouldn't have gone to the trouble," Esther pointed out.

Darlene continued, "Mind you, he's not the first and won't be the last good man ruined in Madame Tildy's den of inequity."

I remembered Evan Clark, the fireman, telling me of his mother's heartbreak of losing her child, and now her husband had gone and squandered their money.

"A fool and his money are easily parted," Fanny declared. "I'd advise Mrs. Clark to leave her husband immediately. I know a little bit about courts granting a divorce."

Esther added, "Jail is the best thing to happen to him. "It's evil to profit from someone else without a fair exchange. Ephesians four, twenty-eight, let him that stole, steal no more, but rather let him labor, working with his hands the thing, which is good. The Good Book shows us the road to righteousness we must all follow."

Darlene leaned forward, "Then, Esther, I believe you should know one of your own slaves was arrested at the same time as Mr. Clark. He was throwing dice when the raid happened."

Esther looked indignant. "Surely you're mistaken, my boys know better than that."

Darlene reaffirmed, "No, I heard correctly. He's one of Rufus Price's slaves, they said. I recall the name was Billy Togen. Of course, my heart goes out to the poor devil. He'll be beaten within an inch of his life for it."

"He deserves whatever Daddy lashes out," Charlotte said matter of factly.

I felt compelled to speak up, "Charlotte, I don't know how you can say such a thing. The white man was gambling just like the slave, but he's not going to be beaten for it."

Fanny patted me like a child. "Mia, grow up, it's just the way things are. He'll have to serve as an example, or else the rest of them will think they can get away with it."

Philadelphia, who had been quiet until this point, inquired, "Darlene, did you say Willy Toven?"

The elderly sister was nearly deaf, and so Darlene yelled back, "No, sister, Billy Togen!"

Philadelphia rambled, "You say Toben? I once hired him to chop kindling. No, now I recall that's the man who invented a ventilation system. Too much carbonic acid fouls the air, but I will not suffer drafts for the sake of it."

Darlene was spelling out the name loudly when Philadelphia pulled out her hearing trumpet from her carpetbag. "No reason to shout sister; I can hear quite well now."

"What does it matter what the name was," Esther fumed. "They are all a bunch of ..."

I found myself yelling, "Esther, don't!"

The ignorant woman stopped, but the damage had already been done. Tears welled up in Liza's eyes, and Miss Emily's nostrils flared with anger. Frightened by the commotion, Little Molly entered the room and ran to hide in her mother's full skirt.

Miss Emily squared her shoulders and stared fiercely at the group. "The man who will be beat for the color of his skin is Billy Togen. He's Liza's husband."

"Oh my," Darlene gasped. "I'm so sorry and never would've brought it up had I known. It's just they all... Well, never mind."

My experiment in social equality was a dismal failure. Ester, unaware her slave and closest companion was even married, was outraged, and Liza dared not raise her swollen eyes from her darning mushroom. I tried to catch Miss Emily's glance, but she too didn't look up as she violently stabbed her needle into the threadbare sock. Darlene mumbled an oath against hearing aids, Philadelphia's knitting needles clicked furiously, and Molly whimpered.

It seemed the only person oblivious to the situation was Charlotte, who cheerily asked, "Have any of you met Miss Rothschild? She's an enchanting young woman recently come to town."

Knowing Miss Emily would go straight to Pappa, I refrained from admitting my acquaintance with Rachael.

In her best imitation, Darlene said in a low nasal twang, "She's typical English, uppity you know. They're always trying to impress us with their lineage and knighthoods, but I heard this girl's father started in trade and has no land to back up a title."

Impressed, Charlotte asked, "How on earth do you gain such insight?"

"My maid, Millie, is friends with the help over at Mosswood," Darlene explained. "She says Captain Biggs' slaves talk of running away because the master sooner hands out a whipping when a kind word would serve better."

"Are you saying this Rachael Rothschild is the captain's niece?" Fanny asked.

With an emphatic glance toward Miss Emily, Philadelphia answered, "Yes, the very one. And Captain Biggs is a character from way back. Isn't he?"

Charlotte warmed to the subject, "They say the captain is one of the richest men in Houston, second only to William Rice, but what's got every girl in a tizzy is the captain's dashing son, Daniel. Why, he's the most eligible bachelor in town, and if I weren't already happily married I'm certain he'd be calling on me."

Fanny sneered, "No doubt he's searching for a passive little creature to tend his hearth and complete his fantasy of domestic bliss. Perhaps I'll introduce myself to this dashing bachelor and show him what a liberated woman is like. Maybe he'll even like my bloomers."

"Why go after the son when it is the father with all the money?" Darlene asked. "My eye is on Captain Biggs."

We all laughed, but Miss Emily had her back up. "Mia, I's had enough, and am ready to go home."

Her words cut through the room, sharp as a husking knife on harvest day. How could I blame her for wanting to leave after placing her in an intolerable position all morning. All I'd wanted was for her to enjoy herself and for the other women to discover how lovely and sweet she was, but it seemed the barriers between them were not to be dismantled in one day at a sewing circle.

Miss Emily and I were gathering our belongings to leave when Charlotte screamed, "Where's my thimble? Somebody here has gone and stole my golden thimble! My mother-in-law vouchsafed it to me as a wedding present! It's been passed down through three generations of Eberhards!" Glaring at Miss Emily, she continued her rant, "You've got it! That explains why you're hell bent on leaving all of a sudden. I demand you empty your sewing basket this very moment, for I'm certain you've slipped it in there."

"Why would you say such a wretched thing?" I demanded. "And how can everyone sit mute when Charlotte is accusing Miss Emily so unjustly?"

I looked to the other women for support, but they remained silent. Liza, who had finally lifted her eyes to take in the scene, rubbed her marble hand cooler to her flushed cheeks, and Philadelphia held her hearing trumpet poised at the ready. I expected Darlene, who had championed Miss Emily, to say something, but she only stared suspiciously.

Charlotte snapped, "This is all your fault, Mia Stein. You brought her here, acting as if she was one of us, but Negroes are not, and never will be, our equals. They're lying creatures who can't be trusted, and your so-called friend has proven it by stealing my thimble!"

Slamming my sewing basket down, I cried, "How dare you say those things, Charlotte. Miss Emily is the finest woman I know. She's smart and compassionate, qualities you don't know the first thing about. She'd never take anything not belonging to her, and for you to accuse her of such a base thing is...is horrible!"

Charlotte stood up, her face red with anger. "You're both a pair of dirty half-breeds. Mia, if it weren't for your father's reputation in this city, you'd be spat upon just like the other lazy Mexicans, who play Monte all day instead of working for an honest wage. And you, Miss Emily, think you're better than the others 'cause you're high yellow, but you're not."

Darlene finally spoke up, "Hold your horses, Charlotte; you go too far. I agree most Mexicans *are* lazy, but there are *some* who fought along side us in the Revolution. Recall our Republic's first Vice President was Zavala. Klaus, like our heroic Deaf Smith, married a Mexican, and their offspring shouldn't be ostracized because of it. Besides our Mia hardly even looks like a Mexican."

Tears streamed down my cheeks. "I can't say which hurts me more deeply, Charlotte's words or yours, Darlene. I thought you believed different."

Liza exclaimed, "Miss Charlotte, there your thimble be under the table. You must've dropped it."

Miss Emily and I locked arms and turned our backs on the small-minded women of the sewing circle. Not a word passed between us until we'd reached the refuge of her front porch.

"I'm sorry, Miss Emily. I should've never ..."

"Hush child," she said, putting her finger to my lips. "As long as Negroes are sold for five hundred dollars on the block, there'll be people like Charlotte, thinking I'm no different than livestock. You can't change them, but if your Ma was alive to see how you've grown up, she'd be awful proud for your tryin'. I know I am."

"I'm who I am because of your teachings. You show me the right way to think and act."

We gave each other a hug, and then Miss Emily said abruptly, "There's one thing you aught to know. Nothin' little Miss Charlotte said, scared me off."

"Then why did you want to leave so suddenly?"

"They was speakin' of Cap'n Biggs, and I ain't ever gonna sit back quietly again when I hear that murderer's name."

CHAPTER XI

WASH DAY

fter hiding behind the garden shed to spy on Daniel and myself, all three of my brothers came down with a painful case of poison ivy.

Scratching the nasty pustules covering his legs, Christian howled, "Ouch! Mia, can't you stop this itching?"

"You have to stop scratching," I scolded. "You'll only cause it to become infected."

Emmett complained, "You boil us alive, slather us with aloe, and wrap us like mummies in plantain leaves, and still we itch!"

"Then shall I leave you boys to your own devices?" I asked.

Sam ran into my arms, and with a fervent hug demonstrated his loyalty.

Emmett shrugged, "I suppose a witch doctor is better than nothing."

"Pappa says Mamma used to call Miss Emily a curandera, and that's what you are now," Christian said.

Smiling at the comparison, I said, "If that's true, I consider it high praise. Now, mark my words, you must all rest in bed today and let these dressings have a chance to work. I've got to be off now, Miss Emily is outside waiting for me to start the washing."

Then biting my lip at the fib I was about to say, I added, "And after that I'm going out to check on a patient."

"Whose that?" Emmett asked innocently.

It was my nature to be truthful, but I couldn't tell him that I'd accepted another of Rachael's invitations to Mosswood, the very home of Captain Biggs, whom Miss Emily had decried as a murderer. Instead I stammered, "Have to see Old Missy Cook. She's burned herself on a stove."

My brothers accepted my word, and Christian asked, "What's for dinner tonight?"

"We just had breakfast, little brother, shall I treat you for tapeworm? Besides, you know by now what we always have for dinner on washday."

"Leftovers!", they wailed in unison.

I gave each a kiss, then ran downstairs where I found Miss Emily bending over a copper pot of boiling water. Careful to avoid a scalding or drop an item, she was using a curved walnut branch to retrieve the clothes.

"Good mornin' Mia, or should I say afternoon?" she teased.

"I'm not that late," I countered. "Had to see after the boys. They all have poison ivy."

She shook her head in disbelief, "I'd think they was old enough to recognize it by now."

Straddling the trestle bench, I braced the washboard against it and took to scrubbing the whites. If I was to be punctual for Rachael's visit, I'd have to hurry my labors. Quick as a wink, I boiled, washed, rinsed, and mangled the clothes.

Taking me to task, Miss Emily said, "Keep up that rough treatment and you'll have a hole in the dress and scraped knuckles to show for it. Now, don't forget the potato rinse, and your green calico has seen better days, some starch will stiffen it right up. Mind you, dry it in the shade to keep its colors from fading."

"Yes ma'am," I said in irritation. Nervously, I checked my pocket watch again, but in my haste, dropped it into a bucket of wash water.

"Fiddlesticks, what have I done?" I cried, frantically retrieving the wet timepiece.

"Is it still workin'?" she asked in dismay.

I nodded with tears pricking my eyes.

Miss Emily pushed back her ringlets, leaving a handful of suds glistening on her brown sweaty cheek. "I been trying to decipher you all mornin'. It's plain as day, you ain't yourself. Quit beatin' the devil around the stump, and tell Miss Emily what's the matter."

How could I tell her my troubling thoughts when she refused to discuss the captain. Besides, she'd go straight to Pappa with my plans, and that would be the end of it. "There's nothing the matter," I answered feebly as I patted my watch dry. Looking down at my hands wrinkled like prunes, I imagined Rachael's morning of leisure. "I suppose I'm feeling sorry for myself. Don't you get tired of working all the time?"

"I'm tired now, but I can't complain about an honest day's work, not when I think of the old days."

Miss Emily had cracked open the door to her past, and I was quick to stick my foot in. "Your master was cruel, wasn't he?"

"Cruel don't quite capture him. More like a monster, and both your Ma and Pa could vouch for it."

"What do you mean? My parents knew your master?"

"I's not answerin' no more of your fool questions. I figure it's your Pa's place to open that can of worms when he sees fit. Now, tell me what's got a fire under you. Is what happened at your sewin' circle, still eatin' at you?"

"I'll never go back there again, nor forgive them for the way they treated you."

"That ain't no way to be thinkin," Miss Emily scolded.

I shrugged, "Percival says Esther Price placed the first order on a sewing machine, and promised one to Charlotte as soon as her baby was born. It was the first I heard she was expecting?"

"They didn't waste no time. Now, tell me what else is the matter. As much as you been checking the time, I's certain you be wanting to be somewhere else."

Finally I confessed, "I'm to meet a friend at one o'clock, and it's impossible to make it on time. That is, unless I left you to finish up, and that would be awfully selfish of me."

"Hogwash," Miss Emily said, pumping the wooden dolly stick with renewed vigor. "I find happiness in what I got to do. It's all in how you look at things. If you're always wishin' things were different, you end up wasting what precious time you have here on Earth."

"But I imagine someone who is rich and at their leisure is a lot happier than us."

"I seen my share of rich folk wiling the whole day away, and they're down right miserable. You get along on your visit, and I'll finish up here. But don't think you got off the hook so easy; there's weeding to be done in my garden, and my back fence needs whitewashing. I'll expect you over tomorrow."

"Yes, ma'am," I said, kissing her cheek, and feeling the strength of her loving arms around me.

Appearing unexpectedly from the house, Pappa asked, "How are you womenfolk getting along?"

"Just fine, Klaus," Miss Emily replied with a shy smile.

"Pappa, I didn't expect you home this morning," I said, unnerved by his arrival. "Though now I consider it, you do often come around on washday."

Defensively, Pappa asked, "As master of my own home, aren't I allowed to come and go as I please?"

"Of course," I answered. "It's just I'm surprised you have any leisure time, considering all the work you've been complaining about at the shop."

Looking flustered, he answered, "Actually, there was paperwork I needed to retrieve, so, I thought I'd be civil and say, howdy."

Miss Emily said, thoughtfully, "Mia, you better get a hurry on, if you don't want to keep your friend waiting."

Taken aback, Pappa remarked, "Mia, you haven't said anything about a new friend to me."

With my heart pounding in my ears, I answered, "She's just a girl I met at the milliner's. I promised to give her one of the kittens."

Relieved, he asked nothing further of me, I quickly took my leave. However, their coy behavior peaked my curiosity, and so after turning the corner of the house, I backtracked the other way round. Feeling foolishly similar to my spying brothers, I hid behind the holly tree and watched them.

Pappa tenderly brushed Miss Emily's cheek with the back of his hand, and the latter puckered her full lips towards him. He motioned his head in the direction of the house, I assume indicating their need to curb their desires. Miss Emily nodded her understanding, and then they parted. Pappa glanced back several times over his shoulder towards Miss Emily, his look was one of unrequited longing.

I wondered how long their romance had existed, and who, if anyone, knew of it. It was ridiculous to think my father had no manly needs and should live like a monk, and yet, I felt an allegiance to the memory of my mother. It appeared, I wasn't the only one keeping secrets.

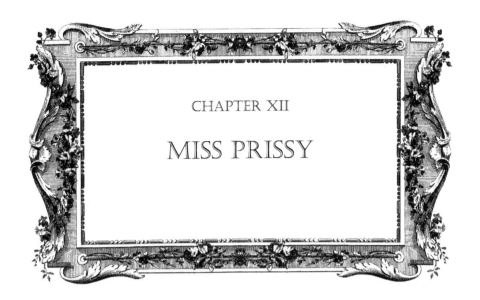

CHAPTER XII

MISS PRISSY

quickly donned my pink cotton frock, one of the few articles of clothing not hanging wet on the clothesline, then
tied on my bonnet at a daring angle atop my coiled braids.
Fetching the intended white kitten for Rachael, I found her contentedly curled up with her black brother. I suffered pangs of
regret as I separated the two, then tucked the mewing creature in
a lidded basket.

"Mia," Christian shouted from downstairs. "Some fellow is at
the door asking for you. Says he's, Ulysses, your driver."

"My what?" I said, taking two stairs at a time.

I'd not expected Rachael to send me a conveyance, and with
Ulysses dressed in flamboyant livery, no less. And though it was
certainly a thoughtful gesture, it provided another chance for
Pappa to discover what I was up to.

Emmett whistled approvingly of the waiting carriage. "A
Victoria, newest in the line. Whose is it?"

"It's Rachael's, and if I'm not off immediately, I'll be late and
will certainly offend her."

Sam clung to my skirt as steadfastly as cleaver in spring.

"I'm sorry little brother, but you can't come, especially with
that rash," I said. "You must rest and stay out of the heat. If you're a

good boy while I'm away, I promise to make flan for tonight's dessert." Sam unclasped his little fingers, but his look of supplication did nothing to relieve my guilty conscience.

With a snap of his quirt to the horses' backsides, Ulysses had us quickly on our way. Driving down Texas Avenue and up Austin Street in so fancy a carriage prompted curious stares of passersby, including Cora Hornsby. I was happy to see she'd recovered enough strength after her bout of yellow fever to give me the evil eye.

On this occasion, my arrival at the Biggs' estate had all the grandeur my initial visit lacked. Ulysses' once foreboding demeanor was replaced with referential niceties. He assisted my descent with an outstretched hand and a courteous bend at his waist. There was no need for the boot scraper, for my shoes remained unsoiled.

Ulysses directed me toward the staircase where the young slave, Sissy, gave a curtsy. While keeping her eyes deferentially lowered, she said, "Just you follow me up the stairs, Miz."

As we passed the door to the library, a strong scent of lavender wafted over me. I looked around nervously for the exotic slave, Rita, who had previously chased me from the room. "Do you smell something Sissy?"

"Nothin' out of the ordinary. This way, Miz Rachael will be waitin' for ya' in her bedchamber."

"Still in bed?" I asked incredulously. "Is she feeling poorly?"

"Oh no, Miss, she's fine. Though, you might say mornin' ill suits her. What's that sound comin' from your basket, somethin' alive in there?"

"Would you like a peek?"

"Yes'm, if'n it don't bite?"

"It's a present for Miss Rachael," I said, lifting the lid for kitty's head to poke out. "Do you think she'll like her?"

Sissy petted the kitten, "What a precious thing. She'll like its blue eyes matching hers, and it'll make for good company. Ain't my place to say, but Miz Rachael has too much time on her hands."

"Is she always a late riser?"

"Yes'm. I always come up about now to help with her dressin' and hair, before she takes tea with Miz Biggs. Some days they play draughts, but more often than not, the old lady falls asleep or has one of her fits. Miz Rachael, she plays game of patience too."

"Is that all that occupies her?"

Sissy stopped as she thought, "There's her letter writin'. I post things for her most every day. Sometimes she works at her scrapbook or does fancy work, then it be supper time, I got to change her clothes again for that."

I couldn't resist asking, "Hasn't her cousin Daniel's arrival altered her routine? I'd have thought they spent a lot of time together."

"You'd think so, Miz, havin' grown up together as they did, but truth be told, Master Daniel ain't never here. He's an early riser that one, and a right gentleman. Always a'workin on the captain's bayou steamer or the property here." Sissy whispered furtively, "I heard in the kitchen just this mornin' that over where he's from, it's against the law to have slaves. They say he's of that mind too. He can't go against his father's wishes, so he plans to do what he can, fixin' up our houses and getting' us more to eat."

Hearing Sissy's praise of Daniel only raised my estimation of him, while her account of Rachael's lackadaisical days made me quite irritated with myself for hurrying my work and leaving Miss Emily.

"You're a healer, ain't ya?" Sissy asked. "My ma got the dropsy bad. But I don't suppose ya look after Negroes."

"Of course, I do, and I'd be glad to see her. I'll make up a tincture with ashes of hickory bark, and bring it by tomorrow."

Sissy thanked me, then took me into the bedchamber. Rachael was still in bed, and without makeup to conceal her freckled cheeks or a corset to create full breasts, she appeared far younger.

After a stretch and yawn, she said lazily, "Darling Mia, do forgive my disarray. I enjoyed Daniel's company late into the evening, and found it impossible to awaken early. I'm sure you understand such matters."

The white kitten poked his head out and mewed.

"And is this my little pussy you've brought? Oh, she's brilliant. How sweet of you to think of me. Whatever shall I name her?"

I wanted to snatch the gift back. "Black as my kitty is, I named him Midnight. He's quite a terror pouncing on anything moving."

"I'll call mine Princess, for she shall live like one. Aunt Edna was displeased when she heard you were bringing a cat. She's certain her pug won't tolerate it."

"They might surprise her and become fast friends."

"It wouldn't surprise me in the least. Just look at us, we're as different as cat and dog, yet we're companions of sort. Sissy, come do my hair."

The young slave untied the rags creating Rachael's 'natural curls'.

Rachael complained, "I completely sympathize why Englishmen are paid a hardship allowance when they're sent to this country. They earn every cent of it having to endure this god-awful heat. Mia, sit down while I finish my toilette, your hovering is making me nervous. Perhaps, watching my routine will be advantageous to you. I think growing up motherless must have put you at a disadvantage."

I'd come with good intentions of teaching her how to be kind, but her acerbic remarks were already getting my dander up. I had to remind myself this spoilt girl was the result of a heartrending childhood, and whose mother was locked away in an asylum. No, she wouldn't provoke me, I promised myself.

Rachael screeched, "Sissy, don't use so many pins in my hair; it gives me a headache!"

The servant rolled her eyes in resignation.

"Achoo! Excuse me," I said. "Achoo! Sorry, I think your perfume makes me sneeze."

"Mia, you're the strangest girl I've ever met. This is the finest eau de cologne from France, scented with ambergris, and it does not make one sneeze."

To me it smelt like something to douse a chamber pot with, but I held my tongue once more.

Sissy laced up Rachael's corset, pulling it tighter with each inhalation. A corset cover followed, a pair of silk stockings, and then eight petticoats. Donning each article of clothing, her movements became further restricted until she was as rigid as a scarecrow.

"Sissy, I shall have my green striped silk today. No, not that one, the iridescent dress with the matching parasol!"

The servant disappeared into an adjoining room which was as large as my bedroom and filled with countless dresses. Reappearing, she asked timidly, "This one, Miz?"

"Yes, yes, get a wiggle on and don't be so lazy."

Rachael fidgeted impatiently as the puff-sleeved bodice was buttoned up her front and its matching skirt attached in back.

Spinning and admiring the flare of her skirt, Rachael said, dismissively, "That will be all, Sissy."

"Don't ya' need help with your shoes?"

"Mia can make herself useful, and she'll no doubt do a better job than you."

"I do my best, Miz," Sissy replied with a pout.

"Your best is not good enough. Now, scat!"

Once alone, I could no longer keep quiet. "Why are you so mean to her?"

"It's not a matter of being mean or nice, but about keeping up the proper relationship. I'm her mistress and there need be no friendliness between us. I made that mistake once with a girl who Father hired at the Mop Fair. She was all efficiency until I started sharing confidences. Not a fortnight had passed before she'd run off with a dozen silver spoons. I learned my lesson with that one, and I'd say it goes double with slaves."

"The buying and selling of slaves is illegal now, and it has always been immoral."

"Well, whether they're black or white or maids or slaves, one needs servants to run a proper household and determine your social standing. Uncle Charles determines where his guests sit at the dinner table by how many servants they employ?"

I threw up my hands in frustration. "That's the most preposterous notion I've ever heard. Don't you realize you'd be far happier if you had some work to do yourself, then by day's end you'd feel a sense of accomplishment."

"Mia, why don't you help me on with my shoes, then you can add *that* to your list of accomplishments."

"Rachael, I've been putting my own shoes on since I was four, surely you can do the same."

"Isn't it obvious I can't bend over in this dress."

Grabbing the tiny shoe and hook, I asked, "I suppose you think this inconvenience a small price to pay for beauty?"

"It's a fashion derigueur, and you should wear more petticoats too; your skirts aren't nearly full enough."

I sighed in exasperation, "So, I won't be able to put my shoes on either? Be practical Rachael, I've no maid to help me dress, and I'd probably catch fire if I tried cooking in such an outfit. Mary Nichols writes, 'We can expect but small achievement from women as long as it is the labor of their lives to carry about their clothes.'"

"Nichols? She's as off her rocker as Stanton and Anthony and all the other women reformers trying to be men. You'll be suggesting I wear bloomers next, which goes entirely against nature."

My faced flushed with anger. "Are you saying your corseted eighteen inch waist is as nature intended?"

"Well, Mia Stein, aren't we impassioned. I was beginning to wonder if you had any backbone at all. I can just imagine your opinion of my using Vermilion for my cheeks."

"Of course I object to slathering on mercury. Why not use Cascorilla, its made from ground egg shells, or just pinch your cheeks."

Rachael took a crystal bottle from a casket laying on her dressing table and pressed it to her lips. Its foul taste made her grimace, but didn't stop her from imbibing. She giggled, "It creates the most delicate hue of skin and dilates my pupils."

"Arsenic! Oh, Rachael, you're surely mad to risk your life."

"Countess Alana is the most exquisite creature you've ever seen, no man can resist her beauty. Her complexion is like the finest porcelain and her green eyes sparkle brighter than any emerald. She was generous to share her beauty secret with me; most women would guard it jealously. I've only just begun taking it in the minutest quantities, but over time I'll increase the dosage. Don't look so shocked, Mia. I'm of high birth and my family has money, so I'm confident of attracting a good husband, but I'd be a fool if I didn't realize my appearance is my most valuable commodity."

"What about your thoughts and feelings, and the love you can give a husband?"

Rachael stuffed folded handkerchiefs into her bodice to augment her figure. "You speak like a naive child. Love rarely comes into play when marriage is involved. Give me a man worth ten thousand a year, and I'll be satisfied."

"I can't believe you mean that."

"Believe it," Rachael said, struggling with her gloves. "Can you get me my hook, it's in the steamer trunk by the door."

"You're trunks are still packed? Do you plan to return home soon?"

"I'd intended to catch the end of the season in Bath. You can't imagine what fun goes on there each summer, gatherings every night in the pump room, and of course, opera and ballet. I'm certain I've missed out on countless proposals, but Daniel begged me to stay, and I can't bear to break his heart."

Striking out at her, I asked, "Did you know Daniel visited me the day after the fair?"

Rachael's eyes fluttered. "There are no secrets held between my cousin and I. Captain Biggs wants one of the estate rooms on the steamboat to be remodeled, and Daniel is in charge of contracting the work out. His purpose of visiting was to employ your father. He's a furniture maker, isn't he?"

I wondered who was lying, Rachael or Daniel, but either way a meeting between my father and Daniel was impossible. "Pappa is the best craftsman in Houston, but he wouldn't be interested in such work. Please tell Daniel, he'd do best to find another carpenter."

Rachael sneered, "You didn't think Daniel was making a social call upon you, in particular, did you?"

Her goading undermined the kind words and attention Daniel had directed towards me. Flustered, I answered, "I've no prior experience with suitors, so, it's difficult for me to judge."

"Mia, you never cease to amuse me. I'll have to tell Daniel that you blush and your voice trembles when you speak of him; he'll find your affection absolutely comical."

"Please Rachael," I begged. "Don't mention my name to him."

"As you wish. Well, I think we've discussed enough nonsense for one morning. We'd best be off."

"What are you talking about? I've just arrived."

"Didn't I tell you? An artist is painting my portrait tomorrow, and I must buy a new riding habit to pose in. My dear uncle is commissioning it; what tremendous fun it will be with a frontier setting of horses and savage Indians in the background. I'll always think of my time in this country when I look at it. You look downcast, Mia. I thought you'd be thrilled to go shopping with me, but if you don't care to, I'll gladly drop you at home on my way."

I stood dumbfounded by the turn of events. I'd expected a friendly visit and a lovely tea to share. Instead I'd been treated no better than one of her servants, delivering the kitten and helping her get dressed. Why did Rachael treat me so coldly? She was like the vine, Carolina Jessamine, beautiful and alluring, but with bitter poison coursing through her veins.

Feeling embarrassed, and as Rachael pointed out earlier, very naive, I managed to say, "No thanks, I'd rather walk."

Self-absorbed as usual, Rachael took no notice of my quivering lip, nor my brusque departure. My intention was to leave the premises as quickly as possible, but curiosity diverted me to an extended tour through the house. It was neither architecture, nor decor I sought to uncover, but rather the secrets undoubtedly hidden there. Not a servant stirred in the silence of those dark corridors. Edna Biggs' room was empty, and I wondered if this was a bad day for her, and she'd been locked away somewhere.

Gathering my courage, I headed to my true destination: the library and attached hidden chamber. Finding the room dark with its shutters locked from the outside, I hesitated with fear at the threshold. Knowing another chance like this might never arise again, I lit a nearby candle and entered. The red leather club chairs and shelves loaded down with books were as I remembered, but this time there were ancient manuscripts splayed open on the table. Though they were filled with grotesque demons similar to what I'd seen before, these were engaged in unnatural acts, like the paintings in the hidden chamber. Knowing Rachael declared no interest in books, it made me feel sick to consider the beholder of such vulgarity could be Daniel. His character appeared upstanding, and yet a predilection for dark deeds could've been inherited from his father.

Though frightened, I couldn't control my desire to know what lay behind the curtained alcove in the secret room. Pushing open the hidden panel, I was confronted once again by the strong aroma of lavender. It had always brought sweet memories of my dear mother, but now it only repulsed me. Then to my horror, I saw pinned to the wall, a small doll. There was no denying it was a facsimile of myself; black curly hair, green eyes, and the straw hat I often wore. The figure had a noose around its neck and pins stuck in its bodice.

This was no doubt the evil handiwork of Rita, the Voodoo slave. She must've suspected I'd return to this room, and was sending me a dire warning to stay away. Any pretense at composure was abandoned, as I ran from that wicked abode. I determined then and there, never to try and uncover the mystery of Mosswood.

CHAPTER XIII

BON VOYAGE

ummer passed with predictable regularity. I rose early, cleaned and cooked before the day's oppressive heat turned me limp, then took an afternoon siesta under a canopy of mosquito netting. The heat even curbed the boys' exuberance; their outdoor play became relegated to the cooler evening hours. I'd had no further communication between Rachael and myself, or Daniel for that matter. I convinced myself it was for the best. When Pappa unexpectedly announced a Galveston holiday, I was ready for the gulf's cool breeze and rejuvenating waters.

At seven in the evening, we arrived dockside at Allen's Landing, loaded down with twice as much baggage as needed.

"This is Houston's birthplace," Pappa pointed out. "Right here where the Buffalo and White Oak bayous converge."

"Why is it named after the Allen brothers?" Christian asked.

"They're the one's who bought the land and got people to move here," Emmett said. "They advertised there was no place in Texas more healthy, beautifully elevated, or well-watered. Considering our city is at sea level and prone to flooding and yellow fever, it leads one to question their honesty."

"Just look around you," Pappa waxed on. "Ships coming and going, they're the true testament to Houston's prosperity, and the bayou is it's bloodline. At first nobody believed a ship could navigate these shallow waters, so to convince them, the Allen brothers paid the captain of *The Laura,* a thousand dollars to bring goods and passengers up from Galveston. The vessel's crew had to cut through vine choked waters, and they ended up three miles past a row of shanty tents, not realizing it was the prosperous town of Houston."

"How long did it take them to get here?" Emmett asked.

Pappa took a draft from his pipe, before answering, "Three days, but dredging and widening has improved the course, and it will only take us twelve hours."

"Which one is our boat?" I asked.

"The double decker side wheeler that Mr. Kennedy is unloading for his trading post," Pappa answered.

From whiskey and pickles to snake oil and coffins, our boat held an amazing array of goods. Everything would be sold at a premium to Houstonians, and triple the price to colonists in the interior. After the bays were emptied, the reloading of freight began; bales of cotton, sugarcane, and lumber. There were also bags of mail intended for civilized relatives in the East, who wondered why anyone was foolhardy enough to live in Texas.

"Look there's Long Jim," Christian whooped.

Amidst the white man's world of boatmen and travelers, the Indian stood as a solemn reminder of when the bayou offered clean drinking water and a dinner of fresh fish. Nearly seven feet tall, his muscular body was immodestly clothed in a deerskin breechcloth and fringed leggings that closely fit his calves. His moccasins were decorated with fine beadwork, and a hawk feather adorned his black, plaited hair. Though his high cheekbones and aquiline nose presented a fetching profile, the strips of cane piercing his nipples and lower lip, and his heavily tattooed skin, made him look every bit the savage.

"He does excite a crowd amongst the newcomers," Emmett noted.

Pappa rubbed his beard, as was his custom, before launching into a philosophical discussion. "I think Long Jim touches a part of us that longs to be free of societal constraints, and makes us question the validity of our so-called civilized ways."

In the past, I'd had many discussions with the Indian. Initially, my interest was in his tribe, the Karankawas, and their use of herbs, but after getting to know him, our relationship had become more personal.

"Pappa, I'd like to say hello to him," I said. "I promise, I'll come back on the first boat whistle."

"Alright Mia, but don't be late. The ship won't wait for you."

As I approached Long Jim, I overheard several women, who had congregated around him.

"Look at those muscles!" one giggled nervously, as she poked him with the end of her parasol.

Another woman stroked his arm with her hat's feather. "Did you know he's a cannibal? Eats the prisoners he captures during battle."

"I think he reeks!" hooted another, clutching her handkerchief to her nose.

"That's bear grease," one said knowingly. "My husband says it's how they ward off mosquitoes."

Long Jim, used to ignoring jeers, stood as still as the carved wooden Indian in the trading post. Finding he wouldn't respond to their provocations, the women finally disbursed. His fox-like dog, thin, but with a fine coat of yellow fur, was named Qüeshe, and he whimpered and wagged his tale in recognition of me. I repeated my salutation to Long Jim several times before reaching beyond the emptiness of his black eyes. He looked down at me, and smiled. "Mia, I not see you for long time. You come to buy fish? I catch fresh drum this morning. Kaxáyi," he said holding up three fingers.

"I'm sorry, no. My family and I are on our way to Galveston for a holiday. I only came by for a quick hello."

"Many tayk ago, I paddle canoe down komkom, and spend winters on there with my family. We call the island, Auia. We were mighty band then, but guns and bad spirits kill us. There are few Karankawa left now."

"Yes, Long Jim, that's dreadful." For the first time ever, I felt his name, so insensitively conferred upon him by white men, was the wrong thing to call him. "May I ask what is your real name? I mean your Indian name."

His eyes glistened with appreciation. "You are good woman to ask. My name is Sekettumaqua. It means Black Beaver. I'm good swimmer and fisherman."

After practicing his name several times in my mind, I said, "My friend, Sekettumaqua, I shall bid you good day."

"Long time since I hear my name. I thank you, Mia. You give big gift. Please take my fish in thanks."

"That is very generous of you, but it would be a bit cumbersome to take them on the trip."

The boat whistled, and Sekettumaqua wished me a swift journey to the big water. Two stevedores were checking our luggage when I joined my family. My brothers scampered up the gangplank as if they were billy goats, while I traversed it with more care. Embarrassed by several men who whistled at me, I almost lost my balance, and was greatly relieved when my feet were safely planted upon the deck.

Sam excitedly whispered in my ear.

"What did he say?" Pappa asked.

"He wants to know if we're going to live like Robinson Crusoe?"

"Not quite," Pappa said. "It's the Tremont House for us, the best hotel in town. But I promise there'll be plenty of time to play at the beach where you can pretend to be that venerable character."

"Why do we have to go, at all?" Christian whined. "I won't have my pianoforte to practice on, and saltwater stings my eyes."

Pappa gave Christian's shoulder an encouraging squeeze. "Come now, son, lay aside your preconceptions and you'll surely find enjoyment. Nature is a tonic to one's body and soul, and these days I'm hard pressed to find enough of it in Houston."

"I don't like tonics," Christian growled.

Pappa gave me a wink, "Well, if you insist on staying. I'm certain Miss Penelope won't mind looking after you. She has a pianoforte, and she'd be delighted to put some meat on your bones."

Believing our father's bluff, Christian didn't argue further. Indeed, his gloomy disinterest quickly turned to wonder as the ropes were thrown ashore and our steamer lurched forward. A tiny tugboat pulled us from the dock and through the many barges crowding the landing. Knowing Daniel often worked on one of his father's steamers, I held a small hope that I might see him there, but no familiar face bid me goodbye. Then a loud popping noise indicated our ship's high-pressure engine had engaged, and the giant paddle wheel began rhythmically slapping the water. With the cool breeze in our faces and the ever-changing flora and fauna before us, we felt the enthusiasm of explorers at the outset of an adventure.

Emmett said excitedly, "I plan to write about our trip, and collect specimens in my vaculum. Christian, you've a good eye for details, maybe you can draw illustrations to accompany my observations."

Pappa maneuvered us to an advantageous position at the stern, where he pointed out a heron bobbing for food among the irises.

Catching the enthusiastic spirit, Christian said, 'Look, there's a family of beavers building their lodge."

Our ship was forced to slow its speed when the bayou narrowed to such a degree that we could touch the cypress and willow trees growing along the banks. Around the bend we came upon a ship marooned on a sandbar, and men, navigating themselves on rough-hewn rafts, used sharp pikes to give aid.

Pappa pointed ahead, "We'll be able to pick up some steam, once we reach Constitution Bend."

"Why is it called that?" I asked.

"The steamship *Constitution* made its way to Houston, only to find it was too large to turn around. It had to retrace its passage backwards till it got to that point where the bayou widens."

Looking white as a sheet, Emmett complained, "I'm afraid the boat's movement is getting to me."

"I've some ginger that will settle your stomach," I offered.

Pappa directed, "Christian, give me a hand with your brother. We'll get him down to the cabin to rest. Mia, you stay on deck a little longer, so Sam won't miss out on the sights. Keep your wits about you, there are ruffians about. Sam, be careful, we don't want a man overboard."

I was grateful to my father, for I didn't want to miss a second of the scenery. "Those are cattails growing over there," I pointed out to Sam. "They make a good ground flour."

A large gathering of people, dressed in their Sunday-go-to-meeting clothes were gathered along the shore. Singing hymns, they watched as a gentleman dunked a woman backwards into the water. She arose sputtering and coughing, and the man slapped her vigorously on the back.

Alarmed, Sam asked, "What's that fellow doing to her?"

"He's baptizing her," I explained.

Perplexed, he said, "But they don't need that much water, and besides, she's not a baby."

"Baptists do it different than Catholics. That's Reverend Hollister, the Negro preacher from Missionary Baptist Church of Christ."

A man sidled up next to me, "Do you liquor, Senorita?"

Before even turning in his direction, I knew by his slurred speech and smell of booze, that the man was of a coarse character.

Intent on discouraging further discourse, I turned away.

Pursuing me, he said, "That's a shame, for a cool drink and attractive companionship makes a trip more pleasurable."

When a pair of alligators appeared along the bank, several men including the drunkard beside me, shot at them.

Noticing Sam was mesmerized by his pearl handled pistols that matched the fancy buttons down his shirt, the gambler said, "Won them in a poker hand in Seguin. Go ahead and feel their handles, they're real smooth to the touch. One day when you're grown, you might become a knight of the green cloth too and win yourself such a pair. Would you like that, boy?"

I firmly redirected Sam's groping hand away from the weapon, while trying to calm my rising anxiety.

"Boy, you got a good sister watching over you, a mighty good sister. Is this your first trip to Galveston, little lady? I can show you round places you never seen before, give you a good time. How about it?"

The man pulled me around my waist, pressing me firmly against him. I was about to scream when Sam grabbed the man's pistol and pointed it directly at him. His tiny hands trembled with the weight of the gun, causing it to waver precariously in the air.

The gambler released me, "Now, now, boy. I'd say don't go off half-cocked, but you might take my meaning wrong. I was just being friendly like. Didn't mean any harm."

I took the gun from Sam, then kept an aim on the man as we walked backwards down the deck. I'd never held a pistol in my life, and though it seemed a small thing, I knew its potential deadliness. When we reached the stairs, I grabbed Sam under my arm and rushed below to safety. Counting on his reticence to speak, I didn't tell Pappa what transpired, nor did I disclose the gun I still had in my possession. The whole degrading experience would surely ruin our trip, and I feared how my father might retaliate.

We ate a delightful supper in the dining room, then spent the rest of the night secure in our cabin. Through the floorboard cracks above our heads, drifted a piano's bawdy ballads and the dust from the shuffling of dancing feet. When I finally lay down to sleep, I thought of how only a few months before, I'd longed to break open the cocoon I lived in. It had been a sheltered existence with Pappa watching over me, and I unaware of what dangers lay beyond. I'd ventured to Mosswood and found evil secrets, and now I was having my first glimpse of a world beyond our city. I had no doubts that I was out of my depth.

CHAPTER XIV

GALVESTON HOLIDAY

n the early morning hours, while the boys still slept, Pappa and I ventured onto the deck. The bayou widened into the San Jacinto River, and after passing Lynch's Ferry, Pappa pointed out where he'd fought in the battle of San Jacinto. The bones of over six hundred Mexicans still lay in the field unburied, though we couldn't see them from the boat. I'd heard the story of the battle many times from people, but never an account from my own father. He didn't like to dwell on unpleasantness, and this occasion proved no different.

Several miles further down the river, we passed the village of New Washington, where burnt slave cabins stood as silent testimony to the Mexican army's pillage. I was surprised when Pappa began to open up.

"This is where the Yellow Rose of Texas lived," he began.

"The high yellow slave that the song is about? I didn't think she was real."

"She was Colonel Morgan's slave, and when he was sent to guard the port of Galveston, she was put in charge of handing out provisions to our passing troops. She and a young boy, named Turner, were there alone when Santa Anna and his army arrived. Captivated by her beauty, the general kidnapped her and ordered the boy to lead his scouts to our encampment. The Yellow Rose helped the child escape, telling him to warn the Texian army of the Mexicans' whereabouts."

"Some say Santa Anna had her in his tent when your army attacked. Is it true?"

Pappa glowered, "That's not something proper to talk about, but many people, myself included, believe the Yellow Rose was instrumental in the final battle."

I was intrigued, but he was no longer inclined to discuss the battle further. After we entered Galveston Bay, and had successfully navigated Redfish Bar, Pappa pointed out three live oaks. "For years they were the only trees on the island, and served as markers to ships coming into harbor. Of course, that's changed since the City Company's efforts to create a tropical paradise."

"I've got to collect plant specimens for Miss Emily; I'm sure there are some unique to the island. I sure wish she could've come with us, she needs a holiday more than most."

"If it were only possible, but Galveston's Strand was once the largest slave market west of New Orleans, and to this day, it's not uncommon for free slaves to be falsely arrested and sold at auction."

We docked at Palmetto Wharf where Williams and Tucker's ocean-going ships waited for the cotton our little steamship was to deliver. With my brothers still groggy, we gathered our trunks, and made our way to the livery stable. It was owned by Captain Cary, a free Negro, who we learned had bought his own freedom for a thousand dollars. We rented a horse and carriage from him for fifty cents a day, and began our drive. At first there were tiny sod grass houses along streets of smelly oyster shells, but as we turned onto the cobblestoned boulevard, we were gratified to see palm trees and sweet scented oleanders from Jamaica. There were also grand houses of Federalist and Greek Revival architecture, many of them topped with widow walks, where wives watched for loved ones returning home by ship.

Pappa pulled our spirited dappled grays to a stop before Tremont House. Completely destroyed during Racer's Storm, as was much of Galveston, our hotel had been elegantly rebuilt. Large white columns fronted it, and its porch was four feet above the ground to protect from future flooding. Texas Presidents, Sam Houston and Anson Jones, had stayed here, as had Foreign Ministers from France and England. Just like at our Capitol Hotel, men took their ease in rocking chairs upon the generous veranda.

We were greeted by Mrs. Pinkerton, the housekeeper. In her starched dress and lace housecap, she proudly showed us the convenient location of her privy and the generous proportions of her dining room. She then had a young slave girl take us upstairs to our suite of rooms. They were comfortable accommodations with two tester beds and a hanging cot, which the boys found exceedingly fun to swing in. We'd barely unpacked our trunks when the dinner bell resounded through the house. We hoped the manner in which the boarders stampeded their way down the stairwell was testament to the agreeableness of Mrs. Pinkerton's cooking.

Upon entering the hall, supper's tantalizing aroma wafted up to greet us, however, a languorous pair of women blocked our speedy progress. Pappa squeezed past them, pulling my brothers along, and though my stomach urged me to follow, I held back, feeling the maneuver to be unladylike.

After my family passed, the older woman, who seemed to be the younger one's dowdy chaperon, snarled, "How uncivilized. No doubt, he's from the interior. You can always tell the upstarts. Just look at the cut of his cheap suit."

The younger one replied, "I've always liked men with beards, and if he has some roughness around the edges, so much better is the challenge to smooth them out."

The older woman rebuked her, "Your mother would wash out your mouth if she heard the way you talk."

Noisily clearing my throat to indicate my presence and discourage further embarrassing discourse, the women turned around and offered me an apologetic smile. Together we reached the dining room, whereupon the older woman parted the beaded curtain for us.

Pappa directed, "Hurry up, Mia, I've saved you a seat."

A bountiful table filled the entirety of the room, with everyone sitting shoulder to shoulder on long backless benches. I squeezed into the narrow spot, saying, "Miss Penelope would be pea green with envy to have this many customers, and the mullet looks very fresh."

"Just wait till you see what's for dessert," Pappa said. "sorbet imported from Boston!"

A man passed a communal bowl of corn dodgers to Pappa, saying, "You've got to take a look at Gail Borden's factory, down at Strand and Rosenberg. It's a marvel of industry."

The stooped, white bearded, Mr. Borden was well known in Houston for starting up two newspapers and designing the layout of our city streets.

"Didn't know Gail had a factory here, what's he making?" Pappa inquired.

"Ever tasted cured pemmican that the Indians make up for traveling?" the man asked. "Borden's meat biscuits are like that. He has an enormous operation, seven thousand pounds of beef a day, most of it going to wagon trains heading west."

Pappa helped himself to buttered grits. "Gail isn't a man to do things half way."

"I couldn't help but overhear you," another man said between gulps of chicory coffee. "Jim Boore is the name. I've forty thousand head on my ranch, and been selling some of my stock to Borden. If you're going to take a look at his factory, I recommend you do it directly, 'cause he's losing on this venture, and the bottom is about to fall out. I always thought it was a harebrained idea, but who's to argue with someone willing to pay high dollar."

A slave walked by, shooing flies away with a palmetto leaf.

"Sorry to hear it," Pappa said.

Boore replied, "Can't feel too sorry for a fellow with pockets that deep. He's got another fool idea about condensing milk and putting it in a can. I mean, who would drink the nasty stuff?"

A lanky young man, whose hair was slicked back with strong smelling cologne, had been following the conversation. Detecting a pause, he jumped in, "Excuse me, gentlemen, it seems you're all businessmen of one sort or another. I'm Gordon Sinclair, and I've recently arrived on the island to start up my service."

"What line of work are you in?" Pappa asked.

Opening his portmanteau and revealing several drawings, the young man answered, "I build privies, which most folks don't give much thought to, except when certain needs arise." With a concili- atory bow towards me, he continued, "I'll put this as delicately as possible out of respect for present company. A lot of thought goes into the construction of one of my buildings of necessity. That's what I'm trying to get people to start calling them. Buildings of necessity, that is."

What a peculiar topic for table conversation, I thought. However, his verve on the subject was contagious, and he most certainly had my brothers' attention.

"I reckon they're pretty simple affairs," the rancher said. "Four walls, a board with a hole in it, and a nail to hang the Sears catalog."

Sinclair shook his head in disagreement. "But there's far more to consider, sir. Take for instance, the distance between the build- ing and the house must be a calculated balance between conven- ience and odor. Then, there's a choice of roof styles. Some folks think pitched construction looks more refined, but I prefer a lean to, there being one less corner for wasps to nest in."

Christian joined in, "You got a good point there."

Sinclair nodded his thanks for my brother's support, then contin- ued, "I prefer to paint my buildings a light color, so that in the middle of the night when you're half-asleep, it's easy to find. Most importantly is whether or not you hinge the door to swing inward or outward; nobody wants to be surprised in the middle of their morning paper."

"Downright scientific," Emmett exclaimed.

Pappa pulled from his pocket, a copy of the Galveston Daily News. "Odd, we happen to be talking about this subject. Did you read the morning's addition? In Bexar County on the fourteenth of August, a man named Hackett was found dead in an outhouse. The deceased was a noted inebriate."

"Why that *is* interesting," Mr. Sinclair mused. "Now, if he'd been in one of my buildings of convenience, he may still be alive."

By this time, the topic of privies had attracted the entirety of the room's diners, and so there arose a collective inquiry into how this might be possible.

Thrilled with the attention, Mr. Sinclair explained, "I install a bell in everyone of my buildings. That way if you run out of corn- cobs or catalog, or are having a health emergency, you need only ring for help."

Mr. Sinclair was debating the benefits of a two versus three seater, and briskly taking orders for his buildings of necessity, when our family finally bid farewell. To stimulate digestion, Pappa insisted we take our leisure along the boardwalk. There was quite the crowd already assembled there: those of the working class, whose holiday was a week rather than the full season, and those of more prodigious means, who were intent on promenading their fashionable costumes, despite the Gulf breeze disarraying their coiffed hair.

We listened to the hurdy gurdy man play a few tunes, and then Sam was indulged with a pony ride. Finally, Pappa gave his approval, and we headed for the beach, passing the timid swimmers tethered to bathing wagons. It didn't take long to reach an isolated patch of beach where Pappa and the boys stripped to their drawers and suspenders. A sand dune and hedge of wild grasses provided me a modicum of privacy to don my suit. It was a hot scratchy wool gown, belted and with bloomers beneath. The milliner, Ophelia Thomas, convinced me it flattered my figure.

"Last one in is a rotten egg," Christian hooted, and without removing his spectacles, he jumped headfirst into the water.

We were all strong swimmers, and soon Pappa and my two oldest brothers had disappeared past the breaking waves.

Having ventured only a foot deep into the murky water, Sam complained, "It's frightfully cold."

"Sam, you know it's warm as bathwater."

Woefully, he added, "But, crabs will bite my toes."

Eventually, the allure of a cool respite from the unbearably hot day had Sam diving through the surf as confident as his brothers. It proved a most delightful day, building sandcastles and searching for shells, and even our sandwiches, coated in gritty sand, tasted delicious. By the end of the day, bone tired and sunburned, we returned to the crisp cool sheets of Tremont House and drifted contentedly to sleep.

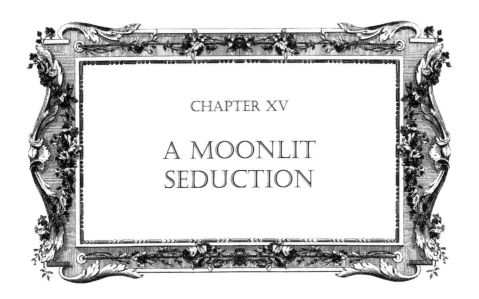

CHAPTER XV

A MOONLIT SEDUCTION

mmett's vacuum was filled with specimens, I'd collected an assortment of plants, and we were all dark as savages, and yet the last day of our holiday came too swiftly for my liking.

Pappa sat down next to me, "How would you like to attend a dance tonight with me?"

I was taken aback. "But, Pappa, you never attend social engagements; except for your Lyceum meetings, and there are no women members."

"Mia, you exaggerate my reserve, but if truth be told, it's the dance pavilion, itself, that holds my interest. The architect was a friend of your Grandfather Stein's, and the craftsmanship is reportedly exceptional. I thought if I took a look around, you might as well tag along. I believe you're of the age for such frivolities."

My trepidation was equal to my excitement. "But, Pappa, I don't even know how to dance, and what shall I wear?"

"Men lead and you follow, and your Sunday best will do just fine."

"But my blue cotton isn't an evening dress."

Pappa's bushy brows went up. "Fine, does that mean you don't want to go?"

"I didn't say that, it's just that... I'm a simpleton when it comes to this sort of thing. What shall I say if a fellow asks me to dance?"

"You curtsy and with your nicest smile, answer, yes."

"And what if no one asks me to dance? To just stand there waiting would be humiliation beyond belief."

Pappa affectionately pinched my cheeks. "My, Mia, a wallflower? I'd bet dollars to doughnuts, you barely have enough time to catch your breath between dances."

My father disappeared for an hour, and returned with two boxes for me. One held a collar, à la Vandyke, made of guipure lace and tied with knotted ribbons, which set off my plain dress to its best advantage. The other box held a pink rose corsage, which Pappa offered laughingly, "For my wallflower."

The pavilion that Pappa was so eager to see, didn't disappoint. Situated amid a landscaped park, with croquet grounds and a bowling green, it magically twinkled with hundreds of tiny lights.

"That's fine marquetry and fretwork," Pappa said admiringly. "Did you notice the star motif carved into each panel?"

My foot was already tapping to the lively rhythm as dancers glided past me. I replied absentmindedly, "Yes, Pappa, that's very nice."

A young man in an oversized suit approached me. "How do, Miss Stein. Remember me, Gordon Sinclair from Tremont House."

How could I forget the enthusiastic privy builder.

"I surely would enjoy to dance with you, or perhaps you'd like a cup of punch first? It is rather warm in here."

Eagerly accepting his hand, I said, "I'm quite refreshed, and would love to dance with you."

I was grateful Mister Sinclair had not been as heavy handed with his cologne as on our first meeting. Together, we mastered the allemande and the do-si-do, though the intricate French rigadoon step was beyond us. We certainly weren't the most graceful dancers, but no one matched our youthful abandon.

I felt no amorous attraction toward my partner, as I imagined happened on a real date, and due to his simple charm, I would've been content to dance the night away solely with him, if it hadn't been for the unexpected turn of events. During a feverish pirouette, I caught a glimpse of Pappa waving a farewell to me before departing the room.

Nonplussed, I excused myself from my crestfallen partner, and made my way through the crowd. I approached the man Pappa had been speaking with and realized he was Pappa's fighting comrade, Henri Dubois. I cannot be faulted for not at first recognizing the Frenchman, for his appearance at the fair had been that of a buck skinned frontiersman, whereas he was now dressed as the quintessential gentleman with frockcoat and silk vest.

"Excuse me, Mr. Dubois, I believe we have met before. I'm Klaus Stein's daughter, Mia."

Giving me the once over, he replied, "Mademoiselle Mia, I remember you well. Très beau. And please, I'm Henri to you." He bowed, then lightly kissed both my cheeks.

Flustered by his European manners, I managed, "And my father, do you know where he's gone off to?"

"To your accommodations. He was tired and ready to take you back, but seeing how much fun you were having, I convinced him you should stay. Please, don't look so alarmed, I promised him your safe return."

I was surprised by Pappa's decision to leave me under Henri's care. However, considering the admiration he felt for the man, and the fact he was twice my age, no doubt he felt it proper. After an uncomfortable silence, and my rejection of Mr. Sinclair's offer of another dance, Henri said, "Would you care to take a walk along the boardwalk? It's a lovely evening, and you'll enjoy the breeze after your exertion."

The question was merely an empty formality, for the Frenchman had boldly linked his arm with mine, and was leading me in the direction of the door. The night was enchanting with the sound of breaking surf and the full moon lighting our way. Henri wasn't inclined to conversation, though whenever I ventured a glance toward him, I found him intensely observing me.

By the time we reached the far end of the boardwalk, the dance music could no longer be heard and we were quite alone. I prattled nervously, "My mother once told me that the man in the moon was sent there as a punishment for gathering firewood on the Sabbath."

Amused, Henri's dark eyes crinkled. "That seems severe. I'm sure I've committed more grievous trespasses on any given Sunday. Perhaps, the man gathered the firewood when the moon was at the full. If so, it's the very fault of that celestial body for his bold behavior."

"Do you mean he was a lunatic?"

"Someone doesn't have to be mad as a hatter to be affected by the beauty of a full moon. I think it simply encourages you to do what you already want to do. We *are* after all animals with primal urges."

With no warning and certainly without my permission, Henri picked me up and carried me down the embankment to the beach. Holding me firmly against his body, I felt the strength of his arms and his breath warm upon my cheek.

Depositing me not so gently onto the sand, he said, "There now, safe and sound."

"You really needn't have done that. I'm quite capable of climbing down a rocky slope."

"I once carried your mother, Francesca, in my arms after she turned her ankle."

"I didn't realize you knew her."

"It was a very long time ago."

Again without asking my preference, he maneuvered me onto a nearby bench, and slipped off my shoes. I started to object, but he quickly explained, "We cannot have a proper walk on the beach with you wearing these trifling things. You'll be far more comfortable without them."

His logic was sound, however, the manner in which he removed them was unnecessarily slow, almost caressing the soles of my feet. I didn't know what to make of him, except perhaps he thought me a helpless girl like Rachael, whom I'm sure would delight in such gallant behavior.

Continuing our walk, Henri asked, "What do you think of Galveston?"

"It's wonderful. My brothers have collected lots of shells and sand dollars. Sam's prized possession is an enormous lightning whelk that holds the sound of the tide."

"And what treasures have you found?"

"I collected plant specimens, mostly marshmallow root, which I make into cough lozenges."

Henri's hand went to his forehead, "Ah, I remember you're the budding herbalist. Your plaster did my cut good, there's barely a scar."

"I still have a lot to learn. Having lived on the island so long, I wonder what you like best."

"The gulf is ever changing, so one never wearies of it. However, my favorite times are the stormy nights when the water churns violently and lightning streaks across the sky. You'd be surprised how many fishermen gamble their lives in those treacherous conditions, in order to collect their most profitable nettings. I also enjoy nights like this, when the water is calm, but something else is stirred."

Henri motioned me to sit upon a large driftwood. This time it was by way of gentle entreaty, rather than his previous commanding manner. His hand ran along the wood, and he observed, "This cottonwood tree has come a long way from home, probably carried here by the Mississippi. I may boast I've wandered much like it, seen every state in the union and much of Europe, but there's something about Galveston that draws me back."

"Does your job as a custom's agent take you away to such destinations? I imagine your work must be quite interesting."

"Yes, it keeps me on the move, and when there are smuggling rings in operation, it can be even dangerous."

"Have you found any smugglers in Houston?"

"You'd be surprised, Madam, how the grandest houses can hide the darkest secrets."

Lingering there for some time, I became mesmerized by the crashing surf, and our silence wasn't broken until he unexpectedly asked, "How well do you know Daniel Biggs?"

Flummoxed, I said, "Excuse me, I'm not sure who you're talking about."

His countenance was serious, and he said firmly, "Mia, do not try and play games with me. Not when grave matters are at hand. I've had every member of the Biggs family under surveillance, and I know very well you're intimate with the man."

I was outraged by his accusation. "I'm friends with his cousin Rachael, but I beg you not to tell my father. He is prejudice against her uncle, Captain Biggs."

His mood softened as he leaned over, and traced my face gently with his finger. "Perhaps we may have an agreement not to share everything with your father." He then took the liberty of kissing me directly on my lips. I'd never experienced such sensation before, and in that moment I didn't reflect upon whether his action was right or wrong. It simply stirred feelings which were agreeable. With unexpected deftness, Henri untied my collar's ribbon, and kissed my neck.

With reason conquering desire, I resisted his approach, crying, "Please don't, you go too far."

Ignoring me, he continued his amorous advances until I slapped him. Cursing in French, he abruptly pulled away, then led me to the boardwalk and onto the hotel. When he left me at the door, his mood had lightened once more, and he blew me a farewell kiss. I was left bewildered and unbalanced.

I wasn't sure if I'd crossed on my own, that indiscernible boundary between childhood and womanhood, or been pushed by Henri. My thoughts went to gentlemanly Daniel, who I was certain would never have dared make such advancements. But, what did I really know of him. I'd only spoken to him on two occasions, and now Henri was saying he and his family were under his surveillance. What did it all mean, I wondered.

CHAPTER XVI

THE HEALING HAND

It was gratifying to return home and find letters waiting. I opened Rachael's letter first, and found it filled with contrition for being so disagreeable to me. She longed for my companionship, swearing she'd be the perfect angel in future, and also expressed her aunt's gratitude for the renewal of good health due to my regimen.

Next was Daniel's missive, and I eagerly opened it. His words were kind and lighthearted, and included an invitation to games of euchre and whist. Imagining the enjoyable company of that gentleman once more, vanquished my resolve to quit Mosswood forever. I knew it meant further falsehoods to Pappa and Miss Emily, but it couldn't be helped. Besides, I'd come to no harm as long as I kept my distance from the library's secret chamber. I quickly shot off a response, promising to visit in the coming days.

The last two letters were for Pappa: one from my uncle Manuel and the other from Henri. I was anxious over the contents of the latter's. Would Henri disclose my dalliance with the Biggs family? Might he twist what transpired between us to reflect badly upon my character? Or were his intentions honorable towards me, and perhaps he'd ask for my hand in marriage. I took the missives directly to my father in his study, then nonchalantly taking up a book, I sat down and waited for him to open them.

Pappa put on his glasses, and read my uncle's letter first. "Why, this is quite remarkable. Manuel says that he followed your advice, and because of it, he and Neeva Jane have reconciled. They've settled in Kentucky, where they plan to breed racehorses."

I peered over the edge of my book, and casually said, "That's good news."

To my dismay, instead of taking up Henri's letter, he began writing a lengthy response to my uncle. The ensuing half-hour was distressing, and just when I'd given up hope, Pappa picked up Henri's letter.

Unable to bear it any longer, I coolly asked, "What does Henri, I mean Mr. Dubois, have to say?"

"Nothing you'd be interested in, daughter."

"Oh, but I'm dreadfully..." Catching myself too late, my father studied my unexpected enthusiasm for a moment, then began reading.

> *Dear Klaus,*
>
> *It was good to see you after so long a time. All the talk in Galveston is of the Compromise, as I'm sure it is everywhere. Though I'm pleased we settled on Pearce's plan rather than Bell's ludicrous idea of splitting us into three states, it's regrettable to lose half of Texas. Better than war, though, don't you agree, my friend?*
>
> *I've got my hands full of a most interesting case involving a prominent citizen of your city. So, expect me for dinner one of these nights. By the way, the Red River Railway Company is starting to lay tracks between Galveston and Houston, which will make future travel most convenient.*
>
> *Your loyal friend,*
> *Henri Dubois*

My voice rising in disappointment, I asked, "That's all he's written?"

Pappa gave me another quizzical look before returning to the letter. "There's just a postscript in which he says, I'm a lucky man to have so lovely a family."

Tears pricked my eyes unexpectedly. Though Henri shocked me by his forwardness, I'd begun to think it was merely the French way of courting. I found my feelings for him were deeper than I'd expected, and was completely deflated by his failure to mention me by name.

"Are you alright, Mia? You look peaked."

"I'm fine," I answered, gathering up my skirt to leave.

Stopping me, Pappa said, "Miss Emily will be arriving soon. You'd better get ready."

"Is it today we're going to Cyrus Harrington's? My goodness, I completely forgot. Miss Emily says the slaves he recently bought are grievously ill from the crossing."

Pappa unexpectedly motioned for me to sit in his lap, like I'd done when I was younger. Though I argued I was too big for such nonsense, I obliged him, and found the arrangement a comfort.

With his eyes dewy with sentiment, he said, "Mia, you're growing up so fast, and I know it's selfish of me, but sometimes I want you to still be my little girl."

"I always will be," I reassured him.

"I expect it will be a trying experience at Cyrus's place. He's not a very nice man, but what you're doing makes me powerfully proud."

I would've gladly stayed longer in my father's protective arms had I not heard Miss Emily's arrival. Giving his bearded cheek a quick peck, I rushed outside to join my teacher.

"There you are, honey child," Miss Emily said, smiling. "Are you ready for our mission of mercy? Mind you, Harrington is probably gonna pay us in ham bones and chickens."

"In the bible the tax man was paid with anise."

"Either way, we be gettin' a heap of satisfaction helping them folks. I been missin' you, Mia. You don't come round hardly enough."

"I'm sorry, I've been busy."

"No need to explain. Young girls are expected to have their diversions. Is it your new friend Rachael been occupyin' your time?"

"I really haven't seen her much, though I plan to this week. She has a mercurial temperament. You know, she runs hot and cold."

"I know just the sort. Have you forgotten our rose water enterprise?" she asked.

"Sold three bottles at Ophelia's, and Mister Kennedy wants a dozen to sell at his Trading Post."

"That's mighty fine. I been thinkin' about your sewin' circle. I know you said you didn't want to go back, but I don't think that's right. That whole thing was just a tempest in a teapot. Besides, it ain't right to hold a grudge, nor be uncivil to your neighbors; even when they're mean as rattlesnake, like Charlotte Price. I mean Eberhard."

"Miss Emily, I'm awfully glad to hear you say that. You're the best midwife in town, and Charlotte will no doubt call on you for her birthing."

Miss Emily threw her head back with laughter. "That woman wouldn't come to me if her house was on fire and I was the only one with a bucket of water."

"You never know what might happen in the future," I offered.

"Lordy, I can't deny that truth."

We rode past the cotton mills and McGowan's foundry, and were soon in the countryside. I was bursting with questions for the wise woman sitting beside me, but knew I must proceed with caution, lest I reveal more than I wanted to. "Miss Emily, you once told me about some slaves who practice Voodoo."

She nodded. "Most white folks fear it, and consider it the Devil's work, but that's not what its about. Voodoo means spirit or God, and it's most powerful for healing."

I continued coolly, "What about the little dolls they use to represent someone. Aren't they made to harm them?"

"Sometimes, yes, and sometimes, no. You can stick pins in the doll to focus healing energy."

What she said might be true, but I was certain whoever tied the twine around the doll's neck at Mosswood had an evil intention in mind. "Do you know any slaves around here who practice Voodoo?"

"Plenty, but they got to do it in secret. If their master found out, they'd be surely beaten, and maybe even hung. Why you askin' all these questions about Voodoo?"

Forced to lie, I answered, "My friend Rachael is from England, and she's very curious about our country and how the slaves have brought their customs here."

She readily accepted my falsehood, and seeing we still had some distance to go, I ventured another question, which had considerably perturbed me. "What is love suppose to feel like?"

Miss Emily laughed at me. "Honey, you do come up with some cockeyed questions, first Voodoo, now love. Hmm, I'll put it this way. When your thoughts just keep going back to that person, and you feel off balance, kinda crazy, but you don't even care. One moment you're flyin' high and the next you're broken. Well, that's not love."

"What is it then?"

"Infatuation, and it don't last. True love is somethin' deep. It's when the happiness of another person is the most important thing in the world to you. There's something about love that makes you overlook the other's failins. You've heard say love is blind, and it's true. A man who loves you thinks you're the most beautiful woman he's ever seen, even when your hair is uncombed and your dress a rag. That's 'cause he sees your insides, not just your outsides."

I reasoned, "But if that's true, then maybe we can't see the real person at all, and they're just a fantasy. I mean, isn't it important to see a person's faults?"

Miss Emily wrinkled her forehead in thought. "Maybe you're right, but in the end, your own faults are the only ones you can count on changin'. Mia, have you got a beau, you're not tellin' me about?"

"Not exactly, but there are two men I often think of."

She clucked her tongue, "I guarantee two men will get messy right quick."

I was considering asking her about her feelings for Pappa when she asked, "What does Klaus think of this situation? I mean the two men, you're interested in."

Horrified, I said, "Miss Emily, what I've said to you is in the strictest confidence. Pappa doesn't know anything about my feelings, and that's the way I want it to be, at least for now. Can I rely on you not to tell him, or need I keep my thoughts to myself in the future?"

"I'm mighty honored you felt you could trust me, and I promise not to breath a word of it. Just don't lose your head over them."

Hugging Miss Emily, I said, "I think you must be the wisest woman in town."

"Can't say as I helped you any. You already got all the answers in there," she said pointing to my heart. "Just listen to them, and you'll figure things out."

Cyrus Harrington's house was situated proudly on a hillock. It awarded him an advantageous view of his sugar plantation, and the ability to see our approach long before we arrived at his door. Surrounded by his pack of hunting dogs, he met us on the road.

With no regard for our presence, the beady-eyed man spat a brown stream of tobacco, then snarled, "See you finally made it."

"Aren't we here at the time agreed upon?" Miss Emily asked, perplexed.

"Yesterday ain't soon enough for me. Time is money, so you best get goin'. They're down a bit past the cattle pen and blue grass field. You'll see a cluster of sweetgums on your left, and the cabins lay a piece further by the river. You can't miss the sorry lot of 'em. I'll settle up with you afterwards, just you keep in mind, I don't mean to pay for those who die."

"Who did you buy them from?" Miss Emily asked.

Harrington growled, "Don't you know curiosity kills the cat, especially when it's a yellow one? I might as well ask who your master is."

Miss Emily shot back in indignation, "I've no master, I'm a free woman."

Harrington blew his nose into a filthy handkerchief. "I suppose a piece of paper, which could easily fly away with a strong wind, proves that. Now, you two best be off to see about my property. Harvest time is in two weeks, and I expect 'em hard at work by then."

The nasty little man made a final spit, as we left.

"Best to choose your fights wisely," Miss Emily said under her breath.

Harrington's directions were precise, and we soon came upon the compound where the newly arrived slaves took shelter. The hovels were in deplorable condition with dirt floors fouled by barn animals, thatched roofs failing, and the log walls unchinked. They were at the mercy of weather and insects.

I'd helped Miss Emily tend slaves before, but never had I seen so miserable a gathering. Many were lifeless specters too weak to move, others huddled together speaking in guarded whispers. No one dared approach us, not even the children with their natural curiosity. They'd been stolen from their homes and shipped across an ocean to a foreign land, and the cruelties they'd endured were etched on their faces.

Miss Emily began speaking in a tongue I'd never heard, and as her words flowed, the people began to stir. Their despairing gaze flickered with expectation.

A young man, covered in sores, came forward. "You be the healers they promise?"

"Yes, I'm Miss Emily and this is Miss Mia. We're here to help."

"My people very sick. The ship's captain kill our botono. He say he too old to be worth anything." He shook his head in disbelief. "Botono most important person of village, but captain is blind to his mojo. Now, evil spirits enter our bodies and steal souls. You come to drive out evil?"

Driving out evil sounded like something a witchdoctor was called upon to do, and I warily I consulted Miss Emily for her response.

"Mia, do you understand what they're asking for?"

"I'm not sure."

Miss Emily chucked me under the chin, as if I were a child. "They need hope that things will get better. Without it, all the cures in the world won't save them." She rolled up her sleeves. "Go on and start unloading the wagon. We got our hands full."

I'd helped her with birthings and healings, but never anything like this. She began with purifying the houses with burning sage, and then began to chant, "I call upon Nana Buluku to bring her healing light. Cleanse these people of all bad spirits. Fill them with sunshine of a new day."

Miss Emily directed me to linger beside each slave with a smudge stick, and encircle their head with a fragrant wreath of smoke. There were a few, too disheartened to respond, but most of them became remarkably revived upon my passing.

The young man, who seemed to be the group's spokesman, approached us again. "It is custom for our botono to sacrifice animal to gods. In this way we give thanks, but we have no animals, no weapons to hunt with. Many people believe your mojo will not work without sacrifice."

Again I looked to Miss Emily in dismay. Waving smudge sticks was one thing, but a sacrifice was too much to ask me to be a part of. If anyone caught us doing this, the slaves would be severely punished, and our reputations would be destroyed.

Miss Emily gave me an understanding smile, then retrieved an egg from our supplies. "This works just as well," she told the young man reassuringly. She cracked its shell, and poured its contents into a shallow bowl.

Miss Emily waved her hands and chanted, "This egg is powerful talisman. Mother chicken gives it life. Now it comes to us as gift to heal our bodies and grow strong once more."

The slaves gathered around her, swaying in unison. Through their clenched teeth, they emitted a shrill chirping that sounded like frogs after a rain. The intensity of that moment was palpable, and when Miss Emily instructed me to place my hands above her own, I felt a tingling warmth pulse through my fingertips. To my astonishment, when we took our hands away, the egg was cooked.

A pandemonium broke out with shouts of praise and heartfelt embraces. With tears streaming down their faces, they threw themselves at our feet.

"You destroy evil eye put on my people!" the young man exclaimed. "You must be our new botono!"

"No," Miss Emily said firmly. "It was *your* people who destroyed the evil eye. They always had the power, but had just forgotten. Remember, no matter what you got to endure, always have hope a better day will come. In this way, your captor don't win. They may own your body for now, but can't own your soul."

A dark expression came over the young man's face, and he said, "Miss, you put hex on Harrington and on captain who bring us here. Then they not own our body either."

Miss Emily stood quiet, almost as if she were deliberating his request. Then she said, "Don't doubt these men will pay the price for their misdeeds. It's the way of Nana Buluku, is it not?"

We took the young man's crooked smile as acceptance, and so began the work of healing their diseased bodies. A restorative concoction of apple cider vinegar and honey was the first remedy we administered. Though their faces screwed up in distaste, they drank it down willingly. Almost all of them suffered from diarrhea, and so we fed them rice and agrimony tea. Ringworm was treated with sweetgum sap, and garlic oil was used for their lice. There were a few men who had been beaten severely, and so we bandaged them as best we could, and gave them bitter willow for their pain.

By the time we packed up our things to leave, the sun was setting, and though we promised to soon return, they cried like motherless children, begging us to stay. It was heartbreaking to drive away, knowing we were leaving them to the misery of captivity and a miserable master.

I could hardly wait to address Miss Emily, "I didn't know you practiced Voodoo."

"I don't," she replied, matter of factly.

"All that gibberish you were chanting? And what about the egg? How did you do that?"

"I knows enough about Voodoo to fake it. As for the egg... That's called slight of hand, like a magician. I expected they might need some convincin' before they'd let me help 'em, so I brought a raw and a cooked egg. Don't generally approve of trickery, but sometimes it be a necessity."

"Miss Emily, you never cease to amaze me."

We had a good laugh, which was welcome relief from the day's drama. When we arrived at my home, night had fallen, but my house was dark.

"That's strange," I said. "Looks like nobody's home."

"Your Pa must have forgotten to tell you. He and the boys went to a town meetin'. I'll come in and scrounge up some dinner for us."

I was making my way through the dark hall when my family jumped from the shadows with shouts of surprise.

"Heavens to Betsy," I exclaimed. "What on earth is going on?"

"Come into the dining room," they directed with peals of excitement. "We have it all ready for you."

Emmett directed me to sit in Pappa's customary head of the table, which was festively draped in colorful shawls. "Your throne, me lady."

Sam, standing on tiptoe, ceremoniously crowned me with a paper circlet, adorned with jewels courtesy of his paint box.

I gazed around the table at my family's beaming faces. "I'm not complaining, but *why* am I queen for the day?"

"It's your birthday," Pappa reminded me. "Eighteen years ago you were born."

"I thought you was foolin' with me," Miss Emily said. "But I see now you really did forget."

Overcome with the day's events, I began to sob uncontrollably, which distressed Sam.

Christian piped up, "Sam, you ninny baby, don't you know women cry when they're happy?"

"You're all so sweet to me," I sniveled.

"You deserve every bit of it," Pappa said. Raising a blackberry cordial in a toast, our glasses clinked together one after another like the notes of a harmonious song.

"I got you a little something," Pappa said. "It's from Ophelia's. She vouches it's the height of fashion. I believe that's what young women these days want to have."

I examined the satin reticule with its beaded fringe and delicate rosette, and began to cry again.

"That means you like it," Sam uttered softly.

I nodded yes, smiling through my tears.

My brothers lined up in front of me, their hands behind their backs.

"We combined our money to get you something extra nice," Emmett said.

"It will come in handy, right now too," Christian added.

They handed me a linen handkerchief, each of a different color and embroidered with their initials. The stitches, executed by inexperienced fingers, were crooked and awkward, but to my sisterly eyes, they were simply exquisite. "I can't believe it. When and how did you keep all this a secret? Miss Emily, I believe you're behind all this."

She smiled, "They worked real hard on 'em. Here now, I brought you a little something too."

By the feel and weight of the package, I guessed it was a book, and was not disappointed to find *The Complete Herbal* by Nicholas Culpeper in my hands.

Miss Emily boasted, "It's even older than that Linnaeus fellow, you're always talkin' up."

"But how?"

Looking toward my father, she answered, "I asked Klaus what would be a good book for you, and this is what he suggested."

"I mean, it must have cost a dreadful lot."

Miss Emily shook her head modestly, but Pappa spoke up. "She's been working her fingers to the bone to afford it. Wouldn't let me help out with it at all. She's too prideful."

"This is far too generous," I stuttered.

"You got no excuses, now. I expect you to one day be the top-notch herbalist in the country."

The rest of the evening was spirited revelry, and the happiest of birthdays. We played Parcheesi and made hand shadows on the wall until it was the boys' bedtime. What with my trip to Harrington's plantation and then the party, I was simply exhausted, but when I was turning in, I noticed the parlor light on.

"Pappa are you alright?" I asked, upon finding him by the hearth.

He answered with a note of melancholy in his voice, "Thought I'd do a little reading. You know how I am some nights, just can't sleep."

I noticed his fingers caressing the frayed hem of his smoking jacket. It was a well-worn gift Mamma had made for him when they were newlyweds.

"Tonight when the boys gave you their handkerchiefs, it got me to thinking about your mother. Just look at the number of stitches she sewed within an inch. When she gave it to me, I don't think I gave her the praise she deserved."

I placed my hand on Pappa's shoulder. "Mamma knew how much you loved her."

His jaw clenched, trying to hold back raw emotion. "Would you mind making something to help me sleep, but not a glass of warm milk."

"How about chamomile with passionflowers? I can't promise it will be as good as your Darjeeling, but it does taste a little like apples."

Pappa regarded me. "You know how proud I am of you, with all the healing work you're doing. It couldn't have been easy going out to Harrington's. Were they as bad off as you expected?"

"Worse. I'm afraid some of them might die from the beatings they received. Apparently the captain who brought them over was pretty cruel."

"I can't imagine what I'd do in their position. The worst has to be seeing your family suffer, and then sold off separately."

"Miss Emily says there's always hope."

"Ja, that's something she'd say."

I came back with his hot tea, and found his depressed mood had not altered. "Pappa, please tell me what's bothering you."

He hesitated, then answered, "Sometimes, it's hard to know what to do."

"But I feel you must always have the answers."

"Not when it comes to love."

"Miss Penelope would marry you in a minute," I teased. "And they say food is the way to a man's heart."

Pappa gave a halfhearted smile. I wanted to talk to him about his feelings for Miss Emily, but knew he must be the one to bring it up.

"You better get onto bed. You'll be needing a good night's sleep."

I kissed his bearded cheek, and went downstairs to check if all the doors were locked. On the front hall table lay a letter for me. It was from Henri. I wondered if Pappa had seen it. I knew he thought highly of his character, or else why did he leave me in his care at the Galveston dance? It was a small packet with the same distinctive handwriting and Customs House return address that I'd seen on the previous letter to Pappa. It read:

> *My delightful Mia,*
>
> *Our meeting on the beach deeply touched me. We barely know each other and yet, many hours are now spent in recalling each detail of our encounter. The way you felt in my arms, the sweet smell of your hair laying softly against my neck. It was as if you'd always belonged there. Please forgive me for my forwardness, which I'm sure you have deemed ungentlemanly. I respect you completely, and didn't intend insult to your character. It was merely my own desires overcoming my judgment.*
>
> *With much love, Henri*
>
> *P.S. I feel it is most essential at this time to keep the affection I feel for you a secret. This will only add to the excitement of our next meeting.*

I studied Henri's short note, finding it difficult to determine how deep his feelings really ran. There were men who toyed with women's hearts, and I didn't plan to fall victim to such folly. He was surely a passionate man, but my feelings for him were unclear at best. However, memory of his kiss excited something within me, and his apology had done much toward forgiveness.

CHAPTER XVII

AN UNEXPECTED PROPOSAL

The onset of school for the boys elicited mixed emotions within me. In times past it was a welcome relief to have my older brothers from underfoot, however this year Emmett was attending only half day, the other he'd work at Pappa's shop, and dear little Sam would be attending class for the first time.

Christian barreled into the kitchen, hollering, "What's for breakfast?"

"I cooked up something special for your first day, buckwheat cakes," I said trying to sound cheery.

"I'll have half a dozen, though they won't make going to school any better," he whined.

"I've heard tell good things about your new schoolmaster, Noah Fairfax. He attended schooling on the East coast, and Emmett even approved after meeting him. Says he's a wizard at mathematics. Most importantly, he understands Sam's shyness and hesitation to talk. He even thinks he might help him. What little boy wouldn't want to benefit from such a learned man?"

Sam whispered, pulling at his newly starched collar, "I don't want to talk to anyone but you, and you're smart enough to keep on teaching me."

I swallowed the lump in my throat, "That's sweet of you to say, but my learning can't hold a candle to the illustrious Mr. Fairfax. Besides, I may not always be here to teach you."

It was obvious I'd said the wrong thing by Sam's disturbed expression.

"Who's the lucky guy?" Christian teased, as he mischievously untied my apron strings. "It ain't that cockscomb who said those gushy things in the garden, is it?"

Defensively I barked, "That's enough, Christian. You don't know a thing about Daniel. Why he's probably one of the most sincere gentlemen I've ever met, and handsome to boot. And just because he dresses well doesn't mean he's a cockscomb."

Christian replied between gulps of milk, "Emmett told me you got a letter from that Frenchy guy. You'd do a lot better with him, even though he kisses men on the cheek. He can hunt and fight, and if we had another revolution, he could at least defend you. I bargain he could beat up that Daniel fellow."

"How on earth did Emmett know about...? Oh never mind, I don't intend to discuss with you any further, either of those men."

"Shall I bring out my crystal ball again and tell you who you'll marry? The fortune teller sees all."

"Stop it Christian, can't you see you're upsetting Sam with all this nonsense, and this being his first day of school. Sam, leave your suspenders on, and quit messing with your collar. It shall be completely ruined by the time you get to class."

Christian continued harping, "Why doesn't Emmett have to go to school with us, he's the one crazy about learning. I should be at the furniture shop helping Pappa, not him."

"Time will come soon enough for both of you to work there, but first there's your studies. Now, if you don't finish up, you're going to be late, and Mr. Fairfax will be putting you in the dunce corner. Both of you have your chores to do, Sam, you need to collect the eggs and feed the chickens, and Christian, please fetch in more wood for the stove."

I'd barely cleared the table of dirty dishes when I heard Sam's frantic screams. Running outside I saw a trail of feathers leading to the coop and my brothers. There they stood staring in horror at a carnage of slaughtered chickens. In the past we'd had coyotes and foxes make quick handiwork of our birds, but this time it was the result of a malevolent person. On the ground drawn in corn-meal was a large pentagram and within it two serpents intertwined. Beside the diagram were the chickens with their throats slit, bodies run through with spikes, and their hearts removed and piled up in a bloody heap.

"The chicks?" Sam whimpered. "I don't see them."

We frantically searched the yard for the babies who Sam had lovingly cared for, but there was not a trace. Heartbroken, we were about to leave when we heard a soft clucking from a lone surviving hen atop the barn's roof. Like a sentry at her post, she'd waited until it was safe to call out her brood. One by one the tiny chicks responded to her coaxing, emerging from the fig tree's low branches and the tangled blackberry brambles. When all of her babies had appeared, the mother hen descended, allowing them to gather beneath her outstretched wings.

Relieved by the chicks survival, our attention turned back to the dead chickens surrounding us.

With his jaws clenched, Christian demanded, "I want to know who did this terrible thing?"

I shrugged my shoulders feigning ignorance, though I was fairly certain who was behind it. The two serpents in the diagram were identical to the ones tattooed on Captain Biggs' slave, Rita. She'd frightened me away from Mosswood's hidden chamber, but apparently she believed I needed further warning with this Voodoo ceremony. "Come on boys, we're not going to figure out anything now or you two will be late for school."

Sam rubbed his stomach as if it ached.

"It's no wonder your tummy hurts with all this excitement, but it's not enough to keep you home today."

"Dose him with cod liver oil!" Christian taunted.

Pulling a tearful Sam onto my lap, I wet the corner of my apron and removed the stray feathers from his hair. My days would no doubt be lonely without him, for wherever I went he shadowed me. However, revealing my angst would only make our separation harder. "You're growing up so fast, one day you'll be too big for me to even hold."

"Then I'll hold you," Sam replied.

I swallowed hard, knowing this love affair was as fleeting as his childhood. "It's time to be off now. Mind you, work hard, watch after each other, and eat all your lunch."

Tears sprung to my eyes as I bade them goodbye from the front porch, watching their youthful figures till they disappeared around the corner. I'd not sat there more than a few minutes when Daniel unexpectedly arrived.

Noticing my red rimmed eyes, he asked, "Mia, please tell me what distresses you?"

I couldn't help but smile at his concern. "I fear I'm softhearted when it comes to my brothers. It's the first day of school and... You must think me silly to be melancholy at their leaving."

"It's endearing, to be sure," he said, taking off his hat.

Realizing my disheveled appearance, my hand flew self-consciously to the kerchief covering my head. "I'm certain I look a fright. It seems you're apt to catch me at my worst."

His eyes twinkled with admiration. "Mia, there's not a woman in this whole town that compares to your beauty."

I blushed under his praise and unrelenting gaze.

"Besides, I'm always impressed by your earnest effort at labor. I only wish you could influence Rachael to employ herself equally. I'm certain it would improve her temperament."

"I shall meet with your cousin soon enough, though I don't intend to bring up the subject of how she passes her days. From my past failed attempts to instruct her, I've learned the only way we're to be friends is to accept we don't see matters eye to eye. Do forgive me, I've been remiss in my manners. Would you like a refreshment, perhaps a glass of ginger beer?"

"No, thank you, and it was I, whose been ill-mannered to drop by without notice. However, circumstance and the desire to give you this book prompted my visit. It's called *The Language of Flowers and Herbs.*"

"This is all the rage," I said, gladly accepting his gift. "A man can apparently send a tussie-mussie to a woman, and each flower expresses a different sentiment. It's a type of coded message, only the lovers will understand."

"Sometimes it's a challenge for men to say what's on their mind."

Flipping through the book's pages, I said, "My mother loved lavender, as do I, and I'm curious what it says it means. Hmm, here it is, and it says, devotion. Definitely something Pappa had for my mother."

"Speaking of your father, I deeply regret not having had the opportunity to meet him, especially due to the change in my circumstance."

My voice quivered with concern, "May I ask what change is that?"

Daniel answered shyly, "There's a matter of import I wanted to discuss with the both of you. I would've preferred to have gone about this in a different fashion, talking with him first. However, my time is limited, for I sail for England on the *Isabella Teague* on Saturday."

Hearing his unexpected announcement, I realized how strong my feelings had grown for him. "You're leaving?"

"It warms my heart to see you distressed at the news, but rest assured that I plan to return, if..." Visibly shaken, he took a deep breath to steady his nerves before continuing, "Though my actions may seem premature, I know my feelings are true and that I must discuss my intentions towards you. What I'm trying to say is that from the moment I first saw you, I was smitten. You were like an enchantress who mesmerized me with one of your spells. Perhaps you used some potent herb to influence me. I care not by what means I arrived at this state, I only know, you are who I want."

"I remind you, sir, I was spitting watermelon seeds at the moment you first saw me."

"I need no coaxing to recall that glorious day," Daniel said with relish. "You wore a white summer dress and your hair was tied back in long braids."

"You're not the only one able to recall the details of that encounter," I said warmly. "You wore a blue frockcoat and striped trousers, and a gold watch fob dangled from your vest pocket. I confess, I initially thought you a dandy except that your tousled hair, and skin tanned from outdoor activity altered that opinion."

Daniel smiled with amusement, "I'm gratified you remember too, and that I possessed some quality to recommend me, even if it was only my tousled hair. Did you not notice my wit or charm in the bargain?"

We laughed together, and I felt once more the ease of interaction between us.

Drawing near to me, he said, "You see the joy we find in each other's company confirms our initial attraction. Dear sweet Mia, there is much about your person that recommends you to me; your intelligence, grace, and perhaps most of all your straightforwardness. You can't imagine how rare that is with young women these days, who are intent on acquiring every affectation."

"Daniel, your commendation is flattering, but ..."

"Please, let me finish. I've been up all night going over a hundred times what I wanted to say, knowing precious time existed before my departure. A lot can transpire in five months to a woman as beautiful as you, and I don't want to risk losing you."

Taking my hands into his own, he continued with his declaration. "I'm situated very comfortably, financially speaking. I inherited a Cotswolds manor from Mother, and even though it's a bit run down at the heels from neglect, I'm sure you'll love it. Hardwick, my caretaker, keeps it from completely crumbling down, and with a little work we could bring it back to its full glory. I've also a seaside cottage in Brighton for holidays. The views are beautiful and after a long winter, it's the ideal place to summer.

"We can live quite comfortably just on the interest from my inheritance. I work for my father, only as a favor to him. Don't think though, I prefer an idle life, for I don't. We can spend part of the year here, and the rest in England or traveling abroad. I'll do everything in my power to make you happy and help your family in any way possible. Am I too bold in my proclamations? Please, Mia, don't just sit there looking so shocked. Say something. No, I can see you'd better not. You need time to consider my proposal, and I understand. You needn't give an answer yet. Only say there's a chance, and I'll return to discover my fate, otherwise I shall remain in England. Darling Mia, I've forgotten to tell you the most important part. I love you."

Our lips came together with a naturalness I'd not expected. Where Henri's raw passion had frightened me, Daniel's tenderness drew me to him.

"Should I take that as a confirmation?" Daniel said hopefully, then kissed me again.

It took all my reasoning and willpower not to impulsively give him the answer he longed for. "I don't think we know each other well enough for me to answer yet. And when you return you must meet with Pappa, and I shall get to know your father as well. But know I'm favorably inclined to your proposal."

"How I dread leaving you even more than before, and if it weren't so pressing a matter to which I was forced to attend to, I'd never consider a parting."

"Did you tell Rachael that you intended to propose to me?"

"I confess I did not. I believe you know her feelings toward me, and though I have never returned them in kind, she holds a false notion I shall change. Telling her about my plans would only have disturbed her, and I feared she might have retaliated against you during my absence. There will be time enough to deal with her childish antics upon my return. Darling, let us not speak of Rachael in these last moments we have together."

We kissed again, more passionately than before, and if it hadn't been for the men at the Capitol Hotel whistling at us, there may have been no end to it.

CHAPTER XVIII

THE FRENCHMAN RETURNS

After Daniel departed, I felt as though I were floating on air. I kept his proposal a secret, reasoning there'd be time enough upon his return to broach the subject with Pappa. That is if I decided to accept it, and this I wasn't at all certain of, especially when that very night Henri Dubois stood at my door with puckered lips.

"Mon cheri, how I have longed for your embrace."

No men were more different than my two suitors. Daniel had offered me marriage in the most refined and tender manner; laying out in logical order his assets and promises for my future happiness. While on the other hand, Henri, roguish in his rumpled coat and muddy boots, proposed only kisses to seduce me.

Hypnotized by his coal black eyes, I moved like a moth to a flame into his open arms, and was saved from this tempting snare only by my father's bellowing voice from the parlor.

"Whose at the door, Mia?" Pappa asked.

Henri's romantic playfulness instantly dissolved, and he pronounced with a contrived formality, "Good evening, Miss Stein, is it not unseasonably balmy weather we're experiencing today?" Then shouting to Pappa, "Dear Klaus, it is I, Henri, your comrade in arms come to visit you!"

Brusquely passing me by as if I were merely a slight acquaintance, he made his way to Pappa, whom he fervently embraced kissing both his cheeks. My father beamed, cordially directing Henri to his favorite chair in the study. "You're a sight for sore eyes, my friend. What brings you to town, business or pleasure?"

"A little of the former and hopefully a prevalence of the latter," Henri answered jovially.

Pappa poured him a glass of our best port, a drink he saved for special occasions. "Do you plan to stay overnight?"

"Yes, but only the one."

"Then you must think of our home as your own," Pappa said with a hearty pat to Henri's shoulder. "No need to spend good money on a hotel when I can offer you the most comfortable bed in town."

"And there's no need to twist my arm with that offer, Klaus. I gladly accept all the Stein hospitality offered."

Henri raised his glass, looking at me through the swirling ruby liquid, and I felt certain his words held some hidden meaning.

Ushering me toward the door, Pappa said, "Mia, Henri and I have much to reminisce over, and I'm sure we would bore you with half of it. Give us a call when dinner is ready."

With the intent to impress our guest, I fetched the fine bone china and embroidered linen napkins, then whipped up a special French bread pudding with raisins and bourbon. I changed into my favorite green dress, which brought out the color in my eyes, then called everyone to dinner.

It seemed all my efforts proved for naught, for Henri offered not one compliment nor even a meaningful glance in my direction. Perhaps wary of Pappa's discernment, he instead pursued dreary discussions on politics and races.

Sleep eluded me that night, for Henri slept down the hall from my bedroom, and I'm certain that towards midnight the floorboards creaked outside my door. By the time daybreak streamed through the window, I could barely rouse myself. However, Henri had promised to take my brothers on an early morning turkey hunt in the countryside, and so I sleepily went to the kitchen to prepare them a picnic lunch.

Henri sat at the table, cleaning his rifle. "Bonjour, mademoiselle. I see you're as beautiful as a dew kissed rose in the morning. Many women would envy you such an attribute, but youth is generous, I suppose. Now you look miffed with me, have I hurt your delicate feelings? You *are* like the rose, with its fragile petals and prickly thorns."

Apparently mockery was a Frenchman's way of making love. "I'm fine, sir, just drowsy as I'm sure you'll find my brothers at this hour. We're unaccustomed to such early rising."

"It's a necessity if one wants to catch the turkeys still roosting in the treetops."

"Then I'd better rouse them, and I promise you it won't be an easy task. Expect at least a half hour's wait."

"Much obliged, and while you're at it, I advise you to put on more sensible shoes. I recall your feet are most tender, and I wouldn't want them ruined by blisters. You look baffled by my instructions. I thought it went without saying that you were to accompany us on this venture."

Taken aback I asked, "And does my father approve of my going with you?"

Henri circled me as if hunting prey. "I'm his respected friend, why would he not trust me to look after you? Besides, it will offer us opportunity to get to know each other better."

Maddened by the game he was playing with my affections, I left the room abruptly. It took a shorter time than I'd expected to awaken my sleepy brothers. They were eager to spend the day with a venerated huntsman, as well as enjoy an absence from school.

My hesitation to go with Henri was short lived. I not only wanted to keep an eye on my brothers, but also to prove to myself I could resist a Lothario's advances. We settled comfortably into Pappa's wagon, myself beside Henri, while my brothers sat in the back. We passed burly wagoneers on their way to Market Square, then crossed the bayou at Preston Bridge. It didn't take long before we came to an open prairie where well-worn tracks led us for nearly a mile into a thick piney forest. We were enjoying the peace of the early morning when a most unexpected sight startled us.

"Jumping Jehoshaphat!" Christian yelled. "There's Indians up ahead!"

I felt completely at ease with my friend, Sekettumaqua, but never had I been amongst an entire band in their natural environment. My brothers' excitement was fearless, whereas I found it impossible to dispel the stories I'd heard of kidnapping and scalping. I said firmly, "Henri, I think we should turn around, right now."

"Calm down, Mia, there's nothing to worry about," he said with a reassuring pat to my hand. "I know these people, and they're quite friendly. Notice how they've reversed traditional roles. The women, in their short cropped hair, are hard at work setting up the wigwams, while the men, wearing the fancy beadwork and long braided hair, are at their leisure.

"The way it should be," Emmett chimed in. "Mia, can I join the tribe? I want to grow my hair long and sit around all day."

Nervous laughter was all I could manage as the tribe's chief solemnly approached our wagon. Addressing us, he said, "Mope-tshoko-pe.""

Henri answered the severe looking native in the same foreign tongue, then translated for us. "He introduced himself. His name means old owl. I told him it's an honor for us to be in the presence of so mighty a warrior."

The chief motioned to a young scout, who brought forward a leather satchel. From it, the chief ceremoniously withdrew a government agent's testimony for Henri to read. It claimed the bearer of the document was a friend of the whites and should be treated in kind.

Emmett mused, "To think that at one time all this land belonged to them, and now they're treated like trespassers, having to bare our government's documents."

Henri offered the chief a friendly handshake, after which a lengthy discussion ensued. I was unnerved by the Indian's constant glances toward me and the laughter that erupted between them.

Finally Henri gave an explanation to their discourse. "Mia, I told him of your knowledge of herbs and your training in midwifery, which duly impressed him. He believes you would be a valuable asset to his tribe, and wants you for his fifth wife. Come now, don't look so mortified, it is an honor he offers you."

"Are you teasing me again?" I asked.

Henri threw back his head in laughter. "Of course, my inno-cent Mia. Actually, he wants to make some kind of trade. He's interested in your necklace, and wants to know what you'd want in return."

"Mamma's locket? Impossible!"

Emmett pointed out with unerring logic, "They look friendly enough and I trust Henri's judgment, but I think it wise to offer something for a trade, or else they may take your refusal as an insult."

Flustered by the situation, I suggested, "Ask him if his healer has a remedy for easing childbirth. If he does, I'd like that in exchange for my sun bonnet."

With the chief's agreement, one of his snaggletoothed wives was dispatched to fetch the remedy. She quickly returned and handed me a pouch full of roots, whereupon I gave her my bonnet. With the newly acquired article perched on her head, she proudly prom-enaded the length of the encampment, inciting jealous bickering amongst the other women. By the time we were escorted through their encampment and shown the skill of their beadwork and blan-ket making, and shared a foul tasting drink they offered us, any hope of finding turkeys still nesting in treetops had vanished.

"No matter," Henri insisted to my crestfallen brothers. "I'll take you to a favorite spot of mine for a swim. We'll park the wagon just beyond that stand of birch, from which it's only a short walk by foot."

The Frenchman's claim turned into a laborious hike through grass as tall as Sam. I was thankful I wore sturdy boots, but my dress was unwieldy, and soon I lagged behind.

"Hurry up, Mia," Henri chided. "You don't want to get lost, do you?"

Christian added, "I don't know why we brought her along. Girls don't have any business in the wilderness."

"Mr. Dubois, are you sure we're not lost, ourselves?" Emmett asked, studying his compass.

Swatting away a persistent horsefly, I pointed out, "That forked oak does looks awfully familiar. I think we've doubled back on ourselves."

"You insult me," Henri retorted. "I'm an esteemed huntsman, and I've never gone astray, unless you count that one occasion in the Black Forest, and I warrant anyone would've done the same in that blizzard. There now, you doubting Thomases, just look ahead and you'll spy the most beautiful waterfall you've ever seen."

We ran to the embankment, surveying the scene which was as delightful as Henri had described it.

"I found this spot years ago," Henri explained. "And never told a soul about it. You're the first I've taken here."

A delightful hour passed as we frolicked in that hidden oasis. The boys were thrilled with Henri's teasing, and even shy Sam warmed to his charm. I was relieved he showed no undue attention toward me, until I emerged from the water. Believing he was stirred by my wet slip immodestly clinging to me, I rushed for cover, but soon discovered his attention was directed toward the leeches covering my legs.

"Get them off of me!" I cried, jumping up and down.

"Quit moving," Emmett directed, as he tried to examine them with his magnifying glass.

Scraping off the gooey creatures, Henri said, "They don't actually suck much blood. In fact, Mia, you, should appreciate their medicinal benefits. Shall I collect some for you to take home?"

"Heavens, no!" I cried with relief when the last one was removed. I'd barely recovered my senses when Sam screamed at the water's edge. To my horror, I found his foot showed the telltale mark of a snakebite.

"It was a large one," Emmett noted with concern. "You can tell by the spacing between the fang marks. The older they are the more venom they can inject."

Henri scooped Sam up in his arms, and we all ran back to the wagon. Seeing Sam's foot and leg double in size, and him vomiting, made me want to panic. However, years of training with Miss Emily taught me to be calm and act quickly in a crisis. Purple coneflower, the most potent remedy for snakebite, was growing plentifully along the trail, and I pulled it up, careful to keep the root intact.

Henri whipped the horses into a lather, and with the wagon jostling us, I found it difficult to force the bitter root upon my little brother. Trying to feign calmness, my trembling voice betrayed my fear. "Please Sam, you must take this, so you'll feel better."

He turned his head away, whimpering from the pain.

Hearing my distress, Henri said over his shoulder, "Mia, did you forget to put in the magic potion? You know, the one from the fairy kingdom. It's guaranteed to make him strong like me and able to catch turkeys next time we go hunting."

I marveled at Henri's natural ways with my brothers, and felt certain he must have grown up with younger siblings. "You're absolutely right, Henri. How could I have been so careless? Sam, I've added the magic potion, the sweet nectar from the flower nymphs."

It's uncertain whether Sam was pacified by our make-believe or only wanted to please Henri. Either way, he chewed the pungent remedy and sleepily begged for his favorite story. I'd told him of the circumstances surrounding his birth countless times before, but on this occasion when I feared he'd not survive the day, the telling held a painful poignancy I could hardly bare.

Cradling Sam in my arms, I began, "It starts with Mamma and Pappa and the love they had for each other. They were already very happy with their daughter and two sons, but when Mamma realized she was going to have another baby, she couldn't contain her joy. Pappa began right away to build a rocking horse for you, the one in the playroom with the real horse hair, and Mamma started sewing your christening gown. She was an excellent seamstress."

"I don't think I remember Mamma," Sam whispered plaintively.

"Well, she was a very beautiful woman who loved us with all her heart. She enjoyed nothing better than taking care of her family and home. Blue was her favorite color, which she often wore. She said she liked it because it was the color of Pappa's eyes, and yours too."

"But then she died," Christian said sadly.

I wiped away my tears. "Yes, when Sam was very young, she died. We were all desperate without her, and cried for a long time."

Doubting me, Emmett asked, "Are you sure Pappa cried?"

Listening to the story, Henri replied, "Men who are brave are not afraid to cry."

With each tender remark, my estimation of Henri grew, and I became convinced his flirting and brash jokes hid his true character.

I continued, "Pappa was most grievous and did cry, for he was at a loss as to how he'd get along without Mamma. He even considered taking us to Grandmother and Grandfather Stein's home for them to help raise us, but an extraordinary thing happened that very night. A flame appeared in the sky, so bright you could read a book by its light, and for the next several days it was visible during the day. Pappa called it Mamma's Comet. You know he isn't church going, but he took it as a sign of encouragement from Mamma to raise us kids by himself."

Sam weakly rasped, "Am I going to go see Mamma now?"

"No, of course not," I sobbed. "I promise you'll get well."

Several hours passed before I knew with certainty whether my words were said in truth. With Miss Emily's help, Sam survived and was resting peacefully late that night when Henri took his leave.

"Thank you," I said to Henri, as we stood on the porch. "You were wonderful with my brothers today. Especially when Sam wouldn't take the medicine."

"I love children," he said sincerely. "But I believe you didn't expect that of me."

"Today you revealed much about your character, I'd not previously suspected."

"I'm glad you approve of these revelations, but I don't want you to think too good of me."

Forcibly he pressed me against the house, and kissed me. I stiffened, trying to push him off, but the more I resisted, the more he was aroused. I knew Pappa was just inside the house, and one scream for help would bring him to my side, and yet I couldn't bring myself to do it.

Suddenly releasing me, Henri strode down the stairs. "You give me extraordinary pleasure, my little Mia. It will be difficult to leave you for so long. You see, I'm going on a little voyage to England on Saturday."

Surprised, I asked, "On the *Isabella Teague?*"

"You think of your friend Daniel Biggs, oui? My path will no doubt cross with that gentleman's. In fact, I will make certain it does."

CHAPTER XIX

COOKING UP A STORM

*S*leepless nights passed as I imagined the crossing of the *Isabella Teague*. Against prevailing winds, the ship would take twenty days to reach England during which time Daniel and Henri were fellow passengers. The two letters that eventually arrived for me only furthered my distress over their meeting.

My Sweet Little Mia,

An ocean separates us, but each night when I lay down weary to bed, I imagine your sweet lips and embrace. You stir a passion in me which I thought was long dead. I can hardly wait to hold you close again.

The crossing proved intriguing and fruitful in every manner, I'd hoped for. I've spun my web and caught the proverbial fly. Let us hope he does not escape. I end on a note of warning. Be wary dear girl, things are not always as you imagine.

Kisses, Henri

P.S. Pray do not run off and marry that chieftain.

Henri was seductive as always, placing the stamp upside down in the left hand corner as a secret way of saying, "I love you". Any doubt I may have fostered as to the identity of the fly in his web was cleared in the next letter, which was from Daniel.

My Dear Mia,

I hope this letter finds you and your family well and happy. The voyage itself was uneventful other than a dreadful case of seasickness, which I'd fully expected. As I confessed previously, I'm no sailor.

London is filled with excitement over the Crystal Palace's construction. It will be the centerpiece of the Great Exhibition in Hyde Park. It's a giant iron and glass conservatory, which will hold thirteen thousand exhibits from around the world. Queen Victoria herself plans to open it the first of May.

I'll visit my country estate next week, and see to work on long overdue repairs. I'm giving my caretaker directions to prepare the soil for a garden in the event someone might want to plant herbs there next Spring.

I met an interesting Frenchman aboard ship, and we've become fast friends. He's taken up lodging near me, and insists I show him a bit of London. I'll indulge the chap only a little, for my focus must remain on the unpleasant matter at hand and returning to you as quickly as possible.

Mia, I leave for last the words that are foremost in my mind at all times. From the moment I left your side, thoughts of you have practically torn me asunder. I can only say that I hope one day you'll understand why there was such need and urgency for this undertaking, and how it will impact the future we may share together.

Your devoted one,

Daniel

The charm and romanticism in each letter moved me exceedingly, as did their hints at gloom and mystery. How I wondered could Daniel's voyage abroad influence our future happiness, and was Henri motivated to follow because of his position at the Customs House or was it a crazed act of jealousy? I felt a puzzle lay before me, but without all the pieces I couldn't put it together.

Soon after their departure, I began receiving nosegays of lavender. I assumed Daniel had arranged for their delivery after I'd said they were a favorite of my mother's and mine. However, when I smelt the bouquet I recalled their fragrance was strong inside Mosswood's hidden chamber, and the beautiful flowers now held an ominous foreboding.

After I'd received the letters and bouquets, the days of Daniel and Henri's absence passed at a snail's pace. I kept busy tending patients, seeing Miss Emily, and running the house, but no matter my occupation, my mind kept returning to the two men across the ocean.

One night late in the hour when I felt at my wits end, I went to the kitchen to cook vegetable pies for the next day. Little time passed before I was disturbed by the whinnying of a horse outside. Pitch black with no moonlight, I could barely make out a pony and rider at the corner. The animal was straining at his bit as the rider deliberated in which direction to proceed. After several minutes of circling, their course was chosen, and they headed directly to our chicken coop. Certain it was Rita up to more of her Voodoo mischief, I picked up a nearby shovel, and steeling my nerves I went forth to confront her. Stealthily moving from tree to tree, I was but a few feet away from the figure when they dismounted from the pony. It was obvious at this distance the rider was indeed a woman, but a hooded cloak concealed her identity.

With shovel raised high, I warned them, "Stop right where you are, or else you shall suffer bodily harm!"

"Well, isn't that a novel way to greet a visitor?"

The tart British accent most assuredly identified Rachael Rothschild.

"What on earth are you doing here at this hour?"

"I've not seen you in ages, and with Daniel gone, it gets lonely in that big old house. The scoundrel hasn't even written a word to me, but I suppose he must be dreadfully detained with business, otherwise I'm certain he would've sent word."

My hand went instinctively to Daniel's letter in my apron pocket, which I kept on my person at all times. "Does your Aunt Edna know you're out on your own?"

"Heavens no!" she answered with alarm. "Auntie is in the midst of one of her fits and doesn't know what's up or down. I'm afraid we've had to lock her up again. Though I hate doing it and loath to hear her cries, it's necessary for her own safety."

"I'm sorry to hear that, Rachael, I know it must be distressing. Come in and we'll talk in the kitchen, if you don't mind. I'm in the middle of making pies."

Removing her cape, she said with disdain, "An odd place to receive a visitor. I've never even been in the kitchen at Mosswood. Do you make bubble and squeak? I suppose not, it being an English specialty. It's simply delicious with beef and cabbage. Haven't eaten any since leaving home, though I've tried countless times to explain it to our cook."

"Why don't you make it yourself?" I asked knowing full well her response.

"Me?" Rachael laughed haughtily.

Ignoring her reaction, I handed her an apron with the instruction, "You can cut the oil into the flour while I chop the vegetables."

Rachael replied, "You must be kidding, this is my best silk dress, and these are real ostrich feathers. I wore it when my portrait was painted!"

"That's what the apron is for," I said, continuing on with my work.

"If I make a mess of myself, I'll never forgive you," she pouted.

I continued with further directions as Rachael fumbled to accomplish the most simple tasks, which even Sam could have done. Eventually she began to show an earnestness in her efforts, and she asked, showing pride, "Have I worked the flour enough?"

"Almost," I said encouragingly. "Cut it until all the clumps are gone and the flour resembles small peas."

"Mia, this is much more fun than I'd ever imagined it to be, though I'd be shamed if anyone but you saw me doing it. You know you're my very best friend and I get ever so jealous when you speak of Miss Emily. You think me the fool and that my concerns for my appearance are frivolous, but I'm not strong and good like you, though I want to be."

Her sincerity touched me, as they were the very sentiment I'd expressed to my mother when I was a child. I offered her similar advice I'd received, "To have a fruitful and happy life, I think we must have a goal each day, something to accomplish and feel good about ourselves. You seem to like cooking, so why not do it at Mosswood. You can even make that ... What was that funny dish called, bubble and squeak?"

We giggled at the funny name, and continued to work alongside each other as congenially as I imagined two sisters would.

"Why are you putting your arm in the oven?" she asked in alarm.

"It's how I judge its temperature," I explained. "If I can bare the heat to the count of twenty, then I know it's a moderate oven and suitable for cooking these pies."

Bending over to put the pies in, Daniel's letter slipped from my pocket onto the floor. Without hesitation, Rachael snatched up the missive, and after an unflattering tug of war, she picked up a poker and kept me at bay as she perused its contents.

"You wretched two-faced, lying thief," she cried with a dark malignancy contorting her features. "Yes, you are truly a thief, for you have stolen my heart's desire. The one man I've always loved and wanted to spend the rest of my life with. How could you be so deceitful, pretending to be my friend when all the while setting a snare for *my* Daniel."

"You had no right to read my letter, nor accuse me of stealing something you never truly had."

"You know very well, I've been promised to Daniel since we were but children. You need to recognize that fact, and see the situation for what it is. Daniel is surely trifling with your affections and the sooner you realize this, the less embarrassment you'll suffer in the end."

With her words hitting a nerve, I shot back in anger, "You should know Daniel has asked me to marry him."

"I don't believe it," she hollered back. "He would never ask a woman to be his wife who is so plainly below his station in life, and his father, Captain Biggs, would never give his blessing to such an obscene union."

Having suffered Rachael's insults one too many times, I pushed her to the floor and proceeded to pull every one of the ostrich plumes from her bodice. It was a childish thing to do, and one I immediately regretted as soon as my emotions cooled.

Jumping to her feet, Rachael grabbed the sack of flour from the table and hurled it at me. "There! That's what I really think of cooking! It's a servant's job, not mine, and mark my words, Daniel will marry *me* not you."

With woeful wails, she fled from the kitchen, leaving me shaken and sorry for the whole incident.

"Is the coast clear?" Emmett asked, poking his head into the kitchen.

"Have you been listening long?"

"Long enough to discover you're engaged to the son of Captain Biggs, the one man our father despises and has warned us against our whole life. How could you betray Pappa's trust like this?"

"Before you hang me out to dry, at least allow me to defend myself. Yes, I've frequented Mosswood on numerous occasions, but the infamous captain has been abroad, and I've never even met the man. As for Rachael, you can reckon by the scene you just witnessed that I'm safe from any future interaction with her. And Daniel has asked me to marry him, but I've not given him an answer. Truthfully, I don't know what I'll say to him, and for now I need not worry, for he's an ocean's length away from me in England."

My brother grabbed the broom and began sweeping up the flour. "I still think you should tell Pappa about all of this. I never took you for one to give untruths."

"Nor has it been part of my character in the past, but for the present, I pray we may keep this between ourselves? More than anything I need time to consider my situation and sort out my feelings for Daniel. He's truly a wonderful person who I can imagine making a life with, but if Pappa finds out, he'll forbid me ever seeing him again. For the sake of love, will you not guard my secret?"

Emmett shrugged an agreement, and I gave him the biggest hug he would allow.

CHAPTER XX

THE GRAVEYARD ENCOUNTER

All Hallow's Eve arrived and as was customary, the boys and I headed for our attic in search of the perfect costume. Only part of the third floor was fitted out for Emmett's bedroom, while the rest remained unfinished, smelling musty of outgrown baby clothes and our mother's moth eaten gowns. The treasures we sought were stuffed in old steamer trunks, once belonging to Pappa's parents. The chest baring their initials and an undecipherable phrase in German was the the only evidence they existed.

"Isn't this the shirt Pappa wore in the Battle of San Jacinto?" I asked holding up the ragged garment.

Emmett nodded. "Fancy he holds onto that, but won't breath a word about his part in the fight."

"I think that's blood on it," Christian said cheerily. "He must've killed a lot of fellows. Probably with a bayonet or maybe carved them up with a bowie knife."

"That's not something to gloat about," I scolded. "Hundreds of men lost their lives that day, and it was surely an awful thing to be a part of."

Raising an old pirate shirt, Emmett said, "I remember this one that Mamma made. Looks like it's Sam's size now. What do you think little brother, do you want to be a pirate this year?"

Sam looked skeptical, pointing out a tear in a sleeve.

"That adds to its authenticity," I said, tying a bandanna around his head. "All pirates are in sword fights or perhaps stranded on an island for awhile, and their clothes get tattered just like this one."

"Can I have that dagger?" Christian asked, pushing his spectacles up.

"Only if you promise to not run with it or poke people," I warned.

Christian and Sam scampered off with a handful of props to play make-believe while Emmett and I picked through the remains.

Emmett confessed, "I don't know what to dress up as this year. Do you think we're too old for such nonsense?"

"Never," I said, ripping out the hem of the pirate pants. "Pappa always wears a costume, and Miss Emily promised to dress up too. I'm going as a sorceress with a black gown and pointed hat, and I'll make magic potions for everyone to drink."

Emmett laughed, "And how is that different, Sister, from any other day?"

Our hurricane lamp flickered as a cold wind blew through the cracks of the walls. Then a melody, lasting only a few notes, played from somewhere in the attic.

Spooked by the music, Emmett whispered, "It came from over there."

Before we even found it in the bottom of a chest, we'd guessed the metallic sounding notes were from a music box.

"Strange how it started playing on its own," I said.

"No doubt a change in barometric pressure," Emmett suggested. "The cooler weather and all."

I rolled my eyes. "Science is your answer to every unknown phenomena."

"And yours is always the supernatural. I suppose you think it's Mamma contacting us from the world beyond."

I said in my best ghost voice, "All Hallow's Eve *is* when the spirits of the dead return to walk the earth."

My brother blew a thick layer of dust off the box. "I wonder why Pappa has this up here? It looks like he might have made it."

By dinner time, the house was decorated with paper lanterns and ghoulish will-o'the-wisps. We were all in our costumes, and the plan was for Sam to jump out as a pirate and frighten Miss Emily upon her arrival. Our guest, dressed as a gypsy in colorful scarf and golden bangles at her wrists, didn't disappoint us as she let out a blood curdling scream. Then, setting down the basket of goodies she'd brought, she daintily fainted on the porch. It was the reaction my brothers hoped for.

Christian knowingly nodded his turbaned head, "It happened just as I foresaw."

Pappa, dressed as a Knight of the Lone Star, carried our damsel in distress to the parlor couch.

Even Sam knew Miss Emily was pretending, but he squealed with delight nonetheless.

"We gave you a fright, didn't we?" Christian crowed, jumping up and down.

Miss Emily's eyes fluttered as if slowly regaining consciousness. "Yes, indeed, I can hardly catch my breath. And I's much obliged to this knight for his gallant rescue. Everyone looks mighty fine in their costumes. Emmett who are you dressed up as? Is that one of your pa's suits?"

Emmett took an imaginary puff from his pipe, "Professor Gall from Vienna, Ma'am. You may recognize my name as the leading expert in phrenology."

"Phrenology?" we asked in unison.

Emmett wiggled his fake mustache, "Scientific study of the bumps on a person's head, of course."

"Cockamamie!" Christian exclaimed.

"I see we have a skeptic in our midst. Young man, allow me to read your skull first, so I may prove my abilities."

Removing his turban, Christian offered, "Gladly, Professor, but keep in mind, I've fallen down a lot and wasn't born with all my bumps."

After removing his gloves, Emmett ran his fingers over Christian's head. "You see, the brain is made up of thirty or so organs, each responsible for a single trait. This enlarged bump near your right temple indicates a musical inclination."

"Exhibit A, the pianoforte," Christian countered. "Tell me something you didn't already know."

"You have a temper," Emmett continued.

"Again, no revelation," Pappa laughed.

Emmett tried again, "I've detected something unusual at the base of your skull. It's a definitive manifestation of a tender heart. However, the bump nearby it, discloses you'll do anything to keep this trait hidden. Christian, my diagnosis is that you're a living paradox."

Christian pulled his turban back on, "Complete hogwash, Professor!"

Emmett crossed his arms. "You've just proven my diagnosis. By immediately denying the existence of your tender heart, you attempt to keep it hidden. Now, I'll read Mia's head."

"If you must," I said resignedly, though in truth, I loved our family's silly games.

"Hmm, quite interesting," Emmett began. "I'm detecting an unusual formation in the top right lobe, signifying an overabundance of conscientiousness, while the middle front portion of the head reveals a streak of curiosity and daring. These traits generally balance each other, however it appears your daring part can easily become dominant if and when the heart is involved. I'm referring to romance."

I suspected Emmett was warning me against my association with the Biggs Family, and didn't appreciate being taken to task in front of an audience.

"A good conscience, I believe, but daring?" Pappa asked. "That doesn't sound like my Mia."

"Come now, it's time to eat," I said, eager to end the charade. "What did you bring, Miss Emily?"

"Chicken feet soup and chitlins," she answered.

"Would that be trick or treat?" Pappa teased.

Miss Emily playfully pulled Pappa's beard. "Why it's a treat, you rascal."

"I made my fortune bread," I said, baring the basket to the table.

"All Hallow's Eve wouldn't be complete without it," Pappa said as we sat down to dinner.

"And be careful not to break a tooth," I warned. "I've hidden three charms in it."

Everyone tore eagerly into their piece of bread. Sam was first to find a coin, which portended of a wealthy future.

"I'll take that," Christian said, grabbing the penny.

Miss Emily scolded, "Give that right back to your brother. It won't do you any good to take it, as you got to find it in your own piece for the magic to work."

"I've found the brass ring," Pappa said, sheepishly.

"Pappa's gonna get married," Christian taunted. "Is it Miss Penelope, we'll be calling Mamma?"

Miss Emily teased, "Yes, Klaus, will you be jumping the broom with Miss Penelope soon?"

I recalled their encounter I'd overheard on washday, and knew they had strong feelings for each other, but if my father suffered prejudice because of marrying my Mexican mother, I couldn't imagine the scandal if he wed Miss Emily.

Emmett gave me a side glance. "Mia, I thought you would've gotten the ring."

"Nope, I've found the wishbone," I said, knowing my only wish was to know which man I truly loved.

We had a wonderful evening with a treasure hunt and bobbing for apples. Christian played songs on the pianoforte, and we danced until we were too petered out to move. Emmett brought out the music box, we'd found in the attic, and we listened to it several times.

When the clock struck nine, we were sad to see Miss Emily leave, but knew she shouldn't stay longer. Slaves had a curfew when they weren't allowed on the streets without written permission from their masters, and though Miss Emily had her freedom, it wasn't prudent to flaunt it.

Pappa grabbed Miss Emily's cloak. "Of course I'll accompany you safely home," he said. "And Mia, I want you to lock up while I'm gone. I'll take my key, so don't wait up for me."

Perplexed, I said, "But, Pappa, in all my days, I've never known us to lock the doors."

"I didn't want to scare you, but a convict escaped from that prison they set up last year in Huntsville. It's a piece from here, but he might think to come South to take a steamer to Galveston."

"What's he sent up for?" Emmett asked.

Pappa hesitatingly answered, "Murder."

As I tucked Christian and Sam into bed, they begged me to tell a scary story.

"Haven't we had enough fright for one night?" I said, blowing out the lantern.

Though Sam pulled his blanket tight to his chin, he insisted I proceed.

"Only a short one then, and I don't want to hear complaints tomorrow morning about you two having nightmares."

"We won't," they promised.

I began, "Once there was a man who everyone was afraid of. He lived in a magnificent house with stained glass windows and lush gardens surrounding it. He was a man of immense wealth, but the source of his money was unknown because he was never seen during the day at any occupation. Only with the cloak of darkness did he venture out, appearing as a shadowy figure on some evil pursuit."

"Was he a vampire?" Christian asked.

"No, but he was not like you or me, for he had no need for company or family. His name was Captain B. and he spent much of his time sailing the Seven Seas aboard his ship. It was during one of these voyages, when his ear was bit off by a, uh..."

"A shark," Sam offered.

"Yes, that's right. It was a shark."

At this point in my gruesome tale, a crow landed outside the window and cawed loudly.

"That's a bad omen, isn't it?"" Christian asked.

A chill ran up my spine. "They say it means a death will soon visit the house."

"Mia, I'm scared," Sam cried.

"Oh you ninny baby," Christian chided. "Come on, Mia, tell us the rest of the story."

"I'd better not say anymore. I've scared you two enough."

Sam declared he too wanted the rest of the story, and so I continued, "One day a woman was hired by the captain to do his cooking. She never saw him directly, but was instructed by letters that he left in the kitchen. His directions included a strict warning to never stray beyond the confines of the house's west wing. However, after finding a bundle of keys, which the captain had forgotten on the kitchen table, the cook's curiosity proved too strong. One stormy night when lightning filled the sky and the rain came down in sheets, she heard her master leave the house, and so took the opportunity to investigate the forbidden rooms. She wandered the maze-like halls until she came to a library. Never having seen so many books in her whole life, she was drawn to study one after another, but when she pulled a large book, the entire bookcase moved, revealing a hidden chamber behind it and a most horrific sight beyond."

I paused for dramatic effect.

"Go on, what was in there?!" they pleaded.

"There hanging from the rafters was the bloody body of a woman, or rather the partial body. Next to her were tables with an ear and a nose on it, and piles of jewelry laid out beside the bloody heap."

Christian exclaimed, "He killed people and that's how he got his money, but why does he keep the body parts?"

"Hold your britches on, I'm getting to that point," I continued. "When the cook saw this carnage, she let out a scream, bringing Captain B. to her side, for he had already returned from his nocturnal wanderings. Her master, who was always concealed by his hooded cloak, now let it fall away. It revealed a horribly disfigured face, eaten off by that hungry shark."

"So, he used the body parts to make a new face, just like Frankenstein," Christian said.

"Exactly, but now, our poor frightened cook was in mortal danger. The monster before her was wielding a bloody hatchet, thankfully she was quick on her feet and escaped despite his pursuit. The captain had lost all sense of precaution, and running after her into the streets, was soon in custody. He'd still be in the penitentiary if not for running away tonight."

Christian wailed, "Oh, Mia, is this true? Is the escaped convict Captain B.?"

"No, silly, I just made this whole thing up."

I knew I'd gone too far weaving my fears and suspicions of Captain Biggs into my story and scaring my brothers. To comfort them, I passed the next hour at their bedside regaling tales of friendly fairies and magic dust. They both drifted into peaceful slumber, but reaching my own bedchamber, I found my own sleep elusive.

The questions, which were tiny naggings during the day, became magnified by the silence of our house. I longed to know the circumstance surrounding my mother's death, but the answers were locked away as securely as her lavender scented bedchamber. I also wanted to know the depth of the secret relationship, which my father and Miss Emily were involved in. A hidden chamber was in the depths of Mosswood, and I couldn't comprehend its meaning or the kind of man who frequented it. I feared Daniel was tied to his father's dark life, and his trip to England was somehow related. Henri was warning me against the Biggs family, but I wondered if it was merely an act of jealousy. I was even suspecting that Henri was stalking me, as he apparently was Daniel.

I hated admitting Emmett's opinion of my personality was dead on, but I *was* curious and daring, and drawn to more and more reckless adventures. On that All Hallow's Eve, I locked the door as Pappa instructed, however, I stood not in the safety of my home, but on the porch in the cold night air. Believing my mother's spirit was more accessible than at any other time, I determined to visit her grave that very night. If no one was willing to reveal the truth to me, perhaps she would.

I pulled the wool cloak tightly around me, but it did nothing to allay my fears. It was a moonless night and an eerie caterwauling pierced the silence as neighborhood cats called for their mates. All Hallow's Eve was a night of folly and mayhem, a time especially unsuitable for a woman to wander the streets unescorted. I passed a youthful group toppling an outhouse, and several men noticeably worse for drink, but no one seemed to notice me. When I finally reached First City Cemetery, all the creepy stories I'd ever heard of ghosts rising from their graves came back to me. Despite my rising fears, I made my way through the high grass to the old oak where Mamma was buried. Francesca Stein, her tombstone read, born eighteen fifteen, died eighteen forty-five.

Kneeling down, I said, "Mamma, I never realized before that you were only thirty when you died. That's so very short a life to have on this earth. How I wish you were still here, for we all need you so desperately. Emmett is growing up into a fine young man. Pappa and I rely on him, more each day. Sometimes his head is in the clouds, but it's only because he contemplates his subjects so deeply. Christian is a rascal, but a good boy at heart. He's a sharp-shooter at marbles and an expert bicycle rider. Sam is a darling child, and though he has no memories of you, I think he misses you most. There's something keeping him from talking, and it's more than just shyness. He needs a mother's love, and though I do my best, I fear it's not enough. And Pappa..."

I couldn't bring myself to mention my father and Miss Emily, and so continued, "I know he never stops missing and loving you."

A lunar moth lit nearby, its eyed wings winking at me. I felt it was a sign that my mother understood everything in my heart.

"As for myself, I'm losing my way. There are two men who proclaim their love for me. Daniel is good and kind, and would be the ideal husband, but Pappa might never accept him, considering his father is Captain Biggs. And Henri, a close friend of Pappa's, is impetuous and passionate, but perhaps too old for me. I don't understand any of this, and wish you were here to guide me. Please tell me what to do, or at least give me some sort of sign."

My heart stopped as the cemetery gate squeaked open and a shadowy figure entered. It seemed to float through the cemetery until reaching a large headstone with a carved angel standing beside it. The figure collapsed and began to wail, leaving no doubt it was a grieving woman. Her body rocked, and she lamented, "Hear me, oh Lord, as I lift up my hands toward the heavens, beseeching your mercy!"

I imagined she was a specter of my mother responding to my beckoning pleas, but the croaky voice revealed she was someone else.

"Cora Hornsby?" I asked, moving towards her.

Her misery was so profound, she failed to acknowledge my presence, and continued to rack her frail body with violent sobbing. She'd always appeared to me as cold and hard, critical in word and action, but now she was but a shell of a person, desperate for help. Feeling words of sympathy were hollow balm, I embraced her, and she held on as if to never let go.

She opened the broach always pinned at her neck, and reverently revealed five curly locks nestled within. To my undiscerning eye there was no variation amongst them. However, Cora's undying maternal love easily identified them.

"This is Jack Henry, he was my first to die. These are the twins Nora and Charlotte, only lasted a few days. Then came William, who lived for almost a year until a fever took him. Little Marie was another stillborn, as was my last child, Edgar. Some folks don't name the ones that don't live, but in my reckoning that's sinful."

She continued to lament, "I still remember how all my babies smelt, sweet like clothes after they've hung in the sun to dry. Sometimes my dreams are so real that I can feel their tiny fingers holding tightly onto my hand, but then God snatches them away from me. I wake up and my breasts are full and aching, and I beseech Him, why? I humbly do His work, and then He strikes my innocent babes down. He's punishing me, and I can't stand it. I want my babies!"

Cora fell into another fit of sobbing until eventually she was spent. We were sitting together in silence, me holding her as if she were a child, when a gang of slaves entered the graveyard. They were a rowdy bunch, hooting and hollering as they made their way to the hanging tree. Pappa had pointed out to me the old willow, where in years past, criminals met their death at the end of a rope. By the light of the moon, the Spanish moss hanging from the branches resembled hair of the condemned.

Cowering behind the tombstone, Cora whimpered, "Lordy, Lordy, what are those heathens up to?"

I noticed Captain Biggs' favorite slave, Rita, was dressed in flowing robes and painted face. I warned, "Cora, we'd best keep quiet."

Ulysses, the butler at Mosswood, drew a bow across the teeth of a handsaw, while others beat drums and rattled gourds. Together they created a haunting tune, as Rita, apparently the high priestess, ceremoniously drew the same symbol on the ground with cornmeal as she had on my chicken coop floor.

Cora's eyes grew wide with fright, "Heaven help us, they be doing Voodoo, the Devil's work."

I pointed out, "It's a forbidden practice, one they'd be beaten or jailed for. Who knows what they might do if they knew we were watching."

Rita sang out, "Damballah, father of all spirits. He who carries on his back our ancestors to the world beyond. Come to me tonight with your white light and give me your strength. I swear on my master's head, I'll do your bidding."

As if possessed, Rita's eyes rolled back in her head, and she swayed to the music like an undulating snake. The others joined her in the dance, chanting, "Damballah, Damballah."

Hissing and flickering her tongue, Rita withdrew a rooster from a burlap bag. She swung it over her head, and with a ferocious chop of a machete, beheaded the squawking animal. Butchering a chicken was an everyday occurrence, but what happened next will forever haunt me. The slaves reveled in the spurting blood, smearing it over their bodies, and crying in ecstasy.

Hours passed before they left the graveyard and we were free to move our stiffened limbs. No matter what had happened between us in the past, Cora and I had endured a terrifying night together, and were forever bonded.

CHAPTER XXI

THE BATTLE

ate November brought our first norther, and with it warmth became as illusive as our sense of security. Pappa had taken to his bed, weeks before with a catarrh, which quickly settled in his chest. Though he hated being treated like an invalid, his debilitating fevers made him too weak to protest our setting him up in the front parlor, where it was warmest in the house. In moments of lucidity, he counseled us in finance and the running of his furniture store, despite our assurances he'd be up and about soon.

We tried, each in our own way, to comfort him. Christian played songs on the pianoforte softer than I'd thought him possible to achieve. Sam shared nature's treasures that he found each day, like a hawk's feather or an empty nest. Emmett built Pappa a bed tray on wheels, which moved easily over the bed and facilitated the serving of his meals. Miss Emily and I cooked his favorite dishes, and treated him with every known remedy, but all of our tender attentions did nothing to halt the progress of his illness.

One night when he was too weak to raise his head, Pappa croaked, "Where's the Texas Telegraph? I want you to read the obituaries to me."

I asked incredulously, "Obituaries at a time like this? Pappa, let me instead find an uplifting passage of poetry or an engrossing novel to amuse you."

"Please, Mia, just do as I ask."

Unable to deny his pathetic appeal, I obliged him. "Wilson T. Lightfoot is listed fist. Says he was a defendant of the Republic at the Battle of San Jacinto, and will be put to rest on his family plantation in Fort Bend County."

"A fine soldier," Pappa said. "As you'll recall his brother William fought and died at the Alamo. Anyone else of note mentioned?"

"I believe you knew Horace Baldwin. He died yesterday in Galveston, and they'll be bringing his remains to Houston for burial."

"A good mayor in his time. Mia, promise me you'll keep my funeral a simple affair; a pine box laid beside your mother, and under no circumstance will I allow preachers."

I shuddered at the casual discourse of his death. "Pappa, don't talk of such things, you're not dying. More rest and steam inhalations are what you need. Miss Emily and I are going to try you on a new regimen of herbs that will surely bring back the color to your cheeks."

Disregarding my cheery prognosis, he stated, "A man knows when it's his time to leave this earth, and I'm not fearing it. Though if I had my druthers, I'd pick a few years later when I've seen my children full grown."

With tears running down my cheeks, I rushed to his bedside and buried my face against his shoulder. I wasn't ready for this reversal of roles. I'd thought previously I was of an independent mind, ready for adulthood, but feeling my one parent slip away, I realized I still wanted and needed my father's protection.

Lifting my chin up, he said proudly, "I admire how you've taken care of all of us. I know it's been unfair to you, having to take on the running of the house, but you've done right good by it, and your mother would be awfully proud. Come now, stop your balling. Go and get your brothers in here. There's something I want to tell them while I still can."

Testing his feverish forehead, I objected, "Pappa, you've already exerted yourself far too much."

Gathering his strength, he pulled himself onto his elbows, and declared sternly, "Mia, there may not be another time. Please fetch them for me."

Sensing the solemnity of the moment, my brothers timidly entered the room, however, with Pappa's coaxing, they gathered round him on the bed. I expected him to deliver sage advice on how we should conduct ourselves in future, but instead he began to tell a story of his past. It was a tale that despite our appeals, he'd never revealed before, and so we hung on his every word, anxious to retain it all.

He began haltingly, "As you know, my family was part of the first group of Americans to settle in Texas. Back then it was part of Mexico and was called Tejas."

"Stephen F. Austin's Colony, the Old Three Hundred," Christian pointed out proudly.

Pappa nodded, "That's right, son. We arrived in twenty-eight and at first all our efforts were focused on just surviving. We built a pole cabin and got our first crops in. As time passed and our colony became established, the Mexican government and its influence felt diminished. The settlers started feeling discontented with their situation, wanting their own representation and to make Tejas a separate state within Mexico. The Mexican government rejected our proposals and began applying restrictions upon us. They increased tariffs on imported goods, and rescinded our ten year exemption from taxes. They'd always outlawed slavery, but now they enforced it, ordering all slaves to be freed. Considering most everyone relied on their labor, especially the cotton plantations, the new regulations weren't taken lightly.

Drawn into the tale, I said, "I'd think you'd agree with the Mexicans, you being against slavery."

"Of course, Mia," Pappa nodded. "It's why I was torn from the word go, as to whose side I was on. My family came to Tejas knowing we'd become Mexican citizens."

Emmett scratched his head, "Then who can blame the Mexicans for imposing their laws? The Texians were invited guests thumbing their noses at their hosts."

"Yes, and these invited guests were outnumbering Mexican born citizens of Tejas, three to one. Fearful of our increased population, further immigration was prohibited, which in turn only made the Texians madder." Pappa took a long draft of water, then continued, "I was content with my life as it was, but my attitude wasn't well received within my family or the colony."

"Did they make you leave?" Christian asked.

My father sighed, "Let's say I felt it time for a journey. At twenty-two I was restless and had always wanted to see San Antonio de Bexar. It was the largest Spanish settlement in Tejas, and the missions along the river were of interest."

Disbelieving my ears, I asked, "Pappa, are you saying you were a practicing Catholic?"

He answered sheepishly, "It was a requirement for Mexican citizenship, which I took to heart at the time. Anyways, I was visiting Mission San Jose when I saw a young woman kneeling in prayer, her long black braid hanging down her back. When she stood up to leave, I noticed her eyes were red from weeping, and so concerned, I followed her."

"Was it Mamma?" I asked with growing interest.

His smile was affirmation enough.

"And why was she crying?" Emmett asked.

Noticeably squirming at my brother's question, Pappa side-stepped it, and continued, "She was a shy thing, actually fearful of me in the beginning, but she came to see I had only honorable intentions towards her. She revealed to me that her father had been a priest at Mission Jose, but had defrocked to marry her mother. Both her parents had recently died, and her older brother, Manuel was taking care of her."

Losing interest in the love story, Christian asked, "What about the settler's unrest? Had the battles begun yet?"

Pappa answered, "The first Anahuac Disturbances happened that summer, again over the issue of slavery."

"Please, I want to hear more about you and Mamma," I pleaded.

My father readily returned to his fond memories, saying, "We were desperately in love with each other, and thought of nothing else than to marry and share our lives together. We decided to make our home in San Antonio instead of returning to Austin's colony."

"Is that because your parents disapproved of your marriage?" I asked.

Pappa's voice broke with emotion, "Yes, because she was a Mexican, they refused to acknowledge her as my wife, and so I swore I'd never see them again. Please, let's not speak of them further when there's more pleasant things to consider. Those years were some of our happiest when our little family was first growing."

"But what of the revolution?" Emmett pressed. "How could there be any sense of content when there were rumblings of war all about you."

"You're right. We couldn't bury our heads in the sand when our livelihood became threatened. The Mexican Congress declared all American settlers who took up arms against the government were to be treated as pirates and shot. Many plantation owners were imprisoned for having slaves and for exporting crops to Europe. Rufus Price was one of them."

I was beginning to understand the circumstances in which prejudice against my mother was born.

"Is that when Santa Anna came?" Christian asked.

"He took quick action after the Texians forced Mexican soldiers out of the settlements east of San Antonio. It was the twelfth of February in thirty-six when six thousand of his soldiers crossed the Rio Grande. There were record low temperatures that day, bringing with it fifteen inches of snow."

"That's not fair, I've never even seen snow," Christian complained. "Or at least, not that I can remember."

Pappa continued, "It's pretty to look at from the warmth of your home or to frolic in for a few minutes, but to flee through it with little more than the clothes on your back and your family in hand, it is utter misery."

Pained by the revelation, Christian asked, "Pappa, you mean, you ran away from them?"

Defending himself, he said, "I had two small children, and your mother was pregnant with you. My thoughts were for my family's safety, besides, at that time I still didn't feel it was my fight. Everyone knows what happened when Santa Anna reached the city; a siege of the Alamo, and all defending Texians losing their life in battle. Santa Anna then went in hot pursuit of Sam Houston and the Texian armies."

"Where did we go?" I asked, trying to imagine the panic my parents must have been in.

Pappa wiped his fevered brow before answering, "Houston knew his men didn't have a chance against the larger Mexican armies, and so he ordered a retreat east towards the United States border. We, along with five thousand other settlers were swept up in what is called the Runaway Scrape. On the way, I stopped at my parents home, just south of Fort Bend. I know I just confessed to never wanting to see them again, but when I considered their lives were in peril, I felt it my duty to see after their safety. It turned out I was too late, for they, with the whole town, had already evacuated."

"I can't imagine how difficult that must have been for Mamma, her being with child," I said.

"I guess I was too young to remember a thing of it," Emmett complained.

"Not me," Christian teased. "I recall all that bumping around with lots of weeping and shouting going on."

Sam was completely enthralled with Pappa's recitation, and whispering to me, asked, "Then what happened next?"

Pappa carried on with his tale despite being completely worn out. "After traveling four days straight, I feared for your mother's health. A steamer called *The Yellow Stone* was taking families north up the Brazos to the states, and so I made the difficult decision to put you all on the boat, so I could join Houston's army."

Emmett acted surprised, "I'm confused. You said you thought the Americans should follow the Mexican laws, and that you didn't believe in what they were fighting for."

"Yes, but this was my home now, and it was either fight or die. I reasoned the Mexicans had taken the land from the Spaniards who in their turn had taken it from the Indians. And who knows what Indian tribes fought over it in the past. I began to think that whoever had the most power at the time were the owners."

The boys hooted with patriotic glee, but the storytelling was taking its toll on my father. "Pappa, hadn't you better take a rest for awhile. You can tell us more another night."

He shook his head, doggedly continuing, "For forty days we were on the move, scorching crops along the way, leaving nothing behind for the Mexican troops to plunder. They were always at our heels until Santa Anna made his first tactical error. He divided his forces into three columns, sending one to the coast, a second back to secure supply lines, and a third with him leading, continued to pursue us.

"Our troops were camping at where the San Jacinto River meets Buffalo Bayou when Santa Anna's men spotted us. They established their camp on the other side of a ridge, so close in fact, I could see their black flag flying. With reinforcements arriving, they had fourteen hundred men to our eight hundred. That night I didn't sleep a wink, and upon hearing their morning reveille, it felt like a calling of arms, but Sam Houston held back our attack until three-thirty that afternoon.

"With my belly full of the beaver we'd hunted the day before, I crawled across that muddy field, only to find the Mexicans sleeping. Our cannons, the Twin Sisters, were loaded with broken horseshoes and incited instant terror, as did our gunfire.

"Remember the Alamo! Remember Goliad!" we roared with vengeance.

"Me no Alamo, me no Goliad," the Mexicans cried in terror, but Santa Anna had shown no mercy to us, and we in turn would show none.

My father's rising emotions threw him into a violent coughing fit, so that I had to hold a bedpan to his chin as bloody spittle foamed from his mouth. I was entranced with the tale, but feared the price my father was paying by telling it. "Pappa, please you must rest now," I begged.

He motioned for a glass of water, then continued, "Just a little more. I'm almost finished."

"Wasn't Santa Anna in his tent with that mulatto slave?" Christian asked.

"The Yellow Rose of Texas is a myth," Emmett countered.

"She's real as you or I," Pappa said, clearing his throat. Looking off into the distance, his eyes welled as if seeing the scene depicted before him. "The Mexicans barely got a few shots off before we were on top of them. It was a slaughter of defenseless men, and though the battle lasted only eighteen minutes, the massacre continued till dark. Houston tried to control his men, but they were out of their minds with revenge. Six hundred and thirty Mexicans lost their lives while only nine Texians died."

"That's something to be proud of," Christian said.

"There's no honor in scalping men with tomahawks and leaving the bodies to the alligators," Pappa countered.

"All wars are terrible," Emmett said sympathetically. "But sometimes you just have to fight."

Pappa laid back into his pillow, spent from the telling.

"Would you fight that day again," I asked. "knowing it would create our great state of Texas?"

Pappa nodded and replied, "Yes, a hundred times over."

CHAPTER XXII

DEAR PAPPA

Pappa's storytelling depleted him of what little strength he'd had, so by nightfall he began slipping in and out of consciousness. I tented him with steamed mint and rubbed his chest with mustard to ease his labored breathing, but my efforts did little to bring about comfort.

Struggling to open his eyes, he mumbled, "Call Doc Abbott to come."

Taken aback by his request, I said, "But Miss Emily will be here soon enough."

"You two done your best, but desperate times require desperate measures. Abbott was a fine surgeon during the Republic, and I'm willing to hear what treatment he may offer. I fear..."

I continued to argue, "Then please allow me to get someone other than him. He's fully capable of treating broken bones and pulling teeth, but since losing his wife, he's turned to drink and his resulting poor judgment makes him a danger to his patients! This is not idle gossip, Pappa, but first hand testimony from many of the people, I see myself."

My father begged plaintively, "Please, Mia, do as I say, I've not the strength to argue."

Reluctantly I did as he requested, but when the doctor entered the room with his gait unsteady and breath stinking of cheap whiskey, I knew I should've refused.

His white bushy eyebrows wiggled like caterpillars as he poked and prodded the thin frame of Pappa, then motioning me to follow him into the hall, he asked sharply, "What nostrums have you used to treat this poor man? Do you not realize he has consumption?"

Though Miss Emily and I both feared this deadly prognosis, it was too frightful to actually say the word out loud. I resented his questioning my treatments and answered hotly, "Hyssop tea and mustard rubs make his cough more efficient, and yarrow aids his fever."

"Miss Stein, what nonsense are you talking? Coughs are to be suppressed and we must stop the fever, not aid it."

I defended myself by explaining, "Suppression is necessary only so far as to bring comfort to the patient. However, our lungs need to cough in order to rid themselves of foreign matter. The same holds true of a fever; too high and it does damage, but allowed to run its course, it will kill infection."

"With no training or license, you and that yellow slave are tramping around town treating folks with this kind of poppycock? It's criminal, I say."

With my hackles raised, I shot back, "It's a far cry better than poisoning patients with mercury and bleeding them to death. And now that we both know how each other feels, I think it best you leave."

The doctor was reaching for his bag when my father called us back into his room, whereupon I was forced to suffer the humiliation of Pappa telling me to hold my tongue and to let the doctor tend to his business. I watched helplessly as Doc Abbott cupped and bled, then dosed him with antimony. As he worked, he spoke of how fine a gentleman Pappa had been, and how every Texian owed him a thank you for his fighting at the Battle of San Jacinto. He praised his ability at pitching horseshoes, and said a finer piece of furniture would never be built by another. He spread lime to purify the room, then tipped his hat goodbye and demanded five dollars of me before leaving. I realized all his words of praise had been spoken as if Pappa's death was inevitable.

In the next few days, Miss Emily and I could no longer deny the critical condition Pappa was in. The citizens of our town called upon him, though none were allowed in his room due to the fear of contagion. Gentlemen from the barbershop stood in the hall, bringing news of politics and yarns of the good old days, while the ladies brought their casseroles and tender condolences. At first Pappa rallied at each encounter, forcing a smile and reassuring them all was well, but eventually the strain proved too much and we curtailed all visitors. It was difficult to turn away our good intentioned friends, especially Miss Penelope, who begged to keep a bedside vigil.

My most unexpected visitor was Rachael, who I'd not seen since tousling on the kitchen floor over Daniel. She stood on the porch with Ulysses waiting at her carriage. Nervously fiddling with her fur collar, she said, "I suppose you're surprised to see me after our disagreement, but after I heard your father was gravely ill, I believed our differences should be overlooked."

"I'm grateful for your visit," I said, swallowing back my tears. "Pappa is sleeping and can't accept visitors, but you can come in and sit in the back parlor with me."

Snatching a scented handkerchief to her nose, Rachael cringed, "Dear me, no, I can't tolerate being near sickness. My intention was only to bring you this basket of goodies. I've got a bottle of the captain's best port, and a tin of biscuits, I mean cookies. I actually baked them myself. Don't look so shocked, Mia. You told me I should learn to cook, and so I've taken your advice and actually enjoy it."

"I'm proud of you Rachael, and thank you for your thoughtfulness."

"You look very poorly, Mia. You need some rest. Aunt Edna says you should change your clothes often or better yet burn the whole kit and caboodle, lest you and your brothers come down with his consumption."

I bristled, saying, "We're taking all necessary precautions."

"I'm sure you know best," she said fidgeting. "Do you think he'll die soon? I've heard this condition can draw out for years or they can be gone in a few days. I know that's an awful thing to consider, but it's better to face facts as they are, so you can prepare yourself. If you haven't any black dresses to wear, I have plenty to loan you. I also have a lovely mourning broach."

I swallowed down the angry words that threatened to escape. Rachael meant well, but she couldn't have spoken any more ill-chosen words. I managed to reply, "He's not going to die."

Pappa's weak voice called out to me like a child.

"Oh my, is that your father? I'm sorry if I've woken him. I really wanted to do what was right this time. I'll let you get back to him. Don't forget the port, it shall probably benefit you more than him."

I sat down the basket on the hall-tree and rushed to Pappa's side. Agitated in the extreme, his eyes searched the room wildly. Familiar with that desperate look, I fetched the chamber pot, but was too late. He vomited on himself and the bedclothes, and though the acrid smell turned my stomach, I kept his head from falling into the mess. I comforted him as best I could, while he writhed with heaves. Finally a calm passed over him, and I changed his nightgown. It was shocking to see his ribs visible beneath his sallow skin.

With lifeless eyes, he cried, "I'm sorry."

"For what?"

"You seeing me sick and pathetic. It's not how a father should be."

I sponged his feverish brow. "Pappa, don't even consider that. It's an honor for me to take care of you."

Wiping away stray tears, he said, "You should know there's money hidden in the newel post. There'll be some expense in burying me and to get things settled, but the business is in good shape."

"Please, I beg you not to speak of these things."

Clutching his chest, he gasped, "Promise me the boys will keep up their schooling. And Sam... He needs extra attention if he's to overcome his difficulties. Mia, I know this is a lot to put on you."

"Just rest, Pappa. I'll take care of everything just as you want."

Gripping my arm, he demanded, "Where's my Emily, haven't seen her in days."

"But she was here this very morning, don't you remember? She had to leave to deliver a baby over in Frost Town, but she'll be back as soon as she's through."

Within the hour, Pappa took a turn for the worst; his pulse growing faint and his face turning ashen. I offered spoonfuls of broth to his parched lips, but he kept his teeth clenched, so that the nourishment he so badly needed, dribbled down his chin. Eventually, he succumbed to sleep, and I, completely exhausted, allowed myself to close my eyes and rest. I was soon lost in the same nightmare that had haunted me, my whole life. Standing in our parlor with black crepe shrouding its windows, I gazed upon a motionless young woman lying on a crisp white sheet. With trepidation, I moved towards the corpse and recognized it to be my mother. I rush to embrace her, but finding her flesh cold and rigid, I'm repelled. Her eyes that are sewn closed, rip open and stare up at me. Beseechingly, her shriveled fingers reach out and she strains to speak. Horrified, I scream and run away.

The nightmare shifts, and I find myself outside in a garden walking with my mother. Once again she is young and alive, and we giggle like girls and share confidences. Becoming confused and not knowing if she's real or a dream, I squeeze her hand, testing its solidity. "Mamma, tell me, are you dead or alive?"

I never hear her answer, for I'm awakened by Pappa thrashing in his bed and calling for my mother, "Francesca, please help me."

"It's me, Pappa, Mia. I'm right here. Everything is going to be alright. Be calm and the fever will pass."

Gnashing his teeth and pulling at his beard in delirium, he cried, "Francesca, forgive me for not protecting you. I tried to always keep you safe, but the day you were killed, I was late from work. I should have been home with you."

"But, Pappa, you're confused. Mamma wasn't killed, she was sick."

Bewildered, he touched my locks, "No, you're my dear wife, Francesca, and you were killed up in your bedroom. Someone strangled you, and our innocent little Sam saw it all. That's why he doesn't talk because somewhere deep inside him, he remembers the horror of that day. He knows who the killer is, as do I."

Stunned by this revelation, I was willing to go along with the ruse and asked, "Who killed me, Klaus? Who killed me in my bedchamber?"

Emmett entered the room and saw the both of us in hysterics. "Mia, what's going on?"

"Please leave us," I barked. "I have to talk with Pappa alone."

"Neither of you are in any state to be having a conversation. You need to calm your nerves. Go to the kitchen and make us some tea. I promise I'll watch over him, and if anything changes I'll come get you."

Never before had I heard my brother speak with such authority, nor could I argue with him, for I was reeling with Pappa's revelation that our mother had been murdered and Sam was a witness. It was the information I'd been searching for all this time. However, a pounding at our front door prevented me from heeding my brother. It was none other than Cora and Reverend Josiah Hornsby.

"It's a gully washer out there," Hornsby said, shaking out his wet slicker on the hall floor.

"I'm sorry, but my father is too ill for visitors," I said, protesting their entry.

The portly preacher raised his hand dismissively. "Then it's the most opportune time for our calling. We are on God's mission to pray for his soul."

He brusquely pushed past me, proceeding to my father's beside.

I turned to Cora, "Please don't let your husband do this. My father wouldn't want it."

The woman who had been so vulnerable at the graveyard and whom I'd comforted and bonded with, stared past me as though I were a stranger. She'd resumed her role as preacher's wife, and would do as he bid.

Hornsby hollered, "Klaus Stein, Satan has had a hold of you. Your weak flesh was at his command, but tonight you can once again be freed from temptation. God is ready to forgive you of your sins. Let Him take you home, and deliver you into the loving arms of our Savior, Jesus Christ."

Arms heavenward, Cora exclaimed, "Praise the Lord and save this sinner!"

Agitated from a deep sleep, Pappa thrashed in protest.

"Can't you see you're disturbing him," I cried.

Possessed with religious fervor, Preacher Hornsby sang out, "It's the Holy Spirit moving your father, wiping away his sins, readying him for judgment. Hallelujah! Pray Children. Get down on your knees and pray your father will be delivered!"

"That's quite enough," Emmett said stepping in. "It's high time you two leave."

"Would you be so callous as to seal your father's fate, Son?" Preacher Hornsby demanded. "Will Satan find another tenant for hell tonight?"

With commanding force, Emmett grabbed the couple by their arms and pushed them out the door. However, hot on their heels was our own priest, Father Muldair. Despite knowing he had the best of intentions, I couldn't help but resent another intrusion.

"My father isn't a member of your church," I said, barring his way.

Standing on the porch with rain dripping off his hat's brim, his piercing blue eyes held an eerie unworldliness. "'Tis true, my child, but he did his duty by seeing you and your brothers faithfully attend. Klaus is a good man and deserves my blessing. Do you not think it wise I perform his last rites? I promise I'll not disturb him."

Too tired to argue, I reluctantly I allowed him in. His sedate composure was in marked contrast to the Hornsbys' frenetic outbursts, and yet his mere presence pointed equally to a finality I wasn't prepared to accept. His shadow danced on the wall as the candle flame flickered. He sprinkled holy water over Pappa's body, and his silver crucifix gently swung from his rosary, just as Mamma's had. However, his words, instead of flowing with a healing rhythm of transcendence, rang empty to my ears. I'd prayed for weeks, offering renunciation of everything I held dear, but Pappa hadn't improved. When he placed a cross in Pappa's lifeless hands, it fell to the ground.

"Let's lock the door," Emmett said after Father Muldair had left.

"Thank you, Emmett," I said, giving him a hug. "I realize you're a young man now. Someone, whom I'll rely heavily upon in future."

His appreciative smile disappeared under the gravity of our situation. "Do you think he'll make it through the night?"

I bit my lip to hold back my tears. "I don't know."

"Shall I stay up with you?"

"No, you have to go to the shop early tomorrow. It's more important than ever that you're there."

Miss Emily soon arrived, wet and cold through. "A breech birth," she said, explaining her lateness. "Did you manage to get any nourishment down him today?"

I shook my head dejectedly. "He's taken a turn for the worse this evening. In his delirium, he didn't even remember you'd been here earlier."

"Mia, you should've called for me to come. I had no idea..." She took his hands in her own, and I noticed his nails had turned blue. "Klaus, honey, it's me, Emily. I'm here and I ain't leavin' your side no more."

Disoriented, he struggled to take stock of his surroundings. "My sweet Emily, where have you been? Promise you'll marry me now. I've been waiting too long to call you mine. Damn the naysayers of this town, you are to be my wife."

"Yes, Klaus, yes," Miss Emily cried with kisses to his cheeks.

Their moment of happiness was short lived, for Pappa's fever spiked and a mad glaze transfixed his sunken eyes. His feeble arms thrashed the air, and his lips pulled back in a painful grimace, struggling to form words. The image was identical to my nightmare of Mamma, and my first instinct was to shrink back in horror, but my love for him gave me the strength to secure his flailing arms within my embrace, and wipe his mouth, lathering with saliva.

A sudden calm came over him, and we watched fearfully as his chest rose with each labored breath. His pulse was only a faint thread, and his half-opened eyes flitted erratically, seeing not what lay before him. He then emitted a guttural rattling from his throat that I'd only heard once before when old Jacob Little's life ebbed away. Pappa was lost to us.

I stood there feeling as dead as the body before me, while Miss Emily in her grief, tore at her hair and rent her clothes. Exposed were the raised scars running down her back, a testament to her days as a slave. When she climbed into bed with my father and kissed his cold lips, I felt an intruder upon the scene. I fled from my home, away from Pappa's lifeless body and Miss Emily's anguished cries.

CHAPTER XXIII

LOST IN THE NIGHT

Cloaked only in the thin shawl I'd hastily grabbed, I roamed the deserted streets of Houston. It was drizzling and cold, but the harsh conditions didn't compare to the pain churning my insides. Like a specter, I haunted places that held memories of a happier time. I went past Pappa's shop and thought of all the beautiful pieces of furniture he'd created with his hands. I couldn't imagine him not ever going there again. Further down the street was Corri's Market Square Theater where my family had watched Lola Fontaine in *The Lady of the Lake*, and listened to countless concerts there. The Lyceum was next, where Pappa had debated the intellectual issues of the day. Then the cafe where Miss Penelope had unremittingly expressed her longing for him. Percival's stalls were across the way, and I pictured Pappa buying his new collar for the fair.

I continued to wander, but the scenes of our happy lives dissolved into the darkness of the night. Shivering in my rain soaked clothes, I ended up at the bayou's banks, forlornly watching a cow's bloated carcass float downstream from Shrimpf's slaughterhouse.

I pondered Pappa's revelation of my mother's death. Had she truly been murdered as he said and Sam a witness, or was it merely a fever fed delusion? I struggled to grasp the finality of his death and the subsequent responsibilities hoisted upon my weary shoulders.

Walking with no direction in mind, I ended up in the seedy side of town where music and bawdy laughter came to life with nightfall. I ventured to look inside the window of Dick Dowling's Bacchus Saloon, and saw my friend Fanny Moffitt. Wearing her suffragette bloomers and chugging whiskey as readily as any man, she was sitting in on a card game. Nothing more than communal wine at church had ever passed my lips, but at that moment I longed for the oblivion hard liquor might offer. Men had been driven to drink with far less impetus than I'd suffered that night.

A Mexican, wearing a broad brimmed hat and spurs as large as silver dollars, stepped up to the bar and requested a drink. The bartender refused him, and a Texas Ranger standing nearby, told the man to move on. The Mexican refused and was unceremoniously kicked through the swinging doors, landing nearly at my feet.

Grabbing up my muddy skirts, I ran from this squalid scene until I collapsed onto the sidewalk, sinking into the darkness of a faint. I don't know how long I lay there unconscious, but I awoke on a crimson sofa beneath a coverlet. A black potbellied stove filled the room with the comforting smell of a crackling fire, while my dress and shawl hung nearby to dry.

I was wondering whose home I'd found refuge in, and what kind person had redressed me in a nightgown, when Madame Henrietta Tildy entered the room. Her scarlet hair shimmered in the firelight, and her breasts were visible through her sheer dress.

"How you feeling, sweetie? Goodness me, you're still shivering. Drink this Tom and Jerry, and I'll get you a hot water bottle for your belly. We'll have you warm in no time."

Realizing I was inside a house of ill repute, I stuttered, "I'm not cold, I'm just..."

"You suffered a shock haven't you, poor thing. I seen the same look on plenty a desperate young girl. It's a rough world out there, and sooner or later it gets everybody. Has a man done you wrong? Has he gotten you in trouble?"

I shook my head no at her outlandish suggestion.

Her garish red lips smiled kindly, "Then shall I have your folks fetched?"

Tears filled my eyes as I realized I no longer had even one parent that would be concerned with my whereabouts.

"You were lucky a proper gentleman found you outside and brought you in. No telling what might have happened to you, otherwise. He said he had an errand to run, but would be back to check up on you."

"I appreciate your help, Mrs. Tildy."

"Ain't been called Missus in a month of Sundays, plain Tildy suits me fine enough now. What's your name?"

"I'm Mia, but I'd rather not disclose my last name if you don't mind."

Accepting my answer, she took up a pair of knitting needles and set to work. It was an odd sight to see such a scantily dressed woman employed with so mundane a chore. Her employees, also in various states of undress, poked their heads in the door to take note of me.

"Is she staying?" one of them asked with a sneer. "If so, she ain't getting any of my regulars."

Tildy shooed them away with her ringed fingers, "Get back to work, ladies, this ain't no circus sideshow." Turning back to me, she asked, "Need a place to stay?"

"No, thank you, Ma'am. I was on my way home when I guess the cold got to me."

"Your exotic looks could make me and you a heap of money, but I wouldn't force this line of work on anybody who had another way."

"I don't think it would suit me," I answered.

My self-righteous answer rubbed Tildy the wrong way. "I suppose you think me and my girls are below your station, but we ain't. Hell, I was once a Shaker up in Kentucky, living in harmony with my brethren and sisters. Only trouble was being celibate didn't seem natural to me, nor God intended. Well, I'm free of them now, got my own place here and am making good money. All the important men of Texas have visited. Ain't naming names though, customer confidentiality."

A man entered the house, whose booming voice I immediately recognized as Reverend Josiah Hornsby's. Only a few hours previous he'd implored our Lord for Pappa's salvation, and now his own was in question. Mercifully, his attention was directed toward picking out a companion, and he didn't notice me cowering beneath the blanket.

"You know him, don't you?" Tildy asked.

I nodded.

"Comes here every Saturday night. I reckon it's his way of blowing off steam before he's got to give his Sunday service. Mind you, he won't be here long. In and out real quick, so to speak."

The walls were thin in the boarding house, and it was impossible to ignore the metal bedstead and springs creaking rhythmically beneath Hornsby's weight. Tildy was right as to the reverend's rapidity, for a mere ten minutes passed before he left the establishment, reciting his sermon to come.

Tildy put down her knitting and lit a corncob pipe. "It's not so bad," she said thoughtfully. "I mean being with all these different gents. It all depends what's going on up here," she said, tapping a finger to her head. "Best to just lay there and think of something else till it's all over."

I was recalling Rachael's governess had said something to the same effect, when a drunken customer tumbled through the door. "Long live the Republic!" he hollered.

Miss Tildy corrected him, "You're a bottle of whiskey and four years late."

Staggering toward me, he slurred, "Hey, I like this youngin' hiding under the cover. Come on out darlin', I won't bite, I promise."

Tildy objected, "Sorry sir, but that lassie ain't available. Giddy on up to the backroom where I got half a dozen just as pretty as her that you can choose from.

Ignoring her, the drunkard yanked my blanket off, saying, "Her eyes are as green as emeralds, and I mean to make her mine."

Tildy had risen up in my defense when another man stepped into the room. Pointing a derringer at my attacker, he calmly offered, "Monsieur, do you prefer to leave this hotel on your own two feet or be carried out in a coffin? Either way, it makes no difference to me."

My savior wore buckskin britches and a fur lined cap, and he was none other than Henri Dubois.

Sobered by the situation he found himself in, the drunkard tipped his hat, saying politely, "Didn't mean no harm, just having a little fun. Sorry if I offended the young lady. Tildy, I'll be back some other time."

Henri holstered his gun, then handed me back the blanket. "Good evening, Mia. I'm relieved to see you've recovered from your faint."

"You were the one who brought me in after I collapsed?" I asked in disbelief.

He nodded, "I arrived in town not an hour ago, where I bumped into Doc Abbott at the hotel. He told me of your father's illness, so of course I went directly to your house. Miss Emily hadn't realized you were gone till then, and she was ready to call on the sheriff until I swore I'd find you. After I brought you in here to recover, I returned to your home to reassure her of your safety."

Alarmed, I asked, "You didn't tell her where I was, did you?"

"Nope, didn't figure she needed anymore to worry about. I'll step outside while you get dressed and then I'll take you home."

I gathered my damp clothing and dressed as quickly as possible. "Thank you, Miss Tildy, you've been very gracious to help me out."

"Weren't nothing. Besides I owed you."

I looked at her quizzically.

"I remember you from the Fourth of July fair. You were right generous, acknowledging me civilly when nobody else in this fool town would, and that meant a lot to me. You're from good folk." She gave me a hug and sent me on my way.

Waiting outside, Henri pulled an old horse blanket from his saddlebags and draped it around my shoulders. He mounted his horse before pulling me up behind him, upon which I clung to him as if he were a lifeboat in a raging sea. I was confused, but didn't object when he returned not to my home, but rather the hotel he was boarding at. With not a word of explanation, he carried me up a back stairwell to his room. It was dark and furnished with the bare minimum of furniture; an iron bedstead, a washstand, and a calfskin chair. I watched numbly as he started a fire in the hearth.

The reality of Pappa's death rushed over me once again, and I fell into a fit of tears. He comforted me with hugs and kisses, and then before I knew what was happening, he deftly removed the pins from my hair and uncoiled the bun atop my head. My hair came tumbling down, and I remembered Mamma telling me how she only let hers down for Pappa. I considered my next confession to Father Muldair as Henri's lips were on mine. I closed my eyes, and floated away down the dark bayou, where the pain of Pappa's death didn't exist.

CHAPTER XXIV

GRANDPARENTS FOR CHRISTMAS

appa's obituary in the *Texas Telegraph* read as follows:

We are pained to announce the death of Colonel Klaus Otto Stein, who died of consumption at his residence in this city, on the 18th of December. A member of Stephen F. Austin's "Old Three Hundred", and a hero of the Battle of San Jacinto, he was buried with Masonic honors as a distinguished member of Holland Lodge No. 1. A large concourse of his fellow citizens followed his body to the grave. Having established his successful business, Stein's Fine Furniture, he was known as a universal favorite. His daughter and three sons will be deprived of an affectionate father, and the community of an honorable man.

Miss Emily and I dressed Pappa in his best suit, then laid him on the cooling board in our parlor, where friends could pay their respect. The memorial was kept simple, but it did nothing to reduce the large numbers of attendants. Miss Penelope, along with the other single women of Houston, mourned grievously. None of course, felt the pain as deeply as Miss Emily, who wore the brass ring, Pappa had found in our Halloween fortune bread, as proudly as any wedding band.

At home, Sam kept asking when Pappa was coming back, and Christian, full of anger, locked himself in his room most of the time. Emmett deciphered the running of the shop, and I ran the house as best I could. One evening as we sat by the cold dark hearth, our only victuals being a potato, Sam asked if we were to move into the orphanage.

"Heaven's no," I cried.

"But we *are* orphans, aren't we?" Christian asked.

"Yes, but Emmett and I are old enough to take care of things. We'll get by just fine."

Christian complained, "I figured we'd have to economize our coal and candles, but I'm freezing."

"Sorry, that's my fault," Emmett apologized. "I'm not used to paying the bills yet, and I forgot to order the coal, but I'm figuring it out."

"I promise to make better meals too," I said guiltily. "Our larder is almost empty, and I've dreaded doing the shopping."

Sam whispered that he'd help out by filling the lamps and trimming the wicks.

"That would be very helpful, Sam, and what about you, Christian?"

He scowled, "I don't want to do anything."

"It's not a matter of wanting to. If we're to make it, we'll all have to pitch in."

"I don't want to, and you can't make me," Christian cried, as he ran to his room and slammed the door shut.

How I longed to follow suit, but I knew such childish antics wouldn't solve our problems. As the sombre evening wore on, Christian reappeared, his shoulders slumped with remorse. "I'm sorry, Mia, I really do want to help, and by hook or crook, we shall make it work."

"No sticky fingers," I said in alarm.

"I've learned my lesson," Christian reassured. "Actually, Percival has offered me a nickel for every rat I catch for him, and I can raise honey bees too."

"That would be just fine," I said, hugging him.

Pulling a crumpled letter from his pocket, Christian said, "And there's this. It came in the mail yesterday."

"Another bill?" Emmett asked woefully.

"It's from Pappa's parents," Christian cried. "I didn't want you to know, 'cause I don't want them to come here and take us away."

* * *

On Christmas day, Emmett and I stood on the porch of the Capitol Hotel, waiting for the *General Taylor*, a Brown and Tarbox stagecoach, to arrive. After learning of Pappa's death, our grandparents were keen on doing right by us, and so had written to say they were coming for a visit. When the distinguished looking couple stepped from the coach, there was no doubt who they were. Wilhelm, who traced his ancestry to German nobility, wore an elegant beaver trimmed hat, and Adelaide carried herself proudly in her ermine cloak and matching muff.

"Schrecklich!" Grandmother cursed, her breath visible in the chilled air.

Grandfather consoled her with a pat of his gloved hand, "There, there, Mutter. Things will soon be put to rights."

Thinking of these two strangers disowning Pappa upon marrying my mother, it was with an awkward wariness that I approached them, "Grandmother, Grandfather, I'm Mia, and this is my brother, Emmett.

The old woman looked uncomfortable. "I'm not accustomed to being called Grandmother. In future, please address me as Adelaide."

Shocked by so cold a sentiment, I withdrew my hand. Had we made a terrible mistake by allowing them to come, I wondered.

Emmett stepped forward, trying to fill the awkward silence. "You must be fatigued. Four days travel is a long distance."

"It was that body!" Adelaide screeched. "They never should've put him up there on top, and they used my good linen as his shroud. It was meant to be a gift to you, Mia."

Wilhelm cooed, "Mutter, you've suffered a shock to your system, but you must calm down. Here are your pills, they will help your nerves."

When the corpse was taken off the stagecoach, the driver offered, "Sorry about your sheet Ma'am. Give us your address and we'll get it back to you tomorrow."

Adelaide wrung her hands, "Are you mad, sir? It's ruined beyond repair. You could at least give us back the money you forced us to pay for the toll. I told you all our fees were paid upfront."

The driver swung the body into a cart. "Sorry, no can do. But on your return trip, I'll try to arrange for you to face forward."

"Who died?" Emmett asked as he took their cases.

Wilhelm explained as we walked home, "Our axle broke on Washington Road, otherwise we wouldn't even have seen the poor fellow. Apparently he fell off his horse and broke his neck."

"An intolerable journey all around," Adelaide complained. "I'm black and blue from broken seat springs and I've got chilblains. I hate to travel!"

Adelaide's diatribe continued until we reached home. I introduced our grandparents to Christian and Sam, instructing my brothers to call them by their given names. Adelaide and Wilhelm showed as little affection towards them as they had demonstrated toward myself and Emmett.

Christian wrinkled his nose at the old woman, "You smell like Mentholatum, are you sick?"

Squinting with disdain, our grandmother said, "I see we'll need to teach you some manners, boy. And no I'm not sick, the rub is for my aches."

Grandfather made himself at home in the most comfortable chair by the fire, and the boys soon gathered round him as he showed off his walking stick. Its silver tip was engraved with his coat of arms, and it unscrewed to reveal a secret compartment. "Holds my gin, for medicinal use, of course."

Adelaide appeared restless. "What about supper? This is Christmas, thought you'd have something special cooking."

"We're in mourning," I reminded her. "I didn't think it right to be celebrating."

A fleeting expression of grief passed over my grandmother before saying, "Klaus wouldn't want you to ignore our Savior's birth. Now lead the way to the kitchen, and I will set to work."

Wanting to escape her dismal company, I offered, "I'll make something, but please rest. I know you're tired from the trip."

Drawing a rolling pin out from her carpetbag, she said, "I've traveled all this way to be of help, and that I plan to do. This is for making spaeztle noodles. I don't suppose you have one of these. It's time you learned how to prepare traditional German dishes."

Reluctantly, I showed her to the kitchen and took down the rack of lamb hanging from the rafter.

Examining the meat, she said, "Das ist gut, the flesh is tender and the vein is blue, but I hope you didn't pay more than eight cents a pound or else you were robbed. Can't ever trust a butcher, I've caught them too many times laying a hand on the scales."

I replied defensively, "Mr. Hudson has been more than generous to us since Pappa died."

"You'll not have to rely on charity now that we're here," she said authoritatively. "My, this kitchen certainly needs straightening up. It's best to hang your pots and pans, and this floor is due a good scrubbing. Ach, a man will not marry a woman unless she's a gut hausfrau. But don't worry we shall have this all in apple pie order soon enough."

I held my tongue, reminding myself she wouldn't be here long.

"Aren't you going to ask me why we didn't visit before?" Adelaide asked, brusquely.

Her directness unnerved me, but I answered, "I think I already know."

"Truth is we couldn't accept our Klaus throwing away his life."

"You mean by marrying my mother?" I asked affronted.

"You know your grandfather got his limp because a Mexican shot him. As we saw it, our own flesh and blood was marrying one of the enemy."

"That's preposterous, and it doesn't have anything to do with my mother. Now, that you've met your grandchildren, do you still think your son made a mistake?"

She stiffened her back, "I suppose not."

Somehow I managed to get through the preparation of that dinner and the meal itself. I'd expected compassion from my grandmother and someone to share my grief with, but she gave neither, instead liberally doling out criticism and petty gripes. Our grandfather proved more friendly. He was genuinely taken with my brothers, and eager to tell them of the good old days of early Texas.

Adelaide harped, "Wilhelm, they don't care about those stories of yours."

Sam's climbing onto his lap was enough confirmation for our grandfather to proceed, "Well, it was just me and your pa who first headed out West. Klaus was your age, Emmett."

"Did you see Indians?" Christian asked. "We met up with a tribe when we went turkey hunting."

"Injuns were everywhere. Why, it's a miracle we weren't scalped. Somehow we made it to Austin's colony, and though we were near death with the ague, the good people there cared for us like we were family. We received a quarter of a league along the Brazos River, just south of the old fort. It was rich land with oats and cane growing wild along the riverbank. I hired a couple of men to help us build a log cabin. It was rough, mind you, with a dirt floor, but it was home."

"Pappa talked fondly of those years," I said.

"When did Grandmother... I mean Adelaide come?" Emmett asked.

"Five years later," she answered. "And the journey took a toll upon me of which I'm still to recover. Our prairie schooner was loaded down with every precious thing I owned in the world, and when a wheel broke, we had to abandon it all and take to foot. Wilhelm searched for the wagon after we arrived, but it was all gone; mother's spinning wheel, the silver, and the embroidered linens from my dowry."

"Then what happened Grandfather?" my brothers asked, obviously preferring his stories over Adelaide's.

"The skeeters were fiercer than the Indians, so when the weather was good, your father and I slept on the roof where there was a breeze. Later we learned the smoke from burning cedar branches was good at keeping them blood suckers away."

"It didn't suit me till we got mosquito netting," Adelaide added.

"Got any war stories?" Christian asked.

"How about the war of eighteen-twelve?" Grandfather asked, hooking his thumbs behind his suspenders.

"Wilhelm, I always get mixed up," Adelaide said. "What year was that war in?"

"Why eighteen-twelve, dear,"

Everyone laughed at our grandmother's expense, which only renewed the hardness to her pursed lips.

Wilhelm was thoroughly enjoying his captive audience. He stuffed a pinch of snuff up his nose then continued, "I was on Old Ironsides herself. Got her name after a Brit saw a cannonball bounce off her side. I was in charge of her sails, since I could scale the rigging faster than anyone."

I found myself unexpectedly enjoying our grandparents' company when there was a knock at the door. I hoped it was Miss Emily, who had been terribly depressed and confined to her home, but I also knew my grandparents would consider her an unwelcome guest. My surprise was great upon seeing Daniel standing there, and even more so by the marked alteration in his appearance. Dark circles were beneath his eyes and a stubble covered his gaunt face.

"Daniel, are you ill?" I asked, pulling him into the warmth of the hall. "Here, please sit down."

I shut the sliding doors to the parlor, hoping his arrival wouldn't be discovered until he'd recovered a measure of strength.

"Have you just arrived in town? You must have suffered a difficult crossing again."

"Sailing never comes easy to me, but it's my concern for you that has weighed upon me. Dear, Mia, I'm so sorry for your loss, and I deeply regret I wasn't here to help you carry your burden."

"It's been a difficult time," I agreed, thinking of how different it may have been with him to support me. "Daniel, now that my father is gone, I want to confess something. Pappa had very strong feelings against your father. Because of this prejudice, I kept my relationship with you and Rachael a secret from him. I can't express the guilt and shame I've felt over my deception."

Instead of defending Captain Biggs, Daniel asked, "Mia, I'm sorry you were put in such a difficult position, but considering your father's objections, why did you befriend me in the first place?"

"It was obvious upon our first meeting, your own character was beyond reproach. I don't believe children should be punished for their parents' sins."

"Did your father explain what he held against mine?"

"No, though I assumed it had something to do with him selling arms to the Mexicans during the Revolution. Is there something you'd like to say as for his character?"

The parlor doors slid open and my family stood there staring.

"Lo and behold, what's this all about?" Adelaide demanded sharply.

"This is my friend, Daniel Biggs. Daniel, these are my grand-parents, Adelaide and Wilhelm Stein."

Daniel bowed, "Mr. and Mrs. Stein, an honor to meet you. May I extend my sympathy for the loss of your son."

They solemnly nodded before Adelaide directed, "Mr. Biggs, it looks as if you could do with some Christmas cheer. Please join us in the parlor, but mind you, wipe your feet well on the rug, I've just scrubbed the floors."

Daniel hesitated.

"Please stay, Daniel," I smiled encouragingly. "I've not felt like celebrating until now."

Daniel's arrival had an uplifting affect on everyone, and though we'd not intended to observe Christmas, Emmett said, "Since we have guests, perhaps I should go get a tree?"

"Please, Mia, let's do," Christian chimed in. "and a Yule log too."

Sam jumped up and down with glee, and Daniel offered to help.

"How can I say no," I answered.

That one night, we let go of our sorrows and embraced the joy of the season. Our house was soon draped in fragrant evergreen boughs and the larg-est log from the shed crackled on the fire. Adelaide insisted a goose feather tree was the proper German

tradition, but when the boys produced a glorious cedar and it stood regally upon the table, even she agreed it was beautiful.

Adelaide scolded my brothers, "You boys eat as many gingerbread men as you hang from the boughs. I don't want to hear your complaining of stomachache in the middle of the night."

When they laughed at her, she laughed back, and I felt a lightness in my heart that I'd not felt for months.

Daniel sat down beside me and with the tenderness I'd come to associate with him, he said, "It's good to see a smile on your face again."

I confessed, "Nary an hour ago did I think it possible to be happy. If only Pappa were here to share this time with us. I shouldn't have told you earlier about his feelings. He was a fair-minded man, and I'm certain once he'd met you, he would've thoroughly approved."

"It was my fondest wish to have known him," Daniel said. "I know this isn't the right time to bring up my proposal, but you should know your letters meant everything to me while I was gone. They're what kept me going."

"Yours were equally looked forward to, and the lavender bouquets you sent me were terribly thoughtful. I suppose you remembered they reminded me of my mother."

Perplexed, he asked, "Lavender? No, Mia, it must have been someone else."

"But you're the one that gave me the Floral dictionary, and we talked about the lavender, remember?"

"Yes, I do recall that, and I wish I'd been the one to think of sending it, but I wasn't. Should I be concerned over another suitor?"

Wilhelm interrupted, "Come now, you two, it's time for games. Shall it be charades?"

Emmett suggested with a mischievous grin, "Let's play 'Guessing Blind Man' and Daniel will be it!"

I said in aside, "Daniel, beware. Our guests often pay the dearest in our family games."

"Forewarned and ready," Daniel winked. "Emmett, is this revenge for the poison ivy you got on my account?"

"Merely a game for fun," Emmett reassured.

We formed a circle with our chairs, then with Daniel blind-folded in the center, we spun him round. The object of the game was simple enough; he was to sit in a person's lap and without a word spoken, was to identify them. The first person he happened upon was Adelaide, who was unable to suppress a giggle when Daniel squeezed her leg. Realizing his mistake, he jumped up with embarrassment and wandered around until coming upon my vel-vet skirt. Sitting down, he confidently announced, "I'm quite cer-tain this is Mia."

It was an uproarious moment when Daniel removed his hand-kerchief, only to discover I'd spread my skirt over Emmett's lap. After this, everyone wanted their turn at being the blind man, and our games continued until Grandfather lit the candles on the tree. Joining hands, we sang Christmas carols and Christian accompa-nied us on the pianoforte. Our hearts were brimming with peace on earth and goodwill to men until Sam yelled, "Fire, get the bucket!"

"So, he does speak!" Adelaide exclaimed.

"When he sees fit," I said.

The flaming branch was doused with not too much destruction to the tree's decorations, and all was soon put to order. Our last tradition was to open our presents. While we had agreed to make all our gifts, our grandparents were very generous in their giving, new suits and pocketknives for the boys, and a proper evening gown for me.

"Thank you, Adelaide and Wilhelm. It was very thoughtful of you to get us such nice things," I said.

Adelaide remarked dismissively, "It's nothing, the real gift is... Come, Wilhelm, tell them why we really came to see them and what we have to offer."

Our grandfather cleared his throat, then began earnestly to speak. "Children, our stubbornness has made us miss out on many birthdays and holidays in the past. It's impossible to make up for this lost time, especially now that our dear Klaus is gone, but it's our intention to do our best by you, given the time we have left. Adelaide and I are all alone, and now you are too. We return to our home by week's end, and we want you to join us."

"You mean to visit?" Christian asked.

"Nein, to come live with us. We've a huge home, a room for everyone. You boys would love swimming and fishing in the river, and the schoolhouse is very near. It would be quite convenient for all concerned."

Disturbed, Emmett stated, "But we've the furniture store to run."

"And *our* home to take care of," Christian added.

Sam ran to me, and hid his face in my skirt.

Adelaide declared sharply, "You can easily sell the shop and your house, and the best part grandfather hasn't even mentioned is, Christoph Amsel. He's a fine young man of good German stock. He's looking for a wife, and I'm certain he'd take to Mia once I teach her our ways."

I was dumbfounded by their proposal, especially the marriage they'd arranged for me.

Sensing our resistance, Adelaide became miffed, and said, "I don't understand. We're offering you a life of ease and security. I thought you'd all be grateful."

"No need to make any hasty decisions," Wilhelm said, trying to smooth over the tense situation. "It's been a long day, and I think it's time for bed. Please consider what we've discussed and we'll talk about it in the morning."

I walked Daniel to the door. He'd been painfully quiet since my grandparents' unexpected announcement.

"Mia, are you considering their offer?"

"It's been hard for us since Pappa's death. Emmett has splendidly rose to the challenge, but I'm not sure if I'm strong enough to handle everything."

Daniel gently pulled me to him, encircling me with his strong arms. "I'm here to stay, Mia. You don't have to do it on your own."

CHAPTER XXV

A RUDE AWAKENING

By week's end my grandparents were gone, and with them their offer of comfort and security. I wondered if I'd made the right decision when our present situation was fraught with so much uncertainty. My first step in securing a stable footing for our family was to visit Pappa's furniture store. It was a task I'd too long avoided.

Emmett stood at the door in his work-apron, a pencil tucked behind his ear. His faint mustache was thickening, and I realized for the first time his resemblance to our father. He took my coat and welcomed me, "Mia, I'm glad you finally came, the books have needed looking over, and you've always been sharp with the figures."

Melancholy for Pappa gripped me, as I gazed around the showroom. "Oh, Emmett, it pains me to see all this beautiful furniture that he's made."

"He was a true artisan, and there are already orders placed on most of his pieces, but I think we should keep some of it for ourselves. Do you like these lyre backed chairs?"

I ran my hand along the fine carving. "They'd be perfect for our dining room, and I can make some needlepoint cushions for the seats. Let's also give something special to Miss Emily, though I'm not sure what she'd like."

"Good idea. I'll have her come in and pick out something, herself. Let's go to the workroom, there's some projects we're working on and changes I've made that I want you to see. We received a large contract to build pews for the Baptist Church. Cora Hornsby brought the order in, and actually expressed remorse for her and her husband coming over the night Pappa died. She said, she realized later it was an intrusion."

"I can't figure her out," I observed. "but I'm sure being married to Reverend Hornsby explains a lot."

The back workroom was a hive of industry, but the men stopped their labors to nod their heads solemnly in my direction.

Eli Bailey, Pappa's loyal foreman, shook the sawdust from his hair and beard, "Miss Stein, it's good to see you."

"I've been meaning to come sooner, but..."

Bailey assured me, "I understand your hesitation. It was hard for all of us to get back to work without Klaus here, and customers worried the quality of our work might suffer with his passing, but they realize now we're staying faithful to the craftsmanship he taught us. As you can see everything is running smoothly, and Emmett has stepped up right smartly. He's got some big shoes to fill, but I have faith he'll do just that."

My brother flushed, hearing the older man's praise. "Mia, trust me, we'd be sinking if it weren't for Bailey's guidance. He's my right hand man, as he was Pappa's."

"And who's been taking care of the books?" I asked.

They shrugged their shoulders guiltily, and pointed me in the direction of towering stacks of bills and orders. I rolled up my sleeves and set to work at deciphering the numbers before me. The rows of figures meticulously entered in Pappa's unique penmanship revealed he'd been running two households, ours, as well as Miss Emily's. His death would impact her livelihood greatly, and so I promised myself to continue helping her.

The ledger also proved the furniture store was a profitable business, but that several large work orders were to date unpaid. The most substantial one was on Galveston Island, and so making arrangements with Miss Emily to take care of the boys, I headed out on the next steamer. Only a few short months had passed since I'd made the same journey down the bayou with my family, and yet I felt I'd been transformed into a completely different person. In my naivety, I'd been eager to shuck away the confines of childhood, but now I knew that with the freedom of adulthood came unforeseen burdens.

Keeping to the safety of my cabin, the voyage was uneventful, and I arrived on the island ready to undertake the business at hand. Staying clear of Tremont House and the cheery memories it held of our summer holiday, I chose instead, the Powhatten Hotel. Though down-on-its-heels, it was inexpensive and would suffice for the one night. I left my portmanteau in the room and headed straight to the bookstore on the Strand, where the owner was delinquent in paying for the shelving Pappa had built him. With my appearance as matronly as I could affect and my attitude professional, our interaction progressed more smoothly than I'd hoped for, and I was done within the hour, proudly holding the handsome payment in full.

With my errand so quickly dispatched, I was considering taking the next steamship home, when I decided on a whim to first see Henri. Since the night of Pappa's death, we had met only once, which was at the funeral. It was an awkward exchange due in part to my overwhelming grief and the confusing emotions I felt toward him.

Unaware of his residence, I headed to his place of employment at the Customs House. Flushed with emotion and anticipation of seeing him, I approached the front desk clerk, saying, "I'm here to see Henri Dubois. I believe he's one of your agents."

The gentleman scrutinized me over his spectacles, "Are you a relation, Miss?"

"A close friend," I answered in a trembling voice.

His eyebrows raised in amusement, and I chafed at its possible significance.

"Mr. Dubois is out to lunch, probably dining at Mick's Place around the corner. Its placard is a blue sign with a crab. Can't miss it."

I left the establishment giddily, imagining Henri's happy surprise at seeing me. He'd no doubt conduct me on a tour of his beloved Galveston with a promenade along the boardwalk. On my way, I came upon a confectioner's shop famed for its saltwater taffy. Wanting to bring a treat home to my brothers, I stepped into the store and was delighted with the variety of candies. With an armload of sweets, I queued up behind a fashionable woman and her two sons. They were adorable children, similar in age to my youngest brothers.

The young salesman, who was obviously smitten by the attractive customer, stammered enthusiastically, "How long can we expect you in town, Mrs. Dubois?"

My ears pricked up at the mention of her name.

The woman purred in a smooth French accent, "At least until the end of the month. Then I return home to France with my sons for the rest of the season."

He gushed, "A pity, Madam, Galveston society isn't the same without you. No one shines brighter at the dances, nor gives fancier dinners, from what I hear."

"How very sweet of you, dear boy, and shall I give my husband, Henri, your regards?" she asked laughingly.

As she turned to leave, our eyes met. She was an extraordinarily beautiful woman; porcelain skin and ruby lips. She flashed a beguiling smile, but I only managed to stare back in shock.

"Are you all right, mademoiselle?" she asked sweetly. "You look as if you're about to faint. Here, take my hand, I'll give you a ride to your home in my carriage."

I stood mute, trying to grasp the significance of this woman.

One of the little boys whined, "But, Mother, you promised us we could look at the ships."

"Little Henri, we will afterwards. You must learn to be gallant like your father, to those in need. Très bien, he is here, and can help us with this ailing girl."

The joy upon their faces as the family came together was the final blow. I turned away, frantic to escape, but Henri blocked the doorway, and his wife was adamant in helping me.

"Henri, this poor girl has been struck ill. We must help her get home, oui?"

A myriad of emotions flashed across his rugged face as he took in the situation, but confusion over why I was there and conversing with his wife was paramount. Fear of what may have transpired between us was next, quickly followed by relief upon realizing she was ignorant of our association. His black eyes that once seduced me, now glared in suspicious anger. It was obvious I was an inconvenience, which could easily complicate his life.

"I'm fine," I reassured with a forced smile. "My lunch didn't agree with me, but it's passed now."

I rushed past them as the child said, "Pappa, I think she's still sick."

"Yes, son, I believe you're right," Henri answered. "But, the young recover quickly. Now, let's go look at the ships."

The sky had turned slate gray and a light misting of rain reinvigorated the fishy smell of the shelled streets. Feeling desperately ill, I rushed in a panic to the hotel to retrieve my belongings, and made it on time at the dock. My steamer arrived in Houston in the dead of night, and I was thankful I'd not have to face my brothers or Miss Emily.

I didn't enter the house straight away, but instead was drawn to the yaupon holly in our backyard. Its evergreen leaves trembled softly in the wintry breeze, calling to me once again as a place of refuge. Unlike in my youth, I found it awkward to climb, but after some difficulty, I reached a nook to sit in. The branches were rough and unwelcoming, and when I spied my parent's initials carved into the bark and the heart encircling them, my pent-up tears washed over me. I felt an impostor in so many ways and hated myself for it. I was the herbalist's apprentice, trained to heal the sick, and yet I'd failed to save my own father. I'd been blind to Henri's true nature, and lead astray by his flattery, while at the same time I'd betrayed Daniel's trust. He was the man who truly cared for me, but how could I face him now.

I studied the native flora around me, desperate to find something to help with my pain. I'd often prescribed the very tree which held me, Ilex vomitoria, to treat rheumatism, but its more potent application is what I had in mind. Long Jim had disclosed to me in guarded whispers, how his tribe, the Karankawa, stripped whole trees of their leaves. Through sleepless nights of dancing and fasting, they boiled and steeped them into an intoxicating elixir. The 'Black Drink', as they called it, brought on violent purging, and when their bodies and minds were emptied, they let go of their world, entering a holy realm of nothingness. I too longed for this loss of self and the pain attached.

The wind stirred and a castor plant revealed itself at the base of the tree. Its brown mottled beans peeked out from the leaves, calling me to it. It would take at least eight of them to permanently end my misery. A painful death to be sure, but one I was certain I deserved.

CHAPTER XXVI

THE HORRIBLE TRUTH REVEALED

"Lordy child, what you doin' here at this hour?" Miss Emily asked, rubbing her eyes.

I stood in my home's hallway, trying to maintain my composure, but it took only her comforting arms for a flood of tears to be released. "I've been such a fool," I confessed.

"Haven't we all been at one time or another?" she said wiping away my tears.

I opened my hand, revealing the poisonous beans I held. "I feel so desperately lost, and if not for the love I have for my brothers, I'd have taken these. Oh, Miss Emily, I'm a sorry soul whose too blind to see what lays before her. How ever can I guide those in my charge when I can barely take care of myself?"

Without rebuke or questioning of what brought on this fragility of mind, Miss Emily helped me to bed. She stayed a week, taking care of the household and tenderly looking after me. My brothers' anxious hovering only increased the shame of considering so selfish an act as taking my life.

One night when Miss Emily brought me dinner, she sat down to talk. "Mia, you won't regain your constitution if you don't eat more."

"Truly, I want to get better," I said, sitting up. "It's just these scenes keep playing over and over in my mind, and I think how I could've done differently to change it all."

Miss Emily confessed, "I didn't get out of bed for weeks after your pa died, but eventually I had to get on with livin' and accept nothin' was gonna bring him back. I learned that hard lesson a long time ago when I was kidnapped and..."

She stopped short, but her unexpected words diverted my focus from my own distress. "Please, tell me more of your past. I want no more of the secrets that have burdened our family."

She pushed back her ringlets with a sigh. "They be demons hauntin' me my whole life through, but I expect you're grown enough to understand them. Feels like it all happened yesterday with every horrible minute seared into my bein'. I was ten and Sis was nine when we was taken. Don't rightly know if Ma was killed or put on another ship, but I never saw her again."

"And your father, where was he?"

"Never did know him. Ma said he was a Portuguese trader. He's where I get my coloring from."

"Was the crossing bad?" I asked.

Miss Emily continued, stoically, "I reckon bad as most. We was herded into the ship's hull like animals, with not a ray of sunlight reachin' us.

"Forced to live in our own waste, people died like flies. The ship's surgeon refused to tend us, said he didn't want to get his

hands dirty. The worst of it came at night when women-folk were led up to the top deck. Sis and I thought we was safe, being so young, but Captain took a fancy to us. He tore into me..."

Miss Emily's voice broke with emotion. "Couldn't hardly walk afterwards, and Sis died from her injuries. They threw her overboard like fish bait."

I comforted my dear friend as best I could, but realized the magnitude of what she spoke of was beyond my grasp. "I was wrong to ask you to tell me this. I see it's too upsetting."

"It tears me up inside all over again, and yet, I think it's good to let it out every once in awhile. My heart gets heavy when it's bottled up too long. There's more if you want to hear it."

"Yes, please, I want to know everything."

She continued, "After Sis died, there weren't no one else in the world I could turn to. Captain kept after me, night after night, and I considered jumping overboard to end it all. Then a dream come to me, where I saw myself a grown woman who was happy. It was this revelation that kept me goin' on the darkest of days, and it's the lesson I want you to be learnin'. No matter how bad things are, there be always a chance for it to get better later on down the road."

"My mind hears the wisdom in those words, but my heart isn't there yet."

"That's a beginning," Miss Emily said with an encouraging smile.

"Did things get better for you when you reached America?" I asked hopefully.

"Eventually, but it was hard at first. After our ship docked in New Orleans, Captain planned to keep me for himself until he found out what a high yellow slave could fetch him. I was stripped naked and put on the block so men could poke and prod me, and size up my ability to work and breed. A bidding war broke out, and Mr. North won it. He give me as a birthday gift to his wife, as a ladies maid. Life weren't what I wanted, but it was a heap better than workin' the fields, and it's where I become an apprentice to healin', just like you're doin' now."

"To Mrs. North?"

"No, another slave who did the cookin'. She knew everything about healin' and midwifin'."

"Is that where you met Hannah's daddy?"

"It was. He belonged to Mr. North too, but when they found out we was seeing each other, he was sold off down the river. Never did know where he ended up or get to tell him I was havin' his baby. Mrs. North was good to me, even let me keep my Hannah."

I shuddered. "You mean some masters take the babies away?"

"They sure do, as cruel as it sounds. But things changed after my mistress died. I was twenty-one by then, and Mr. North started coming after me. You understand what I mean?"

I nodded gravely.

"By then we'd moved to Houston, and Mr. North had opened up his livery stable. He was keen on makin' a name for himself, and when he found out I was with child, he weren't none too happy. Didn't want tongues to wag."

I was shocked by her revelation. "I didn't know you had a child other than Hannah."

She nodded sadly. "Mr. North wanted me gone and was willin' to sell me cheap, just to get me and my growing belly out of his sight. At the time I's seein' to your ma for her birthin' with Sam, and we got to be as close as sisters. Where my thought ended, hers began, and she determined to help me out of my predicament. So, her and Klaus bought me and my daughter Hannah."

Shocked, I exclaimed, "But they didn't believe in slavery!"

"Of course not, but it was the only way they could give us our freedom. A month after I began living with them, I gave birth to a stillborn. By that time I'd learned all about your ma's troubles and how we shared somethin' terrible in common."

Bewildered by all she was revealing, I asked, "You and my mother?"

Miss Emily hesitated. "I's not sure if Francesca's story is mine to tell."

"Does it have something to do with her murder?"

Alarmed, Miss Emily, asked, "How'd you know? Klaus said he'd never told any of you what happened."

"When Pappa was in a fit of delirium, he thought I was my mother. He spoke of her murder, but I didn't know if it was true until this moment. If you know what happened to her, you must tell me."

"Your ma's troubles started when she met a sea captain who traveled to San Antonio de Bexar on business. Smitten with your ma, the man used his polished manners to convince her to accept a marriage proposal. Not much time passed before she discovered his true nature was pure evil, and that he was a slave trader. She begged him to break off the engagement, but the man flew into a rage and wouldn't hear of it. She was at the church prayin' when your father came in. She told him of her sorrows, and Klaus gallantly offered to talk with the captain."

"Pappa told us of that meeting, but he drew a blank as to why she was crying."

Miss Emily smiled, "Klaus remembered alright, for that very day he was in a duel with the captain, gravely wounding him."

I was gobsmacked. "Pappa in a duel?"

"Your pa was a remarkable man," Miss Emily said proudly. "After they married, the captain left the territory, and they believed their troubles ended."

Feeling the answer I'd been searching for was about to be revealed, I asked impatiently, "But the man came back, didn't he?"

She nodded, "Yes'm, and he was so obsessed with your ma that every time she left the house, he was lurking nearby. One day, the unimaginable happened. Klaus come home to find your ma had been strangled in her bedroom. Little Sam was there, crying over her body."

I couldn't believe her words, "Sam witnessed what happened?"

"Don't know what all he saw, but it was enough to make him afraid to ever talk again."

"Was the murderer arrested?"

Miss Emily scowled, "Not enough proof, but we knew in our hearts that the same devil who raped me as a child, also killed her."

The blackguard materialized before me; the bloodshot eyes of too much drink, the scowl that marked his discontent. And to think that it was my own father who had apparently shot off his ear. I'd never met the scoundrel, but I'd studied his portrait enough times and discovered his secret lair filled with grotesque paintings and tools of torture.

"Is the man who murdered my mother, Captain Biggs?" I asked.

"How'd you know?"

"I have something to confess," I said hesitatingly.

"Go on child, as you said you're ready for the family to unburden their secrets."

"I didn't heed yours and Pappa's warnings against the captain. I should've known you two wouldn't hate someone without good reason. Instead, I lied and went behind your backs to visit Mosswood."

Miss Emily fell back in disbelief. "Have you lost your mind?"

"Purely by chance, I met and befriended his niece, Rachael Rothschild, but rest assured I never even met the captain. He's been out of the country the entire time of our acquaintance."

"Blessed be the angels that been watchin' over you, for no harms come to you."

I continued, "I fear it's not that simple. I've fallen in love with Daniel. He's Captain Biggs' son."

All the color drained from Miss Emily's face, and I feared she would be sick. The rest of the night was filled with heated debate. Miss Emily was adamant I should never see Daniel again, and I was equally certain it's what I wanted more than anything in the world.

CHAPTER XXVII

BETROTHED

aniel sat in my parlor, holding my hands tenderly. "Mia, I've been out of my mind with worry. When Emmett brought me your letter saying you were ill, I wanted to come right away, but he insisted I give you a few days rest. I confess there were many nights I stood outside your window, hoping for just a glance."

"Forgive me for worrying you. I'm getting stronger each day and will soon be my old self again."

"It gladdens my heart to hear that. I know your father's death has weighed heavily upon you, as do the responsibilities for your family."

I thought of how Miss Emily had defined love. It wasn't the unbridled passion of infatuation that vanished with time or circumstance, but rather the solid connection that existed when another person's well-being was of the utmost importance to you. This was the bond between Daniel and myself, and yet I questioned was it prudent to give my heart to the son of my mother's murderer? "Miss Emily recently told me your father had been, in the past, an acquaintance of my mother's."

"I was unaware of any affiliation," he answered.

I detected no deception in his clear blue eyes, but considering my failure to see through Henri's lies, his answer gave little reassurance.

Seeming slightly perturbed, he asked, "Did she say it was a close association?"

I lied, "I'm not sure. I believe they first met in San Antonio. Do you know anything about his time there?"

Daniel hesitated, "As I told you before, having grown up with my aunts, I know little of my father, and with his extended absence from Houston, I don't know when that will be altered."

Tiptoeing around the difficult questions I longed to ask, I said, "You've told me your father was in Africa, do you know what kind of cargo he ships from there?"

"I believe, primarily ivory, but enough talk of my father. Mia, you know there's a matter I've long wanted to speak of," he said, whereupon he proffered two small boxes. The first was a slim silver case filled with calling cards, those precious articles genteel women dispensed upon social visits, and which I painfully lacked on my first trip to Mosswood. Each card, bordered in gold and engraved with a nosegay of herbs, was signed with the name, Mrs. Mia Biggs. The second box contained an engagement ring; a lover's knot with a sparkling diamond in its center.

"It belonged to my mother," he explained. "and is the most precious thing I possess. I'll understand perfectly if you prefer a long engagement, a suitable time after your bereavement, but please, Mia, save me from this deplorable limbo and say you'll be my dear little wife."

"I'm not the same woman you first proposed to," I pointed out. "I'm now legal guardian to my three brothers."

"Which is all the more reason to wed, my Love, so I may help you in the raising of them. And don't think my taking on a ready-made family is an unselfish act, for I would glory in the task."

I trembled with the thoughts and emotions swirling within me. My mother had failed to judge the true character of Captain Biggs, and I'd suffered my own delusions concerning Henri. I wanted to ask Daniel pointblank about the hundreds of slaves his father had tortured and killed, and of the grotesque chamber hidden within the walls of Mosswood, but my words failed to come forth. I had to believe Daniel was an innocent pawn in his father's scheme, even unaware of his father's wickedness. It was possible considering the little interaction they'd had in the past. Certain his goodness was true, I answered, "Yes, I'll marry you."

He kissed me with a passion, he'd not expressed before, and I responded as ardently. The one thing I was certain of was our love for each other.

"One more surprise," Daniel said beaming. "I've spoken with my Aunt Edna about us. Rachael has told me you understand her condition, so you'll know the significance of my saying she was in a proper frame of mind when she expressed tremendous joy over the possibility of our marriage."

I recalled my first encounter with Edna Biggs. Unbalanced in her thinking, she mistook me for someone connected to her brother, the captain, and had warned me to leave the house lest a danger befall me. I wondered now if she had known my mother, and confused the two of us. "Daniel, when your aunt is *not* in the proper frame of mind, as you call it, then what does she say of out engagement?"

"Let's not entertain the deranged thoughts of the poor woman. For now she is happy and insists upon giving us an engagement party."

"It would be scandalous to have a party when I'm still in my mourning clothes!"

Daniel reassured me, "From what you've told me of your father, he wouldn't want you to delay your happiness. Besides, I promise it will be an intimate affair. Another surprise is that I've written to my father about you, he's delighted for me. He plans to be home in time for the party."

Thunderstruck by his answer, I forced a smile.

"Then we shall set a date for the party," Daniel said, oblivious of my rising anxiety. "Let's say Saturday, the twenty-fifth of January?"

"Planning a party with your aunt, writing to your father, it seems you must've been quite certain of my saying yes to your proposal."

"A man can hope," he said, twirling me around the room. We laughed and cried, and laughed some more, and it should've been the happiest moment of my life, but the captain's foreboding shadow stopped me short. Until I confronted the scoundrel, and heard from his own lips his confession, I'd not be at ease nor find the happiness I sought.

Several days passed, and with them rose the uncertainty of my making a sound decision. I was further disconcerted by Rachael's unexpected visit.

"Aren't you going to invite me in, I promise to behave myself," she asserted, fluttering in. Her shimmering dress covered in velvet bows swished through the hall and into the parlor. "I wanted to be the first to congratulate you on your engagement."

Taken aback by her reverse in feelings, I asked, "But what of your own affections for Daniel?"

"Nothing more than a childhood infatuation," she shrugged. "Now I only have eyes for Percival."

"Percival Gray of Market Street?" I asked dumbfounded. "I didn't even know the two of you were acquainted."

"I met him while shopping one day, and thought him the most well turned out, charming, gentleman in all of Houston. He's most attentive to me, bringing sweets and flowers when he calls, and it doesn't hurt he's worth eight thousand a year, all due to his own enterprising efforts. This is the necklace he gave me, it's a real ruby. I shall love every minute of being spoiled by him."

The young merchant was as much a cockscomb as Rachael was a social butterfly. "I admit my initial surprise, but now that I consider it, I think it a good match."

Kissing both my cheeks, she chirped, "Now, we can be like sisters with no more quarreling. Here, I've brought you a gift, it's really just a trifle. Do you recognize it? It's the bonnet I stole from you in the shop on the first day I met you. I was such a naughty child then, but now I've grown up. Just as I see Daniel belongs to you, so does the bonnet. Will you accept it with my apologies? Please, say yes, so I know you truly forgive me, and we can begin anew."

Rachael besought me with her cutest pout. Her nature was as mercurial as ever, and I took this newest stance of hers with a grain of salt. "Thank you, I accept your apology, though the hat isn't necessary."

"But, I insist," she maintained with her golden curls bobbing. Dear me, I almost forgot the most important reason for my visit. Daniel asked me to bring over the invitation to your engagement party. Can you believe it, finally a social event in this dreary town? Everyone who is anybody will be there. It will be so much fun; a masquerade ball with dinner and dance. Of course, I, your dearest friend in the world, shall be your bridesmaid, and so will be an important guest of honor at the party."

I felt the ground shifting beneath me. "Daniel told me your aunt wanted to recognize our engagement, but he promised it would be a small intimate affair."

"Don't be a ninny, Mia. Men don't have a clue when it comes to these matters. If you expect to socialize in the right circles, then you must start off on the right foot."

"That is of no importance me, I only want..." I stopped myself short in my argument. Perhaps a large assembly of guests would be exactly the circumstance in which to confront Captain Biggs. "Have you heard from your uncle? Does he still plan to attend?"

"He promises to be here on time, and is excited to meet you. Here, let me read the invitation that Aunt and I have devised.

Captain Charles Biggs & Miss Edna Biggs

begs leave to present their most respectful compliments

to the Ladies and Gentlemen of Houston

& solicits the honor of their company at their

Grand Costume Ball

Saturday the 22nd of February

in the year of our Lord 1851

in celebration of the Engagement of

Daniel Biggs Esquire to Miss Mia Stein.

Dinner at Eight

Good Music and Dance at Eleven

in the well illuminated Dance Room of Mosswood.

"Doesn't it sound divine?" Rachael squealed. "Mia, I'm determined to make your engagement party a spectacular success!"

The next few weeks were busy with preparations, during which time Daniel was a constant source of love and support. There were times I allowed myself to be affected by Rachael's enthusiasm, pretending I was simply a carefree girl whose only concern was what costume to wear to the ball. However, there were also dark moments when I struggled with Miss Emily's anger over my decision, and feared how my meeting with Captain Biggs would unfold.

Rachael giggled as we rushed down the sidewalk toward our appointment, "Hurry Mia, Madame La Fleur does not like to be kept waiting. We will be the envy of everyone, for her creations are sought after from Paris to Milan. Mind you, she's temperamental, but that is true of all genius."

Striking her measuring stick on the worktable, the seamstress said firmly, "Mademoiselles, you're late. Perhaps you do not truly care to have one of my designs. If that is the case, I have a dozen more customers waiting for my attentions."

Rachael whined, "Please Madame, forgive us. My coachman, Ulysses has a toothache, and so Mia took it upon herself..."

"Stop! I do not need, nor want your excuses. However, in future make sure this is not repeated. Am I understood?"

Rachael curtsied prettily, "Oui, Madame, most certainly. What you create with a needle and thread is sheer artistry, and your designs are copied as soon as they are revealed. We want only to possess one of your costumes, so we may be enhanced by its beauty. Don't you think Miss Stein would look good as..."

Madame La Fleur's hand flew up to silence her. Then turning to her work, she disrobed me, then stood me upon a pedestal with no concern for my modesty. With years of experience, she observed my body from every angle, then began deftly draping yards of pale blue silk. Pinning the sleeves into short puffs of fabric, and cinching the dress beneath my breasts with a white ribbon, she attached the final embellishment, a Greek key ribbon, to my hem.

Achieving the affect she sought, she stepped back and admired, "You are a vision, Miss Stein! A perfect image of Empress Josephine, one of the most enchanting women to ever live. And the color complements your skin to perfection!"

Intrigued, I glanced in the mirror, only to see my body completely revealed beneath the thin clinging fabric. "But I'm practically naked!"

Rachael too was shocked, "I'm sure Madame will outfit you with the proper undergarments. A few petticoats and stays would add volume."

Outraged, she screamed, "You ask me to spoil my creation with petticoats? Absolutely not! A simple flesh colored slip will obscure the details of your body, while allowing the silk to accentuate your figure."

"It does move beautifully," I said appreciatively. "Much easier than a stiff ballgown, but I'm afraid I'm going to be chilled."

Madame La Fleur suggested, "A cashmere shawl like the ones Josephine loved to wear will keep away drafts, though you'll not need it after the first dance, I promise you. There it is done, that is if you do not slump. That's right, keep your shoulders back. A backboard would do wonders for your weak spine. Be proud of your beauty, do not hide it away."

Madame turned to Rachael and began draping and pinning her in swaths of vibrant purple accented with bands of gold at the neck and hem. With a mouthful of pins, she exclaimed, "Miss Rothschild you were born to play Cleopatra.

Rachael squealed. "The Goddess of magic, it's perfect!"

The seamstress added, "I will make you velvet slippers embroidered with a golden ankh. Then a little Kohl to darken your eyelids, an asp armlet to represent the snake that killed Cleopatra, and of course, you must don a black wig."

Rachael preened in the mirror. "It's wonderful, but do you not think a bit more décolletage would enhance the dress."

Madame clucked her tongue. "A fine line exists between daring and tawdry, however if you think it prudent, I will lower the neckline a bit more."

"I think our dresses are perfect," I said. "Now, if only I knew how to dance. I confess I've only been to one other assembly before, and my partner and I mastered few of the steps."

"This is no problem," Madame La Fleur said excitedly. "My brother is a master at the Academy of Dance. I promise you half the ball's attendants have been, or will be under his tutelage."

"Splendid," Rachael said. "There's a Polish folk dance that's wildly popular, I've been wanting to learn.

"You speak of the mazurka. My brother, he's an expert in this too."

Rachael twirled in her dress. "Then it's settled; Mia and I shall see your brother, then we'll be the best dressed and the most graceful women at the ball."

CHAPTER XXVIII

DINNER, DANCE & DISASTER

The night of my engagement party arrived and with it a storm of violent weather and raw emotions. I'd not had the opportunity to meet Captain Biggs yet, as he'd not arrived at Mosswood until that very day. I imagined he was well aware I was Francesca Stein's daughter, but I couldn't conceive what would unfold when we came face to face.

Christian and Sam gathered round me as I pinned my hair up. Emmett sat by the fire reading the Telegraph, a custom of Pappa's he'd adopted. He said, "It seems there's been foul play in the disappearance of one of our respectable citizens."

"Who's that?" I asked.

"A Mister Cyrus Harrington," Emmett answered. "He's an owner of a successful sugar plantation, and has been missing since Christmas eve."

"Having met the despicable man and treated his poor slaves, I can honestly say it's a stretch of the imagination to call him a respectable citizen, and I'd wager a lot of people had it in for him."

"Do you mean he was murdered?" Christian asked.

Emmett answered, "Sounds like it, according to Mayor Moore, whose willing to pay a hundred dollar reward to any person who delivers the murderer or any person who aided or abetted the murder."

Christian surmised, "Remember back at Halloween when that prisoner escaped from Huntsville? Maybe he's the culprit. Or maybe that captain whose face got bitten off by the shark needed some body parts."

Sam sidled next to me in fear.

"Christian, what on earth are you talking about?" Emmett asked.

"He's referring to a scary story that I told them, which may I point out, was purely fictional," I explained.

Sam whispered, "Mia, I don't want you to go out tonight. It's too dangerous, and I want to be with you."

My heart broke with his concern and affection. Since Pappa's death, I'd coddled him as much as possible, but my attentions were never enough. "Sam, after tonight I'll have so much more time for fun and games. What if we go eat at Miss Penelope's this weekend, would you like that?"

Revealing a loose tooth dangling from its socket, he mumbled, "But it hurts to eat."

"Heavens, that must be pulled or you could choke on it in your sleep."

Christian examined him. "Let me tie it with a string to a doorknob, and one good yank will do the job."

Sam shook his head in protest.

"That's enough, Christian," Emmett said. "Mia doesn't have time tonight for all this nonsense. I'll take care of Sam's tooth, and I promise it won't hurt too much. Then I'll read a book to the both of them, and I promise to sit beside their beds until they're fast asleep."

"Thank you, Emmett, I don't know how I could manage without you. Can you get my purse, I've got to hurry and get downstairs, Daniel will be here any minute."

"What's in here, Mia, it's as heavy as a rock?" Emmett asked, as he began to open the clasp.

"Don't!" I shrieked, pulling it away. "Don't you know it's inappropriate for a young man to see the contents of a woman's purse."

Emmett's stare held concern, but he didn't press for an answer. He, nor none of the ball's attendants, could ever surmise with what intention I carried a deadly weapon that night. One day I'd tell him everything about our mother's death, but if he knew the truth now, he'd never let me out the door.

Hail, as big as crabapples, pelted down as Daniel helped me into the waiting carriage. I appreciated the hot coal box and fur lap robes, but it was my betroths' attentions that warmed me the most. I fell into his arms and was covered in passionate kisses. When we finally parted I noticed his eyes were troubled.

"Daniel, is everything alright? You look disturbed about something."

He reassured, "I'm to marry the most beautiful, goodhearted, woman I've ever met, someone I adore and want to spend the rest of my life with. What could be wrong?"

His words said one thing, but his expression said another. "Daniel, let's not go to Mosswood tonight. Let everyone have the party without us. I doubt they'd hardly miss us. I could say I'm too sick to go."

For a moment, he appeared to consider my proposal, then uttered, "But we have to." He then lifted his mood, and his grim expression disappeared behind a dazzling smile. "My darling Mia, you're quite a vision tonight. Empress Josephine as your muse suits you, but I, as your devoted Napoleon, can't allow you in public without proper adornment." Removing a sparkling tiara from a velvet bag, he presented me with the gift.

"And are these real pearls and diamonds? Daniel, this is too generous."

Deftly pinning the jeweled circlet on my head, he said, "As my betrothed you'll have to humor me these little extravagances. Besides, you cannot deny it's the perfect accessory. Now, smile for me. No, those perfect teeth of yours won't do. Don't you know Josephine's teeth were rotten to the core. I'll order extra dessert for you tonight as a start."

Happy to see his lightheartedness return, I retorted, "And you are to indulge in sweets too if you're to have the girth of Napoleon."

He laughed, then said solemnly, "Mia, promise you'll save the waltzes for me, so I can hold you close."

Distressed, I asked, "Won't I be your partner for all the dances?"

"If it were up to me I'd never leave your side, but I can't be so cruel to the other gentlemen, who'll be fighting to get on your dance card, and as master of the house it's my duty to make sure there are no wallflowers."

"And your father, will I dance with him?"

I caught a scowl on Daniel's face before he turned to the window.

"There's been a slight change in plans. My father abhors social affairs, and won't be appearing at the assemblage. He prefers meeting you in a more private manner after the dance. Please don't take it personally, it's just the way he is."

I blanched at this new development, but said nothing. It obviously grieved Daniel, and I didn't want to add to his discomfort. I longed for this evening to be over, and yet it was just beginning. As we drove up the long, shell drive of Mosswood, I saw the slave, Rita, standing at a window. She was brazenly staring at me, and I wondered if it was one last attempt to scare me away.

"Daniel, do you know that woman?"

"Who?" he asked distractedly.

"Never mind, I don't see her anymore."

Our carriage arrived, and Ulysses, in his finest livery, welcomed us in with exaggerated formality. It felt like only yesterday, I'd arrived at Mosswood for the first time, overwhelmed by its grandness and frightened by its owner. Those feelings were magnified a thousandfold on this evening, especially when my eyes lit upon the captain's portrait, looking more menacing than ever.

Rachael, in her Cleopatra costume, greeted me, "Mia, you're trembling. Hot rum punch will warm you up."

Appearing eager to leave, Daniel offered, "I'll get a cup for you, Darling."

"Don't you think he looks a bit off?" Rachael opined. "And he's been acting quite mysterious lately. Perhaps he's planning a surprise for you," she laughed with a mischievous glint in her eye.

I was certain the night held many surprises, not all of them pleasant. I'd always felt Captain Biggs' presence in his home; his haunting portrait, his hidden chamber, but now I shuddered to think of his proximity.

"Good evening, Miss Stein."

The voice startled me, as did the appearance of the masked harlequin standing before me.

"Don't you recognize me?" the man teased.

"I'm afraid not," I said, fearing it was the captain himself.

"Then I have you at a disadvantage, for I know you intimately; size seven shoe, dress size six, gloves are a six and a half."

I stammered, "Sir, I don't find your ruse amusing. I respectfully ask that you reveal your identity."

Rachael interrupted, "Mia, it was just a little game I told him to play. Go ahead, Percival, and take off your mask before she has a fit."

"Mr. Gray," I said, feeling relieved.

He bowed grandly, "Proprietor Extraordinaire of Market Square, at your service, Miss Stein. You've been one of my preferred customers for so long, that of course, I would know your measurements. Achoo!" Sniffing vapors from his vinaigrette, he added, "Please excuse me, I fear I've caught a chill."

I sighed, "No harm done. I'm afraid I'm a bit on edge tonight, what with all the activities planned."

"Thank you, Miss Stein, and now since we'll be intimates through our close connection with Rachael, may I offer you a ten percent discount on future purchases."

Always the business man, I thought. "Thank you Mr. Gray, so very generous of you."

A woman, disguised in a medieval wimple, squeezed into our circle of conversation.

"Miss Biggs?" I asked, uncertainly.

"Please, you are to call me Aunt Edna from now on, for you will soon be one of the family. It's ever so much fun to dress up, don't you think, Mia. What a lucky man, my brother is to soon wed you. By the way where is Charles?"

Rachael gently scolded, "Aunt, you're confused. Mia is to marry your nephew, Daniel, not your brother. Don't you remember?"

Confused, she searched about like a frightened child. "Oh, oh, that's right. I'm sorry did I say something wrong? I didn't mean to. Please don't lock me up, I want to stay at the party and see the future Mrs. Biggs. Everyone in Houston will look to her to set the standard."

Sympathizing with her distress, I offered, "Miss Biggs, I mean Aunt Edna, shall I accompany you to the veranda? Fresh air always revives my spirits when my head is a bit foggy."

Rachael scorned, "Don't be ridiculous, Mia. You're expected to stand here and greet the guests as they arrive. I'll take care of my aunt and try to find Daniel, who seems to have disappeared. Come Percival, take my aunt's other hand."

"But Rachael, I don't know what to say to them," I said plaintively.

"Dear, Mia, you're making a mountain out of a molehill. Simply smile and comment on their costume or the severity of the weather."

I'd have gladly cared for a deranged woman over trite conversation with strangers, for the minutes passing in that occupation were sheer agony. Mercifully, Daniel returned to my side, looking flushed and disturbed.

"Forgive me, Mia, I was detained. Goodness, I forgot to fetch your drink. I'll go back."

"Please don't, I'd rather you stay with me."

Rufus and Esther Price stepped into the receiving line. They presented a queer image, he wearing an old Cotton King crown, and she in a dress covered in cotton boll.

"Good evening, Mr. Biggs, Miss Stein," Rufus said with vigor.

"It's such an honor to be invited," Ester said. "We must have you two over for dinner, soon."

Apparently my engagement to Daniel Biggs had instantly elevated my standing, for the same man who had cursed my father at the fair, and the woman, who snubbed me on more than one occasion, had developed a newfound friendliness towards me. I was struggling with an appropriate response when I was further shocked by the arrival of a very pregnant Charlotte.

"Hello Mia," Charlotte said cheerily. "I don't believe you've met my husband, Gunther, yet. We're thrilled to be here, aren't we Honey? I know I'm big as a house and should keep to my confinement, but I wasn't about to miss out on the grandest social event of the year. This is a far cry from Klopper's barn dance in Frost Town."

It seemed everyone in Houston had been invited, regardless of my opinion. The procession moved painfully slow with no other disturbances until Reverend Josiah Hornsby and his long-suffering wife Cora arrived. The two wore no costume other than their usual attire. Hornsby's crisp white cleric's collar threatened to strangle his bulging neck, and Cora had on one of her severe black dresses embellished only with the broach containing locks from her deceased children. Visions of the Hornsbys standing over dear Pappa dying, elicited strong emotion within me.

Hornsby bellowed, "Thank you, Mister Biggs, for inviting us, however, we wish to make clear the motivation which spurred us to attend."

Cora, looking embarrassed by her bombastic husband, pleaded, "Please Josiah, not tonight"

Hornsby silenced her with a stern look, then continued, "I conscientiously oppose both dance and liquoring and the loose moralled revelry that accompanies these, however, we've come to carry out our Lord's divine mission. We must witness firsthand the environs of sin, so we may better save our brothers and sisters from its evil clutches."

Unruffled by their strange behavior, Daniel replied, "Mister and Mrs. Hornsby, had I known your inclinations, I would not have dared affront you with an invitation. But may I allay your fears by saying I do not think too much wickedness will prevail tonight."

I stifled giggles as the two seemingly accepting his response, headed toward the spiked punch bowl. At the stroke of eight, Daniel and myself led our guests in a promenade to the grand dining hall. The room, dazzling brilliantly with candlelight and polished silver, was sweetly perfumed with red camellias and cuttings of fresh pine. I was seated between Rachael and Daniel, and opposite me was Edna Biggs and her escort, who was none other than Doctor Sterling Abbott in flowing robes of an Egyptian. I now rued my decision not to look over the guest list, and most particularly where they were seated.

When the first course, consisting of shrimp bisque, arrived, I nervously surveyed the array of silverware laid before me, and wished I'd had a lesson in table etiquette along with my dance instruction.

Noticing my confused hesitation, Rachael whispered in an aside, "It's not as complicated as it seems. There's no need to know the difference between a melon and a soup spoon, simply use the cutlery as it lay, starting from the outside and moving in toward your plate. Go ahead, Mia, everyone is waiting on you."

I thought of the irony of my situation. Nary a year ago I was a girl with swinging braids and spitting watermelon seeds at the fair, and tonight I was hostess of a grand ball with all eyes upon me. Delicately scooping into my bowl, I brought my spoon to my lips, whereupon the guests followed suit. The following courses were unfamiliar to me, and I only learned their names from the written menu presented on the table. A smoked salmon pate was the next course followed by Chicken Provençal, asparagus vinaigrette, and Potatoes a la Delmonico.

The servants dutifully refilled our glasses with claret punch, and Doc Abbott's table manners declined in relation to the amount he imbibed. Though Aunt Edna was a stickler for etiquette, her double chin jiggled in uproarious laughter at all his drunken antics.

"Got to be careful of what I eat," Doc Abbott complained as he wrestled with his scarlet turban. "Dyspepsia, you know."

Aunt Edna innocently suggested, "I'm sure our Mia could help you. She cured my gout, and just look at me get around now, no swelling or pain. Why she's truly a gift!" Then with a quick follow up she added, "Not to say, you good doctor, did not help me too. Now that I consider it further, I'm certain it was both of your combined efforts that rejuvenated my health."

The doctor glared unreservedly at me through his pince-nez, "It's too bad Miss Stein couldn't have done more for her father, and that I was called to attend him too late."

Overhearing the physician's jab, Daniel said in my defense, "I'm very proud of Mia. She is indeed an accomplished healer possessing knowledge far beyond her years. I'm truly fortunate she'll be looking after me in future."

Daniel's remark put an end to the doctor's attack, though his presence continued to disturb me, as did the rich food churning in my stomach and the uncertainty of what the evening would bring.

Slurping her raw oysters, Rachael asked, "Mia, are you alright, you're looking pale around the gills. Here, have more wine, it will calm your nerves."

"I'm not used to heavy meals, and I've already had too much drink."

Daintily picking his teeth with his personal gold pick, Percival offered, "Women are such delicate creatures. Have a sniff of my vinaigrette, it is certain to revive you."

I felt enormous relief when the dinner finally ended, and Daniel linking arms with me, led me through the arched doorway to the ballroom. Everyone took their positions, and the orchestra, who were seated on the dais, opened the ball with a set of quadrilles. It was a magnificent spectacle as lavishly costumed dancers spun on the polished parquet floor. Though my nerves were jangled and my thoughts obsessed on meeting the captain, I found myself lost in the music and dance.

Daniel whispered in my ear. "You dance superbly, Mia."

"I'm gratified to hear it, though all praise goes to my dance instructor, Monsieur Fleur."

Nuzzling my ear, Daniel asked, "Are you glad we decided to attend the festivities tonight?"

With a brave face, I answered, "Yes, my Love."

The quadrille requires switching of partners, and I found myself paired next with Eli Bailey, my foreman from the furniture shop.

"Good evening, Miss Stein, fine shindig your in-laws have put on," Bailey said with genuine admiration. "How do I look in my kilt? I like the freedom of movement it affords, though my legs are chilled on a night like this."

His hairy bowlegs were a sight, but I managed to say, "If anyone can pull off the look, I'd say it's you, Mr. Bailey. Who is your date tonight?"

"Fanny Moffitt, she's the gal over by the punchbowl, the one dressed like a desperado."

The image of Fanny drinking in the saloon on the night my father died, came to mind. "Yes, she and I are friends. We belong to the same sewing circle."

"She's a lively one," Bailey said with a shake of his head. "I thought it strange for her to come as a man, with a fake mustache, no less, but I suppose it's no odder than me baring my legs. Maybe we make the perfect couple." Confidently twirling me, he added, "I've been wanting to discuss a business matter with you. I know it's not the proper time, but..."

"I'm always willing to talk shop," I said, trying to catch my breath. "Is everything alright?"

"Yes, just wanted to say what a bang up job you've done with the books. You've put things back in quick order. I didn't want to express the doubts I had about the shop's future after Klaus' death, but I can honestly say now, I see it thriving for years to come."

"That's a relief to hear, though I can take only small credit for its success. I'm certain there'd be no business at all without your skill and guidance. Practically every day, Emmett comments on your artistry."

Darlene Campbell, dressed as a Valkyrie with a metal vest a strange counterpoint to her dowager's hump, bumped into us with Noah Fairfax, the schoolteacher.

"Mind your spear, Mrs. Campbell," Bailey reprimanded. "Or have you already forgotten the Fourth of July when I dumped you in the water trough after you abused me with your hatpin."

Darlene shot back, "No, I've not forgotten that unfortunate episode, nor does it alter what actions and weapons I may employ in future."

"Good to see you, Mr. Fairfax," I said. "Are my brothers behaving in class?"

"They're quite subdued after your father's death, but time will heal."

Daniel approached us, smiling broadly, "Bailey, forgive me, but I must steal your dance partner. Our most esteemed guest has just arrived, and I want to introduce him to Mia."

Thinking Captain Biggs had changed his mind and decided to attend the ball, my heart felt as if it had stopped along with the music and conversation. A man and woman strode into the room, and I approached them tremulously, only to discover they were Sam Houston, our esteemed senator and former president of the Republic, and his wife, Margaret. Nearly sixty, Houston, dressed in a scarlet cashmere waistcoat and black velvet britches, still made for an imposing figure. Margaret, twenty years his junior and beautiful in straw colored silk with six flounces of Brussels lace, had retained her girlish figure even after birthing four children.

Our guests quickly encircled us, eager to meet our charismatic leader and his elegant wife.

Extending his hand, Daniel said, "Welcome, Mr. and Mrs. Houston, and allow me to introduce you to my fiancé, Miss Mia Stein."

It was said Houston had the common touch, being equally comfortable amongst the Indians as he was with the most cultured of society, and he demonstrated this quality as he removed his large fur hat and bowed with an exaggerated flamboyancy toward me. "The pleasure is all mine, Miss Stein, for you're a vision to warm my soul on this cold wintry night. I understand you're a daughter of the Revolution, your father having been under my command at San Jacinto. Any man who fought that day is owed a debt of gratitude by his countrymen. I look forward to speaking with him."

Moved by the presence of so famous a man, I stammered, "Yes sir, my father was a great admirer of yours. Unfortunately, he recently passed."

"Please accept my condolences," Houston said sympathetically.

Miss Penelope, dressed as the Queen of Hearts, cozied up to our venerable guest, purring, "Mr. Houston, your costume is quite fantastic, what character have you come as tonight?"

Margaret Houston wittily answered the question, "Dear woman, my husband comes as himself. Is that not character enough."

Laughter erupted, sending an embarrassed Miss Penelope to retreat behind a palm with Evan, the fireman, to console her.

Sam Houston addressed me again. "Miss Stein, you may notice I use a cane. Since having been wounded in the ankle at San Jacinto, it's a necessary article to my toilette, however, it doesn't prevent me from the occasional saltation. May I have the honor of you as my partner?"

I was overwhelmed with equal parts pride and embarrassment as his hand, brandishing gold rings on four of his fingers, took my kid glove with practiced grace. Daniel, in turn, offered Margaret Houston his hand as the orchestra struck up a minuet.

Houston praised me as he maneuvered complex dance steps. "You are light on your feet, Miss Stein."

"Thank you, sir, as are you."

"It feels good to return to this town," he reflected. "Though I still feel deeply the loss of its position as our capital."

"My father often said that the city's economy suffered from its removal, but that we'd benefit from the railroad's arrival. I understand you're in favor of its expansion to our territory."

My comment brought an enthusiastic spark to Houston's eyes. "I couldn't agree with your father more strongly that our country's future prosperity and protection in war, as well as in peace, will be secured when the most distant portions of our Republic has steam cars. I return to Washington tomorrow. If the rail were already laid, I'd be facing a six day journey rather than a grueling six weeks. One day, I'm certain they'll be running from the Brazos to Mexico City. But enough talk of politics, have you set a wedding date?"

"Not as of yet. I'm still in mourning for my father. Even this evening's festivities were against my inclination."

Houston twirled me, "My first attempts at matrimony were unsuccessful, but my union with Margaret has altered me for the better. I highly recommend the institution to the right person. You are so lovely to the sight and gifted intellectually, I hope your young man is wise enough not to delay too long."

I was charmed by Houston's attention and flattery, and when the prompter called the end to the dance, he withdrew a snake skin pouch from his vest pocket from which he disclosed a wooden heart he'd whittled. "Miss Stein, it would give me pleasure to bestow a small token upon you as a reminder of this time we've shared."

"Why, Mr. Houston, how very generous of you. My own father was a woodworker, and often busied himself in his spare hours by the same occupation."

Houston doffed his hat again with a flourish, and kissed my hand before moving towards a gaggle of admirers. I was thinking of my brothers' reactions to such an extraordinary encounter when a gentleman, who was unfamiliar to me, asked for my hand to dance the Chorus Jig. I considered declining in order to take a rest, but the rigadoon, with its simple footwork, was one of my favorites. The music was lively, and as I skipped with my partner, he declared, "I wouldn't value Houston's gift too highly."

As we danced the chaser back up the room, I replied, "Excuse me, sir, what do you mean by that?"

"It's Houston's custom to bestow those trinkets to every woman he fancies. He's an unabashed flirt with a pocketful of them."

Irritated by his critical remark, I asked, "Do I know you, sir?"

"I'm Jake Johnson, overseer at Cyrus Harrington's sugar plantation. I saw you and Miss Emily when you come to heal the slaves. They was in poor shape at the time, and half wouldn't have lived if not for the efforts of you two."

I still didn't recall the man, but was intrigued by his association with Harrington. "My brother read in the paper tonight of your boss' disappearance. What do you make of it? Do you really think he may have been murdered?"

"I got my own theory, but right now I can't say too much on the subject. It's got to do with those slaves of his, and I'll leave it at that."

"Surely you don't think it was one of them who killed him?"

"Now, I didn't say that, Miss. Anyways, everything will be coming to a head tonight."

Disturbed by the conversation, I expressed my fatigue and curtly begged off dancing, then headed toward the refreshments.

Mayor Moore approached the punch bowl and addressed me, "Mia, your soirée is a booming success! And what a grand house! Klaus would be mighty proud of you."

I offered a weak smile, knowing my father never would have allowed me to step foot inside Mosswood. My next dance partner was Mr. Jackson, proprietor of the Capitol Hotel. He reminded me of last Easter when I sat in my bedroom window and how he'd called up to me to go for a walk. His flattery and lightheartedness was a most appreciated distraction, but this too was curtailed by the arrival of Ulysses handing me a note with some urgency. I excused myself from Mr. Jackson then read the missive:

Mia, my love, meet me in the library at twelve-thirty. – Daniel.

Perplexed, I turned to the slave, still standing beside me. "Ulysses, do you know where Daniel is right now?"

He answered nervously. "No, Ma'am, but I believe he's detained with some sort of business."

Studying the shaky handwriting, I felt ill. What sort of occupation could possibly take Daniel away from our engagement party, and what did this ominous message mean? Was it the proposed rendezvous with his father or perhaps Captain Biggs was causing a disruption behind the scenes?

I was contemplating searching the house when a masked stranger approached me. "My lovely Mia, your costume c'est exquis and you're as always très belle."

My voice faltered, "Henri?"

Removing his mask, he said, "I should call you Josephine. That is who you come as, oui?"

His flashing roguish smile that was previously so beguiling, now only repulsed me. Outraged, I declared, "Sir, this is my engagement party. Have you no sense of propriety?"

"I'm here on an official matter, however, there's no reason for me not to indulge in pleasure with a beautiful woman whom I will always consider dear to my heart. Please, let us dance and remember the fond times we shared in the past."

"There are two excellent reasons why we shall never speak to one another again; your wife and Daniel, the man I love and plan to wed."

I turned away from the cad, for the first time feeling completely free from his influence. However, no sooner had I made my way across the dance floor than Gunther was at my side. Wringing his hands and pale with worry, he implored, "Miss Stein, I know it's terribly inappropriate to ask, but please can you come with me? Charlotte's baby is on the way!"

It appeared the evening was one disaster after another. Unable to refuse the distraught man, I followed Gunther to a bedchamber in the west wing. It was far removed from party goers, where Charlotte's screams couldn't be heard.

Hearing the uproar within the bedchamber, Gunther hesitated at the door. "I don't think I'd better go in."

"Best you didn't," I agreed. "But stay close, so I may quickly send word to you."

I found the occupants of the bedchamber arguing. "Make this pain stop right this minute!" Charlotte demanded.

Her mother, Esther, tried to comfort, "Dear child, what you are feeling is the natural pangs of childbirth. It is God intended."

Charlotte shrieked, "Natural? Pain ripping me in two can't be natural! Mia, thank heavens you're here," she said, clenching my hand. "Please, please, I beg of you, get this baby out of me right now, so I may...Ahhhhh!"

"Relax and take a deep breath, Charlotte," I directed. "That's right, see how it lessens the pain. Now, I've got to examine you, and I'll try to be gentle, but first I have to clean up, and so do you, Esther. You'll be assisting me, and clean hands are the best way to avoid childbed fever."

My examination set off another wave of contractions and even louder howls from Charlotte. Dismayed from what I found, I confessed, "Charlotte, I've assisted Miss Emily many times, but never delivered a baby by myself, and yours is breech. His bottom is facing downward."

"It's a boy?" she asked between screams.

"I'm absolutely sure about that, but right now we need to get Doctor Abbott. He's downstairs at the party."

"I'll not have Butcher Abbott anywhere near me. He just killed Mrs. Appleby with chloroform."

Esther added, "Besides, he's completely besotted already."

I couldn't argue against that point, nor did I really want the foul physician. As an alternative, I suggested, "What about Mayor Moore? He was a surgeon with the Buckeye Rangers during the Revolution."

Charlotte shrilled, "And how many babies did the Rangers need delivered?"

Esther piped up, "Why don't we call Miss Emily to come. She was wonderful delivering my children."

Charlotte wailed, "She wouldn't come out in this storm, not knowing it was me having a baby. Don't you remember the horrible things I said to her at the sewing circle? God forgive me, I was awful to her, and now He's making me pay for it."

"You still don't know Miss Emily, do you?" I declared indignantly. "She's the finest woman I've ever known, and if she thinks she can help another person, then she'll try everything in her power to do so, even *if* it's someone who's hurt her deeply."

As I made my point, I realized the preposterousness of asking Miss Emily to come. Would she ever enter Captain Biggs' house, the man who had raped her as a child? Despite my doubts, I sent a distraught Gunther to fetch her, and then turned my attention back to Charlotte. I was horrified to discover she was now fully dilated.

"This is quite unexpected," I said. "From my experience, a woman giving birth to her first child usually has a very long labor. When exactly did your contractions start?"

Charlotte answered between howling, "They started this afternoon."

"You mean before you even came to the party?"

She cried, "I just thought it was another false labor like I had a week ago. Anyways, I didn't want to miss all the fun at this fandango."

It was a harrowing hour that then passed, but mercifully I turned the baby around and delivered him safely. There were tears of joy when an exhausted Charlotte cradled her son in her arms, and Gunther looked on, bursting with pride. I felt only a fleeting moment of relief and exultation, for Miss Emily had appeared, and she was none too happy.

Pulling me aside, she demanded, "Girl, what in blazes are you doin' callin' me to this house? Don't you remember what I told you that scoundrel done to me and your ma? You're grown up now, and I can't keep you from danger, though the Lord knows I wish I could, but I ain't gonna be a party to this."

The clock struck half past twelve signaling the time I was to meet Daniel in the library. With no time for a lengthy explanation, I said, "Miss Emily, every dreadful word you told me about Captain Biggs has left an indelible mark upon me. Trust me, when I say I know what I'm doing. I'm sorry, but I have to go now. Please see to Charlotte. She's not delivered the afterbirth yet."

Not waiting for her to reply, I grabbed my purse and rushed from the room. The ballroom was nearly empty of revelers, and I wondered if they'd left because of the hour or the strange disappearance of their hosts. What few guests remained appeared intoxicated, including an apologetic Sam Houston, whose wife was attempting to lead him out the door.

"There will be no more tippling for you," Margaret Houston affirmed.

"Yes, of course, my dearest," Houston slurred. "But if only the cannon hadn't been shot. We'd surely have returned the capital to this fine city of Houston, its rightful position in government."

When I reached the back hall, I picked up my hem and dashed to the library. With only one candle lit in the room, I couldn't discern if the man standing beside the statue was Daniel or not. He was similar in build and height, but he wore a wide brimmed hat pulled low. As my eyes adjusted to the room's dimness, I saw to my horror, Captain Biggs' bulbous nose and sagging jowls.

"She is so womanly, don't you think?" he asked.

"I beg your pardon, sir."

He rubbed his hand slowly up the thigh of the marble nude. "She's exquisite, but too white for my tastes. I prefer darker skin."

I'd imagined countless times exactly what I'd do in this moment, but confronted by the captain's degeneracy, I was frozen to the spot.

"Don't look so frightened, my sweet Mia. You've come here of your own accord, haven't you? You received my note."

"But it was signed by Daniel."

"Yes, but I think deep down you knew it was me who sent it. We've been playing cat and mouse for long enough."

"I don't know what you're talking about. Daniel told me you don't like social gatherings, and that I was to meet you afterwards, but..."

He pulled me violently to him, clamping his hand over my mouth. I could hear the frenzied Latin rhythm of *La Contradanza* playing in the ballroom, and knew what few revelers remained wouldn't think to look for me. And where was Daniel? Believing my salvation was up to me alone, I kicked the captain and bit down on his hand. He responded with a swift blow to my head, and I sunk into an abyss of darkness.

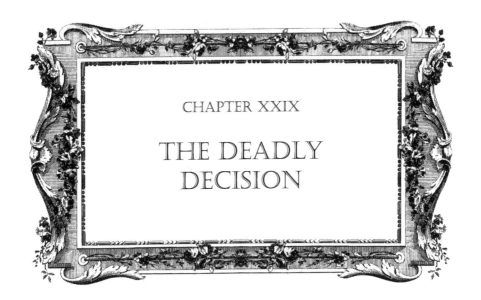

CHAPTER XXIX

THE DEADLY DECISION

awoke in the secret chamber to the scent of lavender. The velvet curtained niche was open, and the flicker of dozens of candles revealed its once hidden contents. It was a perverted altar to my mother, her lifelike portrait staring back at me. Trying to get up, Captain Biggs rolled over, pinning me down with his body.

"Let me go, I cried, struggling with the grotesque creature.

He laughed, "Ah, Senorita, I can do whatever I want. You belong to me. It's true, you lack the fiery dark eyes of your mother, but other than that the resemblance is uncanny. You share her fighting spirit, which makes it all the more fun."

The stench of cigar and hard liquor wafted hot across my face, and I wondered how I'd endure this humiliation for another moment. Surely, Daniel was looking for me or perhaps Miss Emily who would be fearful of my safety in so loathsome a house. But even if they searched, would either know the existence of this room?

Pulling my silk dress up and baring my thigh, he said, "I know this room is not unknown to you. You were here before, but my jealous Rita scared you away. Do you like the lavender? As you know, it was your mother's favorite scent. Do not look so surprised. You knew it was I who sent you the lavender bouquets. You're engaged to my son, but it's the lord of the manor you really want."

"You're completely mad if you believe that's true."

He stroked my cheek. "I wanted to return as soon as my son wrote to me of you, but a few minor complications delayed me; an Italian mistress and her bastard child needed disposing of, and then there was that damnable cargo of dying slaves, nearly impossible to unload. I've been here for some time now, without anyone knowing it, except for Rita, of course. It was delightful watching you go about the house in preparations with Rachael. You seem quite comfortable here, and will be the perfect mistress of my house."

I cried, "Only the vilest of characters hide and spy on women. It's what you did to my mother, isn't it? Hunted her down until..."

I struggled to free myself and in doing so, knocked off his hat. His scarred stub of an ear was inches from my face.

"Don't be timid, take as long a look as you desire," he cooed. "I lost that appendage due to lovely Francesca, but it was a trifle, considering I'd have given my life for her."

The nude statue crashed against the captain's brow, and I was lifted up from the divan.

"Daniel," I cried.

Holding me tightly, he said, "I'm sorry, Mia. I should never have put you in so much danger. Are you alright?"

"Put me in danger? You mean you knew your father was after me?"

"Of course not," Daniel argued. "What I mean is..."

Captain Biggs pressed a kerchief to his wound, "What theatrics, I behold."

"What madness has come over you, Father? To force yourself on any woman is abominable, but to choose my betrothed. Have you no sense of right or wrong?"

Biggs walked to a sideboard, and poured himself a drink. "Miss Stein suffered a fainting spell, and I simply brought her here to recover. No harm was done, and now the happy couple is reunited." He raised his glass in a toast, "Here's to my son and his lovely wife-to-be, may the two of you live happily ever after."

"Come Mia, I'll not stay another minute under this wretched man's roof."

"Not yet, Daniel," I said pulling away. "Not until you tell me what is going on here. I'm certain now, you know far more of your father's despicable activities than you've let on."

Daniel ran his hands nervously through his hair. "I've been in misery ever since my trip to England. I went there to find out if my suspicions of my father were true or not. I heard horrors about him which I could barely comprehend, much less speak of. At first I didn't want to believe any of it, not merely for my own shame, but of what you, Mia, would think of me and my family. I met a Mister Henri Dubois on the voyage, who at first conversed with me in a friendly manner. I came to realize he was a customs agent following me, with the intention of determining any compliance I might have in my father's affairs. Convinced of my innocence, he engaged me to help bring my father to justice."

Captain Biggs snarled, "I've done no wrong, and no one can prove that I did."

"Father, the authorities took your ship into custody at Brig's Landing at the Sabine Pass. There were two hundred slaves shackled in the hull, starving to death. You intended to sell them to the sugarcane plantations, but when you learned the authorities were about to arrive, you abandoned your crew and ship. You vanished and no one knew where you were.

Daniel continued, "Then on Christmas eve, Cyrus Harrington came up missing. During the investigation, Sheriff Franklin discovered you'd sold Cyrus slaves, but because they were sick and dying, he refused to pay you the full amount. The foreman swears you appeared at Harrington's house, threatening to kill him if he didn't give you the money. We then knew you were somewhere in the area."

"Your father told me he's been hiding in this house for weeks," I said.

Daniel took a double take. "I had no idea, otherwise this whole charade would've been unnecessary."

I was stupefied. "Are you saying I was bait to lure your father out?"

"When I wrote to him of our engagement, he was keen to meet you. The authorities believed this would be the surest time to apprehend him. Ask Sheriff Franklin, he's here for that very purpose. You must believe me when I say, I never had any intention of you even seeing my father."

Moving toward the door, Captain Biggs declared assuredly, "Some of Texas' most illustrious heroes trafficked in slaves; James Fannin and Jim Bowie, just to name a few. As for my own business affairs, you think you've figured it all out, but I assure you, there's no document to prove ownership of that vessel, nor Harrington's body to prove murder. Now, if you'll excuse me, I'm bored with this whole evening, and will leave you two lovers to quarrel without me."

The door opened and Miss Emily appeared with a bullwhip in hand. A crack of her whip lashed across the retreating captain's back, bringing him to his knees. Then turning, he said threateningly, "Emily, you damnable yellow slave, you'll pay for this!"

"Whose the slave now?" she asked rhetorically, recoiling her whip. The snake-like rawhide lashed out in quick succession; the first ripping the flesh of his back raw and the second blinding an eye.

"Please, no more," the captain cried out.

"You ask for mercy?" Miss Emily asked incredulously. "Did you show mercy upon me when I was but a child and you raped and tortured me? What of the hundreds of slaves, whose blood you got on your hands? And did you show a shred of mercy to Mia's mother when you killed her?"

Daniel turned to me in shock. "What is she saying about your mother?"

"Then you didn't know about her and your father?"

"Of course not," he answered, his voice rising. "How would I?"

Still unconvinced, I asked, "Then how did you find me here? You surely knew of this room and had seen my mother's portrait. There's no denying my resemblance to her."

Glancing at the altar, he pleaded, "I swear I never knew this existed until tonight. I'd been talking with the sheriff when we realized you were missing. Everyone split up to look for you when

Rita came to me. She said you were in danger and directed me here."

My world was turned topsy turvy as I realized what I thought was true was not. "Rita is the Voodoo slave, who frightened me with effigies and slaughtered chickens, and now you're saying she's the one who brought you to my rescue?"

Captain Biggs moved stealthily towards the door, but Miss Emily's whip lashed out. This time she missed her mark and the captain grabbed the rawhide, pulling her towards him. A tug of war ensued, but Daniel lunged forward, engaging his father in a fight. The captain was like a rabid dog, his mouth lathering and every conceivable foul word emitting forth.

With trembling hands, I grabbed my purse and pulled out the gun I'd been carrying all night. It was the very weapon I'd taken off the gambler on the boat going to Galveston, but now it felt heavier and more frightening than before. "Everyone stop right now!" I demanded, pointing the gun at Captain Biggs. "Daniel, move away from your father."

"Mia, what on earth do you think you're doing?" Daniel asked in horror.

I explained, "When Miss Emily told me of Captain Biggs' crimes, I promised myself I'd bring him to justice."

Daniel argued, "But you can't take the law into your own hands. Sheriff Franklin is here, let him handle the matter."

"Mia, he's right," Miss Emily begged. "No matter how loathsome he be, you can't take his life."

"The law did nothing when he took my mother from me, and he's too powerful and rich for them to do anything now." Closing my eyes, I pressed my finger on the trigger. The anger I'd fostered for this man boiled in me, and I wanted him to pay dearly for it all, but Miss Emily was right, no matter what evils he'd committed, I couldn't kill him. As I put the weapon down, a gunshot rang out through the room, and Captain Biggs crumpled into a motionless heap on the ground. I turned and found the slave, Rita, helping a distraught Edna Biggs sit in a nearby chair.

I had no idea when the two had entered the room, but now the old woman was rocking back and forth, still pointing the smoking gun towards her brother. She cooed, "There now, it's all taken care of. We can go back to the ball and dance some more. Everyone is looking for Mia and Daniel, and Rachael is beside herself with worry. Don't you know it's improper etiquette for the hosts to leave the party before their guests do."

"Here now, Aunt, I'll take that," Daniel said, removing the gun from her clenched hand.

She patted his head affectionately, "Thank you, dear boy. Now, that I sit down I realize I'm quite worn out. I had a lot of punch, and Doctor Abbott was an unrelenting dance partner. Mia, will you fix me up an herbal bath to sooth my sore feet. You're so dreadfully clever that way."

The atmosphere was surreal as everyone ignored the captain laying dead on the floor. "Yes, of course, Aunt Edna, I'll gladly do that for you."

Daniel turned to Rita, "Can you put my aunt to bed. Mia and I will come up to see her after a bit."

The slave, who had scared the wits out of me, nodded and smiled, "Yes, sir. I'm sure glad everything has finally been settled. And Miss Mia, forgive me for frightening you so. I believed at the time it was in your best interest."

EPILOGUE

The authorities were told Captain Biggs accidentally shot himself while cleaning his gun, and though Sheriff Franklin wrote it up as the official report, I'm certain he suspected something else happened on that stormy winter night.

Rachael and Percival soon celebrated their own nuptials, and moved to England, where the industrious fellow opened a string of mercantile stores, carrying only the best of British goods.

Under the care and supervision of Rita, Mosswood remained home to Edna Biggs until she died of natural causes, whereupon the house was turned into a school for people of color. Miss Emily became its most outstanding teacher, guiding her students in the art of midwifery and herbal healing. Miss Emily never courted another man, and always proudly wore the brass ring Pappa had given her.

Daniel and I began our life together at Holly Cottage, where so long ago, Mamma and Pappa had carved their initials into the tree. Our love for each other grew deep as we raised my brothers into manhood. Emmett remained the curious intellectual, but he surprised us and himself as well, when he chose to become a master carpenter, carrying on Stein's Fine Furniture. Never forgetting the day he ruined his hair by cutting it, Christian opened his own barbershop, which became the prime meeting place for the men of our town. Sam, who was too afraid to speak and loved collecting nature's treasures, grew up to be an entomologist, renowned for his eloquent speeches.

We often spent summers in England at Daniel's estate, but it was my Houston home that truly held my heart.

Mamma's dressing room that had been locked up for so many years was finally opened and served as a nursery for our own son and daughter. The secrets which had haunted me were vanquished, and my lavender scented memories became a happy bouquet of love.

The End